Horace Afoot

Horace Afoot

Frederick Reuss

MacMurray & Beck
Denver / Aspen

Published by:
MacMurray & Beck, Inc.
1649 Downing Street
Denver, Colorado 80218

Printed and bound in the United States of America

1 2 3 4 5 6 7 8 9 10

Library of Congress Cataloging-in-Publication Data
Reuss, Frederick, 1960–
Horace afoot : a novel / by Frederick Reuss.
p. cm.
ISBN 1-878448-79-X
I. Title.
PS3568.E7818H6 1997
813'.54—dc21 97–21601
CIP

MacMurray & Beck Fiction: General Editor, Greg Michalson
Horace Afoot cover design by Laurie Dolphin,
interior design by Stacia Schaefer.
The text was set in Granjon by Lyn Chaffee.

For Gail

There are no streetcars in Oblivion. There aren't any streetcars anywhere in America, as far as I know. I don't count the trolley cars in San Francisco. Since I moved here I've been wishing streetcars would make a comeback. I know it's hopeless. I hate internal combustion engines and the civilization that has been built on them. I shouldn't take it so personally. But I read in *Selected Philosophical Essays* that hatred of civilization is not *necessarily* an irrational projection onto the world of personal psychological difficulties. So I know it's not just me.

My house is a rickety yellow thing at the dead end of West Street. The owner moved away and doesn't care what happens to it as long as he gets a check every month. It's a comfortable place, and I sometimes get the feeling that it has remained standing as a favor to me. I'm sure I'll be its last occupant. Every evening I fix myself a plate of beans and rice, pour myself a glass of wine, then go upstairs and eat in bed listening to the night sounds from the woods behind the house. Tonight it is too hot to go to sleep, so I just sit with the empty bowl in my lap trying to imagine someone in China doing exactly the same thing. Of course the time difference would make it daytime on the other side of the world, so anyone sitting up in bed with an empty plate in their lap is bound to be ill or in prison or both. Right? I make a mental calculation. The world's population is somewhere over five billion, so the probability is there. In fact, it is likely that there are thousands of us all around the globe doing exactly the same thing: sitting in bed with our empty bowl, staring at the wall. The process of calculation lulls me into a mild sort of hypnosis, and I find my thoughts wandering from the world of cozy musings in bed to the world of torture described in Amnesty International brochures, the ones that read: right now, today, the horrors of torture and political detention are everyday incidents in fully one-third of the world's countries. I realize that what seems to me a comforting extrapolation, the projection of my measly being into the entire human universe, is also a bloody goddamn nightmare.

I reach for the phone and dial a number.

"Horace here."

"Hello?"

"Right now, today, the horrors of torture are everyday incidents in one-third of the world's countries." I pause, wait for the click of the receiver.

"Is that a fact?" A woman's voice.

"Yes, it is. Do you ever find yourself wondering about the unspeakable things that are happening this very moment around the globe?"

A pause. "To tell you the truth, sir, I do not." Another pause. "But I go to church every Sunday and pray to Almighty Christ that I never have to."

I consider how to respond, but my finger slips and I accidentally hang up on her. I can't remember the number I'd dialed, which is a shame because I would have enjoyed talking to the old lady. There was a grain of frustrated reason in her voice, the voice of a heavy smoker.

I get out of bed and go into the kitchen, put my bowl in the sink, stand at the back door, and watch for falling stars. The outline of a large water tower teeters like a hydrocephalic child against the night sky. The name of the town is painted on it in matte black letters. You can read them during the day. OBLIVION. At night, despite the silhouette of the tower, you can see a big swath of sky. I turn off the kitchen light, sit on the stoop and scrutinize the summer night, listen to the chorusing crickets and cicadas. The sky is clear and brilliant with stars. I wish I hadn't broken the binoculars I confiscated from the kid next door. It would be nice to use them now. I ended up paying for them anyway, and now the kid is spying on me with a higher-powered set from a safer distance.

The evening wears on and I walk to the top of the street, turn left, and follow Old Route 47 out of town. The cornfields are about chest high, and from the slight elevation of the roadway I can see across them. All 180 degrees of the horizon are open to me. A few cars speed past. I step into the shadow of the field and hide as they blow by. At night the traffic on this side of town is light. Few use this road since the new thoroughfare was built several years ago. I like to walk out here for that reason.

Old Route 47 leads to the back of a factory that employs a good part of the town. Semantech, pronounced *semmatech* by the locals. They produce parts for cruise missiles and other weapons, and they've been doing it for long enough now that everybody takes it for granted. A few months ago the president came through and gave a speech.

At eleven the shifts change and the parking lot becomes a sea of clustered headlights. The new thoroughfare, a four-lane road with highway signs and cloverleaf exits, takes this traffic to the east and around to the north end of town, where the new shopping malls are being built. The town has expanded in that direction, leaving the southern end, with its older houses and poorer neighborhoods, to a quiet, slow decay.

At a bend in the road is an ancient mound. Excavated around the turn of the century by the State Historical Society and the Bureau of American Ethnology, it is the highest elevation for miles around. A rotting picnic bench shaded by two medium-sized elm trees and a rusty plaque are the last signs of the state's interest in it. I follow the path that winds around to the top, brushing the tall grass out of the way as I make my way up. The ground is hard and dry and my footsteps fall with a hollow, dusty thud. On top of the mound the nighttime vista spreads out, open fields and the constellation-filled summer sky. Moving directly south from the North Star, I find Hercules low over the horizon. Behind me the town of Oblivion, to my right the factory with its high fence and orange anticrime lamps. These are my coordinates. The rest is a dark sea of fields.

The secret about Oblivion is that it is identical to every other place on the outskirts of the era we live in. The malls and food franchises are here, the idle libraries, the cable and satellite networks, the bad manners, all the septic, inflamed dysfunctions and disorders. An airport was built, but it provides entertainment rather than escape. The corporate moguls who planned it have never come here themselves. If they did, it would only irritate them to see the cars parked along the roadside and the bored people watching the finely logoed airplanes land beyond the fence.

I walk out there now and then to join the fun. Several times a day the big airplanes land. They come in so low over the fence at the eastern end of the runway that people standing there hold their ears and duck. Engines roaring, the flying steel swoops down; puffs of smoke erupt underneath as the wheels hit the ground; the beast brakes, reduces speed. At the far end of the runway it swings abruptly to the left and rolls toward the three-gate terminal, where an eager ground crew waits. In half an hour it's gone again. People finish their cans of soda, pile back into their cars and pickups, and drive away.

I overhear a conversation between a young couple.

"One of these days it'll be me in that thing."

"You ever flown?"

"Sure have."

"Where'd you fly?"

"Florida."

"Vacation?"

"Yup. One of these days I'll be gone for good. I'll take you with me too."

"To Florida?"

"Sure."

They nuzzle briefly. The young man fishes a cigarette from his shirt pocket, puts it between his lips with a proletarian swagger, and lights it, cupping the flame. They stand in silence for a few moments longer, his dry, red-rashed skin a homely contrast to the buttery blue hue that glows under hers, then climb into his pickup and drive away.

I did not arrive in Oblivion by air. I came in on a truck that I'd hitched a ride with. The driver of the rig was a black man from Chicago. His name was Alex, and he said the only reason he picked me up was that he was bored and needed somebody to talk to. He played a tape of songs he had recorded from his collection of old sheet music.

"Everything was published before 1914. My collection stops at World War I."

"Why?"

"No reason. I just decided to keep it that way."

"Why do you collect the stuff?"

"Like to play them. On my Hammond."

"I never heard anything like it before."

"Won't hear nothing like it again, neither. These songs are so old my grandmother can't remember them." The tape played on, leaving me to look out at the passing landscape. He let me out at the interstate exit for Oblivion.

"You sure you want to get out here?"

I said yes.

"Just because you like the name of the town?"

I said yes again.

He shook his head, let out a long and heartfelt Sweeeet Jesus, and let me go, honking the horn good-bye.

I walked the four miles into the center of town and bought a newspaper. Nobody paid attention to me as I sat on the bench in front of the Town Hall. I liked that and looked through the classifieds, saw an ad for a house to rent, and walked out to where I now live. What I liked about the house were the scrubby little bird nests under the eaves of the sinking front porch.

"I'll clear those away tomorrow," the landlord said. He was a small, thin man with missing teeth. He said he'd been living alone in the house ever since his wife died. Cancer got her.

"Leave the nests," I said.

"Whatever you want."

We shook hands, and the following week he moved to Florida.

At the bank Derringer, the manager, waits for me at his desk. Everybody in Oblivion thinks I'm a lunatic. But Derringer just thinks I'm a loafer. He has put the word out, and the word is that I'm not insane, just a rich weirdo. People generally leave me alone. Not because being weird is intimidating but because being rich is. Derringer pats his fingertips together, asks me what I think of such and such and so and so and up and down, and I always say I don't know. This is only a formality. All day long as he manages the bank, Derringer manipulates a rubber ball in his hand. He rolls the ball between his palms, on his desk top, squeezes it. He would like to become my friend. He thinks there's a secret he will discover by making friends with me. He squeezes his rubber ball and leans back in his chair and grins. "How much do you need today?" I tell him, and he always gets it for me. He likes to fill out all the slips of paper, and I don't. A nice arrangement all around.

I leave the bank and sit on the bench in the square in front of the Town Hall, the one I sat on when I first arrived in Oblivion. Across the street are Oblivion's first buildings, built around the turn of the century. Recently renovated, their facades newly painted, they are now occupied by Oblivion's young professional establishment. A lawyer's office in the old mayor's house, a real estate broker, an accountant, a dentist, and the temporary offices of a candidate for the state Senate. There is a sandwich shop that is never open and a movie theater that is losing business to the multiplex out at the mall. In a building on the corner dated 1919, someone has set up a shop called Purrfection that sells things to people who love cats: jewelry with cats, lawn and garden accessories with cat motifs, tee shirts and key chains and toys and games—all having to do with cats. On the next block is my bank, the public library, a restaurant called the Corn Tassel, and a building with an auto-parts store on the ground floor and a secondhand bookstore above it. That block looks slightly shabbier than the one directly across from the Georgian-style Town Hall with the plaza and the bench and the monument to the sons of Oblivion who died in the two World Wars.

I eat a stalk of celery, pretend there are no trucks or cars or foul-smelling air. I sit to pass the time. Sometimes I'll have company on the bench, and sometimes that company will want to talk. I usually go along, depending on the topic. If I've had a string of bad luck on the telephone the night before, I'll try to steer the conversation. It's hard to get people to respond to certain things. On the telephone people are spontaneous.

"Nice morning."

"Yes." I nod and take another stalk of celery from the pocket of my jacket. I chew slowly and think of all the forged and phony Christian sayings I'm capable of, the ones that resemble the twittering of birds and that always dissolve in my mouth before they can be uttered—such as, "The love and peace of Jesus Christ be with you, my brother." Or something like that. I wish I could make myself talk like that. I know that if I did the word would go out that yes, I'm a nut—but a pious one, and if that happened they'd probably want to elect me mayor of the town.

"I remember when that there was a feed store." The man inclines his head in the direction of Purrfection, leans forward with his elbows on his knees, and rubs his hands. "Can't figure how they stay in business."

"With cats, it would seem."

"That's what I mean. I can't figure."

"Was it always a feed store?"

"Feed store moved out, let's see, around 1963, I'd say. Then Harlan's Hardware opened up, stayed there must've been twenty, twenty-five years. Then they moved out. Now it's a goddamn pet shop that don't even sell pets." He rubs his palms together for a moment, then turns and offers me a handshake. "Name's Maver. Ed Maver."

I take his hand. "Horace," I say. "Quintus Horatius Flaccus."

"That's some name you got there, son. What do people call you?"

"Horace. Just Horace."

"Pleased to meet you, Horace. I seen you walking around here for a while now. Been meaning to make your acquaintance. You live in town?"

"West Street."

"That's a fair hike."

I nod.

"You don't own an automobile, I've noticed."

"No, I don't."

He nods, leans back, and crosses a knob-kneed leg. I finish my celery, and we sit watching a large truck maneuver a tight left turn onto Main Street.

"My son-in-law is sales manager over at Chevyland. If you ever get around to it."

"Do they sell cats there?"

Maver laughs. "Not unless you call a Chevrolet a cat." He idly rubs the ankle resting on his knee. "Come to think of it, what in hell is a Chevrolet?"

"A word invented by General Motors."

"It don't mean nothing? What about Chevy? There's a word that's got to mean something."

"It's a variant of chivvy."

"What in hell does chivvy mean?"

"To harass."

Maver looks at me from the corner of his eye. But his instinct is to talk on, to dispel his intuition. "Well, is that a fact? I'll have to tell Pete that. He'll appreciate it."

These sorts of conversations come my way every so often. I find myself going along on a ride I never asked for. Occasionally I'll pop a few questions, the telephone sort. But more often I end up with somebody like Maver whose presence becomes tedious the moment the talk veers into the personal. As expected, he goes right into let me tell you about my this, and I have a that, and such and such reminds me of the time so and so. I sit and chew my stalk of celery while Maver talks.

"I told Pete there was nothing doing. The man can't expect to get up and move his whole family. . . ." His volubility and passion for anecdote soon combine into a frothing storytelling mess that leaves me wondering if he'll ever notice I'm not listening to a word he is saying. I can't stand to listen to people when they launch into anecdotal orbit and drift along as if nobody and nothing else matters. The sameness of people's orations makes me realize how common all individual experience really is. Is subjectivity just an illusion? Certainly, the more a person prattles on about his or hers, the duller and duller he or she becomes. But the marvelous objectivity of this observation doesn't strike me as all that grand in the end, either. Every life is many days, day after day. Funny how this monotonous little statement elevates the fact of everyday existence to the realm of Truth. I like Truth because silence is its natural companion. Facts are loud and boring.

I interrupt Maver. "Someone once wrote that every life is many days, day after day."

Maver turns to me with a puzzled smile, scratches the back of his head, and nods. “True. True.” Then he returns to Pete, his son-in-law manager at Chevyland, whom, I assume, he has mentioned so I’ll go buy a car from him.

I get up to leave and for no particular reason say, “The peace of the Lord Jesus Christ be with you, Mr. Maver.”

Maver is silenced. “Nice meeting you, Mr. Horace,” he calls after me.

I walk up Main Street, the thoroughfare leading into and out of town, and turn onto Liberty, a quiet, shaded street where the well-to-do families of Oblivion built their homes almost a century ago. There are sidewalks here, concrete slabs nicely upturned by the roots of the old elms that grow along the street. The houses are set back from the road, their wide lawns shaded by the mature trees. A car passes by. I hear a thud and a crack. The car slows, stops. The driver gets out, leaving his door open.

“Did you see them?” He approaches me, a man in his thirties wearing a suit.

“Who?”

“The kids.”

“No.”

“This is the second time I’ve come down this street. They’ve been at it all morning.” He fumes and steps back toward his car to have a look. He runs his fingers over a tiny dent in the side door. “Goddamn kids are throwing rocks.”

“What a good idea.”

The man is engrossed in his inspection. I want to tell him the kids are only trying to preserve the tranquillity of their street by discouraging people like him from driving down it. Suddenly he discovers a crack in the passenger window. “Goddamn those little bastards!” He leaps into his car and pulls over to the curb. He slams the door and stalks across a lawn to the nearest house. I try to spot the band of little Luddites. But they are well concealed in the bushes and trees of their neighborhood, tittering quietly among themselves as the enraged driver goes from house to house complaining.

It is noon. The sky is clear. I sit in a rusty, wrought-iron gazebo at the end of Liberty Street. It is set in the center of a small, weedy park that forms the southern boundary to this section of the town. A plaque on the gazebo reads *Bequest of Major Perry Wilkington, USA, in memory of his beloved wife and daughter*. I've seen all of their tombstones in the Presbyterian cemetery. Major Perry Wilkington lived from 1851 until 1920. He is buried with his wife, Ann S. Wilkington; his daughter, Martha Wilkington Murrow; and his grandson, Perry Wilkington Murrow. His wife, who was also born in 1851, died in 1884. His daughter was born in 1871 and died on August 6, 1894. In childbirth, it would appear. Perry Wilkington Murrow, his grandson, lived only from August 6, 1894, to August 12, 1894. I've knitted together an outline of their lives based on the gazebo plaque and the dates on their tombstones, and I imagine the following: Martha married a man named Murrow. Since he isn't buried with her, I surmise that he left the town soon after August 12, 1894, and never returned. I surmise too that Murrow was a cad, a seducer; maybe he married her for her money. When she died, either the old major ran him out of town or he ran away of his own accord. I've found no Murrow buried anywhere in the cemetery. None of the women in the major's life lived for very long. I imagine that the last twenty-six years of his life were spent in kind of dignified sorrow and that he erected the gazebo as a monument to both his family and his grief.

A dog appears at my feet, looks up at me, panting. I glance around for the owner.

"I see we're alone."

The dog pants, sits at my knee, and stares at me.

Stomachs infrequently hungry disdain any commonplace victuals, I quote from my Roman namesake. A car turns up Liberty Street, then screeches to a stop as a hail of stones falls on it. The driver, a woman, gets out to inspect the car, then continues on slowly, scanning the street for culprits. I'm in an expansive mood and continue with a few fragments of Horace's second satire. *Values of simple and frugal existence, good friends, is my subject.*

Not any notion of mine, but the doctrine of farmer Ofėllus, unsystematic philosopher, schooled in no wisdom but Nature's.

The dog begins to sniff around the bench. I pat it and it looks at me, tongue lolling. I take a carrot from my pocket and begin to eat it. The dog sits and watches me, begging.

Now let me name the advantages gained by a plain sort of diet. . . . Have you noticed how pale people look when leaving a multi-course banquet? Not only the body is sluggish . . . but there is also dullness of mind, and our spark of divine upper air is dragged earthward.

The dog continues the vigil, droopy eyed and skeptical.

"I know, I know. Why should I be lecturing?" *I have extensive resources and income. Why must unfortunates suffer privation when you are so wealthy? Why must the ancient and venerable shrines of the gods be left shabby? Why, impious creature, why not devote some of your hoard?*

I hand over the remaining bit of carrot. The dog snatches it and swallows. A long, piercing whistle. The dog's ears prick up and it races off. Not a glance backward. I remain in the rusty little capsule for the better part of an hour. In Wilkington's gazebo nothing can diminish the vivid present. At one point I spot a little band of four or five boys scampering across the wide yard of the gabled and turreted house on the corner. They start across the street but stop short as soon as they see me and dart off in the direction of the woods.

On the way home I stop at Winesburg Wine and Liquor. Mr. Anderson takes out his vintner's charts whenever I come into the store, and I listen to him as he talks about people I couldn't care less about and who probably don't even buy wine from him. He's a puffy little man with a perfectly round belly that juts out like a melon. Whenever I stop in he disappears into the back room and comes out with his latest wares. This time he sells me a bottle of 1982 Château Brane-Cantenac and a cabernet sauvignon from California. He tells me the California vineyard is owned by some Hollywood movie director and it is the best wine they've ever produced. I take it home and drink it, my soon unsober mind trailing off into a casual lugubriousness.

The weather is good. I sit on a battered lawn chair in the back yard, pretending I'm a derelict on the Paris Metro.

"Monsieur, may I invite you to join me in a glass of wine?"

"Oui. Of course. How do you like the view?"

"The view? She is marvelous."

"Do you think a woman should go without makeup?"

"It's vulgar."

"Do you think they should remove the advertisements from the Metro?"

"Never, Monsieur. Never."

Glen Wilkington, the wood behind my house, is thick with leaves. Oak. Maple. Ash. A path leads through it to an abandoned railway line that cuts across the southwestern corner of the town and leads to a crowded intersection on the other side, where the fast-food franchises and convenience stores sprout. Beyond the wood is the water tower, surrounded by a chain-link fence and straddling a small concrete pumping station. Beyond that is a large field, part of which is planted and part of which has gone to pasture, a secluded little meadow. The Wilkingtons of the gazebo owned this land and saved it for posterity. The wood they protected from ax and saw, the meadow from plow, the field from factory. For most of the century the little glen has been the only wooded land left in the whole county. If Major Wilkington had been possessed of less foresight, it too would have been cut down, and the rail corridor that was compromised for in the middle of the last century would now be part of the interstate highway system.

With Mr. Anderson's best wine suffusing my blood, I imagine myself to be the very last locomotive that passed through Glen Wilkington. Mushrooms and other fungi grow in the rot of the old ties. It makes me think of sex, of devouring, self-preserving flesh that feeds on a rotten past to flourish in the rotten present.

A while later I find myself stumbling through the woods.

There are smoke signals coming from the Indian mound. From a distance they look like large clouds grazing the fields. At six in the morning, the sun climbing fast, it is already getting hot. I walk around the base of the mound, then follow the small path up. At the top a few burned logs smolder; a pack of Marlboros lies in the grass a few feet away. There are several left. I remove one, touch the end to the smoldering log and puff it to life, then lie down in a small patch of grass to daydream and watch the sun climb over Oblivion.

The sheriff's car pulls up at the base of the mound. It idles there for a minute, then the sheriff gets out and begins climbing the mound. I hear his jangling cuffs and keys. For a moment I consider trying to hide.

"That your fire?" He stands over me, wipes his forehead with a hairy forearm.

"No. I just got here myself."

The sheriff is a large man in exaggerated physical condition. His shirt, ironed and starched, stretches tightly across his chest. I've seen him in town, but only driving by. He towers over me. I sit up.

"What are you doing here?" He prods the smoldering logs with the toe of a well-polished shoe.

"I was out walking and saw the smoke."

"Where were you walking?"

"Because I enjoy walking, especially early in the morning."

"I didn't ask why. I asked where."

I puff on the cigarette. "Along Old 47."

He doesn't look at me but walks around the fire pit searching the ground, elbows jutting above his belt where his gun and other paraphernalia hang. I try to imagine the invisible pump that keeps him inflated. "Did you see who set the fire?"

"It was out when I got here."

"What about a car? Did you see a car?"

I stand up, shake my head. "No."

"Looked to me like smoke signals." Back turned, he begins to kick dirt onto the smoldering logs. "That what it looked like to you?"

I shrug.

"Yup. Looked just like real smoke signals. You know anything about smoke signals?"

I drop the cigarette and grind it in the dirt, then pick up the butt and put it in my pocket.

"Indians used smoke signals." He turns to me, hooks his thumbs into his belt. "You know anything about Indians?"

"No. Do you know anything about Indians?"

"I don't like your tone, buddy." He jabs a finger at me. "This is an official historical site. It falls under the protection of the State Highway Department."

"I've read the plaque."

He points to the smoldering fire. "Vandalism of an official historical site is a crime."

I look at the charred logs, then at the sheriff. "Are you accusing me?"

"I don't see anyone else up here."

"But I told you I just got here. I didn't light the fire. I came up here to put it out."

"I don't care if you came up here to pick posies."

I am arrested and taken back to town. It is the first time I've been in an automobile since I arrived in Oblivion. The overbuilt sheriff steers the overpowered car with his fingertips; a steel cage separates front from back where I sit. The radio, the assault rifle and shotgun, the deep, plush seats, and the little rack holding a large Styrofoam cup of coffee strike a note of parody.

"Do you have a family?"

The sheriff doesn't respond. He leans over and picks up the radio handset and clicks it twice, then puts it back without speaking into it. I assume it is some sort of signal. I settle back in the seat and watch the town slip by. When we arrive at the police station he tells me not to get out. He walks around and opens the door for me. I feel like a visiting dignitary emerging from the back of the car.

The sheriff marches me into the station. I insist that I'm being wrongfully accused. He shrugs and says, "Sorry, bud."

The fine is five hundred dollars. I should feel indignant but can't bring myself to. The situation is ridiculous. I pay their ransom with all the take-your-goddamn-money smugness I can muster; I actually enjoy paying. Part of it is the thought that freedom must be bought, that these days *autarkeia* means being able to pay. I have no desire to fight the steroid-fed sheriff. It's too much trouble.

On my way back home Tom Schroeder rides past on his motorcycle. He slows down and gives me the finger as he goes by. The kid is a true-blue asshole. One day he'll get killed in a pileup of cars and trucks on the interstate. He showed up on my doorstep one afternoon with a bag full of cassettes and compact discs.

"Want to listen to some music?"

I had been asleep and didn't hear him correctly. I stepped out onto the porch. He'd driven his motorcycle right up the walkway. It leaned precariously on its kickstand like some old, leaky nag. "Music?"

He pulled some compact discs from the bag to show me.

"Isn't it a little hot to be wearing all that leather?"

He examined himself as though he hadn't ever thought about it. His greasy blond hair was fastened to his head by a black bandanna, boots all scuffed and decorated with little chains.

"Keeps me cool when I'm riding." He unzipped his jacket, tee shirt soaked through, plastered to his body. Through it I could see a massive tattoo decorating his chest, some kind of jailhouse angel with cleavage and a Harley Davidson logo and a sneer and wings spread from shoulder tip to shoulder tip.

"I have lots of oldies. Fetus over Frisco. Generation X."

"I'm not interested."

"The Sicfucks. Dead Kennedys. Butthole Surfers. Meat Puppets."

I turned to go back inside. "Not interested."

"Here. Take a look. Check 'em out." He began pulling discs and cassettes out of his bag and stood there holding out his wares, a larcenous grin on his face.

"Do you still listen to them?"

"'Course I do, man."

"They don't bore you?"

"Fuck no, man. Good music is never boring."

I stepped back inside and closed the door on him. Schroeder yelled some obscenities, then stomped down the steps and rode away with a roar of smoke and ripped turf. A few days later he came back with a bag full of pornographic videos and asked if I wanted to borrow them. I told him if he didn't stop bothering me I'd call the police. Now he harasses me at every opportunity.

Back at home I try a few phone calls.

"Horace here."

"Wallace?"

"No. Horace."

"Wallace? Is that you?"

"No. It's Horace."

"Wallace, I thought you were upstairs napping. Where have you gotten off to?"

"I'm not Wallace. My name is Horace."

"You're not Wallace?"

"No. My name's Horace. Hor-ace."

"Don't you swear at me, Mister. How dare you?"

"Who's Wallace?"

"He's my husband. Who are you?"

"I'm calling to ask what you think love is."

"Did you say your name was Horace?"

"Do you have any thoughts on the subject?"

"On love? Wait a minute; am I going to be on the margarine commercial?"

"I beg your pardon?"

"I am, aren't I? The one that goes, *Do you looooove butter? Yes, I looove butter.* Then I try Parks Margarine and you go, *Do you still loooove butter?* That's the one, right?"

"No."

. . .

"Horace here."

"What can I do for you?"

"Define love in your own words."

"Love?"

"Yes. L-O-V-E. Love."

"Well, I'd have to think about it a minute."

"Take your time."

"Let me see. Do you mean what is love for me? Or what is love in general?"

"For you would be fine."

"Love. For me. Well, now, there are different kinds, I suppose."

"Are there?"

"It depends on what kind you're talking about. There's husbands and wives and parents and children. And then there is the love of Jesus, but there's no way of explaining that. You have to strive for it alone."

"Really?"

"Of course. I'll give you an example of what love is."

"Okay."

"Last year I was in the hospital. I had a bypass operation. My husband stayed with me every day. He only went home to change his clothes. I have two grown daughters, one lives in California and the other in Minnesota. They both came to spend time with me even though they have families and it was a considerable hardship for them. Now, if that's not love, real Christian love, I don't know what is."

"I don't either."

It hasn't rained for weeks, and the grass and weeds that sprout up around my house are wilted and turning brown. It is hot and humid. The sun beats down on the tin roof of my little yellow house, and despite open windows and drawn shades the rooms are stifling. The front porch is the only comfortable place, and I rock there all day long in the broken chair I rescued from the dump and restored with nails and glue.

I have been rocking on the front porch for three days now, and I have discovered something: time passes, and I enjoy having it pass. Inactivity is no easy accomplishment, and finding pleasure in it means overcoming conditioned reflexes. My mind wanders. I permit it to. I try to quiet it, slow it down. A period of what I suppose is called meditation ensues. Without effort I suddenly enter a thoughtless, wordless state. Time passes, and I am unaware of it. Leave it behind. This discovery of inactive bliss comes to me as a revelation. It is the wide-eyed empty-headedness of infant life, self-contained, unconnected to the temporal order of things. Nothing precedes it, and nothing ensues. Now I understand why the newer houses in Oblivion have replaced front porches with rear decks. Porches are for being idle. On decks you entertain yourself to death.

Often a distraction from outside breaks the spell: a sudden clap of late afternoon thunder, my neighbor revving his engine or honking his horn, a squirrel racing across the porch. Sometimes the distraction wells up inside, and a spontaneous thought becomes a memory and timeless bliss yields to idle irritation. Rocking restores my equilibrium, a sense of unity with the elements—though not with the neighbors. I watch them come and go, hustling from air-conditioned car to air-conditioned house. They come outside in the early evening to water their lawn and cast sour glances at mine.

A truck with a sign that reads Lawn, Inc., pulls up. A man gets out and ambles up the walk to the porch.

"Mr. Horace?"

"That's me."

"You called for me to stop by."

"I didn't call you."

"You didn't?"

"No, I didn't."

The man scratches the back of his head, puzzled. "Yesterday afternoon a Mr. Horace called, said he needed lawn work."

"It wasn't me."

A pause ensues during which the man makes a quick appraisal of the front yard. "Well, I wouldn't be here if someone didn't call me," he says with some irritation. "Anyhow, from the looks of it I'd say you could do with some yard work."

"I said I didn't call you. And I like my lawn the way it is."

He scratches the back of his head and surveys. Finally he says, "That's not a lawn, sir, that's a disaster area."

"Did my neighbor send you?"

"I couldn't rightly say. All I know is a Mr. Horace called and said he wanted his lawn worked on." The man takes his cap off and slaps it on his thigh, then adjusts it back on his head with military cockiness.

"My neighbor must have called you. I didn't have anything to do with it."

"That's none of my business, sir, if you and your neighbor got problems. And I don't ask for ID when someone calls me up. I just do lawns. It's how I earn my living."

I rock a little and watch him. A board squeaks. I don't want to talk to him, but he doesn't get the message and stands there, gazing out into the yard. "Just taking a mower to it would be a big improvement. 'Course it's only mowing weeds."

I don't respond, just rock. Finally he gives me a business card. "Just in case you change your mind," he says.

As he turns to leave, I change my mind. "I'll hire you on one condition."

"What's that?"

"That you do everything by hand. No power mowers. Nothing that has a motor."

The man looks at me, removes his baseball cap, and slaps it back on again. "What's your point here, Mr. Horace?"

"No point. Those are my conditions."

"But I don't see why?"

"Because I hate the noise, for one."

The man looks at the ground and thinks for a moment. "Well, now, if it's noise you want to get away from I could drop you off someplace and come and get you when I'm finished. The library over on Main Street is nice and quiet inside."

"I'm also against them."

"Lawn mowers?"

"No, motors. Internal combustion engines."

"Well, now, I just happen to have an electric mower. It's quieter than most, don't hardly make any noise."

I shake my head. "No motors. Period."

The man stands in the middle of the walkway and surveys the yard again. "Mind if I take a look around?"

"Help yourself."

I rock while he rustles around in the rear of the house. A few minutes later he returns. "It's a big job, Mr. Horace. You got four-year saplings this big growing back there." He holds his palm to his chest.

"I forgot to mention. The trees stay."

"Excuse me?"

"Those saplings. Leave them."

"I hate to tell you this, Mr. Horace. They're killing the grass."

"That's fine with me."

The man shakes his head and removes his baseball cap and slaps it back on again. "Well, I don't want to argue with you, Mr. Horace. I guess you're not interested."

"I told you my conditions. Take it or leave it."

"I think I'll just leave it, sir. You got troubles with your neighbor ain't any business of mine." He returns to his pickup truck, which is pulling a trailer with a small tractor on it. He pauses for a moment to look at his equipment. Cranking the steering wheel with the heel of his hand, he drives off in a mild huff.

Shortly before sundown I go for a walk and find myself at the airport. The usual pickup trucks and kissing couples are parked along the fence. I follow the fence all the way around and end up in the terminal. I've never been inside before. Lines are forming at the ticket counter for the early evening flight out. It is cold inside the terminal. An old man pushes a dust mop along the polished floor, eyes half closed. The cashier at the newsstand watches him as he shuffles past, her head propped on the heel of one hand.

I look at the departure schedule. Everyone in the airport is destined for Chicago. There are two flights later in the evening, each an hour apart. The first is to St. Louis, the second to Minneapolis. I find a seat among the departees. A young woman sits across from me holding a child in her lap. The child takes in the cavernous atmosphere, wide eyed. An elderly couple sits one row back, hands in their laps. A young man in a rumpled suit sips coffee from a Styrofoam cup and reads a sports magazine. I suddenly notice the Muzak playing softly throughout the terminal. It begins to roar in my ears. I can't swallow the lump at the back of my throat. The woman and her child are looking at me. I stare back. The woman averts her eyes, but the child holds my gaze.

I get up to leave, then sit down again a few seats away. The Muzak croons on. A swirl of black malice pinches my temples. My vision tunnels. But the sightless, thoughtless state doesn't exist.

I leave the airport through the front entrance, walk the length of the parking area and then along the fence to the end of the runway. The grass is dry and strewn with litter blown up against the fence. The airplane roars right over me, engines deafening. I force myself not to cover my ears. The wheels are drawn up into the belly of the huge machine, and it rises and banks away. Soon it is quiet again. All I can hear are crickets in the grass, and all I can see are the blinking red lights of the airplane high overhead.

The clock above the main entrance to the public library reads nine. The door is locked. I knock, and a woman appears on the other side, holds up a finger, and fumbles with a set of keys. She drops them, stoops to pick them up again, fumbles some more, and after several wriggling, jiggling tries succeeds in opening the door. "Sorry about that," she says pushing it open. "Our maintenance man is out sick today, and Mr. Mohr is running late and asked me to open up." I follow the woman down the short corridor into the main reading room. The reading room is an airy place with gilded ceilings and high windows. It must have been a bank once. The floor is covered with carpeting that muffles the sound of footsteps. The place has the atmosphere and smell of a renovated vault.

"Is there something particular you're looking for?"

"No. I just wanted to browse."

"I see. Well, if you need any help, please ask."

I walk between the rows of stacks browsing titles, not bothering to take anything from the shelf. Suddenly I realize there is something I would like to find, and I return to the front desk.

"Where would I find information on the Indian mound outside of town?"

The woman is jotting notes, holds up a finger. A few moments later she puts her pen down. "The head librarian, Mr. Mohr, is the person to talk to about that. Only he can grant access to special collections."

"Special collections?"

"The Wilkington Collection. Local history. There is quite an amount of material in it. Mr. Mohr will be in shortly if you'd care to wait." She nods toward the reading tables in the middle of the library. I withdraw to wait. Feeling lack of sleep, I put my head down on the table and drift in the library quiet, the smell of the old waxed table, and the mild hum of fluorescent lights.

"Excuse me."

A frail man with a razor-scraped face has appeared and is clutching the edge of the table. Mr. Mohr. He has an air of chemotherapy about him that the wig arranged on the top of his head does nothing to belie.

"Mrs. Entwhistle says you're interested in the Wilkington Collection." His speech is slow, a combined effort of articulation and exhalation.

"I'm curious about the Indian mound outside town."

"The Wilkington Mound?"

"Is that the name?"

The man nods stiffly. "It has other names, of course. Depending on the time. And who you talk to." His small barrel chest rises with the effort of speaking, and I find myself staring expectantly at him, trying to anticipate his sentences. "It was once called the Tortoise Mound. Because of its resemblance to a large tortoise. From about 1865 onward it appears on maps as the Wilkington Mound." He adjusts his glasses. "What exactly is it that you would like to know?"

The air inside the library seems suddenly stale. I consider dropping the whole thing and returning home. "Nothing specific," I say at last.

He seems satisfied by this and scrutinizes me from under his ill-fitting wig. The eyes behind the horn-rims are sunken and roll deep in their orbits. The musculature of his face seems completely atrophied. He has the obliging and deserted look of someone without an intuitive sense. "I'll show you what we have," he says.

I follow him up a flight of stairs to a small, windowless room lined with shelves and drawers. In the center stands a table over which an industrial fluorescent hood hangs, casting a bright cobweb of light. The head librarian motions for me to sit down. The first thing he hands me is a small volume called *The Wilkington Mound*. "That will give you details of the first scientific excavation," he tells me. "It was conducted at the turn of the century by the Bureau of American Ethnology."

I thank him and peruse the brittle little book. There are several grainy photographs of canvas-trousered men holding shovels and picks, shirt sleeves rolled high.

Mohr is examining a shelf across the room. "Most excavations of mounds in this area indicate they were used as burial sites." He turns, an ironic grin playing at the corners of his mouth. "Some are simply garbage dumps."

"Dumps?"

"Ancient trash heaps. The ones in this area, at least."

I flip through the book, dated 1904. Mohr slips a large leather folio onto the table. "This was a particularly rich site," he says. "And these are photographs and illustrations of objects taken from the mound. Pipes. Hundreds of pipes."

"Found during the excavation?"

"No. They were discovered much earlier. In 1846. By William Wilkington. He sold them in 1850 to an Englishman named Merrill for 150 dollars. William Wilkington, it seems, needed some quick money to settle his debts."

"Where did this folio come from?"

"A grandson of Merrill had the pipes photographed around 1895. He seems also to have been a gentleman ethnologist man-of-science type. The younger Merrill sent this folio to Major Perry Wilkington. There are letters in the correspondence file that indicate Major Wilkington had sought to buy the pipes back from Merrill. The folio was a courtesy."

"A courtesy?"

"That's how the younger Merrill describes it in a letter. He explains that he intends to publish a descriptive catalog of the collection and offers the photographs as a courtesy to Major Wilkington. There is also correspondence pertaining to a visit the younger Merrill paid to Major Wilkington around the turn of the century. He came out to see the mound just before the Bureau of American Ethnology excavated it. I think there was some connection there."

"Was the catalog ever published?"

"I don't know."

"Where are the pipes now?"

Mohr shrugs. "They seem to have disappeared. A few years ago an archaeologist came here looking for information. A woman named Palmer. She was in touch with someone in London who claimed to know the whereabouts of the collection. She said she wanted to excavate the mound, but I haven't heard from her since then."

The pipes are stone, carved effigies of various birds and animals. The head librarian flips the pages silently, a vague insinuation of beauty and mystery at the corners of his mouth. Halfway through the folio he stops, gathers up the pile, and closes the contents back into their case. He shepherds the oversized volume back to its place on the shelf. "There is quite an amount of material on the mound," he says with his back to me. "The state was going to put a road through it. The papers relating to that dispute are in the county archives. We have copies of most of them."

I watch as he sorts through more drawers. Although his back is turned I can sense his pleasure. Like some neglected child with a collection, his identity seems subsumed by the contents of this room. I have no doubt that he knows the history of this town down to the minutest and most insignificant detail. It is also obvious that he is dying.

"So tell me," he asks as he flips open a file drawer, "why are you interested in the mound?"

I push away from the table. "No particular reason. I pass it frequently on walks and enjoy the view from it."

"That awful factory spoils it." He opens a file drawer and begins to browse.

"I was arrested there the other day."

"At the factory?"

"No, the mound. I saw smoke coming from the top and went to see what was going on, and the sheriff accused me of setting the fire."

"Oh my. And they arrested you?"

"And fined me five hundred dollars."

Mohr lurches between the drawers and shelves and vertical files. I wonder how long he has plied the upper story of this library, what he does after the library closes and he returns home. Does he have someone to dote on him? Does he dote on someone? Does he stand in front of the bathroom mirror and cry?

His voice assumes a strained quality. "There are people in the area who consider the mound a sacred place," he says, hauling an oversized manila envelope from the back of an overfilled drawer.

"Indians?"

"There haven't been any Indians here for over a century. It's New Age types. You're not one of them, I hope."

I shake my head.

"Good. They come in here now and then asking for books. One came in about a year or so ago and handed me this two-hundred-page manuscript and demanded that I place it in the archive. I put it in the Idiot File over there. The Indians who built the mound, he claims, were tuned into some natural cosmic consciousness, and somehow the mound amplifies and broadcasts it for the benefit of adepts like himself who can tune into it as if it were some noncommercial public radio station. Really, I don't know where these people come from. Or where they learn that ecstatic babble."

"I wonder that myself."

"And why they feel compelled to sentimentalize the poor Indians. As if they haven't suffered enough of the white man's stupidities." He puts the envelope containing the manuscript in front of me.

"I think I'll pass."

"If you're ever in need of a good laugh," he says, taking back the envelope and returning it to the drawer marked Idiot File.

"The sheriff called it an official historical site when he arrested me."

The librarian coughs. "Funny. Don't you think?"

"That it is called an official site?"

"That the government has appropriated it. As part of its own official history."

I think about this and find myself wishing there were a telephone handy. I'd prefer to continue the conversation on the phone. Mohr is running out of breath; his sentences are coming out slower and slower. He sets another manila envelope down in front of me, and I pull up tightly to the edge of the table. "What's this?"

"That is some of Major Wilkington's correspondence. The mound was on his property. After fighting in the Indian Wars he became an advocate of Indian rights." Mohr pauses for a moment while I peer into the manila envelope, then continues, "He expended quite an amount of energy preserving the mound. Stipulated that excavation could only be carried out under the auspices of the State Historical Society." He stops, his breath exhausted.

I slide the contents onto the table and select a letter at random. It is written in an elegant nineteenth-century hand that I find difficult to read at first:

Hon. S. H. Parker,

My Dear Sir; I am in receipt of your valued favor of recent date, and beg to say that I recently wrote Congressman Farris that I would take up the matter with Mr. Howell. I rather think your suggestion a good one, that a commission or expert be appointed to investigate the matter. As I never tire of saying, the Indian, with whom over these last years I have had more than passing acquaintance, is being forgotten in the great onward march of civilization. It is only a matter of time when this mode of life will be an uncertain tradition, unless it be preserved in literature or in history. In my association with the Indian I have become aware that they lament this fact, for, like all proud people, they wish to be remembered at their best.

"Don't we all?" Mohr says, reading over my shoulder and leaning for support on the back of the chair.

I put the letter on the table. "Don't we all what?"

"Wish to be remembered at our best." He walks around to the other side of the table, puts a hand on his hip, shifts his puny weight, and fixes a look on me somewhere between disquiet and discomfort. His eyes swim in their broadened orbits behind his glasses. Then he turns away and looks at the ground.

Wilkington's letter is spread before me on the table like so many fragile yet tangible moments of the past. Though I haven't yet seen the lithographed maps and blurry photographs of Wilkington's Oblivion, his handwriting brings it to life in my mind. I can imagine the wheel-rutted road, the billowing elm trees, the corn crop, the dogs and dust, and the barefoot children. A bucolic, sentimental portrait, and I can see it in the major's leisurely, elegant scrawl.

"Will you be looking at more?"

"I don't know. I'm not sure I know what I'm looking for."

"Very well," he says and begins to gather the material up from the desk.

I remain seated, wishing vaguely that I could do something with all this accumulated evidence of the past. But the mound is moot. The past is moot. Nothing remains to be done about either. They simply were.

"Has anyone ever used these materials? Written a book?"

"A history of the town?" He twists his mouth into a smile. "Well, yes and no," he says. "I have been working on something for years. Nothing I'd ever want to publish. There have been county and state histories. But so far nothing about this town alone."

I get up to leave, thanking the librarian for his help.

"Would you sign the log, please?" He slides a clipboard across the table. The last signature is two months old. I sign my name, then print it along with my address. I leave the column marked *Purpose of Visit* blank.

"Your name is Horace?"

"Yes."

"We need your last name as well."

"I never use it."

"We need your full name, address, and telephone number. For our records."

I fill out the form as told and hand the clipboard back to him.

"Quintus Horatius Flaccus?"

"That's my full name."

Mohr looks at me for a moment, disbelieving.

"Do you want proof?"

"I'll be damned," he says, shaking his head. He tries to laugh but begins to cough.

Short, shuffling indeterminism. The phrase pops into my mind on the way to the mound, inspired by my visit with Mohr. The way he spoke in short puffs of breath sent me in search of a metaphor, but all that comes to mind is the phrase *a short, shuffling indeterminism*. I have no idea what it means.

I am interrupted by a flock of blackbirds rising up from the cornfield. Two sharp reports—*pop pop*—and the birds lift up out of the field with a furious beating of wings. The sky fills with animals. They hover for a moment; then as if of one mind, bank away. Another volley of shots. *Pop pop pop*, and in seconds the flock is gone. Short, shuffling indeterminism.

A car rushes past me as I stand on the side of the road. Flutter of dust and dirt, of cornstalks and birds, of suicides—van Gogh. I think Hemingway killed himself in a cornfield too. The lives of both men reduced to—a short, shuffling indeterminism? The phrase rises up and up, some sort of coded message shot from my unconscious like a flare from a lifeboat.

Another car whooshes past. I start walking again. The mound is about a half mile up the road. I stop and scan the sky for more birds but see none. If the road were elevated slightly, I might have a view across the field. But the corn is at its peak, and I am walled in on one side by the field and on the other by the fenced-in grass and asphalt wasteland that surrounds the missile factory, Semantech.

A figure bursts from the tall corn, stumbles in the shallow ditch that runs along the shoulder of the road. About thirty yards ahead. I see that it is a woman. A naked woman. She glances at me, terror stricken, and stumbles, then falls to the ground, where she remains without getting up. I run to her.

Her hands are bound behind her back. She twists her head and I see that her mouth is gagged with a piece of silver tape. She struggles to sit up, but the effort is too much and she slumps back onto her side, turns away from me in terror. I walk around so that she can see me, pat the air with my hands. "I won't hurt you. Let me help you."

She nods, squeezes her eyes shut. She struggles for breath. Her dark hair is tangled, clings with perspiration to the back of her neck and the sides of her face. She has scrapes and bruises all up and down her legs and on her arms and back. I lean toward her to remove the tape from her mouth, peel it away. "Oh God," she wails, gulps in air, and dissolves into a slobbering, whimpering heap.

"It's okay," I repeat like a mantra, knowing it's not. "It's okay. It's okay." It takes a few minutes for her to catch her breath. I offer to untie her hands, and she rolls onto her side. As soon as they are free she rolls onto her stomach and sobs into the ground, cradling her head in her arms.

There is no traffic on the road, so I squat next to the woman and tell her in the most reassuring tones I can summon that I will get help and everything will be all right.

"Were you being shot at?"

The woman is too convulsed to hear or respond. Her head is a mass of tangled black hair buried in her arms.

"Was someone shooting at you?"

The woman does not respond. I begin to pace the side of the road, not knowing what to do. Do I go for help and leave her? No. Waiting is the only option. I pull off my shirt and step back down into the ditch. "Put this on." The woman lifts her head, looks at me, startled, as though she had already forgotten my presence. Her right cheek is swollen and her face is too beslobbered and contorted to judge her age. I hold the shirt out for her and she takes it and slips it on, then rolls into a fetal curl, facing away. I step back up onto the pavement. The sun is high and the heat is beginning to shimmer off the road. Strong sunlight on my shoulders and back. The air feels leaden. The only sound an ominous rustling of the cornfield.

At last a car rounds the bend up by the mound. I walk into the middle of the road, wave my arms over my head. The car slows and then pulls over to the side and crawls toward me, stopping cautiously ten yards away. I jog toward it.

The driver pokes his head out the window. I recognize Ed Maver, the man on the bench. He recognizes me too and pulls the car forward to close the short distance between us.

"A woman. Have to get her to a hospital."

Maver looks puzzled. He doesn't see anyone.

"She's in the ditch over there."

Maver is about to get out of the car.

"No. Wait. I'll get her."

The woman is lying face down. I crouch next to her. "I'm taking you to the hospital. Can you get up?"

She nods, face still to the ground so that all I see is a nest of dark, tangled hair. She lifts her head, allows me to help her to her feet.

Maver's eyes open wide as we approach the car. He leaps out and races around to open the rear door. "Jesus Christ Almighty," he says.

The woman crawls across the back seat and collapses on her side. I get in front. Maver yanks the gearshift down and slams the accelerator, kicking up a fierce storm of gravel and dust behind us.

"What the hell happened?"

"I don't know. She came running out of the cornfield."

Maver looks at me, at my bare chest, then over his shoulder into the rear seat.

"I found her. She ran out of the cornfield and collapsed. I gave her my shirt."

Maver looks over his shoulder again. "Whad'ya suppose happened?"

"I have no idea."

"Did you see anyone else?"

"No."

"Was anyone chasing her?"

"I don't know."

"Looks like she's been roughed up pretty bad."

Maver takes a short cut to the hospital, turning down unfamiliar roads.

"What about the police? Hadn't we better let them know?"

"She needs a doctor first."

"Well, we oughta at least inform the sheriff's office. This is some sure-as-shit big-time trouble you got here." Maver pulls up to the emergency room entrance. I go inside to find a nurse. A minute later the woman is being helped onto a stretcher by two orderlies. Maver stands by as the woman is wheeled through the automatic doors to the emergency room. "I'll go park the car," he says, hops back into the car, and drives away.

At the registration desk a young man is waiting for me. There is no sign of the woman. The stretcher has vanished. "I found her on the side of the road," I tell the man. "She'd been running through a cornfield. Someone was chasing her, but I didn't see who."

"Have the police been informed?"

I shake my head. "Not yet."

"Do you know her?"

"No."

"Do you know her name?"

I shake my head again. "I've never seen her before."

The man looks me over for a moment. "Have a seat," he tells me and points to the waiting area with the pencil he is holding.

"Would you mind giving me my shirt back?" I hug my shoulders. "It's cold in here."

The man behind the desk picks up the telephone. He doesn't respond to me now that he has told me where to wait. I ask again, and he points with the pencil in the annoying way desk clerks have of issuing small orders.

Maver enters through the automatic doors, spots me sitting in a corner of the waiting area, and barrels over.

"What's the scoop?"

I shrug.

He sits down next to me and begins to talk. I tune him out, realizing that he will be impossible to get rid of. I sit with my arms crossed over my chest for warmth.

"You think she was raped?" Maver asks.

A pit opens up in my stomach. It feels like mild stage fright but without the flutters. I look at him without answering. Rape? It hadn't occurred to me. Really. And the fact that it hadn't hits me squarely over the head. How dumb. How could such an obvious thought have evaded me like that? Somehow all speculation stopped when I'd made the connection with the gunshots. Someone was shooting at her, and that was as far as I'd taken it. Rape hadn't occurred to me at all. I leave Maver and go back to the desk.

"Can you get me my shirt?" I ask. "It's freezing in here."

The man looks at me as though he's never seen me before. I notice the way his glasses pinch his fleshy temples. "Just a minute," he says.

"I've been waiting for twenty minutes already."

The man waves an orderly over to the desk. "See if you can find him a gown."

"I don't want a gown. I want my shirt back."

"I'm afraid you can't have it back."

"Why not?"

"Because the police will want it for evidence."

"Evidence? It's my shirt."

He turns away without response.

An orderly appears, hands me a white hospital gown. I slip it on like a robe despite his instructions to put it on with the opening at the back. Just then the sheriff walks through the automatic doors holding a clipboard. He approaches the desk with his permanently askew elbows and brushes past me without the faintest flicker of recognition. I stand a few paces away and listen as he talks to the man behind the desk.

"She's being examined," the man says. After a brief exchange that I can't make out, he nods at me and says, "He's the one who brought her in."

The sheriff turns to me. I sense the you-again in his otherwise expressionless face. Maver is standing by, eager to tell his story.

"What happened?"

"I was walking along Old Route 47."

The sheriff interrupts immediately. "What time?"

"I'm not sure exactly."

"How long ago?"

"Two hours, about."

Maver cuts in. "It was two fifteen when he pulled me over. By my car clock."

The sheriff turns to Maver. "You part of this too, Ed?"

Maver nods.

The sheriff takes the clipboard from the counter and gestures to the waiting area. "Why don't we sit down and go over this."

Maver tells his story first. He has answers to every one of the sheriff's questions about time and place and exactly this and precisely that. They share a dialect that allows each to anticipate and respond to the other with unbelievable precision. Forty yards, forty-two tops. Two—ah—seventeen P.M. by the digital clock in my car. Fourteen minutes, point to point. It must be connected to some element of shared ambition and culture. The military, perhaps. Since I don't share their language or their mutual familiarity, I am cast under suspicion.

They talk until the thread of Maver's narrative arrives at the point where I must take it up, and the sheriff turns to me with a furrowed look that is meant to dredge the truth out of me. There's no trusting strangers, it says. I describe exactly how the woman burst from the field, how I ungagged and untied her and gave her my shirt and flagged down the first car that came by.

"Where are those items?" the sheriff asks, jotting on his clipboard.

"The tape and the cord? I left them there."

"Will we be able to find them?"

The question strikes me as odd. "If they're still there, yes." I try to imitate Maver's forensic precision but see that the sheriff interprets my manner as insolence.

"Also, I think she was being shot at."

The sheriff stops writing and looks up at me with that furrowed expression again.

"I heard shots. Several of them. At first I thought it was the farmer scaring birds out of the field."

"Farmers don't do that," Maver interrupts.

"Quiet, Ed," the sheriff says. "How many shots did you hear?"

"I can't remember. Several. They sounded far off at first. Then the last one or two seemed very close."

"Did you see anyone in the field?"

"No."

"Did you see anyone at all? Tell me exactly what you saw. Describe the scene to me *exactly* as you remember it."

I pull the thin hospital gown more tightly around my shoulders and go over the details. The words *short, shuffling indeterminism* come back to me and with them the whole mystery of memory and pseudomemory, of signs and symbols, of particular things and events and moments that seem to converge and scatter at random. To be absolutely accurate, I would have to say a naked woman burst out of a cornfield into my idea of cornfields, which is connected to my knowledge of the suicides of van Gogh and Hemingway. But then I would have to explain everything to the sheriff down to the last detail, and that is virtually impossible. I might have started from the beginning and explained the overly theoretical sense of self that I have acquired from reading *Selected Philosophical Essays*. I would have had to explain myself as a "knowing subject lost in the object that is known," or as someone "dispossessed of narrative continuity," or simply as a "text." I would have had to explain that, at the very moment I heard the shots, I had somehow linked my existence to the idea of cornfields and the deaths of van Gogh and Hemingway and, by extension, all suicides and the world—the way a French semiologist once linked himself with Proust by captioning a baby picture of himself and calling attention to the fact that, at the time he was learning to walk, Proust was finishing *A la Recherche du Temps perdu*. Why not? If a French pedant can make such connections, then I can link myself and my birth and childhood to events such as, say, the Kennedy-Khrushchev Vienna Conference or the establishment of the World Food Program.

"Can you remember seeing anything else?" the sheriff prods again.

"A car. No. Two cars drove past me while I was walking."

"Which direction?"

I thought for a moment. "One toward town, the other away."

"Do you remember what make?"

"No."

"The color?"

"No. I was standing with my back to the road looking into the field."

"So you were looking into the field."

"Watching the birds. They were flocking because of the gunshots."

"You didn't tell me there was shooting going on when I picked you up." Maver speaks as if I'd betrayed him.

"What type of gun would you say it was?" The Sheriff is making notes furiously.

"I don't know anything about guns. I couldn't say."

"Was it a rifle or a pistol shot?" Maver asks.

"Ed, please."

"Was it a rifle or a shotgun? Or a handgun?" Maver smirks, satisfied with his forensic acuity, crosses his arms over his chest.

I shrug.

"Was it a *pop*," the sheriff asks, "like a firecracker?"

"Or a *crack*?" Maver again.

"A *pop*."

"Are you sure?"

"Definitely. But it wasn't anything like a firecracker."

"Not a *bang*?"

"No. It sounded like *pop* to me."

The sheriff writes this down.

"Probably a .38," Maver says.

The sheriff writes without looking up from his pad.

At last a doctor appears and signals the sheriff. Maver and I are told to wait. The cop swaggers over to the desk, where the doctor is looking over some papers, a surgical mask hanging casually around his neck. There is something leisurely about the way he looks. I think of the smashed-up woman and the antiseptic smells and the doctor's post-emergency repose. A renewed sense of pity wells up, a sense that the danger is past but the suffering is about to begin. The full horror of the woman's plight becomes apparent the way the contours of a photograph slowly emerge in a chemical bath. I can't explain the delayed reaction. Perhaps sympathy can begin only after shock wears off. The image that locks into my memory is the way she twisted and dipped her shoulder as she pitched forward out of the field, the way she stumbled and fell. The hapless moment, the moment beyond help. And the chill in her eyes that said she had already emigrated to that polar region beyond the reach of compassion.

The sheriff returns. "They've sedated her," he says officiously. "And I've got all I need for the time being."

"Was she raped?" Maver asks.

The sheriff ignores the question. "You can leave now," he says.

"Did they say what happened to her?" Maver insists. "Was she raped?"

"That's not your concern, Ed," says the sheriff.

Maver gets up. "Well, I guess I've had about all the excitement I can take." He turns to me. "You need a ride someplace?"

"I'll walk, thanks."

"I'll give you a lift," the sheriff says.

I accept the sheriff's offer for the sheer perversity of it. The sheriff gestures toward the door with his clipboard. "Oh, and Ed. I'll need you to answer a few more questions in the next day or two."

"Right," Maver says. "Anytime. You know where to find me."

This time I ride in the front seat of the sheriff's car.

"You'll be available to answer questions too?"

I nod.

After a pause: "You seem to gravitate toward that mound an awful lot."

"I enjoy the walk."

He shakes his head and is silent for the rest of the ride.

The neighbor's kid is standing in the driveway when we pull up in front of my house. He ogles the sheriff's car, stands stock still. As I get out he drops the hose he is holding and runs inside.

Discounting self-interest and sociobiology, instances of real Samaritanism are rare. I sit and rock on my front porch, thinking of the one or two, my own one or two. I am showered. Fresh. Fresh shirt, fresh pants. No shoes. The kid next door has resumed watering the driveway and is studiously ignoring me. His mother pokes her head out the side door to shout an order or two and glances over. My porch is about even with their kitchen door, and when Dad's pickup isn't pulled all the way up the driveway they have a clear view across the low chain-link fence. I ignore them as generously as I can. But I can sense that the sheriff's escort and the hospital gown I was wearing when I arrived back home have made an impression and renewed their interest in me. Wacko. I can hear the dinner-table talk. Now you stay clear, boy. Hear me? Forks wave. He's wacko.

I lift a leg into the chair, rock with purpose. Into mind pops a line from a poem. *If you never do anything for anyone else, you are spared the tragedy of human relationships.* I like to think the poet meant it. Unfortunately, I think he was just being ironic. I don't at all agree with the idea that a beneficent and thoroughgoing altruism can negate the tragedy of human relationships, can somehow reverse and obliterate it. Human relationships are tragic a priori, and the true Samaritan acts, not to change this condition—but in spite of it. The idea, implanted over the centuries by sentimental Christianity and taken over in our time by political propaganda, advertising, and the movies, is that by good deeds we negate this tragic condition and transform it into something better. But there is nothing better. The world is not so neatly divided. Good is not accomplished merely by negation of the bad.

I get up and go inside. The thought merits a phone call.

"Horace here."

"May I help you?"

"I'm glad you put it that way."

"Excuse me?"

"Do you like Saint Bernards?"

"Saint Bernard? I don't know who you're talking about."

"Not the saint. The dog. You know, the big shaggy things they use in the Alps to rescue people lost in the snow?"

"Yes, I know. Those huge, slobbery animals, the ones with the little wooden barrels around their necks. What about them?"

"What do you think about them?"

"What I think?"

"Yes."

"Not a whole lot. Frankly, I hate dogs. They scare me."

"I see. But what about in principle?"

"Are you calling from the Humane Society?"

"No."

"Because if you are, I'm not interested. I have a cat I took in as a stray, and as far as I'm concerned I've done my duty by little furry mammals."

"I see."

"A dog is out of the question. And a big dog? If you ask me, I think keeping gigantic pets is cruel. They need the outdoors. They need open spaces to run in. I don't know whose idea it was to make pets out of them, but in my opinion they have perpetrated a giant cruelty. Your organization should speak out against it."

"Against pets?"

"Against big pets. Yes. I've seen some of the literature you put out. About neutering and overpopulation and such things. But I've never seen anything about pet size. I mean, how big is big enough and how big is too big already? That's what you people should be concerned with. My neighbor down the street keeps a pig! Can you imagine? A pig. He says it's from Vietnam, but I don't care where he got it. Keep a pig as a pet? In the house? It's disgusting. You people should do something about it."

"I hear pigs are smart."

"Smart has nothing to do with it. My grandson is smart—but do I let him climb all over the furniture? To let a pig into the house—I'm sorry. It's disgusting. Now if you don't mind, I have to go. Sorry about the dog. I hope you find a nice home for it in Switzerland someplace."

A thunderstorm that has been brewing for the past hour finally rolls over Oblivion and pins the town where it lies with bright cracks of lightning and tearing sheets of wind and water. In seconds the weedy lot that is my front yard becomes a muddy bog. Water cascades from the roof overhanging the porch and makes me feel hidden, cozy and safe behind the waterfall. Moments before the storm broke I rushed through the house to close all the windows and have been monitoring the steady drop in temperature by the gooseflesh on my arms and my quickened olfactory sense. I can smell the rain. How clear the air suddenly becomes. Lines seem to straighten and corners sharpen in a thunderstorm. Water flies in dense sheets that sweep past with fierce momentum sustained by wind and the crackling clouds above. The violent crashes of thunder and the monotone *russhhh* of countless gallons splashing to the ground create a feeling of peace and serenity. I have been wondering about the woman in the cornfield for a full day now.

I called the hospital early this morning, but they wouldn't tell me anything except that she is still listed as Jane Doe. I thought of taking a walk out to the hospital to pay her a visit but stalled myself with a swirl of considerations. The thunderstorm is now my best excuse for not going. It's not that I don't want to see her, but that she might not want to see me. It's also likely that, for tightly argued bureaucratic reasons that I can anticipate all too easily, I won't be allowed to see her. Can anonymous patients be allowed anonymous visitors? More specifically, can Jane Doe be allowed to visit with someone she does not know and who doesn't know her? I expect she has already forgotten me. Why humiliate her all over again by forcing her to remember? I can imagine her resting in a state of mild sedation. The sterile atmosphere of hospitals promotes anonymity and all the derivative comforts, primary among them the comfort of knowing one is not alone in suffering. The shapeless gowns with their bare-buttocked openings, the institutional noises and colors and everything on wheels and in flux—a whirlpool of septic humanity passing into and out of existence.

The rain intensifies. I lean in the front doorway, hypnotized by the steady beating on the roof. Water collects in puddles that are rapidly becoming large pools. What will it be like come winter when snow falls and accumulates for days at a time? Since arriving here I haven't thought once about winter. The fireplace in the living room doesn't seem to have been used in years, and I realize it will be necessary to make sure the chimney is clear before lighting a fire. The sudden drop in temperature and the thought of fires and winter send me upstairs to look for a warmer shirt to put on. I lie on the bed and close my eyes, listening as the storm rattles the windows and shrinks me deeper into autism.

When the sheriff arrives to escort me to a lineup my first impulse is to throw *Selected Philosophical Essays* at him. "You want me to stand in a lineup?"

"It's part of the investigation, purely voluntary. You'd be helping us out."

Rather than ask him to explain, I run my thumb over the pages of my book and consider his request. "Purely voluntary," he repeats. He says it as though in volunteering I am exempted from all suspicion, whereas I know that my consent is only a legal formality and that he could just as well haul me into the station in chains. He stands squarely in front of me, filling up the door frame with his bulk. The patrol car idles at the curb.

"If I'd been allowed to visit her, none of this would be necessary. She could have told you it wasn't me."

The sheriff wipes his muddy shoes on the straw mat. The path to the front door is a strip of mud, and there is no way around it except across the soggy yard. "That's not the way it works," he says blandly. "Those rules are for her protection."

I go upstairs to dress while he waits on the front porch. In a sense, I am glad to oblige. I tried twice to visit the woman and both times found the way barred. I left the flowers with the nurse. Now I'm being asked to be part of a lineup. I put on a clean white shirt and roll the sleeves high up my arm so I look like the sort of convict who can deliver long, extemporaneous discourses on nihilism and existentialism. Jean Genet. Someone like that.

"You ought to try laying down some gravel on that walkway," the sheriff complains as we hop across the soggy yard to his car. My neighbor is standing on his front steps looking over with his hands on his hips. To make the pageant complete, the sheriff makes me ride, like a convict, in the back seat.

It is impossible not to think of punishment and innocence and pity and compassion as I ride to the station, a list of accomplished and yet-to-be-accomplished acts ticked off, deed by deed. Protesting isn't appropriate. Instinct tells me that. It would seem too much like whining. Moral perception is like a photographic negative, where the blackest shades develop into the lightest hues and vice versa. The best liars come out of the chemical bath lily white. Those who can't lie take the gray, grim blame. And the more the innocent complain of injustice, the more blackly they are perceived.

The sheriff escorts me into a waiting room. "Want a magazine?" he asks before leaving.

A magazine? Is this part of the shakedown? Part of the *modus tollendo ponens* of the lineup? *Either A or B; not A; therefore B.* We have all been subjected to this logic. Even children understand burdens of proof. It's a part of their instinctual makeup. So is finger pointing. So is lying.

Four others are escorted into the windowless green cube of a waiting room. I take a seat in the corner and look around, legs casually crossed. The others in the room hunker down, scratch upper arms, and look at the floor. I try to imagine the circumstances that have cast them under suspicion and begin to feel relieved. The logical necessity of my innocent presence in a lineup that might include one or more guilty men seems clear. I am the control, the reality check, the standard of innocence against which to measure the guilty. Right?

Good God. A ten-year-old wouldn't fall for that. What if the woman points a finger at me? I can protest all I want: I didn't do it! I swear I didn't do it! For Christ's sake! I glance around again. There is no logic here. My stomach churns loudly as I evaluate my fellow suspects. One of these fuckers is guilty. Not me. My boyhood wits remind me that the best hope of escaping an accusation is to make certain it falls on someone else's head. *Modus ponendo tollens: Either A or B; A; therefore not B*. He did it! It wasn't me!

"Got a match?"

The man is sitting three chairs away. He looks as if he were dragged here straight from a bar stool. An ugly wart grows just above his left eyebrow. His shirt sleeves are rolled halfway up his forearm and reveal a tattoo that has some Vietnam War association: Tunnel Rat.

I shake my head and on impulse ask, "Got a cigarette?"

The man pinches one out of his shirt pocket and offers it to me. Then he turns to the man on his right and asks the question in the same monotone: "Got a match?"

A hand holds out a lighter. I put the cigarette between my lips, and the man passes me his lit cigarette, squeezing it in the middle with his thick, cracked fingers. I decline with a polite nick of the head as the hand with the lighter gestures for me to avail myself. I walk over and lean into the flame, mumbling thanks as I straighten up, inhale deeply, and let my eyes wander down to the other end of the room. A guard is standing just inside the door, keeping a vigilant watch over the five of us. Two other suspects are talking quietly. They seem to be friends. Accomplices, maybe. They are young and, if it were up to me, guilty as hell. I sit back down, enter these faces into the modal logic of my innocence, my permanent, unassailable innocence, the innocence that I bring everywhere to everything—even smoking this cigarette, which has infused a raw and complicated taste into my mouth and the back of my throat.

At last we are shepherded into a long, narrow notch of a room. Three steps up onto a platform. Three other men join us, escorted in from a separate door by a different guard. They look distinctly convictlike. The lights glare. Behind us the wall is marked in feet and inches. We face a two-way mirror set into a frame in the wall like some large and minimal piece of art. The guard calls out instructions. Face right. Turn around. I expect to feel a cold hand clamp down on my shoulder. Come with me. But nothing of the sort happens, and in three minutes it is all over. We file offstage and out the door.

"You can leave now," the guard tells us. The Tunnel Rat shambles off, followed by the others.

"What about those other three?" I ask.

"They're going back to jail."

"Back to jail? Wait a minute." I ask the guard to explain. "How can you come up with suspects from jail?"

The cop frowns, looks at me as he must look at all the countless wastes of time he must endure every day. He is young, blond, with clipped hair that sprouts from his head as though implanted. "They're not suspects," he says.

"Not suspects?" My pulse begins to race. *Modus pollens* bursts apart. *Either A or B; not A; therefore not B?* Impossible! "If they aren't suspects, then what are they doing here?"

The cop closes the door and stands sentry in front of it with his hands behind his back. "It's part of the workup."

"Workup?"

The cop nods. "First we start with photographs. Then we do a drawing. Sometimes we have to look at real people. You know, types. They're supposed to be getting a computer any day now."

"A computer?"

"That can do composites."

"So I'm not a suspect?"

He shrugs. "You'll have to ask the detective."

The cop disappears through the door. I hadn't reckoned with being used as a mnemonic boot to kick the woman in the head with. I thought they had suspects. I thought they were going to arrest somebody.

The air outside is sticky hot. I pause on the steps of the station to wonder what the poor woman—if it were she behind the glass—said when she saw us. Did she recognize me? Or, following the logic of the procedure, did I remind her of someone else? Were the lot of us dismissed with a sigh—nothing, sorry—and a crushed cigarette? Back to the drawing board?

"Excuse me." A young woman has appeared at my side. She had been among a group of people waiting outside the sheriff's office when I was brought in. "May I ask you a few questions?"

"Who are you?"

"Oh, sorry. I'm with the *Sentinel*? The newspaper? Can you answer a few questions about the rape?"

"Who told you to ask me?"

The woman is unsettled by my tone. She fumbles with her bag and takes out a small tape recorder. "Someone inside said you were a witness."

"I didn't witness anything, and I don't want to talk to anybody."

"Could you tell me what you saw?"

"I didn't see anything."

The woman holds the tape machine in the palm of her hand without turning it on.

"I helped get her to the hospital. That's all."

"Could you tell me what happened?"

"I don't want to talk about it."

"Fine. I understand. Could I get your name?"

"What do you want my name for?"

"For the record."

"I don't want my name used." I feel my voice quaver and a wave of tension rising up my neck, the beginning of a headache. "Do you understand that?"

She nods.

"Turn on the tape."

A startled smile comes over her features; she wipes the sweat from her forehead with the back of her hand and holds the machine for me to speak into.

"I am a private citizen, and I want to be left alone, so don't come looking for me."

She nods, eager for me to cut to the details, holding the machine up.

I lean toward it and, measuring my words, say, "If you print my name or mention anything about me in print, including this conversation, I'll sue you and your paper for invading my privacy."

The woman snaps the tape recorder off and stuffs it into her bag. "That was uncalled for." Her face has reddened. "That was obnoxious and completely uncalled for," she says and stalks back into the station.

I skip down the steps and begin walking briskly toward the center of town. Some instinct for escape takes hold, and I obey it. A curious constellation of thoughts begins forming as I walk: the relationship—logical and otherwise—that exists between pairs of opposites, between guilt and innocence, memory and forgetting, anger and sorrow, pity and vengeance, love and hate. And especially the strange transmutation that often occurs between them and binds them together in a unity that seems bizarre until one recognizes it as part of the eternal order of things. I increase my pace.

The sheriff's car pulls alongside. He rolls down the window and leans over on his side. "C'mon back," he says and pops the front door open.

"Why? They told me I could go."

"She wants to talk to you."

"Who?"

"Who? The woman. That's who."

A green-aproned waitress is standing in front of the Corn Tassel, one of only a handful of people outside on this hot day. A few people sit in the diner, visible through the large windows. She lifts a cigarette to her lips and turns to look the other way while pulling on it. Then she turns back to watch, a cloud of smoke issuing from her mouth and nostrils.

"C'mon. Get in." The sheriff pushes the passenger door wide open, spilling some of the cool interior out into the heat. The radio squawks and blinks. I slide into the seat and close the door. Without a word he swings the big police cruiser into a tight U-turn and we return to the police station.

"She remembered you," the sheriff says, getting out of the car. "But that's as far as we've been able to get. She's a complete blank. The doctor says it's shock. The whole thing—*pfffft*—blanked out."

"I wish I could do that too."

"When she saw you she blinked."

"What's that supposed to mean?"

"Just what I said. She remembered you. She's not very talkative, but the doc was able to get her to say she remembered your face."

"Wait a minute." I get out of the car and talk across the roof. "You said she asked to see me."

The sheriff turns and strides toward the station. "You'll see what I mean," he says, and gestures for me to follow him.

"I'm not going in."

The Sheriff turns to me. With one hand in his pocket he jingles his change. "Look. She recognized you, that's all. We asked if you were the man who attacked her, and she said no. The doc thinks seeing you might help her remember more."

"Is that why you brought me into the lineup? To help her remember?"

"Yup. That's right." The sheriff opens the door and holds it for me.

"Why didn't they just ask me to come to the hospital?"

"Because if she had identified you as the man who attacked her, we would have had to bring you here anyway. It saved us a trip." He grins maliciously and tries to put his hand on my shoulder. I draw away. "Relax, pal. It's just a joke. Nobody's making any accusations. You're doing a good deed is all."

We walk down the corridor. The reporter from the *Sentinel* suddenly appears. She shoots me an I-don't-need-you-anyway look and begins to ask the sheriff a question. "Not now, honey. Later." He waves her off and opens the door to his office, where a man is waiting.

"This is Detective Ross." We enter the flag- and mugshot- and plaque decorated room. "He's been assigned to the case."

Detective Ross gets up and offers his hand.

"Where is she?" I ask.

"I'd like to ask you a couple of questions before we go in to see her," the detective says.

My eyes revert to the sheriff, behind his desk now and opening a drawer. "Why didn't you tell me you were bringing me here to be questioned?"

"Didn't think it mattered," he says, then adds with a supercilious grin, "and you didn't ask."

A flash of anger causes my throat to constrict and my stomach to tighten. "What the *fuck* do you want with me?" Heat is rising up into my face.

"Cool it, mister. Just cool it." The sheriff plants both palms flat and leans stiffly over his desk. "Or I'll lock you up."

The detective cuts in. "Calm down, both of you," he says and interposes himself between the sheriff and me. He turns to me. "I just want to get a sense of what happened. There's nothing to be upset about." He pinches his trousers at each knee and sits down in a chair next to the sheriff's desk. He is a middle-aged, flabby black man with a graying mustache, close-cropped hair, and a large cushion of flesh that squeezes above his collar. He is wearing a blue seersucker suit that seems casual and old fashioned among the starched uniforms of the station. He gestures for me to sit down in the chair across from him, ignoring the sheriff, who has his back to us and is unpinning papers from the cork wall at the back of the office.

"Let me see if I got your name right," the detective begins, reading from his notepad. "Quintus Horatius Falcus?"

"Flaccus."

"Flaccus. Flaccus. Quintus Horatius Flaccus," he pronounces. "Mind if I ask where you got a name like that?"

"I gave it to myself."

"Where are you from, Mr. Flaccus, originally?"

"You mean where was I born?"

"That's right."

"New York."

"And would you mind telling us what name appears on your birth certificate?" He eyes me ironically. "You don't have to, but we could find out easily enough for ourselves."

"Be my guest."

"All right, Mr., ah, Flaccus."

"Call me Horace."

The detective grins. "Okay, Horace. Could you tell me exactly what happened the other day? Exactly as you remember it." He pulls a blank pad across the desk toward him and prepares to take notes, his face contracting into a frown of concern and concentration.

I try to recount the episode for him, the shots, the birds, the whole thing exactly as it happened. Ross lets me talk without interruption, then holds up his hand. "Was she walking or running?"

"She was stumbling. Her hands were tied."

"In front or behind?"

"Behind."

"Did it look like she fell? Or did she collapse?"

His questions strike me as completely superfluous. "I suppose she collapsed. That's what it looked like to me."

"How far away were you when you first saw her?"

"I don't know, about a hundred feet or so."

"So she could have fallen."

"I suppose so. What difference does it make?"

The detective jots as I talk. "Just going for as much detail as possible. Bear with me. Now," he asks, leaning toward me, "was she running toward you or away from you when you first saw her?"

"What are you getting at?"

"Just try to remember."

"Neither. She just collapsed."

"Before or after she saw you?"

"I don't know."

"Think about it. Did she come out of the field, turn, see you, and then collapse?"

I shake my head. "She stumbled straight out of the field and collapsed onto the embankment at the side of the road. I have no idea if she saw me or not."

"When you approached her, was she frightened?"

"Scared shitless."

"Did she let you approach her? Or did she try to get away?"

"I said I wasn't going to hurt her and held my hands up so she could see them. She had tape on her mouth and was having trouble getting enough air. She let me approach her to take the tape off. After that I untied her."

"Describe how you did it."

The detective continues writing as I speak, demanding details that finally leave me exasperated. "I just dropped it. I didn't crumple it in my hands. I didn't throw it. I just let it drop on the ground. Jesus Christ, what difference does it make?"

"And that's when you took off your shirt and gave it to her?" The detective leans back, slides a hand into his pocket. I half expect him to produce the cord we have been talking about, but instead he takes out a handkerchief and blows his nose. He folds it and slides it back into his pocket, leaving his hand tucked along his fat thigh.

"Yeah. That's right."

"I guess that's all I need for now," he says, speaking half to me and half to the sheriff. "You can go visiting when you're ready."

They bring me into an adjoining office, and I am introduced to a woman I hardly recognize by a matronly psychiatrist who has accompanied Jane Doe here from the psych ward of the county hospital. Jane sits primly on a bright orange vinyl chair. Her hair is combed up and tied into a straggling black tail that begins high on her scalp. She has sea-blue eyes that seem to water at the sight of anything, and her nose is red, from crying, I suppose. She looks older than I remember her.

Dr. Henley, the psychiatrist, does the talking while I stand across the room. Jane Doe stares at me in blank astonishment.

"How are you feeling?" I ask her.

She looks at me as though I hadn't spoken a word.

"This is the man you said you remembered. Do you still remember him?"

Jane begins to fidget in her lap. A few moments elapse. Then her head bobs.

"Wonderful. Very good," the doctor exclaims.

I feel as though I am sinking into the floor, sensing the shame that has suddenly swelled and thickened the air in the room. I look at the woman, whose eyes are cast down, and guess that I must fit into her trauma as some horrible frill. I glance at the doctor and signal that I am ready to leave, but the doctor sits on the worn wooden arm of Jane's chair and begins talking quietly to her.

"I have to go," I mutter and turn to leave.

"Just a moment, please." The doctor escorts me out of the room with a briskness that defies the sullen circumstances. In the hallway she offers me her hand and thanks me for cooperating. "You can't imagine how important this has been for her."

"You have to hand it to these police."

"You misunderstand. It was my idea. I thought it might help her to remember. The police were very obliging."

"When it's in their interest to be."

"And thank you for cooperating."

I nod my head slightly, wanting only to get out of there.

"She recognized you. It is an important first step."

"So you've told me."

"When you came into the room with those other men, she pointed to you and said, 'I remember him.'" She puts her hand on my shoulder. "Don't worry," she tells me, "she remembers you as the person who helped her. Not as her attacker."

"What's wrong with her?" I ask.

"The symptoms resemble a combination of post-traumatic stress disorder and psychogenic amnesia, a dissociative disorder."

"Was she hit over the head?"

"There are no physical signs of concussion. But she has been badly traumatized, and there's no telling how long the amnesia will persist. She could snap out of it any moment, or it could take weeks, even months."

"She has no idea what happened to her?"

"She remembers what happened to her but has no memory of the person who attacked her or of her own identity. That's why it's significant that she recognized you."

"The police think so too."

The doctor's eyes shift away. "Well, I don't know what to say about that."

"Neither do I."

The faucet in the bathroom drips. Lying awake in bed, I can hear the sound echo down the hallway. It stays in the foreground. In the background the night chirrup of cicadas, a faint breeze blowing in the trees, the pulse of blood in my ear marking lonely time in the dark.

Drip drip drip drop

Squeak

I sit up. Someone is in the house . . . or on the porch. The bedsprings shatter the silence. A thin shaft of blue moonlight illuminates the room. I swing my legs off the bed, stand up slowly. Carefully. A board squeaks underfoot. My pulse beating hard, I am motionless, listen, then tiptoe into the hallway and pause at the top of the stairs.

Squeak squeak drip drip drip

On the porch. Not inside. I exhale slowly through my nostrils, try to control my breathing. My ears are hot. The thought that I have no weapon occurs to me at the same moment I realize I'm naked. I stand at the top of the stairs, motionless. The springs on the screen door begin to crack as it is pulled open. The front door is never locked.

Crack crack. The springs are straining. I imagine the screen door propped open with a shoulder. The front-door latch rattles quietly. A flashlight beam cuts the darkness, illuminates the wall at the foot of the stairs, skates around, and clicks off. My heart is pounding. I put my left hand on the wall for balance. The flashlight beam sweeps the bottom of the staircase again, clicks off. The front door clicks open.

Aaahhhhhhh! I rush down the stairs, testicles bouncing. The door slams. Racing footsteps. I charge down the front steps into the middle of the yard. I strain to see the figure running up the street. In seconds it has vanished. I stand, heart pounding, chest and belly wet with sweat. The hollow pit in my stomach, I realize, is not fear but the slowly dawning pain of free-swinging balls. I have racked myself. I withdraw from the yard onto the front porch, one hand clutching my groin. Breath comes in short bursts. The pain swells as the adrenaline ebbs. A moan becomes a growl becomes a howl: *mmmmmm ohhhhhhhh Fuuuuuck!* I pause for another minute; teeth begin to chatter. In the distance the sound of a motorcycle. The pain in my groin spreads upward, turns to nausea. One retch. Another retch.

I go back to bed but can't sleep. I lie on my back staring at the little orbs of darkness and light that float before my eyes. Sight, in darkness or broad daylight, a function of gathered and filtered globules of viscous light. The pain in my groin has become a dull ache. Words string themselves together in a little rhyme. Do you ever see those little spots? Those tiny orbs? Those puny dots? Do you ever think you're going blind? Walking straight ahead? Staying right behind? Your life is veiled by night mucus. The words stick in my head, forming a little jingle.

By dawn the pain in my groin has become a hollow-stomach feeling. I get dressed and go outside. Mist hangs in the air.

I walk to the police station. The desk sergeant looks up from his mug of coffee.

"Got a problem?"

"Someone tried to break into my house last night."

He puts down his coffee, reaches into a drawer, and takes out a form. He asks me to fill out the top half.

"This doesn't have to be anything formal."

"Are you reporting an incident or filing a complaint?"

"Both."

He reaches into his drawer and brings out another form. "You'll have to fill this out too."

"Can't I just tell you what happened?"

"We'll get to that part afterward."

I fill out the forms and hand them back. The sergeant sips his coffee and glances at the papers. Then he fills in his part and asks me to tell him in my own words what happened.

"I didn't get a good look at him, but I know it was that asshole kid with the motorcycle, Tom Schroeder."

"What makes you think it was him?"

"I heard his motorcycle."

"Did you see the motorcycle?"

"No."

"How do you know it was his?"

"I just do."

The sergeant looks at me over the rim of his coffee cup. "There's not much here to go on, but I'll make a note of it."

"Have you ever had a beard?" I ask him, thinking that men with loose jowls like his should grow beards.

"What's that supposed to mean?" He frowns.

"I was just curious."

He puts his hand to his cheek. "It's against regulations. But it's funny you should ask. My wife used to ask me to grow one when we were first married."

"Did you?"

"I couldn't. I was already on the force. Mustaches are okay, but full beards are against regulations."

"Who made that regulation?"

He shrugs. "Beats me." He taps his pen on the desk. "You think I'd look better with a beard?"

"Maybe."

"Maybe when I retire." He laughs, sips coffee. "I'll send a detective out to look around if you like."

"I've already looked around. There's no need."

"Well then, all I can say is keep your door locked at night and try to get to a phone next time. There's not much we can do at this point."

"What's it going to take for you to catch that little prick?"

"We'll catch him one of these days; don't you worry about it."

I sit at the small table in my kitchen, my notebook open in front of me. On the stove a pot of black beans bubbles and boils as I try to compose a thought worthy of expressing in writing, but except for today's date I can think of no words to inscribe in the spiral bound pad - no words of my own, that is. So after checking the boiling pot and stirring the thickening mass and opening a bottle of the wine I bought at Winesburg Wine and Liquor yesterday, I find myself scribbling disconnected passages from Horace out of ransacked memory. What comes out onto the paper are the words of an ode that once inspired me.

Remember in adversity to maintain a calm and even mind, and when times are good

—what then? When times are good, when times are good . . .

To guard no less against excessive happiness, Dellius,

—and the name sends me scuttering among the overturned tables of all the Horatian poems I ever committed to memory with the thought that by having stored such things inside me, I am partaking more grandly in life by stretching the borders of my own existence backward into time. . . .

Happiness, Dellius, who are destined to die no less if you are forever sad

—Dellius Dellius Dellius, friend preserved in the alcaic stanzas of dead Latin . . .

Than if on every holiday you enjoyed secluded picnics with Falernian
—wine, his own Gevrey-Chambertin . . .
Out of the storeroom's remotest corner.

I put the pen down and read the lines, proud of my capacity to recollect them. I had thought they were gone, wiped out along with all the memories I have tried, with mixed results, to suppress.

I take the pot off the stove, pour the cooked beans into a large bowl, and set them on the counter to cool. If left in the cooking pot, beans acquire an unpleasant metallic taste. An earthy smell now suffuses the kitchen and raises the humidity index of the entire house. I return to the table to look at the shaky black lines I have just put down, sip the wine Anderson sold me—from the storeroom's remotest corner. I bought a case from him and asked if it could be delivered. He said he'd be more than happy to drop it off on his way home. He tried three times to conceal his surprise: first when I told him I'd take the entire case, then when I told him where to deliver it, and finally later that day when he stood politely at my front door and passed the heavy wooden crate across the threshold as though he were introducing something into the house that shouldn't belong there.

I haven't used the telephone now for days. I've resisted the temptation, preferring to let the thoughts popping around my brain lie idle along with the rest of me. Drinking wine is a passable substitute. *Earliest use of the wine jar imparts the bouquet that is longest lasting*. Horace's advice. So I have started using it, reaching for the bottle instead of the cradled receiver, pouring the ruby liquid into a glass, resting my Kilroy nose on the rim to absorb the waft of fumes instead of punching out seven random digits, listening to the clicks and pips, waiting for someone to answer. For the time being, sipping wine has replaced plying questions along the electronic river.

The humid summer heat has the entire town stalled indoors. Everything is still, motionless. Even the trees. I wandered in the woods behind the house for a while yesterday, surprised to find it no cooler than out in the scrubby expanses of my yard. This morning I found a small hand trowel in the cabinet under the sink. I went outside and with monkish intention began to dig in an overgrown flowerbed next to the house. I've always admired the gardening sensibility, the bald-headed, bare-chested simplicity, the solitary attentiveness. But after an hour I sat back on my haunches, smeared sweat from my forehead and chest with a muddy hand, and realized I hadn't the faintest clue what to do in all that newly upturned dirt. I stood up and surveyed what I'd done. It looked like the bed had been invaded by a family of burrowing rodents. I plunged the trowel into the ground to its hilt and left it sticking there, something to mark the effort. *Mollis inertia cur tantan diffuderit imis oblivionem sensibus: Why should softness of indolence so have imbued all my senses and lulled me into lethargy?* Lulled? Am I lulled here? No. Not lulled. Quelled. By my own instincts. Oblivionem sensibus. *Much as if I, in a parching of thirst, had been greedily drinking the waters of forgetfulness.*

I drop the pen and again admire my powers of recollection. It has been years since I committed these lines to memory, changed my name, and re-presented myself to the world as Quintus Horatius Flaccus. The only difference between the Quintus Horatius Flaccus of Augustan times and myself, the QHF of the here and now, is that the first Horace—who retired to his Sabine farm to escape the bustle of Rome—was a social climber and a nice guy, whereas I am without any social ambitions whatsoever and have never considered myself, nor do I know how to be, nor have I ever striven to be—nice.

Still, my identity is bound to the name I have taken, Quintus Horatius Flaccus. Call it an act of forced continuity that has bound me to the name while leaving the poet to roam freely in the surviving body of his work. I have found justification for my wanton act in countless passages from *Selected Philosophical Essays*. It doesn't matter to me which views are current and which outmoded. The thought is the significant proposition, right? So I'll take whatever I can get from philosophers and from poets alike. I am QHF for the present. I might just as well be Diogenes or Marcus Aurelius or Jesus Christ. But, thankfully, I lack most of the discipline and all of the ambition.

It is time to go out and get some groceries. Fortified by wine, I gather my pack and put on my shoes and step outside into the evening. The air has cooled.

The walk is almost twice as far as Foodway, but I won't go there anymore since the manager shooed me away for loitering. I wasn't loitering. I was observing—and with great ethnographic detachment, I should add. Riteway is at the northern end of town, on the strip that caters to the people who live in the suburban ranch tracts, the white-shirted engineers of Semantech who moved here in one of the plate-tectonic shifts of the American economy. Riteway is spanking new, a cavernous bazaar filled not just with household provisions but with all sorts of prepared exotica. Its name suggests the shifting premise of consumerism, a shift from the practical to the fanciful. While the name *Foodway* is pragmatic and informative, the name *Riteway* is precisely the opposite and, in subtle and complex language, suggests the *rite* of consumption as an aesthetic ritual. On top of everything, I hate the walk out here. There are no sidewalks, and there is no way around the four-lane highway or the bottle-strewn underpasses.

I enter the supermarket. The harsh neon stabs at my eyes, and I pause for a moment inside the pneumatic entrance to allow them to adjust. From moonless, starlit streetlight to the hard blue-white, twenty-four-hour daylight of Riteway.

I take a plastic hand basket and begin my search up and down the aisles. My mouth is dry from walking and red wine. I drink an entire bottle of Crystal Mountain Spring Water, to the astonishment of a lady pushing a mountain of groceries. She maneuvers around me, casts a look of suspiscion, her child riding marsupially in the burgeoning cart. I drop the empty bottle into my basket along with another one for the walk home and continue up the aisle behind the moving mountain. She takes up three-quarters of the aisle with her bulk. She moves slowly on tiny running-shoe-shod feet, her head swinging side to side like a tiller as she selects among brand names, a wad of clipped coupons in her fist. She stops and backs her cart up slightly, blocking the aisle. I turn and walk back the other way.

There is a steady flow up and down each aisle. I try to adjust myself to the pace but am unable to get it right. It seems timed; people sweeping along to Muzak down aisle after sterile aisle of colorful packaging and stock display. As I dart up and down I imagine the infrared God's-eye view of this neon-lit parade of hungry organisms.

At last I find the rice. I can choose between boxes or plastic bags or boiling pouches or premeasured, EZ-Pour containers. I heft one ten pound bag of white and one ten pound bag of brown. Twenty pounds should keep me away from here for the next month.

"You can buy bulk out at the co-op," a voice from behind me intones.

I turn. It's the librarian, Mohr, looking pale and splotchy under his wig and behind his thick horn-rims.

"Horatius Quintus Flaccus, I presume." He smiles, a strange clacking at the corners of his mouth, and extends a hand.

"Mr. Mohr. Hello." I grasp his hand lightly, a weak articulation of bones, and almost ask what he is doing here. It is hard to believe that he actually eats.

"The prices are more reasonable at the co-op."

I hold the basket with both hands, bounce it lightly against my knees. "A co-op?"

Mohr nods. "I buy everything I can there. Come here only out of absolute necessity."

I look at the contents rolling around in his basket. It is an effort for him to push the metal cart around. His breathing is audible.

He is still talking. "Out of town a way, about ten miles north on 47. It's in a barn that used to be part of a dairy. It's really very handy."

"Not for me, I'm afraid. I don't have a car."

"Oh. Well, yes. Then it is too far."

We stand there for a moment. Mohr seems unsure what to say next. He is looking into my basket. "How do you manage all of that?"

"I carry it in my pack." I turn slightly so he can see it hanging empty on my back.

"You can carry it all on your back?"

I nod.

"I see," he says, gripping the handle of his cart as if he needs it to hold him up. With the wig slightly askew on his head, he looks like something that came to life under a Christmas tree sometime during the last century. I shift my basket into my left hand and step around him. He moves the cart slightly to accommodate me, looking at my basket as though he were trying to imagine lifting it himself.

"See you at the library." I continue down the aisle.

As I reach the end of it, the fat woman rounds the corner and swings her cart into me. We face off for a startled moment, a tinge of red twisting into her round Dutch-boy face. Instead of backing away so I can pass, the woman tries to maneuver around me, pinning me between a pillar and the row of shelves.

"Back up," I tell her, but she ignores me, suety little arms struggling with the mountain of food.

"Back up," I repeat.

She lets out little puffs of air. "I'm trying!" The child riding in the cart has twisted around to look, a purple fruit bar jammed into its mouth. The woman gives the cart a mighty tug and pulls it backward, but she can't contain the momentum and it swerves into a display, bringing down an avalanche of cereal boxes. The child lets out a yelp. The woman's face becomes a panicked red. "I have a child here," she manages to splutter with indignation. "I have a child with me." I slide around her cart and step over the pile of boxes. "Do you understand? A child!"

I don't have the slightest idea what she means. She says it as though I have violated some subtle supermarket etiquette that gives her the right of way.

"A child. Do you understand?" She seems to want me to respond. I can't imagine what it is she is trying to tell me, so I turn and heft my basket for her to see. "And I have rice. Long-grain basmati rice!"

A clerk sweeps by us and begins to restack the fallen boxes. The woman begins babbling at him. I go stand in the checkout line.

"Can I offer you a lift?"

Mohr has lined up behind me, holding his giant metal cage before him like a battering ram. "That would be great," I tell him, emptying the items from my basket onto the conveyer belt. I follow them up toward the waiting cashier. Mohr pushes in behind me, lifts the items from his cart, and assembles them neatly on the conveyor belt, laying down a plastic rod to separate his things from mine.

The cashier drags my purchases across the scanner, and I put them into my pack.

"Soon we'll have this stuff too." Mohr is talking to me. "Scanning technology. The state is promising it by the end of the year. The information superhighway." He fishes in his billfold as he talks. "Of course, all the technology in the world won't get people to read books. Or return them on time." He pays the cashier, who drops the bag containing his groceries into his shopping cart. "Or stop stealing."

I follow him out the door and offer to carry his bag, but he waves me off with a wobbly gesture, saying he can manage. The arc-lit lot hums with electricity and idling cars and the strains of Muzak piped outside through speakers recessed into the store's awning. Mohr walks slowly. I try to imagine which car is his and am surprised when he stops beside an enormous old station wagon, the kind with fake wooden panels.

Mohr's facility with the outsized vehicle amazes me. We whip out of the lot and into the flow of traffic. He drives with exaggerated ease, the way some older people do, as though the automobile were a giant prosthetic device. The back of the car is filled with boxes that, I assume, must contain books.

"Where do you live?"

"West Street."

He thinks for a minute. "I don't think I know where that is."

I explain that I'm not sure of the best route and point out the general direction. "I've always walked," I tell him.

"I see," he says. "That's a long walk with that weight on your back."

"I'm used to it."

"You would have to be."

We drive in silence for the rest of the way. As he turns onto West Street, Mohr begins to cough, a few light hacks that, by the time we pull up to my house, become a fit.

"Are you all right?" I ask before getting out.

Mohr holds onto the wheel with one hand and with the other holds a handkerchief to his mouth, coughing blindly into it. "Just . . . a . . .

minute . . ." The tendons on his neck strain beneath his collar, his wig askew, face deep red.

"Come inside," I tell him. "I'll get you a glass of water."

Mohr nods, holds the handkerchief to his mouth, and tries to clear his throat. "Just need. A minute," he manages to say.

"You want me to bring it to you?"

He shakes his head, gets out of the car, and follows me up the walkway toward the house.

The back door slams, stopping me in my tracks. "Wait here." I peel the pack from my shoulders and drop it on the ground, sprint around the house. It is too dark to see, but as I round the corner I hear the sound of someone crashing through the underbrush in the woods behind the house. I halt, squint into the darkness. As my eyes adjust I begin to walk across the open yard toward the wall of trees at the bottom of the yard. Without a moon it is impossible to make out anything but indistinct shapes. In the woods a flashlight beam slices through the darkness, then shuts off. I plunge toward it but stumble in the thicket. The beam flashes on again, this time farther away. I cup my hands to my mouth. "I know it's you! You little fucker!" I stand and wait. The beam flicks on again, then off. He has reached the rail line and will follow it out of the woods.

I hear Mohr coughing as I make my way back across the yard to the house. He is sitting on the porch steps when I return. "A burglar?"

I fetch my pack from the middle of the walkway where I dropped it. "Let's see."

The front room is undisturbed. Mohr follows me into the kitchen and stands in the doorway. There is shattered glass on the floor, and the back door is wide open.

"Be careful," Mohr wheezes behind me.

"My wine glass." I stoop and pick up the flat disk that was the base. The empty bottle is still on the table. "He knocked it over when he ran out."

"You'd better call the police," Mohr says.

I leave the kitchen to check upstairs. The second floor seems undisturbed. The bedroom is as I left it, sheets turned down on the bed.

Selected Philosophical Essays face down on the floor, window open. A warm breeze. No signs of intrusion.

"Did you call?" Mohr asks when I return to the kitchen. He is standing by the sink holding a glass of water. It is the first time I've seen him in light other than library or grocery-store neon. He looks less wilted. His wig seems more natural; his features are etched, not sunken.

"I don't think I want to. I've had enough of police lately."

"But someone broke in."

"They didn't take anything."

"You should report it."

I open the broom closet. My case of Château Bel-Air is still there. I lift the lid, no bottles missing. It is the only thing I can think of I might miss. That and my—notebook! I turn to look at the table. The notebook is gone. "Goddamnit!"

Mohr is startled.

"Goddamn, goddamn, goddamn him!"

Mohr puts his glass in the sink. "Call the police," he intones.

"They won't do anything. Goddamnit! Besides, I know who it was."

"Report him."

I go upstairs to call. When I come back down Mohr is standing outside on the front porch. He seems unsure whether to stay or to leave.

"The little bastard stole my notebook."

Mohr lowers himself onto the top step and sits with his back hunched. "Nothing is safe," he says.

"Are you feeling better?"

Mohr nods. "Thank you, yes."

I stay inside, behind the screen. A slight breeze blows through it into the house.

"I have these coughing fits fairly often." He clears his throat, his back still turned, facing into the yard. "I have lung cancer and a touch of emphysema."

I let the screen door slam behind me and sit down on the rocking chair. The chirping of cicadas in the trees fills the silence, and I resist the temptation to say I'm sorry. I rock for a moment, waiting for Mohr to continue. But he doesn't. His shoulders rise and fall with the effort of breathing. "How long do they say you'll live?"

Mohr lets out a weak guffaw that makes his shoulders shudder. He looks back at me with crooked mirth, seeming to appreciate the brutal banality of the question. "I was supposed to die six months ago."

We sit in silence, the warm summer air circulating by a breeze that seems to be picking up. I watch the moths swarm around the bare lightbulb that juts from the wall at the far end of the porch and wonder if it will rain. What is there to say?

The police arrive. The patrol car glides to a stop directly behind Mohr's car. A figure emerges, tests a flashlight beam against the blackness, then approaches.

"Someone call in a complaint?"

Mohr stands up, keeping a hand on the post for support.

"This kid keeps harassing me," I begin.

The cop tucks his long flashlight under his arm and holds up both hands to stop me. He asks if I am the one who called in the complaint.

"Yes," I say and begin to tell him what happened.

The cop interrupts me after a few seconds. "You chased him into the woods?"

"He was already in the woods by the time I got to the back of the house."

"Then what happened?"

"Nothing happened. He got away. I came inside and found a broken glass and my notebook missing."

"Notebook?"

"My journal."

"Mind if I take a look?"

I escort the cop inside. Mohr stays out on the porch. I tell the cop about Schroeder, and he asks a few questions that I can't answer—where he lives, if he goes to school, where he works. We go back outside, where Mohr is still leaning against the post. The cop switches his flashlight back on and says he's going to walk around the house.

"I'll be on my way now," Mohr says as the cop clops past him down the steps. "Sorry about the trouble."

"Do you drink wine?"

"With all the drugs I'm on?"

"Have a glass before you go." The impulsive tone in my voice startles him.

He hesitates. "It's late. I should go."

"It'll do you good," I say with the false authority that can only be used with the troubled, the sick, and the dying.

Mohr accepts with a delighted nick of the head.

The cop reappears. "That about does it, I guess."

"I hope you find the little bastard and lock him up."

"We'll look into it, sir."

Mohr has a nervous tick that I imagine would be more pronounced if he weren't sick. As we sit at the kitchen table he bounces his leg, holding onto his kneecap as though to steady it. It seems to exhaust him, and, unable to sustain the level of energy, he shifts around on his chair uncomfortably, taking unsteady sips from the glass I've poured him. We face each other across the table, each trying to be good company in his own way and to take this unexpected bout of sociability in stride. Mohr seems as unused to amiable conversation as I am. Under the yellow light we begin groping toward a topic of conversation. The Wilkington Mound starts us off. Mohr begins with the Dutch Reformed minister who moved his congregation here in the 1840s and who wanted to build his church on top of the mound.

"Are you prepared to die?" The question pops out spontaneously. I immediately regret having asked it.

Mohr falls silent for a moment. He lifts his glass to his lips and considers his response as though taking up a challenge. "Six months ago I was. Yes."

"And now?" Since I have broken the ice I want to see how far I can pursue the conversation.

He holds his glass in his lap. "When I thought the clock was running out, was set to stop on a given day, in a given month. In a given year. It was much easier."

"When limits were set, you mean?"

"They gave me seven months to a year. Of course, they hedged and said anything was possible. Funny, isn't it?"

"I suppose so."

"Doctors will make a prognosis and disclaim it all at once. Anyway, the general opinion was that I wouldn't last more than a year." Mohr grins the same way he did out on the porch. "And now they say I'm in remission. So in a way, it's like it was before I was sick. Except I'm still sick. I don't think I can explain it very well."

I refill my glass and offer to refill Mohr's. He pauses to consider, then slides his tumbler across the table. "I don't drink."

"I'll get you some water if you like."

"No. The wine is," he sips and smiles so that his face flushes red, "delicious."

It is close to midnight. Mohr is asking me questions.

"You live here alone?"

I nod.

"I live alone too. Now . . ."

A pause hangs between what he has said and what he would like to say. He drinks. I imagine the secrets that are contained in his silence and decide not to pry them out into the open. My intuition will fill in the blanks, as his will have to fill in mine. It's a civilized arrangement. I would never have settled for it on the telephone, that wonderful blunt instrument. But I can't put aside my curiosity about his condition. His affliction.

"How much longer do you think you have?

Mohr thinks for a moment. "I don't know. The doctors say it's a miracle that I'm alive and that I can still take care of myself. I've had a place reserved in a hospice for months. But I can still get around on my own. So why hurry?"

"But what do *you* think?"

"I can't say. I'll just keep going for as long as I can, and then I simply won't be anymore. If I were religious, maybe I'd think otherwise. Religious people are supposed to have a leg up on death. I guess it's because of their faith that something exists beyond it. I think it's exactly the opposite."

"How so?"

"It's their fear that inspires them. I believe that fear of death is an expression of a sort of contempt for the world, for nature."

"How so?"

Mohr clears his throat and recites, "*And nothing 'gainst Time's scythe can make defense / Save breed, to brave him when he takes thee hence.* And I never bred. So there." A long pause ensues that features the battering of flying insects against the screen door. "I don't believe in God—not the Christian one anyway." He waves his hand to dismiss the topic, then sips more wine and continues in spite of himself. "Heaven, being saved, the afterlife, fear of death, danse macabre, and all that kind of thing. It's medieval." His mouth makes a clacking sound, a labial, dental, skeletal blend of noises as he talks. "In my humble opinion, the modern, scientific, atheistic sensibility is a great improvement over that squalid medieval frame of mind." He pauses for a moment, then adds in a stuffy, stoic British accent, "It's a damn shame we have to go. Rather a waste of time, don't you think?" He pauses to drink, then resumes his normal voice. "Do you watch television?"

"No."

"How we worship life and the body today!" Mohr grins. "You see these young, healthy, strong people leading young, healthy lives. No fear, no thought of the end. Just infinite, sunny optimism. A wonderful illusion, a world like that."

"A banal world."

Mohr waves away the remark, lifts his glass. "I love it. The illusion! Television! Especially the advertisements." His head bobs slightly. "They promise everything, and they deliver. In *this* world, *here*, not some other. And it's a wonderful, beautiful illusion."

"What about all the violence?"

"Violence?" He laughs and waves with a theatrical flourish. "It's all fake! Nobody dies. It's a pageant. A danse macabre! A world riddled with corpses—and death is entirely absent from it." He pauses for another grin. "I find it—wonderful! All illusions are wonderful."

"Except the illusion that there is a God and life after death."

"Exactly. That's a dirty, rotten, nasty illusion."

"I don't see the difference."

"You want to know the difference between religion and television?"

"Is there one?"

"Television you can turn off." He laughs.

I refill his glass. "I've never talked to a dying person," I confess after another silence.

Mohr holds his glass in both hands, eyes alight with wine. "Nor have I," he says. "Of course, there are all these groups you can join and therapies designed especially for people in my condition. But I don't bother with any of it."

"Why not?"

"Because dying is not a personal problem."

"What is it if not personal?"

"I don't know. But I am compiling a bibliography."

"How practical! Of what?"

"Of death. I have over one thousand titles."

"Sounds like therapy to me."

Mohr shrugs. "It's something to pass the time."

"Will you publish it? As a form of transcendence, I mean."

Mohr chuckles. "I hadn't thought to. But I like the idea." He tilts his glass and peers into it. "Tell me something, Quintus Horatius Flaccus." He fixes his eyes straight on me. "How did *you* become such a morbid asshole?"

There are four Schroeders in the telephone book: E. C., Frank and Thelma, J., and Schroeder's Shoes. Reflecting on the pros and cons, I decide to take Mohr's advice to recover the notebook myself. It's a matter of principle. Mohr convinced me of it last night before he passed out.

The foundation of a friendship seems to have been laid between Mohr and me, which is strange since neither of us seems much inclined toward making friends. "I was born a morbid asshole," I told him. "I don't know anything else." He laughed until a bout of coughing overtook him. I opened another bottle, and the conversation veered toward the intimate—then crashed there and exploded into the quaintly restrained maudlin. "Don't call me gay," he said with put-on indignation. "I'm too old to be gay. I'm homosexual." Then he told me that he had lived with someone in town for years, a man named Bill.

"What happened?"

"He moved to Chicago. We used to visit each other, but over the years we've drifted apart. He has his life and I have mine."

"You aren't sick with AIDS, are you?"

He shook his head. "No. Just good old-fashioned cancer. And a touch of emphysema. I used to chain smoke."

"Why didn't you go to Chicago with Bill?"

"I didn't want to live in a big city, and I liked my job here." Then, after a pause, "In spite of everything I am actually comfortable living here. I know it's hard to believe. I've lived here twenty-five years."

We went out on the front porch. I offered him the rocker, but he declined, so I took it. He walked to the far end of the porch, holding the almost empty wine bottle by the neck. With his wig askew and leaning against the corner post for support, he cut a quaintly pathetic figure. We didn't speak. His happy delirium made words unnecessary. A short while later he staggered inside and collapsed on the sofa in the front room. "Don't leave it to the cops," he muttered before passing out. "Get the notebook back yourself. And give the boy a good thrashing." I covered him with a blanket and left him to sleep. This morning when I came downstairs he was gone.

I dial the first Schroeder. Three rings. "Hello?" An old man.

"Is this the residence of E. C. Schroeder?"

"It is."

"I'm looking for Tom."

"Tom?"

"Tom Schroeder."

"Don't know him."

"Are you any relation to Frank and Thelma?"

"Who?"

"Frank and Thelma Schroeder. On Ivy Street."

"Never heard of 'em."

"They're listed in the phone book."

"You trying to sell me something, mister?"

"No. I'm trying to locate somebody. Tom Schroeder."

"Let me give you some advice, son."

"What's that?"

"You want Tom Schroeder? Call Tom Schroeder's house. Listen to me, son. You want Thelma? Call Thelma. Did you say Fred?"

"Frank."

"Call Frank. I'm Earl. Now, you want to talk to me, fine. I'll talk to you all goddamn day long. But don't go calling Earl when Tom's the one you want to talk to."

"Thanks, Earl."

I dial Thelma and Frank. No answer.

Next I get a machine. "Hi. This is Jerry. Leave a message and I'll call you riiiiiight back."

I hang up. Schroeder's Shoes is last on the list.

"Schroeder's Shoes can I help you?"

"I'm trying to locate Tom Schroeder."

"Tom?"

"Yes."

"He's not in today. You want to leave a message?"

"No. That's all right. Will he be in tomorrow?"

"He's usually here every day."

"Oh? How long has he worked there?"

"He's the owner."

"The owner? How old is he?"

"Tom? I don't know. I never asked him."

"Does he have a son named Tom?"

"Who is this?"

"Never mind. Does he have a son named Tom?"

"Look, mister. I have a customer on the floor. I can't talk."

In the kitchen I fill a glass with water and go outside onto the porch to sit in the rocking chair. The morning sun has already pushed the temperature from comfortable to warm, and I am hung over. I close my eyes, feeling the seismic waves of headache at the back of my brain. Getting drunk with the head of the local library now feels a little unseemly, a prelude to future embarrassment.

I go inside for a second glass of water. The phone beckons to me from its cradle.

"You want the definition of illusion?"

"Just tell me what you think in your own words."

"An illusion?"

"Yes." I watch a fly bang against the window screen trying to get outside. The noise is like that of a poorly resonating harp string. Does it crash against the screen eye first? Is it trying to break through to the outside? Does it see the screen? I walk over for a closer look. Cradling the phone on my shoulder, I raise the screen. The fly sails out.

"An illusion is something that isn't there, but you think it is."

"Okay."

"That all?"

"Go on if you like."

"Who are you?"

"Horace."

"Horace who?"

"Quintus Horatius Flaccus."

"Very funny. Why did you call me?"

"To ask you a question. That's all."

"You don't think it's a little weird?"

"Weird?"

"Yes. Calling up complete strangers and asking what illusion means."

"I ask other questions too."

"How broad-minded of you."

"And I didn't ask what illusion means. I asked what you *think* an illusion is."

"And I just told you. Something you think is there and isn't. Wait a minute, I'll go get the dictionary."

I lower the screen and stand looking out the window into the back woods. The woman returns to the phone. "Here. It says, 'illusion: (a) an erroneous perception of reality; (b) an erroneous concept or belief; 2. The condition of being deceived by a false perception or belief.' Just like I said."

"How can a belief be false?"

"What's that?"

"A belief. How can it be false?"

"That's a pretty dumb question."

"Then tell me what a false belief is."

"Something you think is true but isn't."

"Like what?"

"Like ghosts. You can believe in them all you want, but it doesn't mean there are such things."

"How do you know?"

"Because there just aren't. Everybody knows there aren't."

"But if you believe in them and, say, something wakes you up in the middle of the night and you believe it was a ghost. What woke you up?"

"A noise. The cat maybe."

"It wasn't a noise. It was just a feeling. I was scared. Can a feeling be false?"

"Are you saying that if you believe in ghosts, then ghosts exist?"

"No."

"Then what are you saying?"

"I'm just wondering what a false belief is. Or a false feeling."

"It's an illusion. A false belief is an illusion."

"A false feeling too?"

"Sure."

"Is a dream an illusion?"

"Of course. They only exist in your head."

"So an illusion is something that can only exist in your head?"

"Yes. And an illusion of *yours* sure can't exist in *my* head."

"Says who?"

"Listen, who'd you say you were again?"

"Quintus Horatius Flaccus. Horace."

"Listen, whoever you are. Don't you think you should get a little help?"

"Help?"

"Yes. You sound disturbed, bothered. Maybe you should go talk to somebody."

"I'm talking to you."

"I don't mean calling people up and asking them stupid questions. I mean professional help."

"Did I ask a stupid question?"

"No, it was a very interesting question. But I think you might have a problem."

"You do?"

"Sure. Why else would you call up a perfect stranger?"

"You're right about that. I do have a lot on my mind."

"So you agree."

"Agree to what?"

"That it's a little weird calling people up to ask what an illusion is."

"Sure it's weird. But it's interesting. Ever hear of the Oracle of Delphi?"

"What?"

"The Delphic Oracle."

"No."

"The ancient Greeks used to go to Delphi and ask the oracle questions."

"And I'm the oracle?"

"No. The telephone is."

"Oh, how fun. You're weird, Horace. Get help, and good luck. I have a tennis game. Bye."

She hangs up before I can ask what number I'd dialed. Too bad. I would have called her back. Despite the cheerful optimism that put her squarely in the camp of those sunny positivists I so despise, I would have liked to talk to her some more.

I reach for my *Selected Philosophical Essays* and thumb through it. I've always bridled at the notion that "help" is available for every human predicament. I won't say "problem" because the word belongs to a vocabulary I prefer to steer clear of. There is no arithmetic of human emotions—problem + help = solution. And I'm suspicious of the "happy consciousness" that is the desired outcome of so much help. My instincts tell me something is wrong. If life is guided by the reality principle, it seems to me that serenity is a more appropriate goal than mere happiness. Happiness is fleeting and too easily confused with pleasure—which elevated to a principle creates the seesaw of discontent that Freud had all of civilization teetering on. Why make life so complicated? Serenity is a state achievable only when all contingencies have been dissolved. A completely autonomous life is free of contingency and requires nothing to sustain it.

So I'm a morbid asshole. So what?

I put the book away.

The sun is shining directly onto the porch. My headache seems to be getting worse despite my efforts to rock it gently away. I go inside for some aspirin. The bathroom mirror reflects a gaunt-faced stranger, blank and bloodshot.

I strip and climb into the bathtub. There is no shower nozzle, just a handheld rubber attachment. A blast of cold water, a quick, shivering lather. I rinse quickly, washing the soap from my tightened skin like a thin film of white paint. I climb out, toss my clothes into the tub, and begin to wash them. A sudden mania for laundry sends me through the house gathering more clothes and sheets and towels to wash. Kneeling over the tub, I try to pretend I am by the side of a clear, rock-strewn stream on Horace's farm outside Rome two thousand years ago—sun shining, world twittering over my head and all around.

Out in the backyard I try to fit all the wash onto the clothesline. I am bare chested, wearing a pair of cut-off shorts. The ground is cool against my feet, the sun directly overhead and shining strongly from a deep blue, cloudless sky. I hang the sheets up first. They shiver on the line and bring to mind backyard images of domestic life that are soothing in a folksy sort of way. The picture is framed by the woods at the bottom of the yard; the little yellow clapboard house; the chain-link fence that encircles the neighbor's property, dividing the citadel of discarded appliances and toys from who knows what; a rusty red-and-white reclining lawn chair set like found sculpture in the middle of the yard—three tattered, procumbent planes ratcheted into odd but supple angles. And the laundry going up on the line.

My hands swollen white with detergent and water, I wring each item before hanging it up, trying to get the last drop of water out, straining my pectorals with each squeeze. There are no clothespins, so I have to balance everything carefully.

"Heard you had a visitor last night." The voice startles me. I turn to see Detective Ross standing almost directly behind me. He breaks into a sweaty grin. "Sorry if I made you jump."

I step back from the line, wipe my detergent-swollen hands on the back of my shorts, and glance at the detective. He is wearing the same blue seersucker I saw him in last time, the same inquiring grin, and a panama hat. "What can I do for you?"

"I have a question or two I'd like to ask." He takes out a handkerchief, removes his hat, wipes his forehead and the interior band of the hat. "You reported a break-in last night."

I nod. A jackhammer pounds away in the distance, a road crew at the top of the street. A dog barks. These distant sounds are amplified by the detective's hard breathing. He looks scorched and uncomfortable beneath his suit and jowly grin. He replaces the hat on his head. "What was stolen?" he asks.

"My journal."

"And have you noticed anything else missing?"

"No."

"Just the notebook?"

"Just the notebook."

"That's a strange thing for a thief to take. Don't you think?" Ross slowly folds his handkerchief and tucks it into the pocket of his jacket. "The Schroeder boy been bothering you a lot lately?"

"So you know about him. Good. The little fucker should be locked up." I pick up the empty laundry basket and swing it to let the water fly. A small arc of droplets lands in the grass with a pleasing little sound.

"What do you think he wants with your notebook?"

"I have no idea."

"How does he even know about it?"

"I'd like to know that myself."

"I guess you write down your thoughts and such in it."

"Yes and no."

"What kind of stuff do you write in it?"

I rearrange the clothes on the line, considering how and whether I should answer.

"That's what most people do, isn't it?" He takes a small pad from his shirt pocket and holds it up. "That's what I do with mine. Take notes. Record impressions. Couldn't do my work without it."

"I recite."

Ross tucks the pad back into his pocket. "I don't follow."

"From memory. I recite passages, texts I've learned."

Ross nods, a look of puzzled appreciation. "What kinds of texts?"

"All kinds of texts."

"The Bible?"

"Ancient poetry and philosophy, mostly."

Ross's eyebrows arch and he nods again as though to say, my, my, but aren't we . . . strange. I continue rearranging the clothes on the line, wondering what he is piecing together in his detective brain. For the briefest moment I'm tempted to invite him to sit down with me in the grass—or, better, on my front porch, my stoa—and discuss it. I might explain to him that my preoccupation with ancient texts isn't as much an exercise in memory as it is an effort to construct—or reconstruct—a self. I might explain that nothing resonates more clearly or more truly, nothing creates a fuller sense of *being,* than the words and phrases that cycle through me; that my essence is memory and that the content of this memory is identical to the content of my being. I might tell him that I believe he too is a sum of texts and that to know them is to know himself, and I might recite to him the opening of the John Gospel, a text that I have no doubt already resides within him—*At the beginning of time the Word already was; and God had the Word abiding with him, and the Word was God. He abode, at the beginning of time, with God.* That you don't even have to believe in God to know this about the Word, and finally that, this being the case, we are epigones, all of us, and thus may—no, must—choose the texts we live by.

"A personal question." Ross holds up a finger. "Just one."

"Go ahead."

"What is a rich, educated, middle-aged dude like you doing in a place like this?" He gestures toward the house, the yard, a fat smile breaking across his face.

I have to think for a minute, and we stand facing each other beside the clothesline. Sheets billow gently. Ross's stentorian breathing is as audible as the breeze. I swing the plastic basket once more and watch the tiny arc of water disappear in a neat, parabolic curve. "I like it here."

The detective, grinning, shrugs his heavy shoulders. "Just asking," he says.

Two squirrels scamper across the far corner of the lawn and up into a tree. I watch them with feigned interest.

Ross continues eyeing me from a discreet, detectively angle. "I thought folks like you preferred big cities, apartments. You don't fit here. Know what I'm saying?"

"You didn't come here to talk demographics, did you?"

His expression turns serious. One hand disappears into his pocket; he shifts his weight, paunch hanging over his belt. "I'll get to the point," he says. "What does that boy—assuming he was the one who broke in last night—what does he want with you?"

"How the hell should I know? He's been pestering me for weeks."

"How long you been living here?"

"Since the spring."

The detective shakes a handful of change in his pocket.

"He started coming around in the beginning, but I made it pretty clear I wasn't going to indulge him."

The detective rocks back on his heels, jingling. "Far as you're concerned, then, he's just trying to get some attention."

"I don't know what he wants. He ought to be locked up."

"And the notebooks—that's just something personal he can lay his hands on. Like a souvenir. Know what I'm saying?"

"Who knows?" I swing the laundry basket again. "The kid gives me the creeps. He tried to break in here a week or so ago, but I chased him off."

"I read the report."

"Who else is he harassing?"

"You're the only one been complaining."

"Why don't you just go and arrest the little bastard?"

An indulgent smile. Ross takes his hand from his pocket, extends it, and we shake. "Thanks, man. You've told me what I needed."

"I have?" We walk together around the side of the house. "How's Jane Doe doing?" I ask.

"As a matter of fact, she's gone home," Ross says.

"She's home? I thought nobody knew who she was."

"*We* knew who she was. They had to keep her until *she* knew who she was. Couple of days ago it all came back to her. Except she still can't remember who attacked her or how she ended up in that cornfield."

We are standing by the front porch. Ross's car is a white unmarked police cruiser with an enormous antenna bent and clamped down to one side of the roof.

"Who is she?" I ask.

The detective glances at me, then looks toward his car. "Let me ask you something."

"Go ahead."

"Did you see anyone else in the field that day?" The tone of his voice and his look demand that I try to remember.

"I heard shots. Then I saw her. That's all."

"Then what?"

"I told you before."

"Tell me again."

"I approached her. She let me untie her, and then I gave her my shirt."

"Then what?"

"Then I flagged down a car."

"The first car that came by?"

"Yes. The first car."

"So. Until that car came along it was you and her alone by the side of the road. Nobody else."

"That's right."

"And you didn't hear any more shooting?"

"No." I put down the laundry tub and lean against the frayed and rotting edges of the porch floorboards. "I told you everything already. What's the point of going over it again?"

Ross takes out his handkerchief, tilts the brim of his hat back, and wipes his forehead. "Just routine," he says unconvincingly.

"Routine," I repeat.

"You sure you remember it exactly?"

"How many times do you want me to repeat myself?"

Ross folds his handkerchief carefully into a small triangle and tucks it back into his pocket. I watch him, thinking for the first time how strange it is that he is a detective. With his big, soft grin and his rumpled looks he'd pass for a preacher or a school principal. "You see," he says, extending his hand for another handshake, "it might be just like you say. And you didn't see anyone else out there that day." We shake, and he holds onto my hand for a beat longer than seems normal. "But that doesn't mean there was nobody there and that *they* didn't see *you*." He turns to leave but changes his mind. "By the way, I did a little check back at the station, like you invited me to." A broad, shrewd smile flashes across his face. "Mind if I ask you a question?"

"What do you want to know?"

"Did you change your name because you just didn't like it? Or are you hiding from someone?"

"It's none of your business." I try to sound evenhanded, but the words come out with a defensive edge.

"I checked it out. You're clean, no record. But you did change your name a few years back. That's why I have to ask."

"I figured."

"Don't worry, Mr. Blake. Mr. William Blake." He winks. "Your secret's safe with me."

I watch him as he lumbers to his car and sinks behind the wheel in that big-man way that looks so uncomfortable and ill fitting. The engine roars to life. He yanks the gearshift into position and drives off. It isn't until he's gone that I realize he never told me who Jane Doe was.

The air is clogged with heat, humidity, and the pulsating chirrup of insects high in the trees. I position the reclining lawn chair in the middle of the yard and lie down. It barely holds my weight. The rotting plastic creaks like dried, worn-out leather.

The detective's visit has settled somewhere near the back of my mind. Discovering that I was once William Blake has aroused his suspicion. *How sweet I roam'd from field to field and tasted all the summer's pride. . . .* It will be amusing when he realizes how irrelevant the discovery is. What do things look like to him? I wonder. The world as puzzle—traces that lead to traces, clues to clues, where everything that doesn't fit must contradict. Telling him I shed William Blake because I was tired of being William Blake will not satisfy him. People don't just shed names like that, he'd say. And people like me don't live in shabby, run-down houses in out-of-the-way places like this, either. Not unless there's a reason; there has to be a reason. And he'll always be on the lookout for it. I should feel sorry for him. Paranoia is the outcome of vigilance.

I might have spared myself this attention had I not tried to help Jane Doe. There's an argument for *autarkeia*: the serenity of not caring. Peace and quiet. I aspire to a state of complete detachment but find myself tugged back again and again by circumstances, conventions, and a weakness for wanting to *be* good, which, like a weakness for wine, only requires a desire to *feel* good. Futile inoculations all. I close my eyes and imagine myself running across the yard flapping my arms, lifting off, soaring on gusts of wind, crashing down, and lifting off again.

When I open my eyes the afternoon has slipped on. The sun has moved, leaving me in the lip of shade cast by the tall stand of trees at the edge of the woods. The clothes on the line are dry. As I gather them, the reddened skin on my chest and arms and face stings, feels cracked.

I carry the bundle of clothes upstairs, drop it on the bed, and begin to fold. The cloth feels rough and warm. I fold with deliberate, pared-down movements: right arm over left, pants legs smooth, one half fold, half again, press flat.

When the clothes are folded I make the bed. The little room is suffused with freshness and calm. I stand in the doorway and look into it as if through a lens: bed along the wall with telephone and *Selected Philosophical Essays* tucked underneath, mattress slightly sagging; a small round carpet, colors faded; a small table I found at some curb, dragged home, and cleaned up, which now it looks expensive and antique; the double-sashed windows through which the sun is slanting so that the whole room has the humble atmosphere of still life, a spirit of place, like van Gogh's room at Arles—or Boethius's prison cell.

The just-so feeling inspires me to go downstairs, put some rice and beans on, and open a bottle of wine. The pots boil, and the afternoon fades to early evening. I sit at the kitchen table, mesmerized by a glowing sense of calm.

The bottle empties. My silent lucubrations give way to alarm. I get up. Pace from room to room. Wine and sunburn combine into feverish restlessness. I go upstairs, look in the mirror. My face and chest are crimson, the skin hot to the touch. My tongue is red, my teeth are red, stained with wine. My whole being is stained, florid and flushed, red and toxic.

I lie uncovered on my newly made bed, too sore for the weight of even a single sheet. In the morning my chest, legs, face, and arms are aflame, swollen with blisters. In the mirror I look like a napalm victim. My lips are whitish, eyelids so swollen I have to tilt my head to see in the mirror. I drink glass after glass of water. It trickles down my chin and chest and belly with flaming cold, seeps into the marsh of pubis, the only unburned part of me. It seems to belong to another body.

The walk to the hospital should take only half an hour. This calculation happens without forethought. I go into the bedroom and sit gingerly on the edge of the bed, rip apart the seam of my shorts, and manage to slip them on, feeling made from cracked plaster. The hospital gown I wore home the other day hangs on the back of the door. I slip it on, leaving it open at the front.

It is dawn, soft light and loud chirping high in the trees. I make my way up the front path to the street, walking like some ghoul from the movies: joints rigid, fingers splayed. A few yards up the street I turn back and return to the house, feeling ridiculous, swearing at myself as I go. Goddamnit. Goddamnit. Goddamnit.

The telephone is under the bed.

"Memorial Hospital."

"Are there any doctors there who will make a house call?"

"You'll have to come to the emergency room to see a doctor, sir."

"I can't get there. Is there someone who could come to my house?"

"I'm afraid not. Do you need an ambulance?"

"No. Just a doctor."

"Have you been injured?"

"Sort of, yes. I'm sunburned."

A pause. "You'd better come in if it's that bad, sir. Do you need an ambulance?"

I hang up. The thought of being carted off makes me feel even more stupid. I go to the bathroom sink for more water, remembering that burns and dehydration go together. Between mouthfuls I consider the prospects. Drink plenty of water. Lie in bed. Try to sleep.

Hours pass. I lurch back and forth from the crisp white sheets of the bed to the faucet in the bathroom. *Selected Philosophical Essays* is no diversion at all. I try to muster all the indifference I am capable of. It seems the only given left to me.

The telephone rings, jarring me up. I reach under the bed and answer on the second ring.

"Hello?" Mohr's voice is unmistakable.

"Yes?"

"Quintus Horatius Flaccus?"

"Hello, Mr. Mohr. How did you get my number?"

A pause. "From the form you filled out at the library."

"Oh, right."

"You don't mind me calling, do you?"

"No." I try to sit up but can't do it without bending at the waist. A painful maneuver. "I'm just a little surprised. Nobody has ever called me here."

"I am honored to be the first." He laughs at his sarcasm. "I was calling, firstly, to say thank you. I enjoyed myself the other evening. Especially the wine."

"I'm glad." I say this with enough of a monotone to let him know that he needn't continue.

"But that's not why I'm calling."

"No?"

"I wanted to tell you that I have just received a letter from Dr. Palmer. A funny coincidence, don't you think?"

"Who?"

"Don't you remember? The archaeologist I told you about? The one who inquired about the pipe collection?"

"Oh yes. The mound. I'd forgotten all about it." I sit up. The ruse of an old librarian. To become more interested in your research than you yourself are.

"She writes that she has located the Wilkington pipe collection."

I had been right in the beginning. The man does lack all intuitive sense. Either that, or he has calculated that taking an interest in my interest will result in further contact between us. I listen as he tells me about the professor's efforts to locate the collection. He speaks as though the information will settle all questions that may be plaguing me. "It happens that the collection is for sale. The university is going to purchase it, and they want the Wilkington papers too."

"Can you sell them?"

"You haven't been listening," Mohr says with a *tsk tsk*.

"I have a small problem."

"Yes. You do," he cuts in with a new, familiar tone in his voice. I realize that this isn't a calculation, it is an act of friendship. I lie back down, resting the receiver between my ear and the pillow. "I was thinking that perhaps you would like to help me."

"Help you? With what?"

"Microfilming the Wilkington Archive."

"Microfilming?"

"It's complicated, legally. The papers can't be sold, so the university is going to pay to have them microfilmed. I was thinking that perhaps you would like to help me. There's a lot to be done before they can be filmed."

A pause. The intensity of light coming into the room has started to bother me. But drawing the shade would plunge the room into darkness and cut off the circulation of air. I can have light and air or darkness and no circulation. Mohr continues talking. "Of course you would be paid for the work." The voice seems distant. The receiver is wedged into the pillow, and my ear has slipped away from it. "Mrs. Entwhistle is too busy, and the job is too much for me to do all alone."

"Mr. Mohr."

"Yes?"

I take the telephone and press it to my ear, propping myself up on one elbow. "Would you take me to the hospital?"

"Good Lord. What is wrong?"

"I'm burned."

"My God. What happened? Never mind. I'll be right. Over."

I lie flat and look straight up at the ceiling. Mastering pain means learning to accept it, but in spite of my best efforts, the searing won't go away. *Autarkeia* is not a theory. It is a state. With help on the way, I manage to have proven that much. As much as I would like to, I have no tolerance for pain because I have no attention span and can't bend my mind away from myself. I'm too narcissistic and have no real experience of pain and don't know how much worse it could be. And I am greedy for sympathy. At any rate, there is a vast difference between lying in pain and waiting for help. Strangely, with help now on the way, I want to feel *worse.* It occurs to me that I am not burned enough.

Should I go downstairs and be ready when he arrives? Or should I let him find me lying here? A peculiar sense of Samaritanism makes me think that I should let him come upon me. Give him the satisfaction of a rescue. A man on death's doorstep, coming to the aid of otherwise hale and healthy me. It seems cruel to ask his help, but it also has the small ring of heroism to it. In a way, I'm doing him a favor.

His car pulls up outside. Doors open and close. He knocks at the front door before opening it.

"Up here," I call out.

"My God, what have you done to yourself?" Mohr stops short in the doorway, then moves in for a closer look. "You look absolutely. Roasted."

"I fell asleep outside." I swing my legs over, and Mohr extends his hand to help me up. "I can manage," I tell him and get to my feet without his help, which I suspect could topple him.

"I've never seen anything like it," he says.

My chest, abdomen, and thighs are one soft, liquid blister, interrupted at the waist by my shorts. I touch fingertips to forehead and feel the same softness there.

"Can you walk?"

"It's hard to bend my knees. The skin feels like it will crack." I stand, dizzy from the effort, and maneuver stiffly past him.

"Go slowly."

"I have no choice."

At the car, Mohr opens the door and winces in sympathy as I slowly fold myself into the front seat. We drive with the windows rolled up and the air vents closed. Any direct circulation hurts. Mohr rambles on about the difference between first- and second- and third-degree burns and goes over all the possible names for my condition with an almost prurient delight. Solar-mediated affliction. Sunburn. Sunstroke. Sun poisoning. At the emergency entrance he opens my door and goes inside to find an orderly. I get to the registration desk on my own and recognize the man behind it. He shows no sign of recognizing me, which gives me small satisfaction.

I am taken to an examination room and told to wait. A few minutes later a nurse appears and asks a few yes-or-no questions. She slides a thermometer into my mouth, jots some notes on her clipboard, and in a modestly conciliatory tone says a doctor will be in to see me shortly. She leaves without removing the thermometer.

I sit at the edge of the table and wait. The antiseptic smell, the extra-wide wooden door with a levered handle, the gleaming porcelain sink, the soap dispenser, scale, blood-pressure unit, poster from a drug company, everything nailed and tiled and stripped down to essentials. The austerity is appealing.

The doctor arrives. He is young and overweight with a scrubbed, pasty-white sheen that looks ghostly under the fluorescent light and comic in contrast to my crimson.

"Looks like someone forgot the sunblock," he says with perfunctory cheer, slips the thermometer from my lips, and reads it. "Slight fever," he remarks, shaking the glass stick and dropping it into a plastic tray next to the table. He tells me to take off the hospital gown, presses the skin on my thighs and chest, evaluates the blisters, jots notes as he goes along. "How long were you out there?" He stands back and puts one hand into his lab-coat pocket.

"All day. I fell asleep."

"Any dizziness? Nausea?"

"Earlier. Not so much now."

"Have you been drinking fluids?"

"Water."

"Good. Keep it up." He makes some notes. "I'm going to give you something to reduce the swelling. Prednisone, a steroid. It'll help reduce the pain too." He writes out a prescription and hands it to me. "You have a serious burn, and it will take several days to stabilize. In a few days the skin will begin to peel."

"I feel like I'm going to split open."

He wags his finger. "Don't use any local anesthetic sprays or creams."

"Why not?"

"False sense of security. The skin will be very tender for the next few days. When you're numb you won't know if you've hurt yourself, and you want the skin to heal, right? The pills will help with the pain. You'll be fine in a couple of days." He extends a hand and we shake.

"Do you know Dr. Henley?" I ask on a sudden impulse.

The doctor pauses at the door. "Henley?"

"She's a psychiatrist. I think she has an office here."

"Yes. Loretta Henley. Ask at the desk. They'll tell you where her office is."

I slide off the examination table, realizing as my feet hit the floor that I'm without shoes.

Dr. Henley is leaving her office when I arrive on the third floor with Mohr in tow. She seems startled. "My goodness. What happened to you?"

"I fell asleep in the sun yesterday."

"Has someone looked at you yet?"

I tell her I was just looked at, but her attention seems distracted by Mohr, who is standing inconspicuously just behind me. The institutional glow of the hospital corridor emphasizes his sickly pallor. Henley is trying and failing to recognize him, and Mohr is embarrassed by the attention. "This is Mr. Mohr. He drove me here."

They exchange nods. Henley seems flustered, turns back to me. "Is there something I can do for you?" she asks.

"I would like to know what happened with the woman."

She shifts her handbag from one shoulder to the other. I can see that she is formulating her complete response on the spot. I've caught her off guard, and the results are evident in a complicated professional calculus that is registering in the shifting of her eyes. At last she opens the door to her office and invites me in, saying to Mohr, "Please excuse us for a minute."

"I'll be downstairs," Mohr wheezes.

The office is a bland mixture of clinical institutional bookishness, a suggestion of esoteric knowledge that, I suppose, is comforting to some. It strikes me as pathetic, the last place I would turn for sustenance or help. I'd rather go befuddled and bewildered through life, crack up, and jump than be diagnosed with reference to a book called *Modern Synopsis of Comprehensive Textbook of Psychiatry IV*.

Dr. Henley puts her bag down and seats herself behind her desk before speaking. She gestures for me to sit, but I tell her I'm a little sore and would prefer to stand.

"I can't tell you anything for a number of reasons," she begins. "But it was thoughtful of you to ask."

"So she remembered who she was after all."

"Yes. Two days after we went to the police station her memory returned. As you can imagine, the whole experience has been extremely traumatic for her."

"Can you tell me her name?"

"I'm afraid not."

"Why not?"

"Privacy."

"I don't want to know the details. I would just like to know who she is. I'm curious."

The doctor eyes me for a moment as though evaluating my claim.

"Look. I don't have any ulterior motives, if that's what you're worried about."

"Frankly, I wasn't. Until you mentioned it." She cuts in with a note of lawyerly psychology in her voice. A brief face-off ensues, with the doctor seated behind her desk trying to read my motives with a look of sanctimonious professionalism on her face that sickens me. This was a bad idea. I can hear the textbook aphorisms tripping around inside her well-coiffed head like so many little marbles.

I open the door to leave. "Sorry I bothered you." For a moment I consider asking her to convey my best wishes to the woman. But I change my mind and close the door on any further imputations.

On the way home Mohr stops at a pharmacy to fill the prescription the doctor has written for me. I wait in the car while he goes inside. It is midafternoon. The heat shimmers off the hood of the car. It feels like it is rising from me too, up into the atmosphere to mix with all the exhausted energy in the universe. The psychiatrist's response still has me bundled up, as if I had been accused. I should have resisted the impulse to know more.

Mohr has left the car running and the air conditioner on. For my benefit. I adjust the air flow away from me, glance at the cars parked all around, each incubating driver and passengers like its own soft guts. The image of driver as organ becomes more vivid still in an accident, when bloody goo is spattered inside the massive steel exoskeleton. I entertain a theory of the adaptive evolution of the internal combustion engine wherein the automobile can be said to have evolved by adapting itself in a symbiotic manner to human needs. Has there ever been an instance of such rapid evolutionary success anywhere else in nature? The Machina, a new taxonomic classification.

Mohr returns at last, collapsing into the drivers' seat with a sigh of exhaustion. "God, it's hot," he wheezes and hands over a small white bag containing the prescription. He reaches into his shirt pocket and takes out a box of Vicks menthol drops, fishes one out with a bony forefinger, and offers the box to me. "They're the only thing. That soothes my. Throat." A menthol smell wafts through the car.

I take out a lozenge and pop it into my mouth. Mohr backs out of the parking space slowly, piloting the station wagon as if it were a large tanker. We drive through town without speaking, savoring our menthol lozenges, eyes on the road ahead.

"Thank you for all your help," I tell him as he pulls up in front of my house several minutes later.

He waves his hand to dismiss my gratitude. "Now you take. Care of yourself. And follow the doctor's instructions." He exhales his mentholated words as I ease myself out of the car and into the furnacelike heat of the afternoon. Mohr leans across the seat. He shuffles the triangular lozenge about in his mouth. It clacks against his teeth. "I'll call you. In a few days. To talk about the. Wilkington project."

I nod, thank him, and close the car door. My neighbor is washing his pickup truck in his driveway. I walk gingerly up the path to my front door, feeling his eyes on me as he lathers the oversized hood. When I reach the door I wave to Mohr, who is idling at the curb, waiting for me to get inside. He waves back, and I enter the house feeling as though I've returned from a long and futile expedition.

The steroid works. As I lie in bed I can feel the swelling go down, almost like air from a balloon. By early evening I feel well enough to try some phone calls.

"Horace here."

"Hi Horace. How's it hanging?"

"You sound cheerful."

"It's called alliteration. When you, like, begin each word with the same letter?"

"What's it like?"

"Alliteration?"

"No. Being happy."

"Being happy?"

"Yes."

"Well, it's hard to say. A little like alliteration, maybe. Who is this, anyway?"

"Horace."

"Do I know you?"

"No. But it doesn't matter."

"How come you called? Is this a prank? It is a prank. I knew it!"

"You can call it that if you want."

"I bet I know you, too. I recognize the voice."

"We were talking about happiness. Let's continue."

"You're in Mrs. Jepson's geometry class. The guy with the red-framed glasses."

"No. That's not me. Let's talk about happiness."

"Happiness? I don't want to."

"You don't want to talk about happiness?"

"Not until I know who you are."

"I told you. My name is Horace."

"Are you recording this? You are, aren't you? C'mon, tell me."

"Tell me what you think happiness is first."

"Okay, let's see. God, this feels really stupid. I can't do it. It's too weird. Is your name really Horace?"

"Yes."

"Then why don't you go first? Yeah, you go first!"

"How about this, then: happiness is the absence of wants."

"You read that somewhere."

"You're right, I did read it. Do you agree with it?"

"It makes sense, I guess."

"It does?"

"Yeah, because it's like, if you don't want anything it's because you already have everything you ever wanted, and so you're happy. Like last week? I wanted to get my hair streaked, but my mom said no, and so I babysat three nights and saved the money and went and did it and now I'm, like, happy as horseshit!"

I can't bear the girl's exuberance. I prefer afflicted teenagers, ones with a little pathos about them. It's the best time of life for it. Their pathos is virginal, hormonally driven, and has a histrionic element to it, in contrast to adult pathos, which is just tedious and generally has its source in some form of emotional dry rot.

I put the phone back under the bed and lie awake looking up at the ceiling. The steroids work their wonders. Time passes in a chorus of insect sounds filtering through the trees. As the first morning birds begin to sing, I turn off the lamp and drift off to sleep.

Seventeen inches of snow have fallen on Oblivion, and the airport is closed. Snow is still falling. A large plow clears the tarmac around a single airplane tethered to the terminal like a captured bird. The ground crew works to keep it free of snow and ice. An enormous orange truck works the runway. The snow arcs high into the air in a dense, finely powdered mist. The plow races back and forth, scraping away the accumulation. Thick flakes muffle all sight and sound, and the speeding plow seems to be doing its work in slow motion. I walk along the perimeter fence that encircles the vast white silence of the airfield.

I've been out since early morning partaking in this drastic transformation of nature. In the snow the visible becomes invisible and the invisible visible. Layers of sediment fall in lapsed time, and the world is buried under a new geology. Dying in the snow must not be a bad way to go. I think of the photographs of frozen corpses littering the battlefields of the Bulge or of Stalingrad. Dead of cold and bullets, bodies disappear under the soft white blanket as though bid a peaceful goodnight.

The airport road has been freshly plowed. Traffic consists of a few four-wheel-drive jeeps, pickup trucks, and a large dump truck spreading sand and salt. I arrive at the terminal, legs heavy from walking. My snowsuit works well, locks in heat. I unzip it in the entrance. The automatic door opens, a blast of warm air and noise. I stomp my feet and enter the hive of bored and impatient activity. Stranded travelers pacing, chasing children, sprawling in heaps, wandering aimlessly between concessions, watching television monitors perched at angles around the terminal.

"Are you from the Marriott?" a woman standing inside the terminal entrance asks.

I shake my head.

"They said they were sending a van out," she explains as I pass by.

I walk from one end of the terminal to the other. The airplane is going to Chicago, but O'Hare Airport is closed. The flight can't take off until both airports are reopened.

"Hey. You been outside?" As I pass by the airport bar a young, pink-faced drunk seated at the center of a group of other drinkers beckons to me. "Hey. Come here." He leans out over the railing that cordons off the bar from the rest of the terminal. "He's been outside," the man exclaims to the group. "Hey! What's it like out there?"

"It's snowing."

"Hey! No shit! It's still fucking snowing. Come in here and have a drink, buddy. Hey! I was supposed to be in Hawaii eleven hours ago!"

I continue on toward the end of the terminal. Heating up, I peel my arms out of the sleeves and roll the upper half of the snowsuit down to my waist, tying the arms so they don't drag along the floor. At the end of the terminal is a door marked Authorized Personnel. I open it and walk to the end of the corridor, call the elevator. I enter and push the top button. The doors slide open again in the control tower, a large glass enclosure that looks out over the entire length of the airfield. I am standing on a platform behind a railing. Five or six people are seated in front of radar screens and telephones.

"Can I help you?" a man calls to me. "This is a restricted area. You're not supposed to be here."

The view is mesmerizing. With snow falling all around, the control tower feels like Olympus, a glass-encased, tranquil sphere of enthroned gods. The silence is broken by pips and squeaks of radio, the clacking of computer keyboards, and quiet telephone conversations. On the tarmac below is the stranded airplane, sprawled like some supplicating beast, red lights blinking nervously at all extremities.

"You're not supposed to be here." The man is coming up the stairs toward me.

"I've always wanted to see what it's like up here. Is it always so quiet?"

The man stops at the top step, holding on to the railing. He is wearing a white shirt and tie, is thin, with bloodshot eyes set deeply into his head behind wire-rimmed glasses. I am standing in a small puddle of water that is dripping from my boots and suit. He reaches out to take my upper arm, but I step back. My evasion makes him tense. "I'll show you out," he says.

"I've never been in a control tower before," I tell him. "Is it always so peaceful?"

The man casts a sidelong look at me. Another man has stood up from behind his console and is watching us. "Need help?" he asks.

"It's okay, I'm leaving," I answer before my escort can respond. "The view is fantastic."

"Yes, it is," he agrees perfunctorily.

"And is it always so quiet?"

He gives me another apprehensive glance, then rubs his eyes with thumb and forefinger. "It's not quiet," he says. "It's closed."

"How much longer will it be closed?"

He signals the man on the floor to sit down and pushes the elevator button. "The storm is moving east. Should be a few more hours."

"Are there a lot of airplanes waiting to land?"

He now doubts my faculties, and his manner eases up. He answers my question as if he's got a big, dumb kid on his hands. "They've been diverted to other airports."

"Beyond the storm?"

He nods. "To the south."

"What is it that everyone's watching on the radar screen?"

The man looks down at his colleagues. "Airplanes above the storm. Between twenty-eight thousand and thirty-five thousand feet." The elevator doors slide open. The man gestures me in. On the way down he asks if I'm on the Chicago flight. I tell him I'm not. The doors slide open. He escorts me to the end of the corridor, opens the door into the terminal, and holds it open for me. "Things'll be getting back to normal soon," he says and closes the door.

I pass through the chaos of the terminal once again, through the main entrance and back into the silent cold. A few cars are on the road now. I cross the parking lot and follow the fence up toward the other end of the runway. The big plows are still working. The snow continues to fall. The terminal recedes. The control tower juts up, splintered panes gazing across acres and acres of whiteness.

At the western end of the runway I discover a large pile of branches left by tree cutters clearing the area around the signal-light posts. It has collapsed to form a crude lean-to. By shifting a few branches, I clear out an area inside and soon find myself sitting under a canopy of snow and branches. Colored strobe lights perched atop staggered towers flash in sync, creating a movement of brilliant blue and white light that descends from on high and races along the ground until it reaches the runway. Split-second, epileptic flashes, an illusion of movement. Cocooned in the body suit that guarantees warmth and insulation down to thirty degrees below zero, I settle in with my back against the rear of the shelter, aping the rustic who waits for the river to finish its flow.

The snowfall slows. It stops. The air becomes still, and a light breeze begins to blow. The clouds begin to lift. Time passes.

The engines of the stranded airplane begin to wind up. It backs away from the terminal, turns, and rolls toward the eastern end of the runway, red lights flashing. Soon I can only hear its winding engines. Time passes. The roar of engines becomes louder. Thunderous. The huge machine leaps up from the snowfield into view, soft silver underbelly exposed, egg-shaped jet engines hanging from under each gracefully swept-back wing. It roars directly overhead. I can see every rivet and droplet of water coursing along its smoothly preened underbelly.

Soon it is quiet. The air becomes still again. Snow falls from the over-laden branches of the trees, is blown along in swirls and into drifts. I leave the shelter and start back in the direction of home. It took most of the morning to get out here, and it takes the afternoon to get back. Along the way I see people digging their cars out of snowbanks. The clouds drift higher and higher. It is twilight when I reach the outskirts of town, dark when I reach my house.

The fire is out. A fresh load of kindling and wood brings it back to life. The stove I bought in the fall heats the entire house. I moved my bed downstairs so I can fall asleep watching the flames through the stove's glass doors. My snowsuit hangs on a nail in the mantel. Boots on the hearth.

The telephone rings. It is Mohr.

"I've been trying to reach you all day."

"I was out walking."

"In this weather? There are seventeen inches of snow on the ground."

"I know."

"I've been home all day myself. The whole town's shut down."

"I know. It's nice."

"And you're out walking around?" He is losing his breath and breaks off to cough. I stare into the flames of the stove and wait for him to finish. "Listen. Horace," he finally sputters. "Could I ask you a big favor?"

"A favor?"

"My car is completely snowed under."

"You want me to dig it out for you?"

"No. I can find someone else to do that."

"What is it, then?"

"Could you open the library tomorrow morning? Mrs. Entwhistle is stuck out at her place. You still have the key I gave you, right?"

"Yes."

"Would you mind? Mrs. Entwhistle will be in by noon or so, and I'll try to get in around then too." He breaks out coughing again.

"Maybe you should stay home and rest," I tell him.

"Thanks again," he says and hangs up.

I have been helping out frequently at the library these days. Microfilming the Wilkington Collection is a tedious affair, and two or three times a week I go in to help with the sorting and shuffling. I've also become a benefactor in the form of a Xerox machine and a security system. Mohr gave me a set of keys as a token of gratitude. I needn't have tried to guard my anonymity. Derringer at the bank knows about my donation because I had to ask him to cut a check. "It's an anonymous contribution," I told him. He looked at me as if I'd insulted him. "'Course it is. Of course." And he winked at me, then watched me through his office window as I carried the check across the street to the library.

When I agreed to help Mohr with his project I hadn't realized how much paper was involved—miles of it, mostly devoted to historical, everyday banalities: *Accepted today of Mr. Johnson in payment for debt outstanding; one saddle and quirt, two sacks flour*. Sorting and keeping it all seems a bizarre waste of energy. These papers of several generations of a family that has long since dispersed itself across the continent couldn't seem more irrelevant. And yet here they are being duplicated and preserved. Mohr refers to the papers as documentation of the town's social and cultural life during the previous century. I think of them as footprints in the sand. To take all this paper and use it in some taxidermic project so that Major Wilkington may, for a few centuries after his demise, stand stuffed in memory's dusty corner—hat, boots, cane, and sidewhiskers. If, as Horace says, we are mere ciphers in life, then what is there to say of our detritus? Time doesn't move forward. It swirls around in confusion and goes straight to the head like a glass of strong red wine. Then it goes away.

The kitchen is the coldest part of the house. I turn on the oven and open a bottle of wine to sip while I prepare a pot of lentils, carrots, celery, and onion, which I will salt and pepper and serve on rice. The kitchen warms quickly, and I sit at the table and breathe in the aromas of cooking food and the rich bouquet from the wine in my glass. I opened the bottle in the morning and left it out all day. It is rich, meaty wine, a perfect complement to the seventeen inches of snow outside. By the time the lentils are cooked I have finished half the bottle and am suspended in a realm of perfect complacence where time seems to hum in my ears.

I reach for the telephone.

"Horace here."

"Who?"

"Horace."

"Horace who?"

"Quintus Horatius Flaccus."

"Say that again."

"Quintus Horatius Flaccus."

"What kind of name is that?"

"A Roman name."

"No kidding?"

"No kidding."

"Is it really your name?"

"Yes."

"Your parents gave it to you?"

"No."

"Aha. So it isn't your real name!"

"Yes it is."

"What name did your parents give you?"

"I've forgotten."

"That's impossible."

"I have."

"Come on. Stop kidding me."

"I've forgotten it. Put it out of mind."

"That's different. So you just don't want to remember it."

"That's right."

"But if you wanted to, you could."

"Maybe."

"So your real name is probably Dave or Mike or George or something, right?"

"My real name is Quintus Horatius Flaccus."

"Was there a real Quintus Horatius Flaccus?"

"I am the real Quintus Horatius Flaccus."

"Was there another one?"

"A poet. He lived in the first century before the Christian era. At the time of Augustus Caesar."

"Is he your hero or something?"

"I like to think we are the same person transposed across time."

"Uh-huh, right."

"To put it another way, the same nature transposed across time."

"Are you a poet?"

"No."

"It doesn't sound possible."

"What doesn't?"

"What you're saying."

"It probably isn't."

"You lost me."

"You lost yourself."

"Sounds to me more like you lost your self and your mind. Like one of those Elvis impersonator types. Or that kid I heard about who changed his name to Trees of North America because he liked the book."

"Whither, Bacchus, am I swept on. Thus possessed by your wine."

"What's that?"

"What are the groves and caves this new self of mine must behold?"

"Sounds like you're toasted, pal."

I hang up, cork the bottle, and make a mental note not to use the phone again after I've drunk more than one glass. I get confused. I'd have liked to pick up on the Elvis impersonation. To impersonate means to act the part of. It also means to embody, and it's in that sense I would use it. Not to copy but to consist and be an expression of. It's not as nefarious or mystical as one might think. Identity is a viscous fluid that spills through all of nature.

The sun breaks through the clouds as I arrive at the library. A transformation from dull gray to blinding white. Snow is piled high along the road. A fine sprinkling of sand and salt melts the bottom layer of ice. I counted six cars on the way over, drivers leaning over the wheel in grim determination. People with shovels work to cut walkways, uncover driveways and cars. The air is filled with the high whine of two-stroke engines. Automobiles idle while their owners groom them with brooms and brushes and scrapers.

A man wearing a bright orange snowsuit is blowing his way up the walk to the front door of the library. The path is only about a foot wide. I circle around him through the deep snow. The engine slows. "Building's closed," the man shouts.

I wave to him and continue wading toward the front door.

"Building's closed."

I dig into my pocket, take out my key, and hold it up for him to see. He nods and waves me on; then the machine winds to life again and snow begins cascading from it.

The front door is blocked by a drift. I wave to the man pushing the blower, but he is spellbound by the machine and doesn't look up. I wade back down the steps toward him. He looks up at last and cuts the motor.

"The door is blocked," I shout.

He can't hear me and cups a gloved hand to his ear.

"The door is blocked," I repeat, pointing to the entrance.

The man nods and points to his truck parked in the street behind a high snowbank. I have no idea what he is trying to say and march toward him. He turns the motor up again and resumes work. When I draw near he cuts the engine. "There's a shovel in the truck." He is flushed—whether from cold or exertion or alcohol or all combined, I can't tell. The snow machine, all blades and blowers, idles on the ground like something Mesozoic. I want to tell him to leave the machine and clear the doorway himself, and I can tell that he is expecting me to say just that. But my response isn't quick enough, and he brings the motor back to life again and lurches forward, looking for all his motorized paraphernalia and orange gear like some plow-burdened peasant borrowed from the Middle Ages.

I begin by clearing the doorway and then get carried away and begin to clear a path toward the steps. Soon I find myself clearing the steps, breaking into a sweat that soaks the inside of my suit. The man behind the plow takes my efforts as a cue to slow his own, and the path he is clearing grows wider and wider and the distance between us greater and greater until he is working his way backward and sideways, clearing the snow in every direction except toward the steps, which, he figures, I will clear for him.

And I do.

When I've finished I plant the shovel into a pile of snow at the side of the walkway and peel the suit from my shoulders. The sun is beginning to get hot, and a slight breeze is blowing. The brightness hurts. The man with the plow looks up and waves, a Tom Sawyer grin on his overripened face. I wave back, finding I have enjoyed the exertion, arch my back to ease some of the stiffness caused by leaning over. One could do worse than be a swinger of shovels, I think, standing in the frosty air with the top half of my suit hanging at my waist and watching as the man blows snow in all directions with his machine. There are many and far greater poverties than that.

The library is like a dungeon inside. I hunt for thermostat, light switches. In several minutes my eyes are adjusted to the fluorescence, and there is nothing for me to do but wait for the heat to come on and for Mohr or Mrs. Entwhistle to arrive. An advantage I enjoy since becoming a benefactor is that I have my own reserve shelf behind the circulation desk. Lined up for my convenience are editions of Epicurus, Epictetus, Lucretius, and, naturally, a volume of Horace. I pulled them not so much because I wanted to read each one from beginning to end but because I've found that in skating over passages and alternating between books, a curious coherence emerges that is like wandering between pictures in a museum. Except the worlds evoked by books seem to me far less remote than those rendered in pictures.

I take down the volume of Horace. I have been memorizing it. The way I test myself is to recite from memory and then check myself against the book. *Mortalia facta peribunt, nedum sermonum stet honos et gratia vivay.*

I have it correctly. *All that mortals make will die and language has yet a briefer span of pleasing life*. Or, *Everything mortal dies, language is easily broken.* Or, straight to the point, *Language, too, is mortal and will die.* I wonder if by uttering Horace's Latin I am proving or refuting his point? In the conjunction of identities that is the world, Horace is dead and I am Horace.

I am alone in the crypt. The dusty clock above the door is dead, a remnant of the days when the building housed a bank. An hour or two passes, and I continue on with Horace. Then I hear the front door open, footsteps in the corridor. It is Mrs. Entwhistle.

"Thank you so much for coming in," she says, entering the reading room. "Is Mr. Mohr not here yet?"

"No. Not yet."

"Has he called?"

I shake my head. Mrs. Entwhistle pulls off her coat and hangs it in a closet behind the circulation desk. She takes off her boots and slips on a pair of shoes she keeps in the closet, telling me about the problems she had with her car and the condition of the roads, and finishes up by saying, "My, it is quiet in here, isn't it? Maybe we'll be lucky and it will stay this quiet all day, and I'll actually have time to get some work done. Would you like some tea?"

I glance at my shelf full of books. "Sure, why not?"

Mrs. Entwhistle hurries off, asking me if I'd be so good as to answer the telephone in case it rings.

It doesn't. I find myself thumbing a book about trees on top of the return pile. Custard Apple, Annona family, asimina triloba, or Paw. Leaves deciduous. Fruit edible. Flowers two inches in diameter, three green sepals. Six heavily veined purple petals.

"Here's your tea." Mrs. Entwhistle hands me a large cracked mug with a spoon and a teabag floating in it. She sits at a long table behind the circulation desk, carefully extracts the bag from her cup, and places it on a small saucer on the table. For several moments we blow steam from our tea in abstracted silence.

Mrs. Entwhistle is a heavy-lidded, middle-aged woman with platinum hair piled and tucked on her head who speaks in high, reedy tones that make her seem perpetually on the verge of a sudden outburst. All I know about her is what Mohr has told me, which is that her husband teaches chemistry at the high school, that they don't have children, and that the two of them devote all their time to organizing summer field trips for the church choir they belong to. I can't help suspecting Mrs. Entwhistle of harboring some secret nastiness, of being the sort of pious, small-town churchgoer who might also belong to the Ku Klux Klan or bomb abortion clinics on weekends.

I finish my tea and begin getting ready to leave. The mailman breezes in just as I'm putting on my snowsuit. Mrs. Entwhistle puts her cup down. "Neither snow nor sleet," she singsongs with phony cheer.

"Nor gloom of night," the mailman booms back in his own overused brand of mock cheerfulness, sorting through his shoulder bag. "There's an e-normous pileup out on the interstate," he says. "Pretty dag-gone nasty."

"Oh my," Mrs. Entwhistle intones. "Is anybody hurt?"

"Don't know for sure yet. Happened just a little while ago."

"Why anybody would get on the interstate in this weather is beyond me." She takes the handful of proffered mail.

"Some people got no choice," he says, implying that he is one of them. "All I can say is I'm glad I don't have to get on it today."

Mrs. Entwhistle puts on her reading glasses and begins to flip through the stack of mail. The man turns to leave, sees me struggling to pull my boots back on. I glance up at him. "Lace 'em up tight now," he says and sweeps past me out the door.

"Goodbye now," Mrs. Entwhistle says without looking up. "And thank you very much."

By the time I arrive at the iInterstate the fire and rescue squad is struggling to right the overturned tractor trailers. I watch from the overpass. The traffic files along slowly; snow piled up on each side of the highway and along the median creates the impression of two long asphalt furrows stretching away into the horizon. The air is filled with the muffled sound of motors, winches, and the hiss of tires on wet roadway.

A crew works to hoist the two overturned containers that have spilled their litter into the snow like a sprinkling of vital fluids. The drivers in the oncoming cars all slow to look upon the scene in curious empathy, then speed off on their way as though personally invulnerable.

Three cars have been hauled to the side of the highway, and one is upended headfirst in the ditch of the median. Rear wheels in the air, it looks more derelict and deranged than the rest. There is no sign of driver or passengers.

"Goddamn kids," a voice mutters from behind. I turn to see Ed Maver coming toward me. His car is parked at the other end of the overpass. He lifts a hand in greeting, then leans over the railing and peers down at the highway. "Saw them being hauled into the station. Little bastards."

"Who?"

"Kids throwing snowballs caused this whole mess." He points out the broken windshield on the cab of one of the trucks. "Driver broke his neck. Had to fly him out in a helicopter. Goddamn kids. Parents probably won't even find out little Johnny's in trouble 'til they get home from work." Maver pushes away from the rail, sticks out his hand. "Long time no see, buddy." We shake. "And you're still without an automobile, I see. What'd you do? Walk all the way out here?"

I nod and watch the trucks working below. Maver steps up to share the view. The truck with the broken windshield has been uprighted and is sagging on its broken axles on one side of the road. The road crew is now standing in a ring discussing the strategy for the next job. "Incredible," Maver shakes his head. I don't know if he's referring to the efforts of the crew or the general scene of the accident or if he's referring to the havoc wrought by a gang of kids throwing snowballs.

"Did anyone besides the truck driver get hurt?"

"Can't say for sure. Three or four people got taken away in ambulances. I'll say one thing for sure, though."

"What's that?"

"Those trucks must've been rolling along at a pretty good clip to wipe out like that. Combination of speed and ice and goddamn snowballs crashing through the windshield." He shakes his head. "They oughta throw the book at the little bastards. Put 'em in boot camp. Straighten 'em out. My oldest, Jim. He began cutting up around sixteen. Couldn't even list the stunts that boy pulled. Dropped out of high school and crapped around, good for nothing. Then he went into the Marines, and boy oh boy, you should've seen his mother's face when he came home after that. It was a different kid standing at the door. His mother and me couldn't believe it. 'It's not Jim,' she kept saying over and over. Now he's got a wife and two kids, and I swear I never knew a straighter goddamn flyer my whole life. Goes to church fifty-two Sundays a year and twice on Christmas, and that's something I quit doing years ago."

As Maver talks I turn and lean against the rail. The sun is beginning to sink and the wind has picked up. Our elongated shadows stretch across the roadway, over the opposite rail, eastward ho. I won't get home until long after dark. A car drives past. Maver waves to the driver.

"Well, I'll be off now." I step away from the rail.

"Lemme give you a lift," Maver says.

"Thanks, but I enjoy the walk."

"Suit yourself," Maver says and offers his hand. We shake, and I turn to leave. "Hold on a second," Maver erupts. "I almost forgot to say."

"What's that?"

"About a month ago. No, wait a minute. It was before Christmas. That's right. It was two months ago. Two months ago I stopped in at Rice's Pharmacy to pick up some flu medicine. Guess what I saw?"

"I have no idea."

"That girl we dragged out of the cornfield last summer! Would you believe?" He cuts himself off and scrutinizes me for signs of shock, surprise, incredulity. It half occurs to me to remind him that neither of us dragged her from the field and that, in fact, all he did was drive to the hospital. "There she was. Working behind the prescription counter. Don't think she recognized me, but I sure as hell remembered her. Couldn't take my eyes off her the whole time."

"Did you say anything to her?"

"Hell no, I didn't. I just stood there looking dumb. Paid and left. What am I gonna say? 'Dragged you bare-assed out of a cornfield last summer?' Hell no. I just paid and left. Said thank you. Truth is, I was pretty goddamn embarrassed. Christ, I even felt my whole face going all red. And that's not something that happens to Ed Maver too easily, I'll tell you that for sure." He pauses to gauge my reaction, then gestures to his car. "C'mon. I'll drive you back into town. You can go in and see for yourself."

I decline the invitation and turn to leave before Maver's good-old-boy jollity forces me to say something nasty. "So long there, buddy," he calls after me, sensing that he has hit a raw nerve.

The walk home takes longer than I expected. Darkness comes quickly, and the way is lighted by a half moon that rises over the bowl-shaped glow of the town like a forgotten piece of celestial furniture. Streetlights begin at the town limit, which is marked by a small sign. The snow, blue in moonlight, turns orange-yellow there.

Jane Doe has merged with my memory of cornfields and van Gogh and Hemingway, no longer imminent but part of a vague diffusion of considerations, cogitations, and ideas. Maver's story has reanimated her. I can picture her across the pharmacy counter handing a bottle of pills to the bug-eyed and embarrassed Ed Maver, who is caught at a loss for words for the first time in years. As I walk she condenses in my imagination. I try to fend her off, sensing an unwholesome preoccupation coming on like symptoms of flu. Don't think about it. Don't think of the left ear of a camel. It's useless. Maver has planted a germ in my imagination that will not easily go away. And the more I am curious about Jane Doe, the more I must wonder what underlies my curiosity. The first thing that occurs to me is that I might go and introduce myself to her, ask her how she is recovering from her ordeal. But that idea is soon submerged by a flood of uncertainties. What for? I can see myself standing across from her at the counter—just as Maver did—and getting a look that says, And now I suppose you have come to collect the reward? Or, Thank you for remembering me. Would you now please let me get on with my life? Or, I've recommended you for the Congressional Medal of Honor. You should be getting a letter from Washington any day now. Maybe I should go in and say, I'd forgotten all about you, but when I heard you were working here I figured I just had to come by and say hello. Or, to indicate that yes, I do have a reason for seeking her out: Could I have my shirt back?

The center of town is deserted. I walk past the library. One of the lamps at the entrance is burned out, and the other is flickering on the verge of extinction. The streets are almost clear. A layer of ice is forming despite all the salt and sand. The temperature is dropping quickly. I continue past the Town Hall and along Main Street. There is a smell of wood and fireplaces in the air. The houses are set farther from the road the farther up Main Street you go. They seem stranded at the end of long, deep trenches cut into the snow from curb to front door. Windows are lit, driveways are cleared, cars are tucked into garages.

I stop at a corner underneath a streetlight and glance back toward the center of town. Not a car on the road. The wind picks up, blowing a fine mist of snow. I imagine myself, an icy statue, standing in this spot forever while people come and go from their houses and cars speed past during all seasons and airplanes take off and land out at the airport and everything slips past in timeless silence.

After three or four minutes my feet get cold, and I continue on toward home.

Snow falls for three full days. I dust and clean, oil my boots, wash clothes, and hang them on a line near the stove to dry. I commit passages from Horace and *Selected Philosophical Essays* to memory, continuing the graft of this fanciful self of mine from the newly cut boughs piling up at my feet. Remaining indoors helps, but despite all efforts of concoction—and with the snow piling up outside to suspend my own and the daily rhythms of the town—a kind of private obliteration occurs so that after the third full day indoors, I find I have begun to play around in Cartesian fashion with doubts about my own existence. The game is surprisingly entertaining, and the hot stove in the living room helps. But it doesn't last long. In the end I am forced to admit that there is no *existence* to obliterate, merely a purely contingent self that finds the roaring flesh satisfying and irrecusable.

The telephone has been out, and this has added to my sense of seclusion. I haven't missed it. The image of toppled poles and tangled wires, of civilization interrupted by a broken flow of electrons (and no one bothering to report it) is amusing. Mohr is the only person who ever calls anyway. As far as spontaneous dialogue, I haven't felt much of an urge.

I haven't seen Tom Schroeder since the summer. I never recovered my notebook, and none of my complaints to the police seem to have resulted in anything. I walk to the police station. The desk sergeant recognizes me. "How about this storm?" he asks. "Holding up against it?"

"So far," I answer. "The reason I stopped by . . ."

"You mean you didn't come by just to say hello?"

"I was wondering what happened with that kid I complained about last summer. Tom Schroeder."

The sergeant taps his pen on the desk, squints into the distance to summon his memory. He picks up the phone. "I'll see what I can find out."

While he talks on the phone I wander over to browse the Wanted posters, a gallery of black-and-white pictures hanging on a corkboard just inside the main entrance. Murderers, rapists, bank robbers, kidnappers, pedophiles. A wall of faces tied to specific acts, blotched and blemished and wearing the sullen look of imprecation that turns each into the hero of his own crime and so poorly masks the secret joy of it.

The sergeant puts down the phone. "The kid left town last August, he says. Hasn't been back since."

"Who told you?"

"The detective."

"Ross?"

"No. Blucher. Ross is in Florida on vacation." The sergeant taps his pen on the desk. "Ross the Boss. Wish I was in Florida."

"What about Schroeder?"

"Kid's in college. Got a scholarship to Notre Dame."

"College?"

"Maybe it'll straighten him out. He's a smart kid. Anyway, if he comes back we'll be keeping an eye on him."

"Were other people complaining?"

"No complaints. Just hanging around a bad crowd. Notre Dame'll straighten him out. I've seen worse," the sergeant says with a lilt, points his pen at me with a flick of his wrist, then resumes tapping it on the desk.

Mrs. Entwhistle nods at me as I pass by the reading room and head for the staircase that leads to the second floor. I've been more or less asked to force myself on the place, and by obliging I seem to be perpetuating a fantasy of mutual need. Mohr, it seems, likes having me around, and I enjoy the welcome feeling.

I find Mohr upstairs hunched over his paper-strewn desk, talking on the telephone. He looks up as I enter and nods at me. He has a furtive, conspiratorial style on the telephone, head dropped, voice lowered, receiver pressed against the side of his head. I peel out of my snow gear and seat myself in an old wooden office chair that squeaks and squeals and tilts back at an awkward angle.

The room has undergone several stages of transformation since my first visit. There are boxes and boxes and stacks and piles of photocopied documents. The originals are piled on a table in the center of the room. The fluorescent hood still hangs over the long table, and the new Xerox machine stands along the wall. Boxes of documents that had been stored in other parts of the building are now stacked against the rear wall of the office. They contain the paper legacies of other families of the town who thought enough of themselves to have left to posterity their yellowing papers and secret diaries and photo albums and letters and genealogies scrawled on grease-stained napkins. The town seems to have been inhabited for a time by a variety of impulsives and obsessives, egotists, graphomaniacs, and collectors. Many boxes are marked Private. One, donated by an anonymous gentleman, contains a collection of erotic postcards from French West Africa depicting native men and women cavorting in their newly colonized Eden. Pith-helmet porn, Mohr calls it. Another box is labeled The Geographical and Geological History of the Region Reconstructed from the Fossil Evidence Collected and Cataloged by Mr. Joseph Goldsborough.

Mohr seems to have been inspired by the offer to purchase the Wilkington material. Some dormant vision for the library has been rekindled, his ambition stoked. He has convinced himself that the entire archive of local history must be duplicated in order to preserve it, so every document is first being Xeroxed onto acid-free paper and the originals packed away. The copying machine I donated has stimulated his appetite for more machinery, and now he has undertaken a campaign to raise money for the library. He seems so contented lately that I don't think it matters if he raises any or not. His efforts are sincere, although I tend to see them as a last stand against his own moribund condition. He is happy with the illusion, call it progress—the perpetual approach to some forever receding goal. The difference between Mohr and me is that having defined for himself a goal he believes to be worth pursuing, his contentment comes from the act of pursuit, whereas I think it is futile to state goals or pursue "progress," unless it be defined simply as peace of mind—and in that case I would say the only worthy pursuit is the avoidance of goals. To see Mohr on the telephone conferring in breathless sentences and behaving as if he were some busy politician garnering votes makes me see how terrified he really is of the end he is facing.

"How are you?" he asks, hanging up the telephone.

"How are you?"

He shrugs meekly, then launches into an explanation of his most recent efforts. I drag my chair up to the corner of the long table in the center of the room and glance casually at a letter from Major Wilkington dated October 2, 1861 . . . *raising an army for the defense of the Union* . . .

"It's a marvelous opportunity. A coalition of businesses in the area is going to donate money and equipment to digitize the entire archive," he says.

I am distracted by Wilkington's letter, in which he describes his efforts to raise a force of volunteers to go off and fight the Civil War. I read the entire text while Mohr talks. "Digitize?"

"It means every document will be scanned into a computer that will convert the image so it can be stored electronically."

"And what happens after that?"

Mohr looks at me as though I haven't understood and pushes his glasses up the bridge of his nose. "Well, most importantly, the material will be preserved. And of course, anyone who wants to look at a document or a photograph can look at it on a computer."

"An image of it."

"Exactly. The originals can be locked away. I've been wanting to do it for a long time. The documents will only rarely ever need to be handled. And searching through the archive will be a matter of keystrokes."

"So all this photocopying has been a waste of time?"

Mohr shrugs. "Not entirely. We will have a duplicate paper archive to fall back on."

"How convenient."

"The technology is very accessible now. Everyone is digitizing their collections. The opportunities are marvelous. Eventually we can make the archive—the history of the whole town—available on the Internet!"

"Internet?"

"The information superhighway. The World Wide Web. It's transforming the way we go about our lives. Don't tell me you never heard of it."

I shrug, not wanting to provoke him further and only mildly shocked at his newfound technological positivism. He picks up the telephone. "Do you have time today?"

"I think I'll go downstairs and read for a little while."

"Come back up before you go."

I go downstairs and retrieve my books from their shelf behind the circulation desk. Mrs. Entwhistle is chatting with an elderly lady about a book the woman is checking out. There are a few people scattered in chairs around the reading room. I go directly to an empty table and sit down, placing the books so the titles on the spines are facing toward me.

As far as progress goes, I suppose the digitization of documents is a step toward the perfect archive—if the perfect archive is simply a place where papers are locked away and preserved over time. The technology that has Mohr so excited permits the separation of the physical document from its contents while preserving the original holograph. I suppose that it is progress of a sort. I browse the spines of the books on the table. They too are an archive. The volume of Horace lying before me, one in a series of regressing shadows, manuscripts labeled *Milan, Ambros. O.136 sup (olim Avennionensis), s. IX/X.* Or *Berne 363, s. IX2*—which was written in a continental Irish scriptorium in northern Italy sometime in the ninth or tenth century. All are shadows of some ancient codex, iterated and reiterated through a warp of time and changing language into the bilingual Latin/Modern English edition lying before me now. *Everything mortal dies. And language has yet a briefer span of pleasing life.* It is a truth that Mohr's digitized archive cannot negate. His holographs, paper and electronic, will be as remote a thousand years from now as the text of Horace's satires copied out in monastic scriptoria are to us today.

In an hour I go back upstairs. Mohr is waiting for me. "It looks good," he says without any preamble.

"What does?"

A sepulchral grin distorts his face. He stands up and walks around his desk. "The money." He leans against the edge of his desk and crosses his thin arms over his chest. "I wouldn't have guessed there were so many people interested in the history of the town. They're practically falling over each other to contribute to the project."

I listen while he spells it all out and then concludes by saying, "It's the technology. That's what has them interested. They think it will make them want to come in and use it. If I were asking for funds to rebind damaged books—forget it. Nobody would give me a dime. But mention technology and everybody says, 'Oh, how educational! It's about time we got up to speed with the technology.'"

"And the archive that has been quietly resting here for the better part of the century will suddenly become all the rage?"

Mohr shrugs and drops his chin to his chest as though in contemplation, then lifts his head back up. "There will be a dedication ceremony," he says.

I pick up his thread. "And people will come for a while to use the new machines. Look up the names of their relatives, show their kids. Then it will collect dust. Just like the books on the shelves do."

"I plan to scan the photograph collections first. The photographs will make a bigger initial impression."

"And after that, Major Wilkington's accounting statements and shopping lists?"

"Say what you like. It's for the good. As long as the collections are preserved." He sits down in his chair behind the desk.

"But by preserving the stuff in a format based in an esoteric technology, all you're doing is making the material *less* available to the future!"

"As long as the information is preserved . . . that's all that counts." He pauses to shuffle some papers on the desk. "You're too pessimistic, Horace. If I listened to you I would do nothing."

"Maybe that's not such a bad idea."

He waves me away with a disgruntled flap of the wrist. "You tire me out, Horace. Really, you do. I don't understand why you say half of what you say." He looks at his watch, a large old thing that dangles on the bones of his wrist like a heavy bracelet. "The library closes in ten minutes. Would you like to join me for dinner?"

"Where?" I ask, surprised by the invitation. Mohr and I have kept our acquaintance to the library since that night of drinking and confession.

"Across the street. The food isn't bad."

"I'm not hungry. But I'll keep you company."

"Great." He hauls himself out of the chair. "I'll be ready in ten minutes."

I go outside and wait for him. The air is crisp and very cold. The lights at the front entrance cast a warm, incandescent glow across the snow. Traffic is moving steadily along Main Street, the rush-hour exodus of people and cars almost over. I lean against the brick wall beside the entrance, saturated by a sense of well-being. The cold air, the steps of the library, the snow; a sense of being completely in the present, of fitness and proportion and charm that I can't sum up but which has descended on me like a momentary state of grace. I take long drafts of cold air into my lungs and exhale large clouds of steam that dissolve in a yellow glow of light.

Mohr emerges from the front door and locks it behind him. We stand together at the top step for a moment, looking at the thin stream of traffic passing slowly up Main Street. "Come on," he says and carefully descends the icy steps, one at a time.

The Corn Tassel is one of those restaurants that changes its atmosphere according to the meal being served. At lunch it is a busy diner. At dinner the lights are dimmed and it becomes a cocktail lounge and restaurant. Mohr chooses a booth. He peels off his overcoat and hangs it on a hook and slides onto the crimson vinyl bench. I slide in across from him as the waitress appears.

"How are you tonight, Mr. Mohr?"

"Oh, same as always," he responds in a voice reserved for the occasion.

"That's good. Can I get you something to drink?" She is a large woman on the edge of matronly middle age with a wide, friendly face. I think I've seen her before but don't remember where. The bank, maybe.

"I'll have the usual."

"Glass of red wine?"

Mohr nods.

"I'll have a cup of coffee."

The booth makes it feel like we're squaring off for something. Mohr fidgets with his silverware and says a few things about the cold and the food at the restaurant. Then, after the waitress has brought him his wine and me my coffee, he looks me squarely in the eye. "I'm going to retire in two weeks."

"In two weeks?"

"And I am moving into the hospice." He lifts his glass to his lips and sips with a mild, bemused expression.

"What about all these plans you're making?"

"My successor can take them over." He sips his wine. "I wish I'd taken to fund-raising a long time ago. I seem to be fairly good at it. People become so friendly once they've decided to part with some of their cash. And you want to know something?"

"What's that?"

"Being sick has come in handy."

"You mean people feel sorry for you?"

He nods and laughs. "It's like taking candy from a baby."

"So how much have you raised?"

"More than I ever imagined possible. Enough to get the collection digitized and the place wired with computers. Mrs. Entwhistle will have plenty to work with."

"She's taking over from you?"

He nods.

"Can't you stay long enough to get it started?"

He puts his glass down and drops his hands into his lap. The lamp attached to the wall in the booth casts a shadow that makes the lines and crevices of his face seem deeper and the hair of his wig seem darker than it actually is. "I'm too exhausted. I've done as much as I can, and now it's time to stop. I go to the oncologist three mornings a week. Then to work. Then home. I'm stoked with painkillers and pep talks from the doctor. It's the pep talks that are killing me." He smiles and reaches for his glass.

The waitress arrives to take the order. Mohr asks for chicken pot pie, carrots, broccoli, and another glass of wine. He gives me a knowing grin. "How about you?"

"I'm fine."

"You're not going to order dinner?" the waitress asks.

"No thanks."

"Have a glass of wine with me," Mohr says.

"Okay," I agree.

"Red or white?" the waitress asks.

"Red."

She jots everything onto her pad and departs to fill the order.

"I have a glass of wine every night at dinner," Mohr says, still grinning. "Since last summer. Of course, they don't serve the good stuff here."

"When are you moving?" I ask.

"Next week." His expression turns serious. "A place came available. I've got to take it or they'll bump me to the bottom of the list." The waitress brings our wine. "My friend Bill is coming from Chicago to help get me settled."

"That'll be good."

"I'm afraid he's in for a shock. We haven't seen each other for several years. I've lost a lot of weight."

"I'm sure he knows what to expect."

Mohr shrugs. "Knowing what to expect and confronting the facts are two different things." He looks into his glass for a moment. "We lived together for close to ten years." His voice has the edge of confession in it. I sip from my glass and wait for him to continue. "How do you like the wine?" he asks after a brief silence.

I shrug, not expecting the detour. "It's not the greatest."

"It stinks," Mohr says. "I've always meant to bring my own bottle, but I always forget, and now I'm used to drinking the bad stuff."

A few more people come into the restaurant, all elderly regulars. Mohr waves to one couple who take the booth behind us. "He used to be the mayor," Mohr says.

"Do you eat here often?"

"Since I stopped cooking, almost every night."

"When did you stop cooking?"

"About six years ago," he says. "When Bill moved to Chicago."

I can tell he would like me to ask about Bill, give the signal that I'm ready to hear his whole story. But I've already deduced the outlines of it from the tone in his voice and don't need to hear it. Don't want to, really. "What about the hospice?"

"What about it?"

"Will they feed you there?"

"Of course." Mohr pushes his glasses up the bridge of his nose. "It's their job. And they do a lot more than just feed you."

"Such as."

"They nurse you to death." He says it with mock sarcasm, the bitterness in his tone stemming, I guess, less from the irony of the observation than from the fact that I haven't given him the opening to talk about Bill.

The waitress arrives and sets Mohr's meal in front of him and asks if she can bring me anything. I shake my head and settle back to watch Mohr as he picks up his fork and begins the motions of eating. After a few dabs and bites he puts the fork down, takes a sip from his glass, and returns his napkin to the table.

"You're not going to eat?"

"I can't."

"Is it because I'm here?"

He shakes his head. "My appetite. It comes and goes at random. It's the medication, I think."

"What kind of medication?"

"Painkillers, mainly. They do funny things." He leans back and stares across the table at me. His black horn-rims make it seem as if he is looking at me through a barrier erected across his face. I can see the air going out of him.

"Do you want to leave?" I ask.

He shakes his head. "Sitting here is fine. You'll have to pardon me. The end of the day is exhausting."

The waitress stops by. "Is there anything wrong, Mr. Mohr?"

He shakes his head. "No. Just resting."

"You want me to clear it away?"

"Leave it. Maybe I'll get inspired."

She smiles indulgently and bustles off, well acquainted with the routine. We sit in silence for several minutes. Mohr makes another attempt to eat, but after a few small bites he puts his fork down again and signals the waitress to take it away. "You know," he says after the table is cleared, "I won't really miss the library."

I wait for him to continue.

"I used to think of it as an extension of my personality. When I started it was a more vital part of the town than it is today. We had money then. For programs. I used to put all sorts of things together. Concerts. Lectures. Seminars."

"What happened?"

"Money dried up. People lost interest. Things change. I hope Mrs. Entwhistle will be able to put more things together than I have been able to these last years." He sips his wine. "Besides remedial reading programs. Read a Book This Week. Read to the Children Day. Reading Is Fun Month. It's depressing. Enough of that. Tell me about your family."

"My family?"

The note of surprise in my voice makes him smile. "Parents. Brothers. Sisters. Tell me about them."

"There is nothing to tell."

"Come now," he says, smiling and on the offensive. "Everybody has a story to tell."

"Exactly."

"Exactly what?"

"Everybody has a story to tell, and mine is no different from any other."

"Don't be so sure of that. Are you estranged from your family?"

"You could say that."

"When did you last see your mother?"

I calculate the years back. "Fifteen years ago. Something like that."

Mohr's eyes widen behind his glasses. "Fifteen years! And your father?"

"The same."

"Brothers? Sisters?"

"I don't have any."

He smiles at what he senses to be a hint of things to come and sits up as straight as he is capable of. The rush to probe has revived him and sparkles in his eyes. To satisfy his pathetic curiosity, I decide to oblige him. "My parents are dead."

"Oh, I, I'm sorry." My statement deflates him momentarily; then he resumes the inquiry. "Were they old?"

"No. They both died fairly young."

"I see." And his tone says, Now I'm beginning to understand.

"I was thirty, I think."

Mohr will not be denied. "Were you close?"

"No. Not at all. I knew from the time I was a kid that I was different from them. They knew it too."

"Funny how that works," Mohr says without a trace of irony in his voice.

"The only way I can think of them now is as stereotypes."

"How do you mean?" The look of engrossment on Mohr's face is too authentic to back out and, in a way, outweighs my reservations about talking.

"Only that they were typical."

"Typical of what?"

"Just typical." I lift the glass to my lips. The sour smell puts me off, but I sip anyway and try to end the narrative. "My father had a heart attack and died at fifty-seven. My mother died at fifty-one."

Mohr gives a grave nod of recognition and presses on. "How did she die?"

"She killed herself."

"I see," Mohr says without changing expression.

"In a manner of speaking," I add, finding it strange that these barest facts can still make me mad. "She drank herself to death. Worked hard at it for years."

"Out of grief?"

"More out of boredom, I think. Boredom and acute self-absorption."

"That is sad," Mohr says. "Where did you live before you came here?"

The waitress sweeps by, offers coffee and dessert, then disappears again. The restaurant is empty except for the former mayor and his wife seated in the booth behind us and two truck-driver types drinking coffee and smoking cigarettes at a table near the door.

"Everywhere."

"Abroad?"

I nod, pausing to consider how much further my little autobiography needs to go. It isn't intimacy with Mohr that causes my reluctance but the decision I made years ago to maintain myself always in the present. The past is a vortex of traps into which it is easy to fall and difficult to get out of, the birthplace of illusions and the graveyard of the self. Danger signs should be erected in the lobe of the brain that controls memory, one going in that reads *Check idylls at the door* and one going out that reads *Deposit all grudges*.

"Where abroad?"

"All over. It really doesn't matter."

"You don't want to tell me?"

"Would knowing make any difference?"

Mohr thinks for a moment. "I suppose not," he says.

"There's nothing to tell. I don't want to talk about it."

Mohr's face goes red. "Talk about self-absorption! Now I know where you inherited it from. I'm not just some nosy neighbor, Horace." His brow collapses in a bundle of knots and his eyes fix on me from behind his glasses and under his wig like submerged points.

His vehemence catches me by surprise. "I didn't mean it that way."

"The trouble with you is you don't ever know what you mean. You're so goddamn blasé it makes me sick. I don't know what you're trying to prove, but you don't impress me with it one bit."

"I'm not trying to impress anyone."

Mohr is rolling and cuts me off. "I don't care what you say, nobody, nobody, nobody . . ."

"Nobody?"

"Nobody can talk the way you just did—as if you were describing some sociological phenomenon. It's pompous and stupid. Have your emotions atrophied completely?" He is sputtering and leans back to catch his breath. I wait for him to continue, but he turns his gaze out into the restaurant. "I don't believe you are being sincere."

"Why not?"

"You're not being frank. You've never sorted yourself out—emotionally." He stops there and dabs his slightly beslobbered lips with a napkin.

"I prefer to live in the present." For a few minutes an uncomfortable silence reigns. I lean back and try to imagine what has prompted his outburst, what has upset him. Mohr doesn't look at me but out into the restaurant like an injured lover. He turns to me, tears welling. I continue, "And my emotional life hasn't atrophied. I have just taken firm control of it."

"Glad to hear it." He seems to want comforting.

"I didn't mean to put you off. I just don't think discussing the past is always the best way of framing the present. I prefer to let mine rest."

"I'm sorry," Mohr says, removing his glasses and dabbing his eyes with the corner of his napkin. "I don't know what got hold of me."

"Now it's your turn. Tell me about *your* parents."

"Maybe I can agree with you up to a point." He replaces his glasses. "But I find that memories can be a source of comfort." He pauses for me to object, then continues, "I grew up in Cincinnati. Mount Adams. As kids we used to call the neighborhood Mount Dumbass." He chuckles, begins to cough, and stops himself, holding a fist against his chest. "Our house overlooked the Ohio River. My father worked for the electric company. He married my mother when she was seventeen. I had an older brother, Jim. He was killed in Korea. It was devastating, terrible, the whole family. Now you know how old I am."

"I never really cared."

Mohr shrugs and continues. "My mother had a nervous breakdown. Back then people got put away for that kind of thing. Lobotomized. Luckily, my father was something of a skeptic and didn't want to leave Mother to a bunch of men in white coats. He took early retirement and moved us to Florida. It was an extraordinary thing to do, I now realize. My father was an extraordinary man. I went off to college shortly after that." He begins to cough and wrests control again. "I visited them whenever I could. Anyway, my mother got better."

"Are they still alive?"

"My father died ten years ago. Mother died one year later almost to the day." He begins to slump a little so that, seen from across the table, he seems to be shrinking. "Lately I think about my brother more than I do about my parents. His death was so—unfair."

"Unfair?"

"He didn't give his life—as the army says in the letter they sent to my parents—he had it taken from him. It was so meaningless and unnecessary."

"How is that different from any other death?"

"I don't know. I will die of cancer. There's no *meaning* in that, I suppose."

"But you say your brother's death was meaningless and unnecessary and unfair?"

"That's right. It was."

"And your parents' deaths were fair?"

Mohr works himself into a more upright position. "Let's say theirs were less unfair."

"And your own?"

He stares at me for a moment, retreating behind the large rims of his glasses. "Less unfair." He removes his glasses again and jabs his knuckle into his eye. "I'm not crying," he says, rubbing. "It's the medication. It dries me out. My eyes get. Irritated." He replaces his glasses. "The real is the rational and the rational is the real. That's what Hegel says." He signals the waitress. "Hegel would probably have said that Jim's death was world spirit working itself out. I used to think that those big philosophical positions explained things. That they contained truth."

"And now?"

"Now? I think they are all a pile of shit."

"And what about the rational and the real?"

"There is nothing rational or real that can't be undone and destroyed by the smallest dose of absurdity." He pauses for a moment, licks his lips. "Call it what you want, *das Vernunftige*, *das Wahre*, bad luck. If Hegel were alive today he'd probably be a systems analyst at the Pentagon." He removes his glasses and resumes rubbing his eye. "And if I had any sense I'd go on vacation instead of checking myself into a goddamn hospice."

"Why don't you?"

He pauses for a moment. "Because I don't have an umbrella," he says, grinning broadly, and when the waitress arrives to take the check she finds us both giggling like schoolboys over a dirty joke.

Mohr pays for his uneaten dinner and for my glass of wine, and we leave the restaurant. I walk with him to his car, parked in a reserved space in front of the library.

"I'll drive you home," he says, struggling to fit his key into the frozen lock.

"I'll walk."

He opens the door and slides into the driver's seat. I stand on the sidewalk and watch him maneuver himself into position behind the wheel. The engine comes to life. He rolls down the window. "Sure you don't want a ride?"

"No thanks." I wave and start off in the direction of home. Mohr passes me slowly, honks his horn. He looks so small behind the wheel of the enormous car, protected from the elements outside by a heavy steel and glass exoskeleton, from the elements inside by sophisticated painkillers and who knows what other kinds of medication. He wears a wig to cover his baldness, thick glasses to compensate for myopia, dentures to enable him to eat. I imagine underneath his clothing he is supported by a variety of trusses and bandages and marked with scars where he has been cut open, probed, and explored. The red taillights of his car disappear into the night, carrying his fragile body away in an intricate and ghostly web of technological contingencies and artificial supports.

Coming out of the bank I run into Jane Doe. She pulls open the glass door adjacent to the one I am pushing through, a pair of sunglasses perched on top of her head. "Hello." I feel my face redden as I realize that perhaps I've spoken too soon. She is startled and glances at me with a puzzled look. Then, in a flush of recognition, her features relax into a look of embarrassment. "Oh, hello," she says.

We stand there for an awkward moment, each holding open a door. A smile breaks across Jane's face, a smile of nervous relief that registers also in her eyes. Had she worn her sunglasses into the bank I might have pushed right by without recognizing her. Now we either continue in our separate directions and let the doors close behind us, or we must speak. She lets go of the door she is holding and steps to one side, lowering the sunglasses over her face. "I'm sorry," she says.

"Sorry? For what?"

"I've always meant to thank you."

"There's no need for that." I can't think of anything else to say. "How are you?"

She shrugs. I notice that she is holding a small bundle in one hand, a canvas cash bag with a heavy-duty brass zipper and the name of the bank emblazoned on the side. She looks at it as if to remind herself where she is and why she came.

"My name is Horace."

"I'm Sylvia." We shake hands. Her grip is light, and she holds my hand for a brief moment before letting go. Everything is expressed in that gesture. There really is nothing else to say. She drops her gaze. "Well, I guess I better . . ."

"Yes. Me too." I step back as she pulls open the door, awkwardly and with a little too much force, and disappears into the bank.

In ten minutes I find myself walking out along Old Route 47. The snow is piled high along each shoulder. My boots make a wet, scraping sound in the gully of slush that runs alongside the sand- and salt-strewn road. Waterproof. Just beyond the town limit, I test the hardness of the plowed snow and begin walking along the top of the ridge. It is slippery and much slower going, but now I have a better view across the flat, empty fields. The snow lies undisturbed except for animal tracks and patterns left by swirling drifts.

The state has erected a fence around the Indian mound. The last time I walked out here there was no snow on the ground, just a heavy mulch of leaves and the usual traces left by visitors—cigarette butts, beer cans, etc. In deep snow the mound looks higher and rounded and more like a tortoise. When I came out in autumn, while the leaves were turning, I didn't think of tortoises at all but of Major Wilkington and his hired men and the horse-drawn wagons that dragged the excavated remains away from the site like plunder from a battlefield. All my visits during the fall put me in mind of the Wilkingtons; visits not just to the mound but to the glen and all over town. Maybe it was the cooling of the atmosphere, the changing colors, the crisp, musty smell of decomposition. I don't know. In autumn and early winter the mound seemed to belong, by conquest, to Major Wilkington and his century. Now, blanketed with snow, surrounded by a new chain-link fence freshly hung with signs that read *No Trespassing,* and looking more plundered and empty than ever, it could belong only to the present.

I make a circuit, holding on to the fence for support, plowing along, shuffling and packing the snow underfoot. Where the path leading to the top begins I find a narrow, padlocked gate secured by a heavy chain. I climb the fence at the gate, drop into the snow on the other side, and lie embedded for several minutes, gazing up into overcast skies.

Getting to the top of the mound is difficult. I scramble up the snow-covered slope, grabbing whatever I can lay hold of for support, and finally reach the top, panting and out of breath. The wind blows a light mist across the surrounding fields. The parking lot of Semantech has been cleared, the snow piled into high mounds around lamp posts that stud the lot and give it a desolate concentration-camp look. In the distance, the sprawl of the town pops up out of the flat monotony of covered fields, its shagginess cloaked by the thick layer of snow. It seems tidy, planned. The spire of the Methodist church competes with several tall buildings for dominance of the skyline. I can see the hospital and a corporate development that is under construction to the north. A high green water tower, relegated to the far western edge of town, juts ungainly from the periphery of the landscape and marks the exact location of my house. Oblivion.

Sylvia occupies my thoughts, and the more I try to turn them away the greater force she exerts—like the light pressure of her hand, which exceeded any crush of words. Sylvia is not the name I would have guessed for her, and I have to force myself not to think of her as Jane Doe. Everything was articulated in the weak pressure of her grip and the forceful way she yanked open the bank door, twisting her small body awkwardly to contain the momentum, slightly pigeon-toed, her sunglasses like big black blinds clamped down over her eyes.

I wander down Liberty Street, take my seat on the curved bench inside Wilkington's gazebo, and look around for my friend, the border collie who now appears whenever I come visiting. Sure enough, he appears, the Hound of Liberty Street, trotting across the little playground, tail wagging. He marches up the steps, lowers his head for me to pat, then begins to nose around underneath the bench. I take a carrot out of my pocket. The dog sits down to watch.

Sylvia. I wonder how often she thinks about what happened to her? I wonder if she regrets that her memory returned? Did bumping into me renew any pain? Perhaps. Maybe she will never recover from her ordeal.

Who am I to say? Maybe she will. Or already has. I don't know what to think, really. And I don't think I can empathize with her. Empathy is dull and empirical, an effort of full, subjective comprehension—impossible, dimensionless goals. Empathy attempts to lead beyond compassion and inevitably spins off into anger and hate, first of individuals and then of the whole vicious congregation of debased nature.

The dog puts its paw on my knee, begging. I bite off a chunk of carrot, offer it. The dog snatches it from my fingers and swallows it whole. We sit staring at one another for some time. Man and dog. It follows each bite I take of the carrot with its eyes, rapt, eager to share. I give up another piece, and again the dog swallows it whole. This irritates me for some reason, and I realize it is because swallowing like that makes it seem that the dog didn't properly savor the gift. What a ridiculous thing to expect! I hand over the rest of the carrot and the dog takes it and swallows, tail slapping the floor.

I wish she hadn't told me her name. Knowing it removes her from the periphery of my attention. Now everything is different. Again, the memory of cornfields and the suicides of van Gogh and Hemingway and the sound of gunshots, the flocking of birds and her sudden appearance on the side of the road. Now everything slips back a little and is replaced by a person named Sylvia.

A car passes up the street, then another. The gazebo is like a shelter from the moment, and sitting in it makes me feel invisible. I get up to leave. Dampness has somehow seeped into my suit, and I begin to think of the fire I will build and the bottle of wine I will open when I get home.

Halfway up the street I turn around to find the dog following several paces back. "Go home!" I shout. A few paces farther I look back again. "Go. Go home! Shoo!" The dog sits in a dry patch on the side of the road. At the top of the street I turn once again. The dog is still sitting there, watching, ears pricked up, anticipating an invitation.

At home I rekindle the fire, tidy up, and eat. Winter has made me realize how fond I am of this creaky little house. As it grows dark outside, I find myself sitting on my bed staring at the orange glow through the creosote-stained glass of the stove. I reach for the phone.

"Horace here."

"Horace?"

"I want to ask you a question."

"Better make it a quick one, Horace."

"What is love?"

"You're kidding me! You selling lingerie or something?"

"Let's say I'm conducting a poll."

"A poll?"

"Sure. On love. Have you thought about it lately?"

"I got a lot of stuff on my mind, pal. I don't have time to think."

"You haven't thought about it at all?"

"Yeah, that's right."

"Have you ever thought about it?"

"'Course I have. Everybody has."

"When was the last time?"

I hear the aluminum crack of a beer can being opened. A pause, a slurp. "Say, you aren't the guy who walks all over town, are you? The one without a car?"

"How did you guess?"

"You said your name was Horace. You know Ed Maver, right?"

"I know who he is."

"I work out at Chevyland. Ed told me your name was Horace." A pause, another slurp. "Ed says you're one hell of a guy." A slurp. "My name's Fowler, Chuck Fowler."

It is tempting to put the phone down and try again, but I can't. "What has Maver said to you?"

"Ed? Oh, just talk, that's all. Told us all about the big rescue last summer."

"The what?"

"That woman you helped him pull out of the cornfield. Say, how come those TV reporters didn't ever ask you about it?"

"TV?"

"You didn't see Ed on TV?"

"No, I didn't."

"Hell, we all wondered why he was getting all the attention. Ed said he figured you didn't want to talk to anyone about it. Said you're a real private guy. Anyway, they sent a reporter from Action News out to Chevyland to interview him."

A pit has opened in my stomach as I remember the reporter from the *Sentinel.*

"So what's this you're asking about love?" A slurp.

"Never mind."

"Hey, I was beginning to get interested."

"Forget it." I depress the button and put the phone away. Television and newspapers. The whole town. The whole country. I get up and begin to pace in the dark. The goddamn news. I can see the headline in the paper. And the news anchor, brow pinched in a theatrical parody of moral concern and straining the resources of an impoverished collective imagination as the news is read from the teleprompter. And next sports and next weather and next and next and next and next. Another awful manifestation of the positivism of the times: keeping up. It implies the struggle to keep one's head above water, implies drowning in an ocean of facts.

I can't sleep. Twice during the night I get out of bed to add wood to the stove and stoke the fire. The house is silent and dark except for the orange glow radiating through the glass door of the stove. As morning approaches I manage to drift off. But then at dawn I am up and stoking the fire again, boiling water for tea and frying an egg for breakfast.

First stop is the police station.

The desk sergeant looks up from newspaper, coffee and doughnut.

"I'd like to see Detective Ross."

The sergeant glances at the clock hanging over the door. "Haven't seen him yet. He usually comes in around now."

"I'll wait."

"I'll see if he's at his desk." He picks up the telephone, punches in the extension. "Nope. Not in yet. Get yourself some coffee. He'll be here any minute." He gestures to a corner where a coffeepot and a stack of Styrofoam cups are neatly arranged on a small table.

"That wasn't here last time."

"Nope." The newspaper rattles. No further comment.

I am drawn, as before, to the faces on the wanted posters. A few minutes later Ross is standing next to me. "Long time no see," he says, looking freshly arrived and ready to start the day. We shake hands.

"Did each of them get the satisfaction of news coverage?"

"Say what?"

I gesture to the wall of faces. "Did they make the news?"

"Most of them. You bet." He stands back, crosses his arms over his chest, and begins to expound. "The criminal is the only *real* celebrity, if you ask me. All you got to do is watch the television or read the papers."

"Celebrity?"

"Sure. Not like entertainers, you understand. It's different. Crime has consequences. You got victims, ruined lives. They both get covered. But the perpetrator, the criminal, he gets the most attention because he claims the most of society's resources. We report the crimes, track down the criminals; doctors analyze them, lawyers speak for them, they get tried and judged and sentenced, and then they get locked up and sometimes we even execute 'em. You know how much it costs to execute a criminal in this state? Average?"

I shake my head.

"Three hundred fifty thousand dollars. Average. It's about the same as keeping them locked up for life. I read it the other day. And you and me? We pay for it. So take your pick." He waves at the wall with a heavy hand. "That's what I call real celebrity—when *society* pays. You and me." He goes over to the coffee table and pours himself a cup. "You come in to see me?"

"Yes."

He gestures for me to follow him through the doors that lead into the rear of the station. His office is third down the corridor, a room not much bigger than the desk and the filing cabinet it contains. He sits behind his desk and motions for me to take the chair opposite. "What can I do for you?"

"I'd like to know what you've learned about the rape last summer."

"The cornfield rape?"

"Is that how they put it on TV?"

"What would you prefer?"

"How about just the rape?"

"Which one? We got a bunch we could talk about. Cornfield. Gas station. Liberty Street."

"There was a rape on Liberty Street?"

"Double. Mother and daughter." Ross sips his coffee, regards me over the rim of his Styrofoam as if jotting a mental note, and leans back in his chair. "Surprised you don't know about it. The whole state does."

"I don't read the papers."

"Obviously not. Anyway: case unsolved."

"Tell me what you know so far."

"Right up front? Nothing."

"You don't have any clues? No suspects?"

He shakes his head. "Except for you and that other fellow, Maver, we haven't got any witnesses."

"What about the woman?"

"Well, sure. If she decides she wants to talk about it."

"What has she told you?"

"Can't tell you that."

"Why not?"

"All I can say is: case unsolved."

"What about the other ones?"

"The gas station we got. Some guy driving through. Pumped his tank full, put in a quart of oil, raped the cashier in the restroom, and drove away. Finally caught him in Nevada."

"And Liberty Street?"

"Case unsolved."

"Do you think they're connected?"

Ross shrugs.

"Would you tell me if you did?"

"Probably not."

"Why not? I have a right to know."

"And *I* have a duty not to make statements that aren't fully backed up by facts."

"You want to know what I think?"

Ross puts his cup on the desk. "Always."

"I think you know exactly who did it."

My accusation annoys Ross, and his easygoing, extra-large manner disappears. "What kind of bullshit is that? What did you come in here for?" He glowers at me across his desk. "What do you want?"

"I want to know what you know."

"Look. I'm not going to argue with you, Mr., ah, Mr. Blake."

"It's not my name."

"Well, it *used* to be."

"My name is Horace."

"Look. I got work to do." Ross's temper has puffed his eyes larger.

"I'm not asking for anything unreasonable. I have a right to know."

"You got no rights, Mr. Blake. Your duty as a citizen is to obey the laws and stay out of my way."

"Stop calling me Blake. My name is Horace. Quintus Horatius Flaccus."

"Look, I don't care what you call yourself. Horace Quintus Superfly. Let's stop the fucking around." Ross puts his coffee cup on the table and reaches for a notepad and pen. "You're so interested in the case? Let's go over your story one more time. What were you doing when the woman came out of the cornfield?"

We lock eyes. "I was walking."

"Walking where?"

"Along Old Route 47."

"Why?"

"Because I enjoy it."

"Where were you headed?"

"The Indian mound."

"The mound? What for?"

"Because it intrigues me and I like the view."

"Okay. So you're walking. What do you see?"

"A woman coming out of the cornfield."

"Before that. Think. Close your eyes and try to remember every last detail."

My instinct says not to, but I do as the detective says and close my eyes. At first all I can think of is Ross sitting directly across from me, watching. "Take your time," he says. I hear his chair squeak and open my eyes to see that he has risen and is turning toward the high file cabinet in the corner. "Take your time," he repeats.

I close my eyes again, sink down into the chair, and try invoking the dubious conveyance called memory. Short, shuffling indeterminism. The phrase leaps up. *Pop pop*. Blackbirds. Ernest Hemingway and Vincent van Gogh. A short, shuffling indeterminism. What is a short, shuffling indeterminism? The general view that for every event there are any number of unknowable conditions that may or may not apply? *Pop pop.* Blackbirds aloft. Hemingway and van Gogh. A lonely country road on a hot, dusty summer afternoon. *Whoosh.* A car.

I open my eyes. "A car."

Ross is standing in front of an open file drawer. "A what?"

"A car. I saw a car. No. Two cars."

Ross returns to his desk and flips through a notebook. "Describe them."

"I can't."

"Try to remember. Close your eyes and go back."

I do as the detective asks but can't couple the general memory with specific details.

"What color?"

I try to remember but can't.

"What make?"

"I don't remember. I don't know makes."

"What do you remember?"

"Standing next to the field. Hearing shots. But they don't register as shots. Just background noise. Seeing birds flock."

"You heard the shots before seeing the cars?"

"Yes."

"What direction were they headed?"

"Toward the mound."

"Away from town?"

"Yes."

"And the only car you saw after that was Ed Maver's?"

"Yes."

"Which direction?"

"Coming toward town."

"The opposite direction of the other two cars?"

"Yes."

"What color is Maver's car?"

"I can't remember."

"Try."

"I really don't remember. Blue?"

"Okay. Enough. That's good. Leave it for now."

I open my eyes and Ross is jotting notes in his little book. He glances up at me with an expression I haven't seen him use before. "Good. Very good. You did good," he says as he jots. "Maybe it'll come back to you later. When you're not forcing it. Happens all the time."

Later in the library with back issues of the *Sentinel* spread before me on the table, I try again to recall details. But can't. The reason is simple: you can't recall what you didn't notice in the first place. Reading the newspaper accounts forces this realization. And I feel somehow implicated, as if my inability to recollect points to a larger defect, a general failure of perception.

> *An unidentified woman was brought to the emergency room of Memorial Hospital yesterday by two men who discovered her in a ditch along Old Route 47. According to police, the woman was found by Edward M. Maver of Locust Lane and another man who requested that his name be withheld. A spokesman for the sheriff's office says that the case is being investigated as a rape and that there are no suspects. The victim, whom police would only identify as a woman, 30–35 years of age, was admitted to Memorial*

Hospital at 5:30 p.m. A hospital spokesman stated that she is being treated for severe trauma.

The brutal rapes of four women in less than one month have left police and citizens worried for the safety of the community. The latest rape, which occurred two days ago, has contributed to a growing atmosphere of fear and focused attention on the problem of crime in the community. "I haven't seen anything like it in my thirty-two years as pastor," Rev. James Ball, Pastor of Bethlehem Methodist Church, stated. "People are stunned. They're confused. They ask me how it is that such horrible things can be happening in our community."

I skim the rest of the article and find this quote by Ed Maver at the end: *"It's the breakdown of the family, if you ask me. Same thing that's happening all around the country. Nobody taking responsibility for anything anymore. We're finally getting a taste of it here in our little neck of the woods."*

Article two:

The Nevada Highway Patrol working with the FBI has apprehended a man charged with four rapes in four separate states. He is believed to be the same man responsible for the rape committed here less than two weeks ago. The man, identified as George P. Mullen of Madison, Wisconsin, was apprehended by FBI agents and Nevada State Highway Patrol officers as he left a motel early on the morning of August 6. Police say evidence collected at the time of the arrest identifies him in connection with four rapes committed in four states over the last two months, including the July 22 rape of a service station employee here in Oblivion. According to a local police source, the man was tracked by charges made to his credit card during his drive across country. "We're glad to have this one cleared up," says a spokesman for the local sheriff's office. "Now we can concentrate all our efforts on solving the other two cases." The spokesman would not comment, however, on the status of either case, saying only, "We're devoting all our resources to them at the current time."

The reading room is busier than usual. Mrs. Entwhistle has been behind the circulation desk all morning without a break. When I came in earlier she told me that Mr. Mohr was at home and she hoped the day would be a quiet one. I fold the newspapers and return them to the counter.

"Anything else?" Mrs. Entwhistle asks without looking up. She is slipping due cards into the pockets of a pile of books. I glance over at my reserved shelf of books and briefly consider spending the rest of the day here.

"Find what you were looking for?" She sweeps the papers from the counter and puts them in a stack of others to be filed away.

"Yes. I suppose I did."

"What was it?"

"The rapes last summer."

"Terrible. Just terrible." She takes off her reading glasses and lets them drop on their little gold chain onto her bust. Her broad features pucker into a look of consternation. "I hear the whole family has moved."

"Family?"

She wheels her chair closer. "The house is empty. For sale. They just picked up and left town practically overnight without saying a thing to anyone. I heard they moved to California or some place out west. Couldn't stand to be reminded, I guess."

I realize she's talking about what Ross called the Liberty Street rape. The mother and daughter.

"Between you and me," Mrs. Entwhistle continues, "I think it's probably for the best."

"Who can say what's best?"

"Well, that's right too," she says with a wary note in her voice, suspecting I might be harboring an opinion. "It's so tragic." A tear wells up in the corner of her eye, and she wipes it away. "I don't know what I'd do," she begins but then stops short.

You mean if it were you? I'm tempted to say, but finishing her thought for her would be as impertinent as is her empathy. The tendency fascinates me, the persistent reframing of the world into hypothetical personal experience. The only purpose I can see in the whole exercise is the manufacture of a flattering self-image. "If it were *me*, I'd . . ." Mrs. Entwhistle fidgets delicately with her reading glasses and the gold chain around her neck, aware of the nasty spot where empathy has landed her. I can hear the wheels grinding—"If it were me." Finally she looks up and changes the subject completely. "Mr. Mohr has told you of his plans, I assume."

"He has, yes."

An elderly man approaches the desk holding a thick volume in both hands. "Things aren't going to be the same here without him." She slips on her reading glasses and pedals herself away to check out the old man's book. I consider the possibility of a double meaning, a "When I'm in charge things'll be different," but decide to take her statement at face value.

"Will he be in later?"

"Tomorrow morning," she says, her librarian cheer returned, all subjects having been returned—on time—to their proper shelf.

The sky is threatening more snow. I cut across Main Street at the blinking traffic light and find myself walking in the direction of Liberty Street. It is hard to make sense of all the news that has been shoveled under my nose in the last day or so, the lifting of the veil of blissful ignorance. Sylvia is at the core of a morbid curiosity I know better than to indulge but which I am indulging nevertheless. Until now I had not wanted to know anything of the town's doings. Now it seems a whole hidden world has come to light, and I am allowing myself to be pulled into it.

At the top of Liberty I pause as a car backs out of a driveway, blocking the sidewalk. The driver looks at me and waves. I wave back. A man I don't remember seeing before, he rolls down the window. "Anything I can help you with?" His voice is friendly but inquisitorial.

"Just out for a walk."

An elbow juts out the window. The man nods. "I've noticed you sitting in the gazebo," he says.

I nod.

"It's a nice spot." He twists his body around, poking a hand out the window. "Tom Schroeder," he says.

We shake. "Schroeder's Shoes?"

"That's me. You been to the store?"

"No. Not yet."

"Well, come on out." He peers down at the boots on my feet. "We'll fix you up."

"You have a son named Tom, don't you?"

"I do indeed. You know him?"

"In a way, yes."

"He's off at college. Got a scholarship to Notre Dame. I didn't catch your name."

"Horace."

It is hard to make any connection between the two Schroeders. The father seems thoroughly innocuous despite the interrogation that he is trying to make as pleasant as possible. I consider unleashing a stream of complaints about his son, but it would be pointless. We seem to have arrived at the end of the conversation. Schroeder checks his rearview mirror. "Well, have a good one." He backs out into the street, waves to me again as he drives off.

I continue down the street. The house with the For Sale sign is the last one on the block, which dead-ends in woods. It is a little farther down from Wilkington Park and the gazebo. If the sign was there the last time, I didn't notice it. The house is a hulking gray old Victorian with a turret on one corner and a large front porch that looks as if it settled into place fifty years after the house did. A wide yard at the front and a tall row of hedges separates the property from the neighbor on one side, and a driveway overhung with elm trees seems to blend the whole place into the woods on the other side and makes it feel gloomy.

I walk as far as the end of the street, then turn back. Had Schroeder not stopped me I might have been tempted to walk around and inspect, but I now feel that I'm being watched and am a little intimidated. It's not just gloom that surrounds the place but an air of affliction. I can't imagine that anyone ever wanted to live in it. I pass by the house again, thinking of Mrs. Entwhistle. The gossip of the town seems just as likely to have caused the evacuation of the house as the rape itself.

The Hound of Liberty Street rounds the corner and bounds up to me, barking and wagging its tail. It crouches up against my legs, tail and rear end waggling furiously while I pat its head. We stand at the curb looking across the wide yard at the house, the dog and I. Snow begins to fall.

I haven't set foot outside for days except to bring in wood from the porch. It is quiet. The only sounds are water dripping from the roof, the crackle of the stove, the occasional hiss of car tires on the street. The snow and muck and damp air aren't really what has kept me indoors these several days. I am afraid to go out—afraid of stumbling onto more contingencies. And the longer I remain inside the greater my fear seems to grow. I'm not sure I understand completely, but I think it's fairly common—the disinclination to participate in the riot of unintended incidentals and possibilities and truth values derived apart from propositions and conditionalities and the general roaring in the ears of all the finite facts of the world.

Standing on the front porch, I listen to the water trickling from the roof, a load of musty wood bundled under one arm. Damp air and a falling barometer have affected the functioning of the stove, and the raw, sodden smell of creosote and smoke permeates the air inside the house. After stoking the fire I go back outside and slog through wet snow to the side of the house to check on the chimney. Rather than rising in columns or plumes, the smoke merely oozes asthmatically into the atmosphere and hangs in the air above the house. I can't tell what is causing the problem—if the chimney is blocked or if it has something to do with changing barometric pressure. As long as smoke is coming out, I figure there is nothing to worry about.

A quiet knock sounds at the door. It is the kid from next door. He is standing on the porch holding a snow shovel that is almost as tall as he is. "Want your walk shoveled?" he asks timidly.

I motion him inside. He leans the shovel against the side of the house and enters cautiously. He stands just inside the door and glances tentatively at my living room quarters as though captive on foreign soil. I judge him to be about ten or eleven. He has the idle air of a young boy with a secret or two tucked under his belt. He didn't expect to be invited inside and is already formulating his description of the weirdo neighbor's house, which he will relate to Mom and Dad at dinnertime.

"How much do you charge?"

"Ten dollars."

"It looks pretty deep. Can you do it alone?"

"I did our walkway in less than an hour. My dad did the driveway. He has a plow."

I pull the curtain aside and look over. The riot of plowing that has been going on every morning for the past three days has created a high mound of snow that rises up at the end of the neighbor's driveway. Dad's truck with the snowplow attachment is parked before it in an attitude of casual victory. Mom's car is parked just behind, beneficiary of the big-boy violence of snow moving. The boy snuffles, swipes his nose with a torn glove, and stands on the mat with blank preadolescent insolence.

"How many walkways have you shoveled today?"

"None."

"I thought you said you did yours in under an hour?"

"Yeah. But that don't count."

"Why not?"

"Don't get paid. It's part of my chores." He twists to look out the window, embarrassed by his admission of domestic servitude.

"Did your parents suggest you come over here?"

"No. I mean, well, sort of. Dad told me if I wanted to get paid I had to go out and find work. He don't pay for chores 'cause he says Mom don't get paid for housework and he says he don't pay himself for chores, so why should he pay me?"

"What do you want the money for?"

"A TV." He makes reproachful eye contact. "I'm saving up."

"What do you want a TV for? Don't your parents have one?"

"Yeah, but I want my own so I can watch what I want to watch."

"How much have you saved?"

"Thirty."

"How much do TVs cost?"

"The one I want is two hundred."

"That's twenty shoveling jobs."

"Seventeen," he says and swipes at his nose again.

"If I hire you, will you stop spying on me?"

The boy looks down at his feet. A shit-eating smirk and more shifty embarrassment.

"That new set of binoculars you got last summer. They work pretty well, don't they?"

"I wasn't spying."

"I bet you're glad I broke that first set."

"I wasn't spying. I swear."

"I've seen you sneaking around back there in the woods with them."

"I was looking for deer."

"You were looking for them in the direction of my house."

"I was looking all around. I swear."

"If I hire you, will you promise to stop?"

"I wasn't spying," he insists, eyes filled with mock hurt and resentment.

"Promise me you'll cut it out."

"I wasn't spying."

"What are you going to do for money when the snow is gone?"

"I don't know."

"I have a proposition. Since you're so good at spying, bring me information and I'll pay you for it."

"Whad'ya mean?"

"Tell me what's going on, what you see and hear."

"Stuff from the news?"

"Whatever you think is important. I'll pay you."

He considers the offer. "What about the snow?"

"I'll pay you to shovel my walk. Afterward, though, I want information."

"Okay," he says, shifting nervously. I open the door and he slips outside without looking at me.

In twenty minutes he has cleared a path halfway from my porch to the curb. I watch him through the window. In a few days he'll have his television set, and his interest in binoculars will evaporate, and they will collect dust in a closet with all the other gadgets he's grown bored with until the day he packs to leave home.

Getting through the shrink-wrapped cornucopia of industrial farming that is Riteway is not pleasant or easy. Time inside is slowed by some mysterious effect of light and sound so that people's movements seem drowsy. It takes an effort of will not to succumb. I dart up and down the aisles dropping what I need into the basket and ticking it off my mental list. In the fresh produce section I browse among hybrids flown in from distant points around the globe. I'm always curious but rarely tempted by lettuce that actually comes in the size and shape of a baby's bib, square tomatoes piled neatly into pyramids, apples powered by their own internal sources of electricity, oranges that can talk, carrots that will serve as entrenching tools, and bananas that will lift payloads many times their weight into low satellite orbit.

"Hello."

I turn. Sylvia is directly beside me, standing behind an empty shopping basket. "Do you roll them in your palms to test for freshness?"

I look at the tomato I'm holding. "Actually, I'm trying to see if the corners can be rounded out."

She picks one from the base of the pyramid and holds it out, gripping firmly. "I see your point."

I select another tomato and roll it vigorously between my palms. "You can't make them round."

Sylvia smiles broadly. Her eyes look bloodshot under the neon lights.

She holds the tomato flat on the palm of her hand, then lets it drop to the floor. "They don't bounce too well, either." She takes another tomato from the display, holds it up. "Observe," she says, then hurls it. It lands noiselessly somewhere at the other end of the fresh produce section. "They fly pretty good. Horace, right?"

"That's right." I am still looking at the spot where the tomato landed, wondering if it hit anyone. "And you're Sylvia."

"That's right."

She is drunk. Her eyes blink in slow motion. Her smile fades a little, and I notice that she is holding on to the empty cart for support. She is bundled into a bright red down jacket that looks like an inflated raft and highlights the red in her blue eyes, the flush of her cheeks. She is wearing an old brown fedora, and her dark hair falls to her shoulders in weather-blown tangles. "Do you like kiwis?" She pulls one from the pocket of her jacket.

"I haven't had one in a long time."

She holds it in her hand, regarding it for a moment. "I was going to steal these." She pulls another from her pocket. "I mean, how can they make people pay for things that look so—goddamn ugly. Know what I mean? It's like ginger or potatoes. How can they charge for things that look so pathetic?"

I nod, wondering what else she will pull from her jacket pockets.

"Anyway, I came here for kiwis. I had this craving." She mimics a southern accent, pronounces it *cryving*. "And you know what, honey-bun?"

"What?"

"Ah just don't know what the fuck to do with them. Ah mean, do you peel it first? Or are you supposed to slice it and then peel? Ah cain't decide."

I lean against the tomato bin, holding my basket with both hands and bouncing it lightly against my knees, amused.

"Fuck it. I'll pay for them this time. Figure out what to do when I get home." She drops both fruits into the cart. "Does that ever happen to you?"

"What?"

"You get a *cryyyving* for something you never had before? Or maybe you had it someplace but never made it yourself."

I shrug.

"Or maybe you even just saw a picture of it in a magazine and you go, 'Boy, that there sure looks delicious,' and you just have to have it."

Her sentences ramble together, and she sprinkles her speech with mock southern inflections.

"Or maybe you been eating them all your life and you just don't remember. That ever happen to you?"

"No."

"They look so good when they're cut up, like on cheesecake." She leans forward and half whispers, "But they got all this fur on 'em."

Her sotto voce deadpan makes me laugh, that and the sheer surprise of her bloodshot, bantering personality. We stand in uncertain silence for a moment. I double-check the contents of my basket. Sylvia wanders over to a large bin filled with pineapples. "Fresh Hawaiian." She lifts one from the mound and hefts it in her hands as if she is about to hurl it. Then she drops the fruit into her basket and turns to me with a devilish grin. "Hey, Horace! Let me buy you a drink." She starts toward me with her cart, peels the sleeve of her jacket back, checks the time on her watch. "It's three o'clock. Three peeee emmmm." She lets her arm drop. "There's plenty of time. You're lucky."

"Why is that?"

"It's my day off. My only goddamn day of the week off. C'mon, Horace. It'll make me feel good."

Fifteen minutes later we are sitting in a booth at some place called Andy's. It's two parking lots up from Riteway. I insisted that we come here.

"I hate this place," Sylvia sulks. "I want to take you to Jack's."

"I said I'd have a drink with you, not crack up your car."

"I can drive just fine."

"I believe you. But not with me in the car."

She waves me away. "I'm not even drunk." She leans back into the corner of the booth and glares at me. The bartender sets our drinks down on the table, a glass of wine that I can tell will be undrinkable and a Jack Daniels and Coke for Sylvia, which I see she'll have no problem with.

The place is empty except for the two of us and an old man at the bar reading a paper. A more generic vinyl atmosphere would be hard to imagine. We clink glasses. "To my only goddamn day of the week off."

Conversation does not come easily, and in the beginning Sylvia talks about her job at the pharmacy. She says she is the pharmacist's assistant and tells me that she plans to get licensed as a pharmacist but hasn't gotten around to taking the courses yet.

"How old are you?"

She regards me over the rim of her glass. "Thirty-one."

"What are you waiting for?"

She shrugs. "Not really into it. I used to work at Semantech. It's why I moved here in the first place."

"What happened?"

"Pink slip."

"What did you do?"

"Nothing. I swear." She holds up a hand and laughs. "Just kidding. I was an assembly coordinator."

"Assembly of what?"

"Circuit boards."

"For what?"

"Missiles. Conventional guided. Everybody thinks they make bombs there. But it's only circuits and wiring harnesses. Anyway, it's all over for me. They cut over half the work force. The old guys were given early retirement. The middle managers are being retrained or are leaving. The assembly line is down to one-third and shrinking."

"Where were you?"

"Right in the way of a pink slip."

"How long did you work there?"

"Seven goddamn years."

We sit in silence for a few minutes. Sylvia stares across at the television over the bar. A soap opera. When she lifts her glass to drink she keeps her eyes fixed straight ahead. She hasn't removed her hat, and in profile her features seem aquiline, hardened. She is wearing small silver earrings. Her fingernails are chewed. Since she mentioned Semantech the broad outlines of her redneck stoicism have begun to emerge. She's a good ol' girl. The incongruity of it allows me to ask the question that has been on my mind from the beginning. "Did seeing me in that lineup help you remember?"

She turns to me. Her features soften in an I-was-waiting-for-you-to-ask-that look. She tears at the napkin stuck to the base of her glass. "Yes," she says. "Well, sort of."

"Do you mind me asking?"

She shakes her head.

"I stopped by the doctor—what was her name?"

"Dr. Henley?"

"Right. I stopped by to find out how things were."

"She told me about it. I said I didn't care."

"Did your memory return completely?"

A shrug.

"You don't want to talk about it, do you?"

"No."

"Sorry."

"It's okay."

After a brief silence I continue asking questions anyway. "Are you still seeing Henley?"

She shakes her head. "I quit."

"Why?"

A shrug. "Didn't want to continue." She sips her drink and looks up at me with a weary expression. The military stoic again. "Didn't think it mattered one way or another."

"Mattered?"

"I went to group therapy for a while afterward. It was okay in the beginning, but then I just got tired of all the goddamn whining and complaining. Anyway, it doesn't matter anymore."

"Why not?"

"I don't know." She sips her drink and looks me in the eye for one completely sober and uncomfortable second. The geography of her features changes as the outline of a hidden rage comes to the surface, then sinks below again. She finishes her drink and signals the bartender for another. "You want another one?"

I shake my head.

"You don't like the wine?"

"It's pretty awful."

"Get something else."

"That's okay."

She shrugs. The bartender sets the second drink down in front of her and she stirs it, first with the plastic swizzle stick, then with her finger. "The therapists all say you have to come to terms with the anger. What the fuck is that supposed to mean? You know? Come to terms? It's a bunch of bullshit." She stirs the swizzle stick around with her finger without looking up. "There's only one way I can see to come to terms," she says.

"What's that?"

"Get even." She jabs her finger back into her glass and puts it in her mouth, then looks at me, completely sober eyed.

"You'd have to remember who it was."

She puts her finger in her mouth again, then lifts the glass to drink. "That's right," she says with a wily glint in her eye. "That's absolutely right."

It takes about fifteen minutes for her to finish the second drink, and during the interval conversation stops. She sits wedged into the corner of the booth, one leg up on the bench, staring idly at the soap opera on television, poking her finger alternately into her glass and her mouth. I align myself in the same position so that we are parallel, facing into the bar. I take intermittent sips of the sour red wine, which leaves an aftertaste in my mouth that seems appropriate to the occasion.

"I wonder where they find the assholes that act on soap operas?" She knocks back her drink.

"Same place they find the assholes that watch them."

Sylvia looks at me and smiles. "I'll remember that," she says and signals the bartender.

"I have to go." I reach under the table for my backpack.

"Just one more. I'll be quick."

"You said one drink. Not three."

"It's my day off."

"Mine too." I let the backpack drop back under the table. "How do you plan to get home?"

"My car."

"You're too drunk to drive."

"I'll manage."

"I don't think it's a good idea."

"Listen to you!"

"It's dangerous."

"Then why don't you wait for me and you can drive?"

"I don't drive."

"What do you mean you don't drive? Everybody drives."

"I don't know how."

An alcohol-fueled guffaw erupts from her. "I don't believe you. You telling me you've never driven a car before?"

"No. I don't like cars."

"I don't believe you."

"It's the truth."

"Do you have a phobia or something?"

"Something."

She nods her head. The bartender arrives, takes her empty glass, replaces it with a full one. He glances at my unfinished wine and then loafs off without comment, wiping his hands on a towel slung over one shoulder.

"Have you ever been to Mexico?"

I reach under the table for my pack and put it on the bench beside me. "Years ago."

"Where did you go?"

"All over."

"What did you like best?"

I lift my glass and swirl the remains, trying to think of an answer. "I liked different places for different reasons."

"C'mon. Just answer me. What places did you like best?"

"Mexico City."

"Mexico City? That's supposed to be one of the most polluted places in the world."

"That's part of its charm."

"C'mon, be serious."

"I am being serious."

"Everybody says stay away from Mexico City because it's too polluted and too huge."

"It's a good place to get lost." I let the comment drop casually but watch to see her reaction. Does she want to run away? Plan an escape? Her expression doesn't change.

"What about the beaches?"

"Are you planning a vacation?"

"Maybe." She sips her drink, regarding me with aqueous blue eyes. It is a little discomforting the way she fixes them on me. I find myself unable to look directly back. If she senses my discomfort, it is only making her stare more overtly. I don't know why I find it so unsettling. Maybe because underneath it all I sense that in her drunkenness she is revealing something to me that I would rather not know, inviting me to share in some secret plan she has concocted.

"Do you come from around here?"

She takes her eyes off me and settles back into the corner again, keeping one hand on her glass. "Not by a long shot."

"Where did you grow up?"

"I grew up all over. My dad was in the Air Force."

"How did you end up here?" I am asking all the questions of her that I would refuse to respond to myself.

"Semantech."

"You moved here to work there?"

She nods, hefts her glass, mock macho. "You want to hear the story?"

"Not really."

She sips. "Well, I'll tell you anyway. I was working at a resort down in the Virgin Islands. Just finished my first year of college. A group of Semantech brass were having their annual getaway conference. I got friendly with the president, and he offered me a job."

"You got friendly?"

"It's not what you think. He was just a nice old guy. Dick Georges. He died of a heart attack during my first year on the job."

"And you took him up on the offer just like that?"

"Why not? I was planning to take a year off school anyway, and I figured what the hell. The job was pretty decent, and the pay was great. I figured I'd go work for a year and then go back to school."

"Did you?"

"No."

"Why not?"

"I guess I got trapped."

"What happened?"

"For a guy who doesn't want to know anything, you sure ask a lot of questions."

"Change the subject."

"Fuck it," she says, then continues with her story without any prompting. "They made me a team manager. One day they called me in and said I could make section head if I decided to stay. What about my degree? I asked. They said as far as they were concerned my on-the-job was more important to them than a degree. They wanted me to stay. What they didn't say was that they figured they could save money by putting me—a woman—in a dead-end job that they would have to pay a man more for and eventually promote him out of anyway. It's the fucking truth, and I was too young to see it."

"What happened?"

"Everything was fine. I liked the job. Anyway. Last year—I get a pink slip. Cutbacks. Blah blah blah." Her eyes glaze over.

For several minutes there is silence. The television drones; another man appears and sits at the bar and begins telling the bartender a loud joke. Sylvia's story is not particularly moving. Maybe it's the way she told it. People talk about themselves as though their life story were some uncomfortable obstruction, best purged early in an acquaintance. The process is called "intimacy," and, for reasons I don't understand, people seem to attach an element of moral necessity to "telling all." I prefer the quiet, blank absorption of the present. *Non semper imbres nubibus hispidos: the clouds do not forever pour murky rain.*

Our eyes meet for a moment, and I look away. The man at the bar roars with laughter at his own joke. The bartender grins and shakes his head, then leans forward and says something that causes the man to slide off his barstool and do a sort of laughing pirouette. Sylvia shakes her head, smiling into the heel of her hand. It's a good thing she can't remember everything. I'd like to tell her so. Her doctor too. What possible good could a complete return of memory be to her? Who would wish to know?

Sylvia drains her glass. "Do I have time for another?"

"Why are you asking?"

"Because you're my escort."

"I am?"

"You think I'd stay in this shithole alone?"

"Do you go to other bars alone?"

"Bars suck," she says and holds up her glass to the bartender.

"I can't believe I'm doing this."

"Shut up and drive," Sylvia says, slams the door. I adjust the seat and the rearview mirror. "Think you can manage?"

"What kind of car is this?"

"It's not a car. It's a Bronco."

"A Bronco?"

"Four-wheel drive."

"It feels like being in a truck."

"This here's a sport utility vehicle," she says in mock cowboy talk, patting the dashboard. "Never lets me down. All this here snow? Never even notice the stuff."

"It's too big."

"Quit complaining, Horace. Just start it up and let's get outa here."

"What's this?"

"That's to shift into four-wheel drive."

"Do I need to do that?"

"Not unless you plan on driving in the snow."

"What's this?"

"That there's a CD changer, pardner. Want to listen to some music?" She touches a button and the speakers in the rear erupt.

"Turn it off!"

"You don't like it?"

"No!"

She touches the button and there is silence. "That was my favorite band. Nirvana."

"Sounded more like Hell."

"You never heard of them?"

"No."

"The singer killed himself. Blew his head off. Now his wife's a big movie star. You must have heard about that."

"No. I didn't."

"They're great. I saw them in concert once."

"I don't think I want to drive this thing, Sylvia. Let's see if we can find a cab."

"A cab? In this town? There aren't any cab drivers here. The last one starved to death a few years ago." She reaches over and twists the key in the ignition. The engine roars to life. "There ain't any buffalo either. C'mon. I'll give you a lesson. Put your foot on the brake."

I depress the pedal and she yanks the gearshift into reverse. "Now. Back out slowly. No gas. Just ease off the brake."

I do as she says, and the truck begins rolling backward. It is dusk, and there is a pink midwinter slant to the last bit of daylight. I look into the rearview mirror, and when we've pulled clear of the parking space Sylvia tells me to cut the wheel and reaches over to help. I brush her hand away. "I can do it." I step on the brake. We are thrown back in our seats.

"Fucking hell, Horace! Go easy." Sylvia snaps on her seatbelt and tells me to do the same.

"I didn't realize they were so sensitive."

"Just go easy on 'em. Everything's power. And you forgot to turn on the headlights."

She points to a lever and I pull it out. Everything inside lights up. "Drive around the lot until you get the feel of it," she says.

I steer the enormous vehicle toward the emptiest part of the lot.

Night is coming on quickly, yet the lot is illuminated by tall lamps, the headlights of cars, and the neon emissions of Riteway.

Sylvia hiccups. "Shit," she says. "I hate when this *up* happens."

I'm too busy concentrating to pay attention. The moving vehicle has a momentum all its own, reacts at the slightest touch of the steering wheel.

"Easy," Sylvia instructs. "You're *up* doing fine."

"I haven't even touched the gas yet. The thing just goes by itself."

"It'll *up* do that."

I make a few turns around the lot, stopping and starting again while Sylvia slouches in the seat next to me holding on to a strap above the passenger window and trying to stop her hiccups by holding her breath.

"Are you all right?"

She nods her head.

"Can you give me directions?"

"Left out of the lot. Take the *up* bypass north."

"The bypass?"

"North *up*."

"Where the hell do you live?"

"Outside of town."

"How far?"

"About *up* fifteen miles."

I put on the brakes. We are thrown forward.

"Shit, Horace. You're *up* going to make me *up* puke."

I put the gear lever into park.

"How am I supposed to get back?"

Sylvia rests her head in the crook of her arm. "You can *up* take the *up* car."

"I don't want to drive at all!"

"You can *up* stay at my place and I'll take you *up* home later."

I drop my hands from the wheel. "What the fuck am I doing here?"

Sylvia lifts her head from the crook of her arm. "Relax, Horace. I'll *up* drive."

"You can't even keep your head up."

"What's the big deal?" She drops her arm into her lap and shifts so that she is sitting straight-backed in the seat. "Now drive. Will you? Before I puke."

The bypass north is crowded, and I stay in the right lane hugging the shoulder while cars whip past. Being at the wheel of this growling box has set every fiber of every nerve on edge. Magnitudes of horsepower. The pedal under my foot responds smoothly. I fix my eyes on the road, unable to ignore the caroming around of all the other vehicles, each one inhabited by a placid-faced driver, blissful and complacent in the conjunction of power and private convenience.

Near the end of the bypass Sylvia directs me onto a quieter road. It grows darker, and all that is visible are the melting heaps of plowed snow along the roadside and the parallel beams of the headlights. I try to keep the car centered in the lane.

"Sit back, Horace," Sylvia laughs at one point. "You're all hunched up like an old lady. Makes me nervous." I glance over. Her hiccups have gone. She is sitting primly, looking forward, both hands in her lap. "You really never drove before?"

"I told you that."

"I didn't believe you."

I lean back in the seat and ease up on the accelerator. "I've never wanted to either."

She looks over at me. I keep my eyes on the road ahead and try to return her look peripherally, driver-style. "Still, you gotta admit. Driving's fun."

"For pathological cretins, maybe. I wish they'd all disappear."

"Pathological cretins?"

"And their cars."

"Why?"

A car approaches in the other lane. I slow down, trying to avert my eyes from the headlights without taking my eyes from the road. My pulse quickens. The car whooshes past and the road ahead goes dark again. "Why?" she asks again.

"Because they've turned the world into a big, noisy, stinking brawl."

She giggles and says with drunken sarcasm, "Aren't we being sensitive?"

The darkness unrolls toward us, and we drive in silence for several more miles. The throbbing engine creates a mysterious lull that hangs between us, two people strapped in a seated position and hurtling through the night in radium-green stillness. The mound comes to mind, the diagrammed attitude of its human contents shut up in silent darkness and hurtling not through space but through time.

"Turn left at the third mailbox up ahead."

I take my foot from the gas, touch the brakes. The machine responds nicely.

"Not here. Up there."

I coast, bring it to a stop with the lightest pressure of my foot on the brake pedal. A driveway appears to the right of the mailbox, and I turn into it. The tires crunch onto gravel. The headlights illuminate a large white house set back from the road behind a wide, snow-covered lawn and a stand of tall trees. Lights come on on the porch and the first floor.

"Motion detector," she says. "It turns on the lights automatically."

I coast the truck to the end of the drive. "You live in this big place all alone?"

"I got a roommate. Laura. But she spends most of her time at her boyfriend's."

She shoves open her door and climbs out. I follow her as she weaves her unsteady way toward the house, stoops down, and reaches underneath the first porch step to extract a hidden key. "My secret," she says.

Inside is a jumbled mess of furniture strewn with clothes, shoes, books, magazines. Everything looks as if it has been shoved aside with a sweep of the foot. A sofa and coffee table stand in the center of the room. A television set, wilted potted plants, a stereo.

"Excuse the mess," she says, going into the next room. "Want a drink?"

I follow her into the kitchen, a large, spacious room with a solid-looking square table at one end. There is a faint smell of food left out.

"I don't have any wine." She yanks open the refrigerator. "I'll make you a bourbon and Coke if you want."

"I'll have a glass of water."

She takes a large bottle of Coke from the refrigerator and retrieves a half-gallon bottle of cheap bourbon from a cabinet. "In case you're wondering why I drink so much. I have trouble sleeping. And I'm afraid of sleeping pills. Dr. Henley wanted to prescribe some to me. But she said it wouldn't be a good idea unless I agreed to go to AA. Fuck that. I told her I could do just fine without the pills." An ice tray crashes to the floor. I pick up the scattered cubes and put them in the sink. She hands me a glass and drops some ice into it from the tray. I fill my glass at the sink while she tends to her drink, which she mixes in a large glass beer mug filled to the brim with ice. "God! I almost forgot!"

"What?"

"The kiwis! I left them in the car. They're probably frozen by now."

I offer to get them and return outside, knowing I should not have come. I crunch across the frozen gravel toward the Bronco, retrieve both my backpack and the paper bag containing Sylvia's kiwis. All this is done in a daze, and before returning inside I pause in front of the house and breathe a few drafts of cold air to clear my head. It is much darker out here than on West Street with its pathetic streetlight at the corner and the kilowatt-hungry neighbors piled one against the next. The stars shine brightly. A few dark wisps of cloud move across the sky.

"I bet these will go great together." Sylvia holds up the brown oval fruit. "Just peel the fur off." She hands the kiwi to me and takes a knife from a drawer.

I peel and slice it for her, sampling a piece of the sweet-sour fruit. It tastes good and cuts the sour wine taste left over from the bar. I haven't eaten all day, and now that the adrenaline from the drive has subsided I realize I'm hungry.

Sylvia takes two slices of the kiwi and drops them into her drink, stirs them in with her finger. "I gotta show this to Laura. She always comes up with weird drinks." She wanders into the living room.

"Do you have a girlfriend?" Sylvia asks, sipping off the top of her drink.

"What do you mean?"

"You know, a girlfriend? G-I-R-L friend." She sips and grimaces. "This is sour!"

"Why do you ask?"

She shrugs. "Just curious." She sits down on the sofa, reaches underneath, and pulls out a mirror. She puts it on the coffee table, takes a small vial from her shirt pocket. She taps a small mound of powder onto the mirror, chops it up with a razor blade, and in a few deft swipes creates a few thin parallel lines. Then she holds a plastic straw to one nostril and snorts. She turns to me, her eyes bluer and more aqueous. She offers the straw, fingers long and slender, each tight little bone in her hand articulated.

"No." I am fascinated by the seriousness she brings to the little ritual. She slides a finger across the surface of the mirror, rubs a little powder onto her gums as if brushing her teeth. At last she looks up, slips her finger from her mouth with a satisfied slurp. "You want to fuck me?" She hurls the question like a sharp object. It's not embarrassment that prevents me from answering but the intuition that a simple yes or no is not the correct response.

"I don't know how to answer that question."

"You do," she says and reaches for her mug.

"I hadn't thought about it."

She regards me now through the rearranged furniture of a new mood sprung suddenly upon her—hostility mixed with uncertainty, alcohol, cocaine, eros, thanatos, sour kiwi, and a thousand unnameable little gouges. She drinks again with a swagger. "You're lying," she says.

"I don't know what to say, Sylvia, but you're mistaken."

"Why not?" she demands.

I don't want to say anything else to provoke her, so I say nothing and turn to leave the room.

"Where are you going?"

"To get my pack." I pause for a moment to try and gather whatever it is I must gather in order to make it out the door. I can hear her snort another line, rub the surface of the mirror with her finger. The ice cubes clink in her drink.

"You're not going to run away now, are you?"

I hoist my pack onto my shoulders and return through the dining room. She is standing in the foyer at the bottom of the staircase. "C'mon, Horace," she says. "Why don't you ask me if I want to fuck you? Go ahead." She begins to unbutton her shirt.

"I have to go," I say, unable to look at her. My chest is thumping with fear. I do not understand.

"What's the matter?" She is leaning against the wall with her shirt open and one hand on her hip. Mock whore posture. The drunkenness has suddenly and mysteriously evaporated from her speech. "You've been wondering, right? Don't deny it. I can tell. You asked if I could remember what happened. What you really meant was, I wonder if she still likes to fuck? Am I right? Tell me. Am I right?"

I can't answer her.

"Go ahead, ask me. Ask me right now."

"I don't know what you're talking about."

"The hell you don't. You want to know, so ask me. Go ahead."

"I don't want to know anything."

"So then stay here and fuck me and find out for yourself. C'mon. What are you afraid of?"

"I want to leave, Sylvia. You're not making sense."

"You mean you don't want to fuck me? Why not?" The tone of her voice is now unsteady and uncertain and drunk again and has an edge of unpurged misery. "I'm a good fuck."

I twist the door handle. A blast of cold air sweeps into the house. Sylvia follows me out the door.

"Stay, Horace. I'm sorry." Her tone is now conciliatory. "I was just . . ." she breaks off, standing on the porch buttoning up her blouse.

I turn to her but can't find any words to say. I start off across the gravel, the crunch of my boots obliterating the silence.

"The truth, Horace. You want to know the truth?" she shouts in a taunting voice. I pass by the Bronco and continue on down the drive toward the road. "I remember everything. Everything! You stupid asshole! I never forgot. I remember it all!"

I pause for a moment, adjust the straps of my pack, turn around. She is standing on the porch, a silhouette, breath condensing in thick clouds above her head. I have nothing to say to her that would make me turn back now.

"You coward!" she shouts at my back. "I remember everything! You goddamn fucking coward." The door slams just as I reach the end of the drive.

Daffodils are blooming all around the house. The ground is soggy and until a week ago was just a cold bog of muddy turf. Now flowers are coming up everywhere. I came outside this morning and there they were, a sea of yellow flowers to drive away the winter.

The neighbor's kid is at the door and rattling away excitedly. "A man in Florida killed his wife and put her in the car and they caught him."

"Slow down, slow down." I step out onto the porch, where the kid is standing with his hands crammed into the pockets of a battered jacket.

The kid continues at a fast clip. "He went to a drive-through and the man at the window saw the body in the back seat of the car and called the police."

"He went to a drive-through? What for?"

"A hamburger, I guess." The kid swipes his damp nose with the sleeve of his jacket. "He was hungry."

"Where'd you hear this?"

"My TV."

"So you got it after all. A television."

"Yeah. Are you going to pay me?"

"How much do you think it's worth?"

The kid looks at his feet. "I don't know."

I hand him a quarter.

"That's all?"

"How much do you think a recycled old story from TV is worth?"

"I don't know."

"I think a quarter is too much. Next time get me something more interesting. Closer to home."

He slides the coin into the pocket of his pants, turns to leave, then hesitates a moment. "You want me to, like, spy on people?"

"Not spy. Just keep your eyes and ears peeled."

"For what?"

"Anything that you think I'd want to know about."

"Okay," he says and scuffs his way down the porch steps.

I go inside to make a few telephone calls.

"Tire shop."

"You sell tires?"

"Yes sir. Any brand you can name."

"Are the daffodils up over there?"

"Beg pardon?"

"The daffodils. Flowers. Are they blooming over by you?"

"To tell you the truth, I haven't noticed. Hold on a second. Hey, George! We got flowers coming up out front? Daffodils? Daffodils! Someone on the phone wants to know. Beats me. The landscaper, I guess. Who am I talking to?"

"Horace."

"Says his name is Horace. What? Okay. I'll tell him. Hello?"

"Yes."

"The boss says if you planted 'em they should be there. He says come out and take a look for yourself."

I hang up to try another number.

"Have you seen the flowers blooming?"

"Flowers?"

"Outside. Spring is here."

"I don't go outside anymore. I need a hernia operation."

"Look out the window."

"Can't. Don't want to. I'm in bed, and I need an operation."

"Go have one, then."

"Can't."

"Why not?"

"Don't want to."

"Why not?"

"I'm afraid. Anyhow, I feel fine. Long as I keep still and don't move too much."

"You have someone looking after you?"

"Yup. My daughter."

"Can I talk to her?"

"Nope."

"Why not?"

"She's deaf. Been deaf all her life. Anyway, the hernia. I've had it for years. Happened just after my wife died. Who'd you say you were?"

"Horace."

"Don't believe I know you."

"You don't."

"What're you calling for?"

"To find out if you've noticed the flowers."

"You ain't a social worker, are you?"

"No."

"I been telling you people over there to stop pestering me."

I try a few more, but nobody seems as distracted by the news as I am, so I put the telephone away and eat an early lunch. Around midday I head out to the mound to see if the archaeologists have turned up yet. Mohr says they've got all the permits they need. About a month ago the professor from the university came to go through the archives one more time. I didn't have a chance to meet her. I was sick with a cold I caught walking back from Sylvia's house. It was the worst cold I've ever had. It lingered for weeks. I haven't seen or heard from Sylvia since that night. Every now and then I consider going over to the pharmacy to say hello. But something keeps me away, and I don't know what it is. Or maybe I do.

All the way out Old Route 47 I notice the daffodils. The air is cool and clear. Small puffs of cloud move across the sky. A recent selected philosophical essay informs me that there is an *ordo amoris* at work in the world, a basic ethos. It is, simultaneously, the subjective ordering of love and hate that lies at the center of our perception of the world *and* the objective order of what is worthy of love in all things, an independent order that can't be created or destroyed but simply is. On the subjective side, it can be trampled and deformed and confused by any number of things: personal trauma, world events, the tenor of the times. The damage is not easy to repair. I wonder if Sylvia's can ever be fixed?

Early spring is when the *ordo amoris* is most apparent—when the vast world swarms and stirs the heart and the passions and rekindles a many-sided interest in the things of this world. The philosopher wrote that the *ordo amoris* is what attracts and repels us to everything. It is what makes flowers beautiful. I have been struggling to get my *ordo* to work properly so that on this fine spring morning I may feel myself drawn outside toward whatever fate has in store for me. The daffodils help. And as I stride along the shoulder of the road I remind myself that without the *ordo amoris*, I could easily slip back into fearing contingencies, as I did for most of the winter, rather than offering myself up for them to do with me what they will.

There aren't any archaeologists at the mound when I arrive. The padlock that secures the gate is rusted and shows no signs of having been opened recently. The ground is too soft for digging. They must be waiting for the weather to get warmer and the ground to dry so they can dig and sift more easily.

I climb the fence at my usual spot near the gate and drop into the perimeter, feeling more like an intruder than I did in winter when deep snow blanketed the ground. The path is muddy and slick. I lose my footing twice on the way up and wipe the mud from my palms on the trunk of the elm tree growing near the top. The snow has melted to reveal the same old charred logs in the fire pit. It is comforting to recognize these little details of the ground after so long and deep a winter. Something of a surprise too. I search for and find the remains of the empty Marlboro box in which I found the cigarette I smoked when the sheriff came to arrest me. I wish I had a cigarette to smoke now. The grass is damp, and I sit on a fallen branch on the side of the mound that faces town. The fields all around have been plowed. Brown furrows extend for acres in machine-dug parallel lines. The parking lot of Semantech is almost empty.

I sit for an hour in the warming rays of the sun. A few cars blow by but do not stop. They don't even slow down. Birds in the elm tree keep up a steady chirping. I watch one high among the branches as it builds a nest. It flies away and returns again and again carrying the small twigs and sticks of its new home in its beak. The *ordo amoris*—if it is anything—is what comes to life at the observation of all these little facts of the world. I wonder where the bird's old nest is? Was it corrupted by the passing of time? Did it fall? Or do birds abandon their homes and build new ones every season? The image of the abandoned nest begins to crowd my thoughts and forces an urgent inspiration.

It is time, again, to change my name.

At Town Hall a clerk shuffles through a filing cabinet and hands me a series of forms, circling the instructions with a pencil. "Come back when you're done with step number four," he says, scratching behind an ear with the end of the pencil. "We'll fix you up with a court date."

"The paperwork isn't enough?"

"Not in this state it ain't." He taps the papers with his body-prober pencil. "Just do what I said and follow the instructions." The petty authority in his voice is irritating. I gather the papers up and leave, feeling the man's extruded presence cleaving to me until I've left the building.

I walk over to the library to fill out the forms. Mrs. Entwhistle and Mohr are standing next to the circulation desk when I enter the reading room. Mohr is not wearing his wig. His head is shaved, and he is dressed in a stylishly cut dark suit and tie.

"Horace. I'm glad you're here," he says with his usual difficulty. Mrs. Entwhistle stops speaking and nods curtly. Since Mohr left, a little over two months ago, she is growing less and less tolerant of my presence in the library. My reserve-shelf privileges are already being threatened on the grounds that space behind the circulation desk is limited. She makes a point of being nice to me. This she does in a nasal middle American vernacular so overladen with phony pleasantry it actually hurts to hear it. Horace, I just haaate to have to have to aaask you. I hope you don't miiiind . . . etc., etc.

"I like your suit."

Mohr produces a dark gray fedora and perches it on his bald head, tugging the rim down rakishly to one side. The hat is a good touch and looks better than that awful wig; it adds some weight to him and gives the attenuated, lonely tendons at the back of his neck something to support. He looks like Fernando Pessoa—or one of his heteronyms, Bernardo Soares, maybe, Assistant Bookkeeper of the City of Lisbon—or just any mortally conscious poet from the first half of this century. He steps back so I can regard him more fully, produces a cane, and leans forward on it, both hands on the polished silver handle.

"Very elegant. Where are you off to so dressed up? An audition?"

Mohr grins his clacky dentured grin. "Just the oncologist," he says. "I like to put my best foot forward."

"For radiation?"

Mrs. Entwhistle shoots me a horrified look and returns to the circulation desk.

"For chemo," Mohr says.

"Why bother getting all dressed up for that?"

Mrs. Entwhistle emits a little gasp. If I were her son or her husband she'd probably swat me.

"I've found that they stop treating you like a hopeless case when you're well dressed." He asks Mrs. Entwhistle if she would mind if I accompanied him upstairs.

"You two go right ahead," she says, her mock cheer regained. "Just make yourselves at home."

The suit hides Mohr's advancing sickness well. I follow him upstairs as he tells me that he has had to force himself to stay away from the library.

"Maybe you should come back to work," I say as we reach the second floor.

Mohr waggles his cane. "Too late for that. And anyway, I'm settling into my books. You'd be surprised how long it takes to get back to real reading after a lifetime of noisy distraction. But also what a pleasure."

"What is real reading?"

Mohr doesn't respond. We enter his old office, and he stands in the doorway for a moment, leaning on his cane. The blinds are drawn, but a fair amount of light filters through the slats. "It's stuffy," he says and advances toward the window to pull up the blind. The room is transformed by the light. Mrs. Entwhistle has cleared away the boxes that cluttered the floor but left the room essentially the way it was before Mohr left.

"I don't understand," Mohr says. "Why hasn't she moved in? This is the head librarian's office. Why doesn't she use it?" He sits down behind his old desk and twirls his cane between his knees. The desk top is clear except for the telephone and an old blotter pad decorated with decades of Mohr's own doodles.

"She's waiting for you to die," I blurt.

Mohr looks up at me for a moment, holding his cane between his knees. "I think you might be right."

Now I know I don't like her. Some macabre sense of propriety is preventing her from staking her claim. She wants the place completely and absolutely to herself and doesn't want even to be reminded of Mohr. The worst is that she would never admit it.

"What are those papers you have?" Mohr indicates the legal forms rolled in my hand.

"I'm going to change my name."

Mohr's brows arch slightly. "But Quintus Horatius Flaccus is such a—nice name. Why change it?"

I shrug, not really in the mood to explain myself.

"Have you decided on a new one?"

"Not yet."

"Do you have any ideas?"

"A few."

"Tell me."

"Flavius Arrianus. Arrian for short."

Mohr nods his head appreciatively. "Whom are we referring ourself to this time?"

"The author of the *Discourses of Epictetus*."

Mohr nods again, continues twirling his cane. "Why not go all the way?"

"What do you mean?"

"Call yourself Epictetus."

"I can't."

"Why not?"

"I lack *prosopon*."

"*Prosopon?* As in *prosopopoeia?* Or *prosopography?*"

"*Prosopon* is Greek for person. But Epictetus meant it in a special way. For him, *prosopon* meant the proper character and personality of a person."

Mohr continues his nod, repeats the word *prosopon* several times.

"It's a Stoic idea. When one finds one's true character and personality—one's nature—it is one's obligation to display it to the world."

"So you don't think you're up to Epictetus. But you can handle his amanuensis?"

"You could put it that way. I'd rather think Arrian *is* Epictetus in the same way that, say, Plato is Socrates. Or the poet Fernando Pessoa is Bernardo Soares, Assistant Bookkeeper of the City of Lisbon. You look like him, by the way."

"Like whom? Pessoa?"

"No. Like the Assistant Bookkeeper of the City of Lisbon."

"Thank you, Horace. But that's enough. I'm getting confused."

"If Arrian didn't call himself Epictetus, how can I?"

"I don't know what to say about the logic of it," Mohr answers in an indulgent tone of voice. "But your reasoning is interesting." He pauses for a moment. "What about Horace? Do you think you had the *prosopon?*"

"Maybe. But it's time for a change." I walk over to look out the window. It is late afternoon, time to go home, drink a few glasses of wine, watch the daffodils. The sun's rays slant long and golden. The big white house behind the library looks almost yellow in the light.

Mohr's chair creaks as he leans back in it. He is amused by our conversation and wants to continue. "Can I offer a suggestion?"

"Be my guest."

I sit on the edge of the desk. A glint escapes Mohr's eyes that I haven't seen since the evening we drank together at my house. Maybe it's the suit, his new dapper look. He leans forward, placing one hand over the other on the hilt of his cane. "Forget Arrian," he says.

"Why?"

"You're too young for Stoicism. And too healthy. Save the forbearance stuff for later. When you're in my shoes." He stops for a moment to clear his throat, then continues, "Besides, I don't think you really believe that the whole, undivided universe is really all *good*. Do you?" Before I can respond he continues, "And there is a theistic element in Stoicism that can't be escaped."

"So?"

"So. You have always struck me as more agnostically inclined." He smiles, reshuffles his hands on the hilt of his cane. "I was going to suggest something more eclectic, in the direction of Cynicism."

"The Cynics are too demanding. The wallet and staff thing is too much. I don't want to live in a barrel and harangue people and beg. It's too noisy and extreme. Besides, they'd throw me in jail."

Mohr waves off my objections. "I agree. I don't see you barking at people in the street either. Or hugging icy statues and masturbating publicly." He breaks into strangely noiseless laughter and drops his cane. His whole frame shakes weakly, and a few tears erupt from the corners of his eyes, which he wipes away with the back of his hand. There is something unfunny about his outbreak, and I can't bring myself to laugh with him, so I just smile and look down at the floor and shake my head in mirthful sympathy. He recovers and bends to pick up his cane. I twist around and look past him through the window. The tops of the trees just outside the window are swaying in the breeze.

"I'm sorry," Mohr says. "I didn't mean to be so. Silly."

"Then let's have your suggestion."

"I was thinking of Lucian. Lucian of Samosata."

"I don't know him."

Mohr drops his cane again and bends to pick it up. "You don't know Lucian? Shame on you."

"Was he Roman?"

"Not one bit. Samosata was some backwater in Syria, I think. He lived at the time of Marcus Aurelius. A satirist—with a Cynic bent who lived to expose shams and phonys. He traveled the world of his day delivering diatribes on every subject. Mainly he poked fun at the bigmouths and the pompous philosophical schools of the day. Best of all." He rests his chin on his hand and continues with a wry grin, "He thoroughly despised his own epoch."

The door opens and Mrs. Entwhistle pokes her head into the room. "I'm not interrupting, am I?"

I want to say she is, but Mohr waves her in. "We were just having a little philosophical conversation."

Mrs. Entwhistle steps in, leaving the door open behind her. "Memories, memories," she says in a sickeningly cheerful voice. "I hope you don't mind. I've done a little straightening up."

"Not at all," Mohr responds with his shaky reed of a voice, returning cheer with cheer. "But tell me. Why haven't you moved in yet?"

Mrs. Entwhistle crosses her arms over her narrow bosom. "Well, Mr. Mohr. I just haven't had one extra minute since you left, and until my position is filled I don't see any reason to begin moving things around. And besides," she pauses to choose her words carefully, "I just can't get used to not having you up here."

Mohr swallows the bait. "Well, Mrs. Entwhistle, I honestly can't get used to it either." A moment of subdued silence ensues, and I slide off the corner of the desk and make for the door. "Leaving us?" Mohr asks.

"I still have some things to do." I hold up the rolled papers in my hand. Mrs. Entwhistle begins to rearrange a stack of papers on one of the shelves along the walls.

"I wanted to tell you before we got off the subject. The archaeology team arrives next week. They've told me we can come out to watch the excavation. Would you like to join me for an afternoon?"

"I'd like that."

"I'll call you to arrange a time."

I detour through the stacks and locate a battered old bilingual Greek/English edition titled *The Diatribes of Lucian*. Mohr's suggestion intrigues me, and, testing my library liberties, I leave a note for Mrs. Entwhistle informing her that I have taken the book.

On the way home I stop in Winesburg Wine and Liquor. I haven't visited for over a month, since I bought a case of 1981 Château Léoville-Las-Cases and a case of Hattenheim Steinberger that Anderson became sold on after a short trip to Germany last fall—as he did on everything German. He happily shows off his newest selections and invites me to sample a bottle he has just opened.

We stand in the neon light of the small store, and I listen while Anderson tugs at his walrus mustache and rambles on using jargon taken from magazines and his growing collection of wine books. He keeps them on a shelf near the register for the benefit of his customers, whom, he says, he has been trying to educate for years. Anderson sees himself as something of a novelty in the town, but in fact he is the kind of man who lives contentedly by all the accepted conventions of taste—a true connoisseur, in other words. We stand facing each other, Anderson's belly pressed up against the counter, savoring the wine.

"Full bodied," he says, swirling his glass. "Nice tannins." He pokes his nose back into the glass, snorts and sips and smacks with red-lipped relish. "Big. Very big," he says from under his walrus mustache. He delivers his appraisals and opinions with guarded enthusiasm—amusing, since I know that none are his own. He has adopted wine to substitute for a basic lack of originality, which is to his credit because without the veneer of connoisseurship he wouldn't have anything to think about at all and would just be a slave to his alcoholism—like me.

A motorcycle drives up to the door with a loud rumble. Tom Schroeder, wearing black leather from head to foot, dismounts and marches into the store, closing the door behind him with a bang. "How's it goin'?" he asks, taking the two of us in at a glance.

"Now, Tom," Anderson begins, "you know better than to come waltzing in here like that."

Schroeder holds up his hand, reaches into his jacket, and brings out a driver's license, smirking. He is spattered with mud and wearing leather gloves that leave the upper halves of his fingers exposed. "Turned twenty-one last month. Ein und zwanzig." He saunters over and presents the laminated plastic card to Anderson with a ceremonial flourish. "And I got the stretch marks to prove it." He turns to me. "Horace, right?"

"That's right." I turn to browse the bottle rack.

"See? I remember." Playing the wiseass, he breaks into a stubble-faced grin.

"Do you remember the notebook you stole from me too?"

Schroeder shuffles toward me with a creaking of leather. He is smiling broadly. Up close he smells of tobacco and leather and several other unidentifiable odors. His straight blond hair is tied back, lighter and longer than I remember it. He has a purple bandanna tied around his neck. The current of youth that runs through him overwhelms his seediness; the dirt and grunge are a form of adornment. "Of course I remember," he says in a confidential tone. "In fact, I still have it. I was going to give it back. You're one hell of a poet, Horace."

Anderson hands the license back to Schroeder. "Well, Tom, congratulations. Have a glass of wine."

"What the hell," Schroeder says and slides the laminated card into an inside pocket of his jacket. I peruse the wine rack.

Anderson gives Schroeder a glass. "Happy belated birthday," he says.

Schroeder empties the glass in one gulp and puts it back on the counter.

"That's not how you're supposed to drink wine," Anderson chides him.

Schroeder ignores him and strolls over to where I am browsing. "I'm not bullshitting, dude. I'd never admit I took it if I didn't dig what I found." His voice still has an adenoidal edge to it.

"What you stole."

"Whatever." He grabs a bottle from the rack, gives the label a cursory glance, then puts it back. "I gotta tell you, though, the poems helped me. No shit. They did. I been writing some stuff myself. Lyrics. Some dudes I know in a band are going to put 'em to music. If you want I'll show 'em to you."

"What I would like is to have the notebook back."

"It's at home. I just got back yesterday."

"I thought you were in college."

"I was. I mean I am. I cut out early."

"Or they threw you out."

I move down the aisle a few steps. Schroeder stays with me. Now I remember what I hated about him, his lingering presence. "I'm not the only one who likes your poems. My English professor liked them too."

"You showed them to your English professor?"

"Yup." Schroeder grins and grabs a half-gallon bottle of Jack Daniels from the shelf. "He gave me an A for them."

I want to laugh but keep a straight face. "Your English professor is an idiot," I say, examining the bottle in my hand.

Schroeder grins, bounces the half-gallon bottle against his thigh. "Don't knock it, dude. It means he liked *your* stuff."

"If he'd known *his* stuff, he'd have flunked you for plagiarism."

Schroeder's grin is undiminished. He gives the bottle in his hands a few aimless hefts, as though practicing with weights. "How's he supposed to know I copied your poems?"

"Because *I* copied them."

"No shit! Who'd you copy them from?"

"Horace."

"Horace who?"

"Quintus Horatius Flaccus."

"Who's he?"

"Just one of the more famous Roman poets."

"No shit! Never heard of him."

"Nor has your professor, it seems."

"What'd you do? Copy them out of a book or something?"

"I copied them out from memory."

Schroeder's eyes widen along with his grin. "No shit!" He scratches the stubble of his cheek, then slaps his leather-clad thigh and laughs. "That's fantastic!"

"I can't believe your professor didn't catch you."

"Well, I changed them around a little so that they didn't sound, like, too old-fashioned. It was fun, man. And know what?"

"What?"

"I made 'em better." He strikes a pose and recites, "You rotten old bitch/my cock ain't hard/'cause every tooth of yours is black/and between your flabby legs/a hole as raw and nasty as a cow's . . ."

"All right, that's enough!" Anderson shouts from behind the counter.

"It's a poem, man."

"I don't care what you call it. Get what you came for and leave."

Schroeder saunters over to the register, where Anderson is waiting with a scowl. He reaches into his pocket and pulls out a wad of bills. I watch the transaction, my anger at Schroeder dissipating, a mysterious effect of his oafish charisma. I return to the rack and take down another bottle.

"Don't bother coming in here again unless you know how to behave yourself."

"Hey," Schroeder calls on his way out the door, "I'll bring your pad back later." He pushes through the door, and both Anderson and I watch as he packs the bottle into a saddle bag, mounts, and drives off.

"I've known that kid since he was this high," Anderson says, coming out from behind the counter and chopping his fat thigh with the side of his hand. "He's been trouble for years, and his father pretends not to notice."

"What about the mother?"

"That's how it all started. She killed herself about ten years ago. They say she did it right in front of the boy—with a shotgun. I don't know if that's true or just gossip. It doesn't matter one way or another because the whole town thinks it's what happened, so the kid gets away with pretty much anything he wants." Anderson shakes his head wearily, puts his reading glasses back on. "If he were mine I'd've put him over my knee a long time ago." He pulls a bottle from the rack. "This is one I really like," he says, picking up where he left off earlier.

It's dusk by the time I get home. The woodpile on the porch is nearly depleted, and while daylight fades I restack what's left and sweep the porch before opening the Château Bel-Air Anderson sold me. I drag my rocking chair onto the porch and sit outside, despite the chill. The wine is full bodied and very pleasant, although Anderson's opinion was that it still needed some time in the bottle. Maybe he's right, but I'd never let considerations like that prevent me from drinking it. The air grows colder. The street is quiet, and it is nice to breathe fresh air after the long winter in front of the stove.

I find myself wondering if I can still despise Schroeder as I have in the past. His ludicrous story did it. I even found his dirty leather swagger and his de-bowdlerized Horatian epode amusing, if only because Anderson was so repulsed. If he does return the notebook I'll ask him about his mother—and the score between us will be settled.

Night falls, and it is too cold to stay outside. I bring in a few logs and some kindling to start the fire. The wine has taken away my appetite, but I go into the kitchen out of boredom and make a pot of rice to eat with the last of the kidney beans and squash I've been eating for the past three days. An orange for dessert cuts the lingering aftertaste of the wine, and rather than finish the bottle as I'm tempted to, I cork it and return to the living room to read more about the *ordo amoris* in *Selected Philosophical Essays*.

After a few pages the relation between the acts of love and hate and cognitive acts and acts belonging to the sphere of striving and willing confuses me and makes me restless. I put the book aside and turn to the copy of *The Diatribes of Lucian* I brought home from the library. It is not long before I am engrossed.

Time passes.

By early morning Lucian is a roaring atavism within me. I can hardly contain him, and I take out my copy book and begin to transcribe, copying first the Greek and then the English on facing pages. I remember the words of Dionysius of Halicarnassus: *The reader's spirit absorbs a similarity of character with what he reads by the act of continuous concentration.* It's what I intend to do, but after several pages I stop, realizing that I will have to work on my Greek, which is rudimentary.

At dawn I go out onto the porch. I am Lucian. Lucian of Samosata. Lucian the Slanderer. Lucian the Blasphemer. The Atheist. The Mocker.

I walk through the woods behind the house to the abandoned train tracks. The first light of dawn filters through the trees. I strip myself naked, pull off the boots that saw me through the winter and begin to dig a hole. The ground is soft, and I am able to dig with my bare hands. After I have dug through the layer of topsoil the earth grows hard and I need a stick to break it up so I can scoop it out. Soon I am sweating from the effort. When the hole is a few feet long and a foot deep I lay my boots in it, cover them with my shirt and pants. Then I fill it in, tromping down the earth with bare feet, the air on my soil-streaked skin cool and invigorating.

I stand in the clearing and listen to the birds singing my name in the trees—*looshen, looshen*—then make my way slowly through the woods, stepping tenderly through the undergrowth. I emerge into the sea of daffodils that surrounds my house. The morning sun is bright and the dew heavy on the ground, my stagnant little house an emanation on the horizon. As I approach it, the neighbor appears, clomping toward his truck in the driveway. He raises his hand, then stops short.

I run across the yard trampling daffodils, bound up the porch steps and into the house.

The pavement is warm against the soles of my feet. The sun is bright. By the time I've reached the top of the street I am damp with perspiration. I unzip my snowsuit as far as my navel to let the air circulate. The world has taken on a mild hallucinatory aspect, as though I am viewing a quiet avalanche of things through a clear but solid barrier, a pane of glass. On the way into town I think about the new name I have chosen and how it both binds me to and isolates me from this remote, shimmering world.

At the bank Derringer rises to greet me. "Run out in a hurry this morning?" He looks me up and down, extends his hand across the desk. "You forgot your shoes. Sit down. Make yourself comfortable. Can I get you some coffee?"

"No thanks." I reach into the inside pocket of my suit and take out the documents from the court. They are limp and wilted looking. Derringer has seated himself in his fake leather chair and removes the yellow ball from the top drawer of his desk. He sits back, squeezing the little orb. "What can I do ya fer today?"

"I need you to notarize this form."

Derringer takes the document and glances at it for a moment. Application for Change of Name. His left hand pumps the ball as he reads. He looks up at me with cheerful inquisitiveness and then continues reading the document, returning his yellow ball to the drawer and fishing out his notary tools without taking his eyes from the form. "Lucyann? Have I got it right? Lucy-ann of Same-es-atta?"

"Looshen," I correct him. "Looshen of Sam-os-ahta."

Derringer repeats, pronouncing it more or less correctly. "What is it? French?"

"Greek."

"You like them Greek names, don't you? Isn't Horatius Quintus, whatever it is. Isn't that Greek too?"

"It's Latin."

"Well, it's got a ring to it. I'll say that." He turns the document over and hands it across the desk. "You have to fill in the second part," he says, pointing with his finger. "Number three. Reason for Change of Name. Can't put my chop on it 'til you got it all filled out correctly."

"I left it blank intentionally."

Derringer shrugs and smiles superficially. "Well, you have to put something down. I can't notarize an incomplete form."

"What if I don't want to explain myself?"

Derringer leans back, shrugs his heavy shoulders, and reaches for the rubber ball. "Put 'none' down. Not applicable." He rolls the ball on the top of the desk with the flat of his hand, then sits back in his chair and begins to squeeze.

"Why do you squeeze that ball all the time?"

Derringer seems a little surprised at my question and transfers the ball from one hand to the other. "Keeps me calm," he says. "Relaxed. Used to smoke. The doctor says this is one hundred percent healthier."

As Derringer speaks an answer occurs to me, and I fill in the blank box on the form: Expression of personal identity. I slide the paper across the desk.

"Well, it's a free country, I always say. And a man's gotta do what a man's gotta do." Derringer puts the ball away, takes the iron clamp, and squeezes tightly, embossing the seal at the bottom. "Paper's a little damp," Derringer says, examining the mark. "Could be a little crisper." He waves the form as though to dry it and then signs with a flourish and returns it to me. "Now, what else can I do ya fer?"

"I need some money."

"No problem," he sings, peeling a withdrawal slip from a small stack at the side of his desk. He turns to his computer terminal. "By the way." He begins tapping on the keyboard. "You'll have to bring all the paperwork from the court so we can make the changes in your account."

I nod. Derringer keeps pecking at the keyboard, then copies numbers onto the slip. "I see your certificates of deposit are coming due. Want to talk about that now, or do we wait?"

"Just do whatever it is you did before."

Derringer finishes on the computer, then swivels in his chair so he's facing me. "You know, there are a variety of other financial tools available for someone in your position." He has completely changed his tone of voice, speaking now with what he must consider to be the authority of his profession but sounding more like a precocious child trying to talk like a grownup. "If you're interested I can put you in touch with our investment division. They'll discuss the full range of options with you. Equities. Annuities. Mutual funds. That kind of thing."

"I don't really care."

Derringer gives a professional shrug and pretends indifference. "Just thought I should say something. With your level of liquidity, you could be looking for higher returns."

"I don't want to think about it."

Derringer gives a sagacious nod, then shrugs again. "That's what money managers are for," he says, pushing his chair back and getting to his feet. "Just wait here a minute and I'll go to the cashier for you." He lumbers off. I take the notarized form, fold and return it to the insulated dampness of my pocket.

The walk to Schroeder's Shoes takes twice the time it should because I have to stop every ten minutes to give the soles of my feet a rest and to cool down inside the suit. By the time I get out to the strip of development that bulges like a tumor from the northern end of town my feet have been thoroughly tenderized. I had considered doing without shoes and even thought the suit might make a sort of cowl-less habit. But asphalt is too hard to walk on and the suit is too hot for late spring weather.

When I enter the shoe store Tom Schroeder Sr. is nowhere to be seen. A bangled and teased-up young woman approaches me, a smile splashed across her face. Her name tag says she is Cathy, the manager. She takes one look at my feet and bursts out with, "Wow! Do we need shoes or what?"

"Is Tom Schroeder here?"

Cathy shakes her head vigorously. "Nope. He hardly comes in since the new store opened."

"New store?"

"Out at the Pavilion."

"Pavilion?"

"The new mall. Since they opened up out there, traffic's down here by about half. They got a food court and a cineplex and a virtual-reality arcade called Hyperworld."

"I'm looking for a pair of walking shoes."

Cathy motions me over to a display. "These are what you want. Lumberlands." She lifts up an object that looks like something for incubating eggs in. She turns it over in her hand and traces a finger along the sole. "They've got a patented insulation system, vacuum sealed to create a cushion of air between your foot and the ground. Try it on. It's like walking on air."

"I'm not interested in walking on air. What about a plain leather shoe?"

"This is no gimmick. These are the best shoes on the market. Everybody who buys 'em loves 'em. I got two pairs, I like them so much."

"I just want a normal leather shoe."

"These shoes let your foot breathe."

"I don't want my feet to breathe. I want them to walk."

"Very funny." She puts the shoe down. "Plain vanilla? We got plain vanilla." She marches across the store, beckoning me with a crooked finger. "Here's what you want." She holds up a boot that is all laces and thickly notched sole. "A hiking boot."

I shake my head. "I just want an ordinary shoe."

"An ordinary old shoe," she repeats. "Sit down. I'll bring you the plainest oldest ordinariest shoe we got."

I sit and watch the dazed procession of shoppers moving past the display window. Cathy reappears a few minutes later and hands me a pair of white socks. "You'll need to put those on first. These are the plainest oldest shoes we have," she says, kneeling. She begins threading the laces. "The company has been making these sexy things since 1921 and hasn't changed a thing about them. Not even the color. They only come in black." She grabs my foot to slip the shoe on.

"I can do it." I take the shoes from her and put them on.

"How do they feel?"

I stand up and take a few steps toward the front of the store. "I'll take them."

"Need anything else?"

"More socks."

"No problem." She grins, snaps a bright red fingernail. "I'll even let you keep the ones you have on for no extra charge."

Across from Schroeder's Shoes is a clothing store where I buy three pairs of jeans and four shirts, two white button-down and two black tee shirts. I've not bought or worn new clothes for over two years, and when I emerge from the mall wearing shiny black shoes, stiff new jeans, and a white shirt, a peculiar self-consciousness overwhelms me. I look at my reflection in the glass doors at the mall entrance. A stranger looks back. It occurs to me that the physical forces that bind me to the reflection in the glass are analogous to the semantic forces that link name and identity together; and that amid this phantasmagoria of names and things, to be named Lucian of Samosata is nothing more than to cast a reflection.

I walk back to town carrying a bag containing my new clothes and the snowsuit. Passages from *Selected Philosophical Essays* filter through my mind along the way, passages containing words like *Being, Transcendental Ego, Subject, Object.* What good is a name for a thing—a being—that transforms itself spontaneously by nature or by an act of willing? From nothing to egg to zygote to embryo to fetus to infant to child to adolescent to adult to geriatric to corpse to decaying flesh back to nothing. Or from

Quintus Horatius Flaccus to Lucian of Samosata? Is there a single identity that inheres and abides throughout? Or is identity an accretion that builds up like a crust around a name and even continues for a time after death like hair and nails growing on a corpse? If it is nonsense to say that two things are identical and meaningless to say that a thing is identical to itself; and if the universe is an infinity of names with different meanings—what then of identity?—except to say that it is a stream running through all of nature—and names are the hooks we use to fish in it.

At Town Hall the obnoxious clerk reviews the notarized form. He stamps it and scribbles on it, then disappears into another room, finally returning with another form that he hands to me. "That'll be fifty dollars," he says.

I pay him the money and he writes out a receipt.

"Go down the hall, left, to courtroom number one and wait inside. They'll call you."

"Today?"

The clerk looks at me as if I've asked exactly the wrong question. "I just said so, didn't I?"

"You didn't say anything." I pick up my shopping bag to leave.

"Not tomorrow. Not yesterday. The judge will see you today."

"Drop dead."

"Same to you, Mister," the clerk chimes back as I close the door.

Courtroom number one is a sleepy, windowless chamber. I sit in the rear, my bag between my feet, while the bailiff calls out name after name and the judge, a tired-looking gray old man, dispenses one by one with landlords and tenants, debtors and creditors, licenses and permits of all classes until, after a little over an hour, the bailiff calls, "Quintus? uh, Horatius? uh, Mr. Flaccus?" I am told to approach the bench.

The judge doesn't look up from the papers he is reading but leaves me to stand suppliantly before him. At last he looks up and, appraising me from head to foot, says, "Expression of personal identity—would you mind explaining yourself a little more, ah, completely?"

"I don't know that I can."

The judge seems to regard this as an evasion. "You just feel like changing your name. Have I got it right?"

"I don't feel like it. I want to do it."

The judge pauses to consider this response. "And this new, ah, appellation, Lucian of Samosata. Why exactly have you chosen it?"

"Everybody needs a name."

The judge nods. "Why not George or Harold, say, or even Lucian? Lucian's a fine name." Then, to demonstrate his fatigue and his infinite patience, he takes off his reading glasses and rubs his eyes. When he realizes that I am not ready with an answer, he puts them back on and looks at me over the rim. "What I'm asking, sir, is what exactly is it that you think will be, ah, conferred on you by this change?"

"A new identity."

The judge leans back and regards me with a frown that rises over his brow and into the baldness of his pate. "You trying to run away from something?"

"No."

"You sure?"

"Yes."

"How about someone? You got someone chasing you?"

"No."

"No family?"

"No."

"Creditors?"

"No."

"Bankruptcy?"

"No."

"I see here that you listed your occupation as 'retired.' Mind telling me what you retired from?"

"I'm retired from society."

The judge glances up from the paper, then nods his head. "Fair enough. Sometimes I wish I was too. Ever been convicted of a felony?"

"No. I answered all those questions on the form."

"I'm just making sure. Have you ever been married?"

"No."

"You'll have to explain yourself more fully. I'm having trouble understanding you. A name change is not something that this court takes lightly. Nor should you. So please tell me what you mean by, ah, a new identity."

To appease the judge, who by his look seems the sort of man who will continue to listen to a complaint despite having formed an opinion, I reach for an answer from *Selected Philosophical Essays*. "Identity is a relation that obtains between the names of an object."

The judge's eyes shift from the paper he is holding back to me, then to the paper again. "Between names, you say?"

"Yes."

"And you want to change yours," he says, putting the papers down and taking off his reading glasses again.

"Yes."

"From Quintus Horatius Flaccus, which, I see here, has been your name for, ah, five years. Before that you went by . . . William Blake?"

I nod.

"*And did those feet in ancient time* William Blake? William Blake the poet?"

I nod again.

The judge pinches the bridge of his nose, closes his eyes. "Because . . ." he loses his train of thought, passes his hand over his brow. "Because . . ." He waves the docket of papers at me. "This is a pretty esoteric little hobby you're practicing here, son. And I don't find it amusing. This is a court of law, not a place for frivolous games. Now tell me: Why do you want to change your name?"

"Because I want to."

The judge's eyes narrow. "Tell me what you said about identity again."

"A relation that obtains between the names of an object."

"Between the names or the objects themselves?"

"Between the names."

"Explain."

"What kind of car do you drive?"

"A Ford."

"If I had a Ford we would say that we both drive the same car, right?"

The judge nods and looks over at the bailiff, who is standing near the bench, smiling.

"But my Ford and yours are in fact two different cars. The relationship between the name, Ford, and the object, car, is purely a matter of convenience. In fact, it obscures the real relationship between your car and my car—which are in fact two entirely different objects sharing the names *car* and *Ford.* Strictly speaking, a thing can only be identical to itself, so identity can never obtain to the relationship between objects because no two objects can be the same object. Identity can only obtain to the *names* for objects."

There is silence for a moment.

"And I want to change mine."

The bailiff is still smiling. The judge picks up the docket of papers, puts his glasses back on, and skims through it once again. Then he looks back at me. "I don't know if you're trying to be funny or if you're just nutty or what." He picks up a pen and signs the papers. "I'm going to go along with you because"—he measures out his words—"because I *want* to. And because I believe in freedom of expression." He hands the papers down to me. "But don't expect to come back into this courtroom again with another frivolous request because I'll send your logic-chopping carcass right back out."

On the way out I stop to read the paper the judge has handed me. It is an Order of Publication and reads:

> *Quintus Horatius Flaccus, having filed a complaint for Judgement changing his name to Lucian of Samosata and having applied to the Court for an order of publication of the notice required by law in such cases, it is by this Court this thirteenth day of April, 19— ORDERED that all persons concerned show cause, if any there be, on or before the thirty-first day of May, 19—, why the prayers of said complaint should not be granted. PROVIDED, that a copy of this order be published once a week for three consecutive weeks before said day in The Sentinel newspaper.*

I step out into bright sunshine. New clothes, new shoes, new name. Maybe the judge would have been more sympathetic if, instead of citing Gottlob Frege's selected philosophical essay, I'd told him about the birds I watched out at the Indian mound, their existence defined by seasonal migrations and continual reconstruction of habitus. Now, walking down Oblivion's Main Street and carrying my packages, I feel like one of them, an anonymous migrant inhabiting little more than an ostensible name—and that too subject to change.

The Sentinel Building is farther down Main Street. It is one of the larger buildings on the block, with a hammered tin cornice peeling green paint that names the building and dates it to 1919. The entrance is not off the street but in the rear next to an old loading dock that functions as the delivery entrance for the store called Purrfection on the ground floor.

I climb the steep stairs to the second floor, feeling like an intruder. At the top of the stairs is a glass-paneled door that reads *Sentinel,* Editorial Office. I knock and enter a light-filled room that runs the entire length of the building. It is cluttered with desks and drafting tables and old letter-presses that have not been used in years. The walls are decorated with yellowed maps of country, state, and county. There are issues of the paper mounted in wooden frames and political posters dating back over decades, and the whole place smells of machinery and ink and bristling brittleness. A young man stands up behind a desk in the center of the room. He is wearing a shirt with sleeves rolled up in reporterly fashion and a dirty tie and looks as if he has been awake all night. "Can I help you?"

"I want to place an announcement in the paper."

"I'll take care of it, Brian," a rusty-sounding voice calls from an office partitioned near the back of the room. An elderly woman puts her head out and beckons me over. "You just finish what you're working on."

The young man sinks back down behind the desk, and I make my way through the clutter toward the office in the rear. A small brass nameplate next to the door reads *Muriel Maydock*. A printed sign taped under the nameplate reads *Don't ask me why. I just own the goddamn thing.*

"Come in. Come in," the woman calls from inside the office. "What can I do for you?" She is standing over a drafting table where the next edition of the paper is being laid out. "It's only Brian and me today. We're down to four, and one is out sick and the other one is out chasing the only goddamn story we have for the week." She talks without looking up at me. "If this paper goes to bed by Friday I'll drop dead from amazement."

"I need to run an announcement."

The woman waddles over to a desk and picks up a paper and pencil. I hand her the announcement, which she glances at and puts in a box on the desk. "Are you a subscriber?"

"No."

She glares at me from under her white helmet of hair, then dismisses me with a wave of the arm. "I should have guessed. You probably don't even read. None of the young people do anymore. The flat fee for notices and announcements is thirty dollars," she says, returning to the drafting table. "Since this has to run for three weeks I can give you ten percent off the total."

"Twenty-seven?"

"Twenty-seven times three. Eighty-one dollars," she turns to me, "for three weeks. It's a bargain."

I reach into my pocket and take out the last of my cash, still damp from the pocket of the snowsuit. Muriel Maydock jots a note to herself on a slip of paper and takes the bills from me, noting their soggy condition. "I'll get you some change," she says.

"Keep it." I turn to leave.

"Hold on a minute. I know you. You're the fella walks all over town, aren't you?" She comes around for a better look. "I almost didn't recognize you in those new clothes." She moves into the doorway and crosses her arms, blocking my way out. "You threatened one of my reporters last summer."

"I did?"

"You did. You said you'd sue me if we printed your name in the paper."

I lift my shopping bag up underneath my arm, not able to recall exactly what I had said but remembering an encounter in front of the police station.

Muriel Maydock stands in the doorway holding an elbow in the palm of one hand and with the other probing her scalp through taut white hair tied back on her head. "You have some nerve coming in here," she says, looking up at me. "I heard the tape. Janet played it for me. You said you'd sue this paper if we printed your name or ever mentioned anything about you in print. Remember now?" Her look condenses into a frown. "Never mind the stupidity of it. The press has certain freedoms in this country, in case you weren't aware." She pushes past me into the office. "I'm sure I can dig up the tape somewhere. I made Janet give it to me."

"I meant it in connection with the rape case."

But Muriel Maydock is already rummaging through her desk. "This paper has never, ever been sued, and it's been around since 1919. And nobody has ever threatened us with a lawsuit as far as I know either." She slams the drawer. "Never mind, I can't find it."

I stand in the doorway ready to leave, holding my package. Muriel Maydock strides toward me, holding out the money I've just given her. "I won't take it," she says, waving the bills at me. "You intimidate one of my reporters. You threaten to sue this paper for printing your name. And now you want to *pay* me to print it? Forget it, Mister."

"I don't want it." I turn to leave.

"I don't want it either. Take it back." She follows me through the office. "How dare you come in here? What for the love of Christ were you thinking? Ever hear of freedom of speech? We didn't take your little threat too seriously, I want you to know. But we didn't print your name either. Janet wanted to, but I said no. Not because I was afraid, Mister. Oh no, I wasn't. Only because it didn't matter one way or another."

I yank open the door and start down the stairs, wanting only to get away from the woman's carping voice. "Go find another paper to print your goddamn announcement!" She is standing at the top of the stairwell. "And take your goddamn money back. It's no good here." The office door slams. At the bottom of the stairs I glance back to see the soggy bills scattered down the staircase. For a moment I consider retrieving them, then decide to leave them. I know that Muriel Maydock will do it after I've left. Or she'll send Brian to.

When I arrive back home the neighbor's kid is waiting for me.

"I got some news," he says eagerly.

"Okay, let's have it."

"Miss Foster is pregnant."

"Who?"

"Miss Foster, the gym teacher in the high school."

"That doesn't sound like big news to me, kid."

"I'll tell you who did it to her for fifty cents."

"What do you mean, did it to her?"

The kid flashes a dirty grin. "You know, who made intercourse with her. She ain't married."

"I don't know about this, kid. Do you even know what intercourse means?"

"Sure I do. It's fucking."

"I asked if you knew what intercourse means."

The kid senses a trap and says nothing.

"It comes from Latin. *Inter*, between, and *currere*, to run."

"Will you pay me if I tell you?" The kid resumes as though I haven't spoken.

"Tell me what?"

"Who, um, *ran between* Miss Foster?"

"Very funny, kid." I try to keep a straight face but find that I'm failing. "I don't think so."

"Why not?"

"It's none of my business."

"But you said . . ."

"I said I'd pay you for news. Not dirty rumors."

"It's not a rumor!" The kid sees me smiling and thinks he has me.

"Or gossip."

"It's not gossip, I swear. Everybody knows about it."

"Well, I'll be the only one who doesn't, then. Haven't you ever heard of invasion of privacy?"

"But it's in the paper!"

"The paper?"

The kid nods.

"The *Sentinel?*"

Another nod. "They arrested her and everything."

"Arrested her? For what?"

"For, um, *running between* one of the seniors. The paper didn't say who 'cause he's only seventeen, but everybody knows who it is anyway. Want me to tell you?"

"I told you, I don't want to know about it."

"I'll tell you for a quarter."

"Forget it."

"A dime, then."

"Not interested."

"Okay," the kid says, bursting with the need to tell and unable to hide his merriment. "I'll tell you for free!"

"I said I don't want to know. Go find something else to tell me."

"But it's in the news!"

"I don't care. Bring me something else. I don't want to know about it."

The kid backs off a little. "Do you feel sorry for Miss Foster or something? 'Cause they arrested her?"

"Yeah, let's say I do. So next time how about bringing me something a little further away from home."

"My mom says they should abortion *her*. Not the baby."

"The word is abort. What does Dad say?"

"Nothing. He said Miss Foster is cute."

"What do you think?"

"She should name the baby Tiger."

"Tiger?"

"That's the basketball team. The Tigers."

I reach into my pocket and flip the kid a quarter.

"I thought you weren't going to give me nothin'?"

"It's not for the news." I close the door.

"You want me to give you a definition of love?"

"If you'd like."

"Well, there ain't one, I hate to tell you. Not unless you're talking about the love of Jesus."

"I was thinking more about love in general."

"You ever been in love?"

"I don't know. I don't think so."

"Well, you'd know it if you had. I don't think there's any defining what that feels like."

"Webster defines love as (1) an intense affection for another person based on familial or personal ties, shared interests and experiences, or (2) an intense attraction to another person based on sexual desire."

"Sounds like you got your definition right there."

"I don't like it."

"Why not?"

"Because it's lacking."

"What's it lack?"

"An element of necessity, a moral dimension."

"You mean it's gotta be good and everybody's gotta get some?"

"Not exactly."

"What the hell you mean, then?"

"By necessity I mean that its existence is not predicated on anything, that it is because it is and it cannot be reduced."

"And the moral part?"

"The moral dimension must result from the necessity of its existence."

"So why you calling me? All them fancy terms—sounds like you got it all figured out for yourself."

"I'm looking for more."

"More? What more?"

"I don't know, exactly."

"Well, all as I can say is I'm satisfied with what you said. Can't think of anything to add to it. I'm not a preacher or a philosopher. I just go for the basics like most people. Love is as love does, I always say. Love your spouse or hate 'em. Love your neighbor or hate 'em. And if you love 'em you leave 'em alone. Let 'em be."

"And if you hate them?"

"Well, you do exactly the same. Leave 'em alone. Let 'em be. No need to go around smashing up things just 'cause they don't set with you. I don't see as you got much choice. Let things be. Don't go causing trouble. World's got enough trouble already."

I hang up and sit for a while to think about the old woman's pragmatic view of the world. It is a disposition I often wish I could share. The conversation incites more calls, and I spend the rest of the evening punching numbers randomly into the phone and mostly getting nowhere.

Mohr calls at seven the next morning.

"Horace?"

"It's Lucian."

"Lucian? Ah, yes. Excuse me. Lucian of Samosata. Of course. Lucian. Lucian."

"I should thank you for your advice. But there has been a snag."

"Snag?"

"The *Sentinel* won't publish my notice, and I don't know if there is anything I can do about it."

"They won't publish it? Why not?"

"It's a long story. The owner took a dislike to me."

"Muriel Maydock? She is one of our more enlightened citizens. I'd have thought you two would see eye to eye."

"We didn't. Now I have to come up with an alternative that the court will approve. I was thinking of posting notices around town."

"Does the announcement have to be in a local paper?"

"I didn't think of that. I'll find out. How are you feeling?"

"So so. Listen. Today's the day."

"The day for what?"

"The dig. It starts this afternoon. The people from the university are here. Are you still interested?"

"How about you? Are you up to it?"

"Don't worry about me. I don't need an excuse to get out of this damn place. Should I come by to get you?"

"You're still driving?"

"I'd be stuck out here if I didn't have my car. I'll probably drive it to my grave."

"I'll walk out and meet you there."

"Fine. I'll get there around noon."

"See you then."

Mohr has already hung up.

I am too restless to wait until midday, so I get dressed and drop *The Diatribes of Lucian* into my pack along with an apple and a banana and start out for the mound. It will be the last time I have it all to myself before it gets ripped open by archaeologists.

The streets are quiet this time of morning. It is Saturday, and the people of Oblivion sleep late on Saturday. It has been so long since I have tracked the days of the week that I only recognize Saturday by the quiet early morning and Sunday by the car-jammed parking lots of Oblivion's churches.

Everything is crisp this morning. The air is crisp, the light is crisp. My legs make a swishing sound as I walk. I pause at the bend where Old Route 47 turns suddenly from south to westward. A flock of birds passes overhead. The fields have begun to sprout and are covered in a fine green silk that captures the morning light and absorbs it directly into the earth. The trees in the distance also shimmer with this same light-green essence, and standing by the side of the road I feel like some solitary vessel that has slipped its mooring and is drifting in a vast expanse of quiet.

In the last few days I have committed eight short pieces by Lucian to memory and have begun to copy the Greek into my notepad. I know the alphabet and pronounce the words as I copy them down. The English translation follows line by line, and a dictionary is not necessary. As each paragraph ascends into memory and takes its place with all that already resides there, Horace slips into the background a little and a reassuring vagueness sets in that resembles the vagueness of personality with all its unaccounted-for latencies. Horace will remain a part of me as long as I continue to incubate his words. Besides, short of complete and total amnesia, Lucian's Greek couldn't displace Horace's Latin any more than Horace's Latin could displace any of the other texts that reside within me, all packed and bundled and bound. At times they run together willy-nilly, and it takes a great effort of will and concentration to separate them. Thus, the luster of the present hour is always borrowed from the background of possibilities and *Das Dasein ist ein Seiendes, das nicht nur unter anderem Seienden vorkommt* and *Beatus ille qui procul negotiis, ut prisca gens mortalium . . .* Were I blind and bumping into walls I would still have these words to recur to.

As I round the bend and continue toward the mound the rising sun is at my back. All the excess preoccupations of the morning begin to melt away, and a rising tide of good feeling begins to well up. Can this be?—and the moment the question breaks the calm surface of the mood a measure of it drops away, and I stop walking for a moment to try to recapture it. Horace comes up gasping:

Vitas inuleo me similis . . .
You keep fleeing from me, Chloe, the way a lost
Fawn darts off to the wilds seeking his timid dam
Scared for nothing at each slight
Breath of air in the forest trees;
If the coming of Spring rustles the leaves for one
Instant, or if the green lizards go whisking through
Tangled briars, he stops dead,
Terror stricken in heart and knees.

I can't recall the rest of the ode but stand for several minutes caught in this freakish conjunction of poetry and nature, waiting for the good mood of moments before to reassert itself. The flow of words slows to a trickle, and the gentle breeze across the newly planted field blooms across my shoulders and trembles through my hair. If I had a walking stick and a topcoat and were standing atop the light-drenched peak of a mountain like Caspar David Friedrich's Wanderer, I think my mood would be no different—except that that wanderer was stirred by some powerful Germanic evocation of wild Nature and Spirit, and I am standing not in a wilderness but on a paved road beside a cultivated field, and on the horizon is an ancient mound about to be excavated and a high-tech munitions factory, and the only Spirit stirring within me is the quiet flight of words and the decocted meanings of texts that I have learned and taken too much to heart.

Parked behind a tree at the base of the mound is Tom Schroeder's motorcycle. The bike has been positioned so that it is not visible from the road. Schroeder is nowhere to be seen. I conclude from the dew on the seat that it has been parked for some time and wait beside it for a few minutes just in case he suddenly materializes with a can of gas or a wrench or whatever it is he has had to fetch to restart the machine. After a short wait, it occurs to me that maybe he is up top. I walk around to the gate and climb over it at my usual spot.

Instead of going up along the path, I circle at the base and start up from the opposite side. Near the top I crouch behind a thicket. A jackrabbit bursts from underneath, speeds down the slope, and disappears into the undergrowth at the bottom. A minute or two passes. I am unable to see over the crest, so I inch forward, staying near the tangle of weeds and branches sprouting around the bush. Suddenly a low moan breaks the silence, accompanied by a laugh and a woman's voice. My pulse begins to race, and I shrink back for a moment. A few seconds pass and a chorus of moaning begins. I creep forward again until over the crest of the mound the naked figure of Sylvia rises in outline against the blue morning sky. She is bent over him, back curled, hands planted on the ground beside his shoulders. They are lying on a sleeping bag beside a small heap of clothing. A fire smolders lightly; a half-gallon bottle of Jack

Daniels is planted in the grass near to hand. I begin to inch back as Schroeder's supine body heaves upward; lifts the straddling Sylvia, flips her, and sets her down underneath him. Her legs curl up around his thighs, and he begins a rapid tupping that in a few seconds breaks up in spasms and a strained howl. After a few moments he pries himself away and leans back on his haunches, glances down at his slackened penis, grabs the bottle by the handle, and drinks from it. I can see the angel tattooed on his chest. When he tips the bottle upward his long, stringy hair falls away and I can see his face as he drinks. His gorge rises once, twice, three times, and when the retching stops he grins stupidly and hands the bottle to Sylvia. She rises up on one elbow and drinks, spilling down her chin. Schroeder leans forward and slurps the dribbled liquor from her face. She lets out a peal of laughter, plants the bottle in the ground, and pulls Schroeder down to her. He falls toward her with a grunt, toward one more possibility of possibilities.

I back away, crouched, keeping low to the ground. When I've dropped far enough from the crest I stand and walk quickly back, climbing the fence at the gate. I sit down at the ruined picnic table in what was once a shaded pull-off and now serves only as a muddy turnaround for cars and trucks and a place to hurl garbage.

Sylvia and Schroeder? I glance toward the summit, and the thought of them mingled together combines with the memory of my awful encounter with her, and I see that garrulous asshole seizing his opportunity without a moment's hesitation. It was bound to happen, only a matter of time before they beat their miserable paths toward each other. It's not my business, yet I am disturbed by what I have seen. I don't think it is concern or outrage or jealousy or lust or moral indignation but merely the hollow vertigo, the primal thrill of peeking.

I return home and read for a few hours, turning to the essay on the *ordo amoris*. But the phenomenological shadings and gradations of the various powers of love don't clarify much for me, and if it is true that loving can be characterized as correct or false—insofar as acts of love can be in harmony with or oppose what is worthy of love—then is it possible that what I have seen is an aberration? That Sylvia and Schroeder's coupling is a gross mistake? All philosophizing aside, my instinct tells me it is—and that the answer to the question, What draws them together? lies with Sylvia, not Schroeder.

The neighbor's kid pounds on the door, his knock now irritatingly familiar. I put the book down and go to answer it.

"My dad said you're an asshole."

"Oh yeah? When did he say that?"

"I heard him talking to Mom last night."

"What else did he say?"

"Will you give me a dollar?"

"Okay."

"He said you're a nut and they should put you in a stray jacket and lock you up."

"It's *strait*-jacket."

"That's what I said, stray jacket."

"What else did your dad say?"

"He says somebody's going to run you over one day."

"Did he say who, by any chance?"

The kid shakes his head. "He said that people don't like the way you just walk around doing nothing and that you should get a job like everyone else and you're asking for trouble."

"What did Mom say to that?"

"She said he was right and that she heard you were a millionaire but she thinks you're a shady character and you've been giving her the creeps since you moved in."

"What else did she say?"

"Nothing."

"What about your dad?"

"He says you're not a millionaire but probably got a record or something."

"What else?"

"He said never trust a man without a car."

I laugh. "That, my friend, is worth two bucks."

The kid grins and takes the money. "Thanks!"

"Do your parents know you come over here like this?"

"No."

"Would they be mad?"

"I only come when they're not home."

He dashes off in a thrill. I go into the kitchen and heat up a small portion of leftover beans and rice and walk back to the mound. Schroeder's motorcycle is still leaning up against the tree when I arrive, and there is no sign that anyone else has been here since I left. I sit down at the bench, facing the nearly empty Semantech parking lot across the road. A large flock of blackbirds has landed. They seem to be feeding on something. I cross the road and stand at the fence for a better view. It isn't crumbs they are feeding on. They are drinking from a large puddle of bile-green antifreeze that has spilled onto the asphalt. I search the grass for a stone and hurl it into the middle of the flock. They scatter into the air, then return moments later for more. I throw a few more stones, but the birds return each time.

A while later Mohr arrives. He pulls off the road and crunches to a stop near the picnic bench. With a look of fierce concentration he raises the gearshift and twists off the ignition before lifting a hand and waving to me. He has difficulty opening the door, and I walk over to open it for him. He takes his time getting out, reaching for his cane and a new safari hat that he dons as soon as he has extracted himself from the car. A costume of stiffly pressed khaki trousers, shirt, and multipocketed bush jacket hangs like drapery from his tiny frame. The shiny brown leather boots on his feet are laced neatly to the top—the merry anthropologist. "Are we the first to arrive?" he asks, making directly for the picnic bench with a less than steady gait.

"Not exactly." I close the car door and follow him over. The bench creaks under our weight.

Mohr takes his hat off and adjusts the band. He is completely bald underneath, his head a tiny orb protruding from the stiff collar of the bush jacket.

"The owner of that motorcycle is up there with a woman. They're having sex."

"You don't say?" Mohr says without a trace of sarcasm. He puts the hat back on and looks over toward Schroeder's motorcycle.

"I went up there a few hours ago and found them going at it."

"How funny. Did you tell them they were about to lose their privacy?" He pronounces *privacy* the British way—as in privy.

"I figured they'd come down soon enough."

"And they haven't?"

I shake my head.

"Well, good for them!" Mohr lets out a laugh. "But they're in for an unwelcome interruption." He reaches into the breast pocket of his jacket and takes out an antique gold watch on a chain. He fumbles to open the cover. "It's just after noon. They should have arrived by now."

"Are you well enough to be out here?"

Mohr tucks the watch back into his pocket. "No," he says flatly. "But I'm not well enough to *be* anywhere." He parses his words as if inured to them. "So it makes no difference." After a short pause he begins rummaging through the pockets of his jacket. "Besides, I have bought all these new toys and I want to play with them." He begins placing them on the picnic table, naming them as he goes. "Compass. Magnifier. Knife. Measuring tape. Spyglass. Camera. Snakebite kit. Brushes—soft, medium, hard bristle. Pocket flask." He twists off the cap. "With real brandy!" He sips and offers me the flask. The brandy settles into my stomach with a nice burn.

"They look like antiques."

"They are antiques! Except for the camera, of course. It's the newest model I could find." A whirring of tiny gears as he slides the black compact case apart to demonstrate all the camera's features.

I examine the rest of his gear, taking each item and turning it over in my hands. They are wonderful old brass instruments, cleverly hinged and solidly fitted together in early industrial fashion. The spyglass is tucked into a felt-lined leather case and looks as if it might have belonged to John James Audubon himself.

We make small talk and fidget with the various instruments. I photograph Mohr and he photographs me, and I set the camera on the end of the table and set the timer to photograph the two of us together. Mohr lifts his arm across my shoulder for the pose and I place my arm across his, feeling his scrawniness underneath and the poignancy of the gesture as the camera's timer winds a self-conscious infinity into the moment.

When the picture-taking is over Mohr fills me in on library gossip. Mrs. Entwhistle, he says, is beginning to sabotage his project to digitize the archive collections. She wants to spend the money buying more books and periodicals and was surprised to discover that the funds Mohr had raised came with strings attached. He begins to chuckle and for a moment seems about to launch into a coughing fit but settles back against the picnic table, cane across his knees. "She was indignant," he brags, "accused me of arranging it so that she had no discretion over the money."

"Did you?"

Mohr grins. "Of course I did. She thinks the archive doesn't belong there. Too much trouble. A bunch of papers. She'd like to transfer it all somewhere else. Preferably the State Historical Society."

"Maybe that's not such a bad idea."

Mohr shakes his head and taps the end of his cane in the dirt. "The archive was set up by the Wilkington Trust. The library didn't come until much later. It would be like moving this mound to another county to be with the mounds there." He cuts off abruptly and takes a handkerchief from his pocket and holds it to his forehead for a moment, wiping underneath the brim of the hat. "Besides, my manuscripts are part of that archive now. The idea of moving them somewhere else is upsetting."

"Manuscripts?"

"My history of the town. From trading post until today."

"I'd forgotten about that."

"And my bibliography."

"Bibliography?"

"On death."

"I thought you were joking about that."

"It's no joke. I now have over a thousand sources."

"What about the history? Is it finished?"

Mohr shakes his head. "I never meant to finish it."

"Why not?"

"Where to end it?"

"You could end it anywhere, couldn't you?"

Mohr turns loose a big dentured grin. "Little by little and was by was."

I stand up and pace out to the road. There is no traffic, and the afternoon has already begun. The sun has long since burned off any dew or moisture on the ground, and I can feel the verdant blooming and budding all around. I tell Mohr to wait while I go up to check on Schroeder and Sylvia.

Instead of ascending on the far side as I did earlier, I walk up the main path, trying to make as much noise as I can. I stand under the elm tree at the top and call over to them but receive no response, then make my way across the top of the mound. Side by side, naked in the grass, they do not stir. The fire is completely out. In the sunlight their bodies are pale and small and look like matter left to the elements. Schroeder is lying next to a reeking puddle of vomited whiskey. Sylvia is curled fetally beside him, covered partially by the sleeping bag, the empty bottle an arm's length away. But for the subtle rise and fall of her abdomen, she looks dead.

I shake Schroeder, but he only rolls onto his face. I tug the sleeping bag out from underneath Sylvia, whose skin is mottled and blue, and open it out and spread it over the two of them.

I return to the base of the mound. The archaeologists have arrived. Three of them, two women and a man, are talking to Mohr, who is seated in sartorial splendor on the bench pointing with his cane as he makes the introductions. "Lucian of Samosata. Drs. Palmer, Norris, and Middleton. They have come to excavate the mound."

We shake hands all around. The archaeologists are all dressed alike in tee shirts and jeans and down vests with the insignia of their university emblazoned on the breast. Dr. Palmer is the leader, a woman in her forties with spiky blond hair and a cracked red complexion. Dr. Norris is large and hairy with a cigarette-singed beard and turquoise jewelry and an aura of mild dissipation. Dr. Middleton looks to be the youngest of the group and could be an Indian herself. She is a tall woman with an olive complexion, deep brown eyes, and a long black pigtail that falls over her shoulder and hangs to her waist like a coil of rope.

"Are the rites of spring over up there?" Dr. Palmer asks.

"I think they need to be carried down. They're both unconscious."

"Unconscious?"

"There's an empty half gallon of whiskey on the ground next to them."

"Jesus Christ," Palmer says, annoyed.

"I'll call an ambulance," Norris says and ambles off toward the van. The other two follow him over and begin to unpack equipment while Norris fidgets with a cellular telephone and paces back and forth as he places the call for help. Mohr and I remain at the picnic bench watching the production unfold with mild interest. They unload a tripod and several small crates. "Surveying equipment," Mohr comments. "To unlock history."

The ambulance arrives, and after brief consultation the medics follow me up the mound, carrying their portable kits and two pole stretchers. The sheriff arrives as we are about halfway to the top, and now the base of the mound is a turmoil of revolving lights and idling vehicles. Mohr is seated at the picnic bench talking with Dr. Palmer and the sheriff. The other two archaeologists are fussing with equipment next to their van.

The medics kneel next to the unconscious bodies and begin their ministrations. They peel back eyelids and shine lights, take pulse and blood-pressure readings, test reflexes. Then they cover them up and place them on stretchers. The sheriff huffs up next to me.

"If it isn't the happy wanderer," he says, keys jingling. "I should've guessed you'd be up here."

"I came to watch the archaeologists," I reply as dryly as I can. We both watch as the medics adjust the blankets and straps on the stretchers.

"What's the verdict? They gonna live?" the sheriff asks.

"Alcohol poisoning," a medic responds. "Acute. Class four, I'd say."

"What's that mean?"

"Means they're drunker'n shit." He struggles to adjust the straps on Schroeder.

"I can see that, Charlie," the sheriff says, ill humored. "What's the class four business?"

"Means they're comatose. No response to stimuli. No reflexes."

The sheriff bends to pick up the empty whiskey bottle lying at his feet. "Goddamn. I'd be comatose too drinking this shit. You boys gonna manage with those stretchers?"

"One at a time we will."

"Want us to give you a hand with 'em?" The sheriff waggles his thumb to indicate he means the two of us. "Horace here is in pretty good shape. Isn't that right?"

I ignore the question and step back as the two medics position themselves to lift Schroeder. "What you can do is watch to make sure she doesn't vomit and start choking."

"I think we can handle that," the sheriff says.

They hoist Schroeder up. "He's one heavy bastard," the medic grunts. Schroeder, with his dirty blond locks falling over his shoulder, lips dry and slightly parted, looks as innocent and semiretarded as I've ever seen him. I glance down at Sylvia, who doesn't bear the same look of innocence but, strapped tightly down under the blankets, looks tiny and gaunt and wasted. Her face is a void, dark hair knotted and tangled with bits of grass. I try to remember how she looked that day in the grocery store on her search for kiwis. It was only three months ago, yet it seems to me that she has aged.

"Some orgy they had," the sheriff says as the medics carry Schroeder away. He picks over the clothes piled next to the fire pit and begins to search the pockets. "Uh-huh. Here we go," he says and removes a small plastic bag and a pipe from Schroeder's leather jacket. He opens it and sniffs. "Sinsemilla. Them two'll be out for days." He puts the bag and pipe into the pocket of his windbreaker and continues to search the clothing. I turn to leave, but the sheriff stops me. "Hold on a minute, bud. I got a few questions for you." I stand a few paces back while he finishes rummaging. He gathers the clothes back into a pile, then stands up, dusting his hands. "Booze and dope and puke," he says with a disgusted expression. "I seen too much of this shit to think it's cute. Families oughta be ashamed of what these kids are doing to themselves. Buncha degenerates."

"Don't tell me you've never been drunk before."

He turns to me as though I've challenged his integrity. Then his look softens a little. "Of course I have. Everybody has. But it's a lifestyle with these kids. I see it every day."

"Maybe they're bored."

"Bored, hell. They're spoiled."

"Maybe it's fun."

The sheriff looks down at Sylvia and shakes his head. "She don't look to me like she's having fun." The medics return and pick up the stretcher. As we walk down the path together I outline what I have seen for the sheriff.

He interrupts. "Wait a minute. Isn't that the girl who was raped out here last year?"

"I don't know."

"She looked familiar. Goddamn! It *was* her."

I say nothing. As we pass through the gate at the base of the mound he pats me on the back. The comradely gesture strikes me as strange, and I realize that our little exchange up top has somehow made him see me in a different light, as though we share an outlook and values, kindred spirits of a sort. I'd like to disabuse him of the idea but see no point in it.

An hour later he has asked his questions, inspected the archaeologists' various permits, and departed.

The archaeologists are taking their first measurements. I escort Mohr up the path, carrying his folding chair and a loaded picnic basket. He declares that he has come for the entertainment. The archaeologists are amused, and Dr. Norris calls Mohr the founder of a new sport—spectator archaeology—and promises hours of competitive digging.

We set up our little picnic underneath the elm tree. The archaeologists discuss how they will proceed so as not to harm the tree but are not making any promises. Norris thinks it will have to come down. Middleton thinks they can work around the roots. Palmer is noncommittal.

I sprawl out in the coolness of the grass and listen to their discussion and watch the sun-dappled limbs of the tree swaying overhead. Schroeder and Sylvia. I can't think of it as a gross mistake anymore. The outcome was too pathetic. A misadventure, an accidental bacchanal. A spontaneous inversion of the *ordo amoris*, neither in nor out of harmony with anything, echoless, without consequence. Still, I can hardly comprehend it—and not for any abstract moral reason but only because it is not on any map. I can put it in terms of Lucian's geography, where the Fountain of Coma gushes before the Temple of Reality and Illusion. The temple is open to those who can pass by the fountain without being tempted, but the plaza outside is littered with the unconscious bodies of those who prefer the comfort of sleep. Among them I see the bodies of Sylvia and Schroeder, who will wake up in the detox ward wondering how they got there.

My own secret is that I have suppressed and denied all my erotic impulses. *Autarkeia* means not having to be reminded of them. It is deliberate, an effort to acknowledge the loneliness that is the condition of our organism. And to live with it. In the *bios theoretikos* I inhabit, the flesh is mitigated by this simple acknowledgment. Mind over matter: the sublime sublimation. The meat-hungry world becomes more and more distant, and all the sorry flailing and wailing begins to seem a little absurd, if not plain funny—the hands down the pants, the slobbering, panting, gimme-gimme of it all that lasts as long as the body lasts and determines so much of its living. As a strategy of nature it is beautiful. Sure it is. That our bodies are driven to leave a substitute behind is very convenient. But I find ducking nature's urges much more sublime than merely going along with them. And whether we give them up out of high purpose as I am attempting, or sublimate them for the sake of civilization, or take the bypass and practice the instincts for sport and entertainment—fucking and feeding and fighting and fleeing—the end is just as inevitable and just as difficult to face.

"Do you think about sex much?" I ask Mohr.

"Almost always," he answers.

I prop myself up on an elbow to face him. Seated in his collapsible chair, the Victorian gentleman with his khakis and walking stick and cut-crystal wine glass. "Isn't it a little strange?" I pause to formulate exactly how to put it without using the word *death*.

Before I can continue Mohr answers with an emphatic "Yes!" He grins and takes a sip from his wine glass. "But it's sex!"

I pull at a clump of grass. Dr. Norris pounds a wooden stake into the ground nearby, cigarette smoke curling through his beard into his eye. Mohr keeps his gaze focused ahead as though he were watching a game and stoops to lift the bottle from the grass. "More wine?" I hold my glass out for him to fill. Dr. Norris looks over and nods his approval. "Save me some," he calls. Mohr lifts his glass and toasts him. Dr. Palmer, crouching over a map spread on the ground, motions her colleagues over.

"I wish I could dig too, damnit," Mohr says. "I would enjoy getting my hands dirty."

"When was the last time?"

"I got my hands dirty?"

"No. The last time you had sex."

Mohr looks down at me and arches his brow, lifting the brim of his hat. "That's a very personal question."

"You don't have to answer."

He shifts his gaze back across the mound. "And I won't. Except to say that it was a very long time ago."

"Do you miss it?"

After a few moments, he answers. "No. What I miss is having someone to have sex with." He looks down from his chair, a confessional smile playing on his features. Then he looks back at the archaeologists, sips from his glass. "But tell me, Horace."

"Lucian."

"Sorry, I keep forgetting. Why all this talk of sex? Are you becoming desperate?"

The question comes as a surprise, at least the way Mohr has formulated it. Desperate? I hadn't thought about it in exactly those terms. But since the morning prurient thoughts have been welling up inside me. I'm trying to figure out how those two got together, what Sylvia wanted with Schroeder. I am conscious of the half truth of my answer. I am not desperate. That is Mohr's archaic term for it. But why can't I get the image of the two of them out of my mind? The two of them fucking. "Schroeder is the kid who broke into my house and stole my notebook last summer. You were there, remember?"

Mohr nods.

"And Sylvia is the woman who was raped last summer. Right out there in that field."

Mohr tilts the brim of his hat back. I tell him the story of my encounter with Sylvia, leaving out the one important detail. "What would make her want Schroeder—of all imbeciles?"

Mohr is silent. Dr. Middleton veers over. "Bored yet?" She takes her long pigtail and tucks it into her vest.

"Not in the least," Mohr answers cheerfully.

"Nice day for a picnic." She kneels down by one of the stakes that Dr. Norris has pounded into the ground and ties the end of the string to it. She unrolls the string, going from stake to stake until, slowly, a grid begins to take shape on the surface of the mound. It includes the burned logs and the area of grass where, earlier, Sylvia and Schroeder lay. Dr. Palmer continues measuring and marking and referring to a chart spread on the ground. As Mohr's silence prolongs itself I recall Sylvia's words to me that night at her house. I hadn't understood them at the time, hadn't seen her gesture as anything other than a drunken misstatement of anger and frustration. Now I realize that she meant to charge me—all men—with this one base motive: the need to know the sexual constitution of *every* woman and to aspire to become part of that constitution.

As if reading my thoughts Mohr suddenly asks, "Is it possible that you are a little jealous, Horace?"

"Stop calling me Horace. I'm Lucian."

"I'm sorry. Lucian." Mohr looks at me from the corner of his eye and then resumes following the movements of Dr. Middleton, who with her ball of twine is still pacing out the rows of the grid.

I don't answer him. Jealous? Is it possible? What is there for me to be jealous of? I have never desired Sylvia. How then could I be jealous? Mohr's question riddles my brain with uncertainty, and now I must consider the possibility. If jealousy is what I am feeling, then it must be the most primitive, primordial kind—sexual envy. Entangled instincts. Competition. The desire to substitute one's self for all other possible selves, the desire to be the one singular being occupying and reproducing the universe.

Mohr's enthusiasm for the dig is greater than his stamina, and by late afternoon I am porting him and his empty picnic basket down the side of the hill. The archaeologists interrupted their work long enough to share the cornucopia—fruits and cupcakes and cheeses and a second bottle of Pouilly-Fuissé. Dr. Norris, crumbs in his beard, estimated that it would be a few days before they began to uncover anything and recommended waiting a few days before resuming the watch.

At the car Mohr confesses that he has overextended himself. "It will take me a few days to recover from this," he says from behind the wheel. The sun is dropping toward the horizon. My shadow stretches along the ground beside the car. Schroeder's motorcycle is still parked underneath the tree. A bright orange tag dangles from the handlebar. It reads *Tow.* I lean on the window while Mohr fusses with keys and straps and adjusts the mirror. He is saying something about an opera he was taken to as a child. I ask if he is alert enough to drive, and he reassures me that he is and pulls away slowly, pausing to honk his horn and wave before driving away.

Ambling back to town, still lightheaded from the wine, I find myself following the shortcut that Ed Maver took to the hospital that hot summer day.

An ambulance is parked at the emergency entrance, and a stretcher is being tugged out the rear doors. I stand aside as the stretcher is wheeled through the glass doors. A plastic bladder drips fluid into an arm. A blue-green oxygen mask covers a face.

Tom Schroeder Sr. is in the emergency room. He is sitting alone, one leg crossed over his knee, a magazine open on his lap. It looks as if he has come directly from the golf course. After a short wait at the information desk I walk over.

"How is he?" I ask.

Schroeder glances up from the magazine with a puzzled expression, trying to place me. "They're waiting for him to come out of it." He flips the page of the magazine. "Do I know you?" he asks.

I sit down, leaving an empty seat between us. "We met last winter. You were pulling out of your driveway."

The elder Schroeder searches his memory, flipping the pages of his magazine. He has one of those domesticated faces that abound in advertisements for hardware and lawn products, flabby and plain with wide-open features that do not lend themselves easily to preoccupation or very deep thought. It is not a face that seems acquainted with sorrow or tragedy either, and I wonder at what depth beneath the regular-guy features the grief over his wife's suicide is submerged. Or if it has simply been jettisoned.

"I didn't catch your name."

"Lucian."

"Right." He nods his head. "Now I remember." The passing untruth of his statement turns with the last page of the magazine in his lap. He flips it into the empty chair between us. "You've come for the girl, I guess."

I nod.

"You a relative?"

I shake my head. "Only an acquaintance."

Schroeder glares at me for a moment, then shakes his head. "Word sure gets out fast around here."

Rather than explain the circumstances, I simply agree and leave it at that. But Schroeder wants to know more. "Mind telling me how you heard?" He uncrosses his legs, leans forward, and plants his elbows on his knees, hands clasped, preparing to hear me out.

"I was out at the mound when they took them away."

"Big party, huh?"

The sarcasm in his voice is irritating. "I was with the archaeologists," I answer with more defensiveness than intended.

Schroeder's head bobs slightly. He purses his lips.

"What did the doctor tell you?"

"Not much. Only that it was alcohol poisoning and they want to keep him on an IV until he wakes up." He leans back in the chair and shakes his head. "Idiots drank near to half a gallon of whiskey. Of all the goddamn stupid things. And that damn girl he's been hanging around. She's a regular piece of business."

"What do you mean by that?"

Schroeder glances at me as if to size up the exact nature of my professed acquaintance. "Only what I know and what the sheriff told me."

"What did he tell you?"

"She's no goddamn good."

"Did the sheriff tell you she was raped and beaten last summer?"

"Yeah, he told me that too." He shakes his head. "The boy sure knows how to pick 'em, don't he?"

Schroeder's words set off a flash of anger. I feel the blood rushing to my temples. "You talk as if she were some whore he picked up."

Schroeder turns his puffy face to me. "Yup. That's exactly what she is. A fucking whore."

Our eyes meet, and a clarity descends on me that propels everything into sharp black perspective. Blood is pounding in my temples. My mouth feels dry. When I open it words spill out, measured and even. "No more than your son is, you stupid son of a bitch." I am shaking with something I can't name, stand, start for the exit. Before I've gone three paces I feel Schroeder's hand on my shoulder. I spin. A hot shudder of adrenaline. Schroeder's fist mashes into the side of my face. A crack. A ringing in my ears. I am wildly conscious, yet I sink to the floor on one knee. Two orderlies pull Schroeder away. "You piece of shit," he yells. I manage to remain balanced on one knee, holding the side of my face, a pointillist cascade of light trimming the edges of my vision. "I'll fucking kill you!" Schroeder is shouting. The orderlies shove him into a chair and stand over him. I rise to my feet just as a nurse appears at my side, takes me by the arm. A warm viscosity smears the side of my face. A ringing in my ears. The electricity fails. Everything swells shut.

A crow has landed in the backyard and is cawing loudly. I stand in the open doorway on the kitchen stoop watching it flutter and flap in the grass while inside a pot of beans boils on the stove. It is the first day of hot weather, and the air in the house is stifling.

The bird is distressed. It caws and caws, dancing a circle around a wing extended in the grass. I make my way slowly across the yard, moving toward it one step at a time. The bird stops its dance and hunkers down in fear. Its jet-black feathers are matted and wet and the grass around speckled and smeared with blood. It breaks into a loud, pitiful cawing, then falls silent and surrenders.

The bird puts up a feeble struggle as I pick it out of the grass and wrap it in a towel. I carry it around to the front porch and put it into an empty kindling basket. It cocks its head from side to side, black eyes appraising.

I call a vet. No luck with the first two listings in the telephone book. The first caters only to house pets, the second to farm animals. Both suggest calling an animal rescue league. I decide to try a different ploy and call the third number listed. A woman's voice answers.

"My dog was shot."

"How long ago?"

"Half an hour."

"Where?"

"Behind my house."

"I mean where is the wound?"

"The wing."

"What?"

"It winged him."

"Where?"

"In the leg."

"Fore or rear?"

"Rear."

"Have you been able to stop the bleeding?"

"Not really."

"Is the dog conscious?"

"Yes."

"Is there an exit wound?"

"I don't know. You'd better come see for yourself."

"Can you bring him to the clinic?"

"I don't have a car."

"I'll see what I can do. I'll have to call you back."

Ten minutes later she calls back to say she'll make the trip over. I go out onto the porch to wait. The bird is calm now. In shock, I suppose. Yet it's coal eyes seem vigilant and alert.

"What's in the box?"

I start. Tom Schroeder is standing at the edge of the porch, a supercilious grin plashed across his face.

"Goddamn! The old man really popped you good."

I stand up, trying not to startle the bird.

"How many stitches you get?"

I touch my cheekbone. The stitches at the corner of my eye are hard and feel like needlepoints protruding from numb skin. "Four."

"I came by to apologize, man. I'd sue if I were you. I hate the fucker. Hate his guts." Schroeder sits on the porch step with a creak and a jangle.

"What for? Spoiling you?"

"I hate him for being a fucking pig."

"Is that what you came over to tell me?"

Schroeder reaches into his scraped and stained and thoroughly filthy-looking leather jacket. "Nah. I came by to give you this." He pulls my notebook out with a casual flourish and hands it to me. I take the pad and fan through the tattered pages. It almost seems foreign to me.

Schroeder jams his hands back into the recesses of his jacket. "I took it to find out what you wrote about Sylvia."

"What made you think I'd written anything about her?"

Schroeder shrugs. "I don't know. Just thought maybe you had. I was looking for clues."

"Clues?"

"Proof."

"Proof of what?"

"That you raped her."

"You thought *I* raped her?"

Schroeder flaps his elbows, shrugs.

"How did you know I kept a notebook?"

"I didn't."

"Then why did you break in and steal it?"

"I didn't come here to steal it, dude. I came here to kill you."

His macho gravity makes me want to laugh. I bend down to look at the crow. The bird tries to pull its head into the towel like a turtle retracting into its shell. But the towel is wrapped too tightly. I try to loosen it, but my efforts only agitate the bird. Schroeder is watching, waiting for my reaction. I go to the rocking chair and sit down. "You thought I raped her?"

"Yup."

Now I return his stare, rocking. "What made you change your mind?"

Schroeder leans against a corner post, looks down at his feet. "The notebook. I saw it lying on the kitchen table, so I started reading it. Then you came home and I figured I'd see if I could find written proof first."

"Then what?"

"*Then* I'd come back and kill you."

The floorboards of the porch creak under the rocker. Schroeder's melodrama makes me want to laugh.

Schroeder shrugs. "Anyway, I decided you didn't do it."

"How did you conclude that?"

"Because you didn't write anything down."

"So?"

"So what's the point of writing and keeping a notebook if you don't use it to confess something?"

His comment surprises me. It's the most intelligent thing I've ever heard come out of his mouth.

Schroeder continues, "I read everything and couldn't even find a hint. Just stuff like—*Suppose a painter chose to place a human head upon a horse's neck.*"

"That's the beginning of the *Ars Poetica*."

"Whatever. I read it enough times. Anyway, I figured if you were weird enough to write poems, I figured you'd have written *something* about Sylvia."

"But I didn't."

"Nope."

"So you decided not to kill me."

"Yup. I thought maybe it was, like, code and I tried cracking it. The part about putting a human head on a horse's body?"

"What about it?"

"Sounded like, maybe, you were talking about a kind of code."

I fan the pages of the notebook.

Schroeder shoves away from the corner post, grins at me. "Besides, I know it wasn't you." He stoops down to look at the bird in the basket. "What's wrong with the bird?"

"How? Did Sylvia tell you?"

"Maybe."

"Who was it?"

Schroeder shrugs. "Never mind. What's with the bird?" He bends down for a closer look.

"How were you planning to kill me?"

"What happened to the bird?"

"First tell me how you planned to kill me."

"You really want to know?" Schroeder tries to touch the bird, but it pecks at him and he pulls his hand back.

"Yes."

Without looking up from the bird he reaches into his jacket and pulls out a gun. He holds it out for me to see. "Saturday night special, dude. Clean. No numbers." As he speaks a car pulls in front of the house. He slips the gun back into his pocket.

"What are you carrying that around for?"

"My security blanket."

"You walk around with it in your pocket?"

"Yup."

"Loaded?"

"Fucking right."

"You didn't have it with you the day you passed out at the mound."

"I left it behind. Sylvia wanted to play roulette."

"Roulette? With the gun?"

He grins stupidly.

"I don't believe you."

"Then don't, dude."

The vet strides up the walk carrying a little black bag. "Where's the patient?" she asks in a friendly, down-to-business voice. She is young and tall with long, fiery red hair. Schroeder, hands crammed conspiratorially into his jacket, nods to her and stands aside as she marches up the steps. By some instinct she ignores him and directs her attention to me.

I point to the basket. Schroeder backs up a few paces and sits down at the other end of the porch.

"Didn't you say your dog was shot?"

"Yes, I did."

She regards my swollen, stitched-up eye. Finally she kneels down next to the basket, turns to me. "Why'd you tell me that?"

"Because nobody would come out here for an injured crow."

She returns her attention to the bird in the basket and for a few moments says nothing. Then she stands up. "Is there a place I can work inside? A table?" Her tone suggests that she is irritated and that I had better not bother her.

I watch from the doorway, fingering the stitches at the corner of my eye, as she works at the kitchen table. She examines and dresses the wing, working swiftly and without comment. A splint is fashioned from a tongue depresser. The bird submits to her competent hands as if by instinct. "This is a wild bird," she finally says, gently winding the wing with gauze. "Where did you find it?"

"In the backyard."

When she is finished she places the bird in the basket. "I'll take her back to the clinic. When the wing is healed we'll let her go."

"I want to take care of her."

The woman says nothing and begins repacking her bag. "Caring for an injured animal is not easy," she says. "Especially a wild one."

"I'd like to try."

The woman continues packing her bag. A brass nameplate on the side reads *Jane.* No last name, no initial. Just Jane. "You were right, the bird was shot. With a .22, I'd say. The bullet broke the bone and passed through the wing. It should heal fairly well."

"You'll let me keep her?"

Jane shrugs. "If you want to."

"Thanks." I feel silly and a little overly enthusiastic. My eager gratitude seems to break the ice a little, and Jane smiles. An uncomplicated, straight, bright smile that makes me realize I am in the presence of an utterly direct person. She exudes clarity, seems wise. By contrast, I feel all convoluted and contorted, unspontaneous and foolish.

"Crows eat carrion," she says at last. "Put some hamburger in a dish and leave it in the basket. Some water too."

"Should I keep her inside?"

"Where you had her is fine. If it gets cold at night you can bring her in. The less you do, the better."

"What if she tries to get out of the basket?"

"She won't. The splint is too cumbersome."

"How long will it take to heal?"

I follow her back through the house to the front door. "I'll come back toward the end of the week to check on her. We'll see."

I hold the door open and step out on the porch. Schroeder is still sitting there, a leather-bound malfeasance. I ignore him and walk with Jane to her car. Before getting in she gives me a business card. "Call me if there are any problems."

I take the card. "What do I owe you?"

Jane puts on her seatbelt and thinks for a moment. "Let's see how she does first."

"Let me pay you for your time."

"Don't worry about it."

"Are you sure?"

She starts the car. "You can pay me if the wing heals," she says.

"And if it doesn't?"

She pulls away without an answer. I watch as she turns into the neighbor's driveway, backs out. "By the way," she calls out the window, "I would have come out for a crow." Then, without a glance back, she whips up the street. The card in my hand reads *Jane's Veterinary Services.* No last name, just an address and a phone number.

Schroeder has not moved from the porch. "What are you still doing here?"

He drops his chin into the palm of his hand and scowls. All I can think of now is the gun in his pocket. It makes him more pathetic than dangerous, and his confession of contemplated murder angers more than frightens me.

"I need money, man." He has adopted the tone of a downtrodden teenager.

"For what?"

"My bike. The cops towed it. I need three hundred bucks to get it back."

"That shouldn't be a problem for a man about town like yourself."

"Fuck you, man."

"What about Dad?"

"The fucker won't help me out."

"Gee, that's tough."

"Fuck you," Schroeder grunts.

I walk into the house and close the front door as a signal for him to leave. The crow is still in the basket, splinted wing akimbo. The white bandage and the black sheen of its feathers contrast beautifully and make the contorted bird look like some sort of appliquéd Maltese Falcon. I sit down and watch it for a few minutes, wondering why Jane refused payment. I decide that she is one of those people who are able to act without needing a motive and whose actions always seem right and proper and balanced. I lift the basket carefully and carry it back out onto the porch.

Schroeder has still not moved. “How about lending me the money?”

I ignore him and place the basket under the window on top of the small stack of firewood left over from winter. It is not completely stable. After a slight reshuffling of logs the basket sits nicely.

“What do you say, man? I can pay you back in a week.”

“I don’t think so.”

“Why not?”

“I don’t even want to explain why not.”

Schroeder stares out into the yard. “Look,” he says after a short silence, “I’m sorry about the notebook. I should have returned it right away.”

“The notebook has nothing to do with it.”

“Then I’m sorry I told you I wanted to kill you. I probably wouldn’t have anyway.”

“Well, at least you came prepared.”

“Very funny,” Schroeder grunts.

I reach for the broom leaning next to the front door and begin to sweep the porch.

“If I had my bike back I could get my shit together, man. Get the fuck out of here. And take Sylvia with me too. She wants to go to Mexico.”

“Why not get the money from her, then?”

“She’s broker than I am. Lost her job at the pharmacy. Even had to sell her truck.”

A cloud of dust has picked up. I move toward Schroeder, trying to keep it away from the bird. “Just out of curiosity . . .”

“Out of curiosity what?”

“What is it between you and Sylvia?”

Schroeder lifts his knees and crosses his arms around them. “What do you mean?”

“How long have you and she been—an item?”

Schroeder casts me a why-the-hell-do-you-care look. "We been together on and off for a couple of years."

"She's older than you are."

"She's thirty-one."

"That's quite an age difference."

Schroeder rests his chin on top of his knees. "In lots of ways I'm older than she is. Less fucked up, too."

I continue to sweep. Schroeder looks more and more pathetic the longer he sits there—despite or because of his concealed weapon, I can't decide. "We're both fuckups," he says after a short pause. "She's totally fucked up. Very, totally fucked up. I mean it. I'm fucked up too. That's probably why we're in love."

I put the broom back and go over to look at the bird. It cocks its head, wary. Its vigilance is astounding. The effort must be exhausting. It stares at me. I stare back, a game to see who blinks first. "Tell me what you know about the rape," I finally say.

Schroeder looks over at me. "Will you lend me the money?"

The bird blinks. "I'll think about it."

Schroeder rearranges himself so that he is leaning up against a corner post. He stretches his legs out in front and makes himself comfortable, boots, chains, concealed weapon, and all. "Promise?"

"I said I'll think about it."

"No money, no story."

"How do I know you're telling the truth?"

"When you hear it you'll know it's the truth, man."

"Tell me one thing first."

"What?"

"Did your mother really kill herself in front of you?"

Schroeder doesn't bat an eye. "Yup." He fixes me with a level gaze, ready for another.

The unnecessary cruelty of the question hangs heavily, but Schroeder shows no sign of anger. "Sorry." I look away. "I'll lend you the money."

"Fucking perfect," he says and settles back against the post. He pulls a pack of Marlboros from the interior of his jacket and lights up with a studied expression. Inhales deeply and holds it as though the beginning, middle, and end of his story will condense in his lungs. "The names have been changed to protect the guilty," he begins. A long exhalation of smoke.

"Why not change the story while you're at it too?"

Schroeder flicks his ash, grins. "Maybe I already have. The guilty need as much protecting as anybody."

Who am I to argue the matter of names? Symbol and thing and the copula is—the third singular present form of *to be* and a terrifying predicament all around. I let him continue.

"It all started when she got fired from Semantech."

"She said she was laid off."

"She got fired, her and another line worker. For fighting."

"She said she was a manager."

"She worked the line. Assembling whatever the fuck it is they assemble there. Bombs, I think."

I watch the crow while Schroeder takes long drags from the cigarette and reinvents Sylvia for me.

"She and this dude worked the same shift. He used to sell her blow and it got so they started doing business together. He'd front her and she'd cut it and sell it out at Jack's and take the profit in product. That's when I met her. I used to cop from her there. I started getting in there when I was seventeen. First time at the door the guy asks me for ID and I pointed to my Sportster and said, 'There's my ID, dude.' The guy just opened the door right up and nobody ever asked me for ID there again. At Jack's a Harley is the only ID you need."

"You had that bike when you were seventeen?"

"My dad gave it to me for a graduation present. Four point oh GPA and the highest SATs in fucking school history. Got scholarships from three colleges." Schroeder flicks his cigarette into the yard. "I deferred a year. Then I deferred again, and I would have deferred again, but they said I had to start or lose the money, so off I went."

"Where?"

"Notre fuckin' Dame, man. And don't give me that good school shit. They threw me out. That's why I'm here."

"I'm sure you deserved it."

"I'll tell you about it some other time." Schroeder takes another cigarette, lights up, and continues. "So anyway, Sylvia starts fucking up with this dude, and I know all about it because by that time me and her are hanging out together pretty regularly. She gets burned a couple of times and keeps taking her cut anyway. Then she starts getting greedy and stomping on it so bad pretty soon she's just selling pure inositol and nobody wants to cop from her."

"What does all this have to do with getting raped?"

Schroeder drags on his cigarette. "I'm getting there, dude."

"Let me guess. Mr. X raped her."

"The man's a fucking genius! How'd you guess? But there's more to it." He flicks his ash. "By now Mr. X is all over her big time. He wants his money, and Sylvia doesn't have it. She blows him off and blows him off until finally it boils over and he smacks her one day at work and they both get fired. So then he starts harassing her at home. I offer the guy my goddamn bike so he'll leave her alone. He says he'll take it, but then he decides he wants to get paid his own way, and so one day he drags her out into that field and rapes her and tries to kill her, but she manages to get away. You know the rest of it, dude."

"You're lying."

"I am *not* fucking lying."

"Why should I believe a word of what you're telling me when you just told me you thought *I* raped her?"

"*That* was a lie."

"Why did you lie?"

"Why not? Why should I tell you the truth? It wouldn't make any difference. Not to me, anyway."

"Why did you break into my house?"

Schroeder runs a hand through his dirty hair. "Because we thought you saw who raped her and didn't want you to talk to the cops."

"Wait a minute." I stand up and walk to the end of the porch. "You were going to kill me because you thought I would lead the police to the *rapist?*"

Schroeder climbs to his feet. "You don't get it, do you, dude? I'm rubbing your fucking nose in it and you just don't fucking get it. You want me to make you up a sign?"

"You're right. I'm stupid. I don't get it. So explain."

Schroeder comes to the end of the porch and stands directly in front of me. His hands are crammed into his jacket, unzipped except at the very bottom. His black tee shirt is spotted with sweat. Besides a gun and the hideous angel tattooed on his chest, I wonder what else he is concealing. "You're going to have to figure it out for yourself, dude. I can't tell you any more. I already told you more than I should have."

"Then you're going to have to get your three hundred bucks someplace else."

"I told you everything I can. Not just because I need the money."

"Why else?"

"Because I figured you'd understand better than most people and because someday, you never know, it might come up again, and I'll be glad I told somebody." He holds the end of the cigarette to his lips with pinched fingers, sucks on it, and flicks it away with a macho swagger. "You don't want to know any more. Believe me."

The neighbor's kitchen door bangs shut and the kid runs outside. He stops short at the sight of Schroeder. Then, regaining confidence, he hops over the fence and races up to the porch.

"Some terrorists hijacked a school bus and now they're surrounded by tanks and army."

"Where?"

"In the Middle East."

"Which country?"

"Jerusalem."

"Jerusalem is a city, not a country."

"In Israel, I think it said."

"You sure?"

"That's what it says on the news. Anyway, the terrorists are going to blow up the kids unless they get what they want."

"What do they want?"

"I don't know."

I hand the kid a dollar. "Let me know how it comes out."

The kid jams the dollar into his pocket and runs off.

"What the fuck is that all about?"

"My news service."

"You pay him every time?"

"Only for good stories."

Schroeder laughs. "At least you're consistent, man. Now where's *my* money?"

"I have to go to the bank."

"I'll come with."

"No. Wait here."

"Jesus, dude. Why do you always have to fuck with me?"

"Keep an eye on the bird until I get back. And stop calling me dude."

It isn't until I get to the bank that the story gels. Derringer is at his desk and is about to begin the back-slapping but notices that I am preoccupied and, for the first time ever, skips the buffoonery and goes about getting my money. What Schroeder wouldn't come out and tell me is that they intend to avenge the crime. That is the only obvious conclusion. And that they are determined not to let the opportunity slip—and to keep the police out of it.

Derringer hands me the money. "Looks like you had a nasty run-in with a blunt object."

"A fist." As if to remind myself, I run my fingers over the stitches.

Derringer shakes his head. "Hope you gave as good as you got."

I ignore the remark, count the money he has given me, and slip it into my pocket. We shake hands and Derringer begins saying something about scars adding character to a face and his football days, but I turn and leave without letting him finish.

I cross the street and sit on the bench in front of the Town Hall. My business there remains unfinished. I have not placed the required announcement and thus, legally, I am still Quintus Horatius Flaccus, although I haven't *been* Horace for weeks. Or felt much like him. Horace wouldn't give Schroeder a penny. He'd turn him in. Let Caesar watch over the state. Steer clear of insane contention. But vigilante justice has a certain visceral appeal to Lucian. He prefers self-assertion and direct moral satisfaction to the coercive, bureaucratic apparatus of the state. He distrusts monolithic structures.

I get up and begin walking, though not in the direction of home. Soon I am on Liberty Street and headed for the gazebo. The Hound of Liberty Street comes bounding up. It has been some time since I've visited, and the dog wags its tail and yelps. I pat it and continue on in an empty haze, trying not to think.

Winter has taken a noticeable toll on the iron gazebo. The paint is peeling in great gobs, and rust is slowly taking over. I climb in and sit down facing the street. A large moving van is being unloaded at the house at the end. The movers come and go from the house, directed with new-owner vigor by a man in a black jogging suit. No sign of wife or children or pets. I imagine the neighbor who will trot over tonight to welcome him and try to learn what he knows of the house's ghastly history and who, when he discovers his new neighbor's innocence, will inform him in confidential tones and with expressions of deep regret and much head-shaking.

I watch for a while, wondering what sort of retribution and punishment the mother and her daughter would call for, and soon find myself begging the question of *ordo amoris.* If there is an objective order of love and hate that underlies everything and is at the core of our humanity, then the question of justice must be closely tied to it. Not justice as in the law of state or jungle, but justice as it pertains to acts of love and hate. According to *Selected Philosophical Essays*, the heart is a structured counterimage of the cosmos of all possible things worthy of love and to this extent is a microcosm of the world of values. The same must hold for hate. The heart must contain everything—love and hate and the infinite and undefinable shadings and gradations that fall in between, a stew of apples and oranges and things palatable and unpalatable, benign and malign, right and wrong, that call us to act or shrink away from acting.

But beside this *ordo amoris* is another *ordo* that compels me equally. I call it the *ordo tranquillus*, the order of tranquillity and peace of mind. This *ordo* holds that the cosmos is undiscernible, unstable, and indifferent and that nothing definite can be said about it except that nothing definite can be said, so you can take your *ordo amoris* and your microcosmos of the world of values and stick them up your ass because the only appropriate way to survive here is to strive toward a state of complete *ataraxia*, imperturbable tranquillity, to suspend all judgment and be, forever, silent.

Time passes, and the early summer sun casts a lazy pall over everything. It would be nice to lie down in the grass and take a nap, and as soon as I decide to do just that I realize what my course of action with Schroeder should and must be, and I hurry home.

He is sitting in the rocking chair on the porch when I return.

"Where the fuck have you been, man?" He flicks his cigarette into the yard and stands up. "You said you'd be right back."

"And here I am."

"You've been gone for three hours."

"Has it been that long?"

"Fuck you." He follows me into the kitchen. "I can't hang around, dude. So if we could, like, just get down to business."

I motion for him to sit down across from me, which he does with a great show of impatience. "I have decided to lend you the money on the condition that you pay it back next week, like you said."

"No problem," Schroeder says.

"But there is one more thing I have to ask."

Schroeder stands up. "But you said . . ."

"I want your gun."

Astonishment.

"As collateral."

Schroeder is silent, and for several seconds the atmosphere in the kitchen resembles that of a bad western. Doubt flickers. He sits down and leans back in the spindly chair, which creaks under his weight. Then he reaches into his jacket, takes out the gun, and with a manic smile points it at me. "I'll give you collateral, you asshole." He stands up and kicks the chair away, holding the gun on me, finger on the trigger, strands of hair falling in his face.

My pulse begins to race. I try to return his gaze as evenly as I can, feigning composure.

"Give me one good reason why I shouldn't just *take* the fucking money."

I say nothing. Fear has now welled up, and the only way I can think of to avoid panic is to hide it. Remain absolutely still. Try to stare him down.

Schroeder switches the gun from one hand to the other. "Fuck borrowing; I could just rob you, dude. I could take your goddamn money if I wanted. Couldn't I?"

My gaze is locked. The image of Schroeder, a boy, witnessing his mother's suicide races through my mind and with it the understanding that he could easily murder, has been waiting all his life for the opportunity.

"Goddamn right I could." The volume is rising, the pitch is rising, his voice is wrong, cracked, and I begin to see that he is pushing himself toward some threshold and at the same time deciding whether he will cross it. He swipes the hair from his face, prods the gun. "Say it! Go ahead, man! Say it! Say I could rob you if I wanted."

I say nothing.

Schroeder grips the gun in both hands, arms stiff out in front, police style. "Go on, asshole! Say it."

I say nothing. Stare.

"Okay, then. Say 'You could could kill me if you wanted.' Say it!"

I continue to stare and say nothing.

"Say, 'You could kill me if you wanted.' Say it!"

A chill works its way through my limbs. Panic. My heart is pounding. Schroeder is a panicked contortion towering over me. He has scared himself. I open my mouth to speak, but nothing comes out.

"*Say it, goddamnit! Or I'll blow your fucking brains out!*" Spit flies. He trembles.

The words spill out of my mouth in a rush. "You could kill me if you wanted." Schroeder stands trembling over me for several moments. Blank fear. Ringing ears. Then, like air escaping, his arms go limp. He stands for a long minute in complete silence. Then he tosses the gun onto the table. Something condenses in the air around us, palpable, unnameable. I take the three hundred dollars from my pocket and lay it on the table beside the gun. Another minute passes. Then, without a word, Schroeder picks up the money, counts it, and quietly leaves the house.

Sunset.

Twilight.

The house grows dark. Cicadas begin their nightly chorus in the trees.

I listen for a while, fingering the stitches at the corner of my eye, able to make out only the faint outline of the gun lying before me on the table like some malignant new infection. The neighbor's truck pulls up next door. Headlight beams pierce the kitchen. A glint of the revolving cylinder. Copper and silver cartridge ends. Then blackness again. Slamming doors. I lift the gun from the table, carry its dead weight upstairs, slide it underneath the mattress of my bed. Then go downstairs to check on the injured crow.

Mohr has taken a turn for the worse and has been unable to come to the phone for two days. The nurse at the hospice keeps saying I should call back later. She says he is in a weakened state. I decide to go out and pay him a visit.

I pack some provisions for the trip and feed the crow. It has been gaining strength and now spends most of the day perched on the rim of the basket, tethered there by a piece of string. With its splinted wing dangling magnificently at one side, it looks like a convalescent prizefighter. The bird seems to like me now. It squawks whenever I approach—a greeting, not a warning—and allows me touch it.

The hospice is seven miles outside town. By midmorning I am at the airport. Instead of following Route 38 I cut across the parking lot and follow the footpath behind the hangars and along the fence. The lean-to of cut branches that I found last winter has been cleared away, and now only deep tire tracks mark the spot. I stop to eat an apple. An airplane takes off in the other direction. It rises and banks away to the south, then disappears from sight.

Around noon I arrive at the hospice, an old farmhouse set back from the road and surrounded by a flat expanse of lawn fenced off from fields at the back and on either side. A single elm tree at the back provides the only shade. The house is a large white rambling structure that looks as if it grew to its present size by slow accretion and was then suddenly arrested by an iron fire escape trussed up along one side of the building.

I climb the steps. A man stationed by the front door in a wheelchair lifts a hand from his knee in weary greeting. Two other men sit in wicker chairs playing checkers. The office is just inside the front door. A young woman in a white uniform greets me cheerfully. When I tell her I'm here to see Mohr, her expression changes. "He's not doing too well," she says.

"Can I see him?"

She tells me to wait and disappears into the house. A few minutes later she returns. "He's asleep," she says. "You can sit with him if you like. Just don't disturb him. He's very weak." I follow her through the house to Mohr's room. She pushes the door open and peers in before allowing me to enter.

Mohr's bed is next to a window at the far end of the room. The blinds are drawn, and the room is dark and quiet. Mohr is connected to an oxygen tank by a long plastic tube attached to his nose by a clip. The room smells of unwashed laundry and urine and alcohol swabs and air conditioning. A large leather chair and a table covered with books and papers dominate the center. A bricked-up fireplace with a broad wooden mantel takes up one wall; shelves filled with books occupy the remaining wall space. The floor is bare except for an old, tattered Oriental rug. I approach the bed, floorboards squeaking.

"Hello, Horace," Mohr says feebly and opens his eyes.

"You're awake."

He nods his head. "I am."

I peel the pack from my shoulders and set it down at the foot of the bed. "The nurse said you were asleep. I hope you don't mind me coming unannounced."

Mohr's lips part in what must pass for a smile. Against the pillow, and with the plastic tubes coming from his nose, his head looks shrunken. He is covered to the chin with blankets. "I've been waiting for you to come, Horace. What's wrong with your eye?"

"Lucian," I correct him. "Someone hit me a few days ago. Mind if I pull up that chair?"

"It looks awful."

I drag a cracked leather chair across the floor. A book lies face down on the cushion. I glance at the title. *Treasure Island.*

"I loved it as a boy," Mohr says, turning his head to me on the pillow. "Would you mind opening the drapes?"

"Gladly." The room is flooded with light, transformed. It feels like a college dormitory, littered with books to be studied. I imagine Mohr leaping out of bed, restored to youth and vigor, but he closes his eyes and drifts back to sleep. I sit and flip through the pages of Robert Louis Stevenson's novel. A 1911 edition, illustrated with N. C. Wyeth paintings of iron-jawed buccaneers brandishing swords and pistols.

Time passes. I wander around the room browsing books, waiting for Mohr to wake up. On the table in the center of the room is a large photograph album, the old-fashioned type with velvet pages. I flip it open in the middle. A young woman and two boys in front of the Cincinnati Art Museum, Mohr and his brother, hair combed flat, eyes squinting. I turn the pages and look at more photographs. Mother, father, boys, car, house, pony ride, Christmas tree, high school graduation, and, at the end of the album, a portrait of a young man in military dress. Mohr's older brother. A letter slipped into the back panel begins *With great regret and heartfelt sorrow it is my duty to inform you of the death of your son, Pvt. James M. Mohr, in action at Heartbreak Ridge, Korea, on September 10, 1951.* I close the album, thinking it strange that such a letter should be kept like any other memento.

Mohr is still sleeping. Sunlight has warmed the room slightly, but the shuttered atmosphere remains. I sit down again in the chair. Mohr stirs. "Do you like Robert Louis Stevenson?" His voice is clogged with phlegm, and he strains to clear his throat.

"I suppose I do."

Mohr lifts his head from the pillow, then lets it fall back. "I love Robert Louis Stevenson." He closes his eyes and drifts off again.

The afternoon wears on. I stand at the window and watch as clouds roll in and the sun disappears behind them. A flock of starlings hops and flutters around a bird feeder standing on a pole a short distance from the house. The view from Mohr's room takes in a good swath of lawn, field, and a barn off in the distance, huge and red and ornamental looking.

The nurse puts her head in the door.

"He's sleeping."

"No, I'm not," Mohr says and opens his eyes.

She rolls a cart into the room. "Dinner," she announces and pushes the cart to the side of the bed. "Do you need help sitting up?"

Mohr lifts an arm. The nurse hoists him upright and slides a large pillow behind him.

"Chicken noodle," she says.

Mohr glances over at me. "My favorite," he says with a wry smile.

"Do you want to try sitting at the table?" She speaks in the nursing tone of phony cheer.

"I'll stay where I am."

She adjusts the cart so that it becomes a bed table and leaves the room as efficiently as she entered it. Mohr takes the spoon from the tray and motions for me to come closer. "Pull up a chair," he says.

I move the chair to a spot near the foot of the bed so that Mohr can see me without turning his head to the side. He lifts the spoon to his lips and slurps. His hand is remarkably steady.

"So, Horace, you finally made it out to visit."

"Lucian."

"Ah, right. I keep forgetting. Lucian of Samosata. I guess Muriel Maydock finally printed your ad?"

"No. I'm placing it in another paper."

"Which one?"

"The *Los Angeles Times*."

"That's convenient." He smiles, puts a cracker between his lips, breaks an edge. Crumbs fall. He lifts two or three more spoonfuls of soup, returns the spoon to the tray, and leans back, sated and exhausted at the same time. The look of desertion that I noticed the first time I met him is in full bloom—conveniently, because it banishes pity and wards off sorrow. He tilts his head so that he is looking out the window and I see him in bony profile.

"Have you been out to the dig?" he asks.

"Not since that first day."

"I would like to go out there again." The comment drifts into the room and fades.

"I have a new pet."

"A pet?"

"A crow. It was shot right out of the sky over my house."

"Have you given it a name?"

"Not yet."

"A pet needs a name," he says and gazes out the window as the sun returns from behind a bank of clouds. Time passes while I consider crow names. Corvus. Corax. "You know," Mohr says, after a long silence, "I don't believe there is a God." He turns to face me, licks his dry lips. "I decided it a long time ago. But you know what I do believe in?"

I shake my head.

"*Treasure Island*." He chuckles weakly at his remark.

"Would you like me to read it to you?"

He nods enthusiastically, tubes shaking in his nose. "I'd love it. From beginning to end. The whole thing." He pulls a cord, and the nurse materializes. She readjusts Mohr on his pillows and rolls the tray out of the room.

I open the book, move the chair to take advantage of the light coming in the window, and begin:

Squire Trelawney, Dr. Livesy, and the rest of these gentlemen having asked me to write down the whole particular about Treasure Island, from the beginning to the end, keeping nothing back but the bearings of the island and that only because there is still treasure not yet lifted, I take up my pen in the year of grace 17—, and go back to the time when my father kept the "Admiral Benbow" inn, and the brown old seaman, with the sabre cut, first took up his lodging under our roof . . .

I read the first chapter, glancing up at the end to see if Mohr has fallen asleep. He is wide awake, lying back on his pillows, eyes moist, unfocused, and wandering in a warm rain of fantasy. "Go on," he says. I turn the page, settle back into the chair for the long haul, and continue the liturgy. But for a few interruptions—glasses of water and helping Mohr to the bathroom—I read the entire text. It is late when I close the book. Mohr is lying on his side, cheek mashed into the pillow, staring into the room, lost to time. I stand and stretch, place the book on the table in the center of the room. "I have a long walk home."

Mohr's eyes remain fixed in the intermediate distance. "Stay here." His voice is flat.

"I need to walk. I've been sitting for too long." I lift my pack from the floor and thread my arms through the straps. Mohr has not changed his expression or looked at me since I closed the book. I stand at the side of the bed. An artery in the hollow of his temple pulses; his scalp is a jaundiced-looking yellow. He has not been shaved in days, and the gray stubble makes his cheeks look gaunt and sunken. The plastic breathing tubes affixed in his nose look almost natural.

"I'll come back tomorrow." I bend down and kiss him on the forehead. The spontaneity of the kiss surprises us both. Immediately I go for the door, pull it open, glance back before leaving. Mohr is smiling, his hollow little face illuminated by the bedside lamp, a mire of tubing, snot, and tears.

Briskly through the house, down the porch steps and the long driveway. The warm night air is a welcome relief from the conditioned chill of the house, and I am glad to escape from the shuttered quiet into the riotous croaking of toads and the chirruping of cicadas high in the trees. I can still feel the touch of his dry skin on my lips, smell the uric atmosphere of the room. From the road I glance back at the house. Blue television light flickers in a few upstairs windows, and the fluorescent light of the office pokes out of the window just beside the front door. Even set against a clear, star-filled sky and open to the breeze blowing across the broad lawn and fields, it is a place that seems long ago to have suffocated itself. The Welcome plaque hanging on a post at the side of the road is a cruel touch of irony too deliberate to be overlooked.

I have one question. Why is it that Mohr hasn't killed himself? I consider turning back to wake him up, take him from the confinement of that narrow bed, and walk him outside to look up at the stars. It would frighten him. I'm certain it would. I see the dry hollow of his face lying back on the pillow in contented delusion. A complete self-contained world, the world of Treasure Island: uncharted, bursting with buried treasure. Sail to it, explore, and then leave. An island to be discovered anew, over and over and over again, and I'm sure that the worst dreams Mohr ever has are when he hears the surf booming about its coasts.

At the airport I follow the trail around the perimeter fence and stop to rest at the old site of the lean-to. The red lights of a jet pass high overhead. I watch it move between constellations, Ursa Minor, Ursa Major, Cassiopeia. I think were I Mohr, I would kill myself. And I would do it thinking of Treasure Island, and I would do it right here. Looking at the stars and watching jets take off and land.

I am tempted to bed down here in the grass, but something impels me onward, and the rest of the walk becomes an endurance test, a long march home to bed.

At last I reach the top of West Street to find the police at my house and lights and neighbors and the squawk of radio. Sylvia is being escorted to the patrol car by two policemen.

"Fucking Jesus Christ, Horace. Where have you been?" She struggles to be released. Her hands are bound with a plastic tie.

"You live here?" the cop asks.

I nod, look around. The entire neighborhood is awake.

"Someone reported a break-in." One of the cops takes me off to the side; the other stays with Sylvia, holding her by the elbow. "We found her inside. She broke in through the kitchen door. Smashed the glass. Tore the house up a little."

Sylvia is being told to cool out.

"She says she's a friend. That true?"

I slip my pack off. The neighbor returns inside, turns off the porch light. "Yes, she does. I mean she is. Yes."

"Tell 'em to let me go." Sylvia calls to me.

The cop tells her to cool it.

"We will place her under arrest if you decide to press charges."

"No. Let her go."

"She's intoxicated," the cop adds, as though I might change my mind.

"She's a friend. Let her go."

The cop shrugs in a beats-the-hell-out-of-me way and motions to his partner to let Sylvia go.

"See. I told you," she taunts the cop as he cuts the plastic ties around her wrists. When he releases her she saunters over, follows me toward the house muttering under her breath. "Goddamnit, Horace. Where the fuck have you been? I thought you'd never show up."

The cops wait until we are inside and the door is closed before driving off. Sylvia stands just inside the front door, a sheepish smile. I go into the kitchen. The cabinets are flung open, contents strewn along the counters, shattered glass on the floor.

"Mind telling me what you want?"

She is standing in the doorway looking down at the floor.

"What do you want from me?"

"Did Tom do that to your eye?"

"No. His father did."

"Big Tom hit you? What for?" Her tone is conversational—to override my anger. If she is drunk, she is hiding it well. With puffy eyes, straggly hair, and dirty tee shirt with faded logo, she looks like any unhappy, middle-aged insomniac out for a midnight jog.

Not to be distracted, I repeat the question. "What did you come here for?"

She crosses her arms and looks at the ground, declines to answer.

"You came for the gun, didn't you? He sent you here to get his goddamn gun."

"No, he didn't," she says calmly.

"That's what you came for, though. Isn't it?"

No answer.

"Tell your young boyfriend that I'll give it back when he repays the loan. Tell him if he has any questions he can come here himself and not to send you here to do his dirty work."

"I don't know what you're talking about. He didn't send me here, and I don't do dirty work for him—or anyone else. And I don't know anything about a gun either." Her brow condenses into a frown.

"Then tell me what you broke into my house for."

"For money, goddamnit! Okay? I need money." The hardness in her face melts and tears well up in her eyes, and she turns away. "Look," she says, "I'm not trying to hurt anyone. I just need some money, okay?" Wiping her eyes with the back of her hand, she goes into the next room.

I remain in the kitchen, unsure and not wanting to be swayed by her tears and histrionics. She has to be lying. It seems impossible that she doesn't know about Schroeder's gun. But then, maybe she doesn't. She is sitting in the living room, face in hands. "I'm not going to ask you to leave," I find myself saying. "But I am tired and I am going to go to bed. You can sleep on the couch if you like. If not, close the door when you leave."

She doesn't respond but remains bent forward, hiding her face in her hands. I go outside to check on the crow. She is in the basket, alert. Half of the meat in the dish is gone. I adjust the towel draped over the back of the basket and return inside.

"Good-night." I climb the stairs.

Sylvia does not respond.

My room is undisturbed. Evidently the police arrived before she made it upstairs. The gun is still under the mattress. Without bothering to undress, I get into bed and turn out the light.

Sylvia's presence downstairs makes it impossible to drift into sleep. I lie awake, conscious of her being in the house, listening in the darkness. I try to distract myself by thinking of the visit with Mohr, of *Treasure Island*—but sex swarms in and I am unable to obliterate it from my thoughts. A torment. How can I think of sex?

A creaking on the stairs. I start, shut my eyes, pretend to sleep.

"Horace," she whispers.

Heart pounding, I don't respond.

"Horace. You asleep?" A creak of footsteps coming toward the bed. A few moments pass—eternally long. My eyes flutter under tightly clamped lids. Rustling. The sheet is lifted, and her warm body is suddenly next to me.

"Hey!" I open my eyes.

She puts her fingertips to my lips, fumbles with the buttons on my shirt. I twist away. She leans over, presses her lips to mine, and my body goes slack. I lie motionless while she struggles with buttons and zippers. Begin to cooperate, hands seeking her. In moments the bed is a tumble of sheets and clothes. She straddles me. "C'mon, Horace," she whispers, manipulating me with her hands, her lips. It is dawn and the room is growing lighter. I lift my head from the pillow and watch while she tries to lick and suck me into hardness. Minutes fly. Nothing happens.

"I can't." I twist to break away, dejected, also half relieved.

"It's okay," she says softly and slides her slender body alongside me. "It's okay."

"I want to," I find myself saying, half true, half false.

"I know. Don't worry. It's okay." She runs a hand through my hair. "It's better this way."

"Why do you say that?"

"I don't know. Because it just is." She cuddles next to me. The bed is too small for the two of us. I feel the lump of gun underneath the mattress. We lie together in silence while the room grows slowly light. A din of contradictory longings—withering desire. Contentment and unfulfillment. Have I been waiting for this all along? I think I have. I don't know.

"Why did you come here?"

The question is ambiguous. She doesn't answer immediately. "I'm lonely," she says after a while.

I want to ask her about Schroeder, but jealousy prevents me. Already I am making calculations. "Why did you break in?" I wait for her to answer, and when she doesn't respond I follow up with the first tallied sum. "Obviously it wasn't because you wanted to fuck me."

She sits up, embraces her knees. "I told you already," she says. "I need money."

I am already sorry for what I have said but am also helpless and can't stop the whirring of calculations. I see the vertebrae of her spine, a gentle arch. I begin to count them. I begin to count everything, arms, legs, fingers. I am helpless for counting. I want to count her, to trap her with my counting. "To pay off debts?" I ask.

She shakes her head.

"What for?"

No response. I begin to feel myself giving in to the modal logic of emotional need. "What for?"

"To get out of here."

The room is light now. Dawn gives way to early morning. I am tumbling, drawn to her and repelled, happy and disgusted with myself—

flaccid prick and all. Were we to make tender love, go away, and live together happily ever after I don't think my self-disgust could be allayed. Neither could it were we to reaffirm all the delusions of love and romance to each other and strive instead for friendship or some variation of the platonic ideal. Neither could it were we to go our separate ways and pretend this little interlude never happened.

I climb over her and go to the window. Sylvia remains in bed. We do not speak but quietly take in the strange languor of the morning. I am unembarrassed by my nakedness.

"How much money do you need?"

She turns to me, unsmiling, and pulls the sheet to her chin. "Enough for me and Tom to get to Mexico. Or farther."

The mention of Schroeder's name sends the calculator whirring again, jealousy, plain and simple. She turns her face to the wall, intuiting my reaction. I lean against the window, cold balls on the sill. "Meet me at the bank this afternoon," I tell her, calculator spitting tape out all over the floor. "Don't tell Schroeder. Just come alone."

She turns to me. Her face betrays nothing. She throws off the sheet. "I want to fuck you for it," she says evenly. "I want to fuck you for every cent of it."

"You can have the money."

"No way," she says. "I want you to pay it to me."

She is lying on the bed, breasts splayed across her chest, hands moving across her pubis. An effort of arousal. I notice her sour smell, alcohol and perspiration, the wrinkles at her eyes, the cold stubs of her painted toes. The calculator crashes. She is as remote from me as any stranger, and I am a stranger to myself. She cannot know me nor I her and as these thoughts fly through my head a vacuum yawns inside and my prick begins to stiffen.

Around noon I am awakened by knocking. Sylvia has gone. I go downstairs and open the door.

The neighbor kid is on the porch examining the crow in the basket. "They attacked the bus and killed all the terrorists," he tells me.

I stand in the doorway, shirtless, uncomprehending. The kid thinks I'm waiting for him to continue. "They killed seven civilians too."

"Wait a minute." I go into the kitchen to get my money. When I return the kid is patting the crow on the head. "Careful. She's been hurt."

"Can she talk?" the kid asks.

"You're thinking of mynah birds. She's a crow." I hand the kid his dollar. "Thanks for the update."

The kid crams the bill into his pocket, gives the crow one last stroke with his finger. "Good girl, Dracula," he says and then leaps from the porch and races off.

The police are at the mound. I see their cars from a distance, sheriff, deputy sheriff, State Highway Patrol. The sky is cloudless, the air hot and stagnant. There are no flocks of birds today. Passing by the field—a short, shuffling indeterminism—I don't think of Hemingway or van Gogh and suicides but of her. All morning I have had little else on my mind. Despite all efforts to dissuade myself from thinking so, today seems marked off from all previous ones. Making love with Sylvia has caused some ineffable change in the chemistry of the universe. Things look different, color, shape, the arrangement and dispersal of objects in space. A reaction has occurred that can't be reversed, and I am helpless over and against it. Strangest of all, my feelings seem completely independent of my will. All morning I have tried to take it in stride. A fuck is a fuck is a fuck. It is what I will have to think when, later today, I meet her at the bank to pay her for it.

I return once again to the question of *ordo amoris*, where the logic of the heart doesn't borrow from the logic of the understanding and the heart can love blindly and the understanding hate insightfully ad infinitum and vice versa. There is no law in this strange *ordo* that stipulates that the two can or must ever be in accord. What then of the *ordo tranquillus?* Or, at the very least, a dumb state of the emotions where the conflicts between heart and head have been put down and our inner language no longer riots at our core but we are internally bathed in the rhetoric and psychology of contented feeling states. Is that happiness? I hope not. I can't decide which is worse—loony riot or stupid contentment. Both seem equally bad.

The first person who comes into view as I approach is Detective Ross. He is conferring with the sheriff, Dr. Palmer, and two others. An ambulance idles at the far end of the lot. Middleton and Norris are sitting on the rotten picnic bench smoking cigarettes.

Ross sees me from the corner of his eye and waves without breaking the conversation. I go to the bench. The two archaeologists nod hello.

"What's going on?"

Norris puffs on his cigarette and gives his beard a tug before answering. "We found a body."

"Remains, more like it," says Middleton.

"Remains, body." Norris puffs again, waves his cigarette. "Intrusive burial."

Middleton, toying with her black braid, chuckles. "That it was, for sure. But not, strictly speaking, of an archaeological nature."

"More of a forensic one, I'd say, wouldn't you agree, Dr. Middleton?"

"I've dug up my fair share of bones, Norris."

"Wearing jeans and Nikes?"

They are both amused.

"Where did you find it?"

Norris points up to the summit, where poles and stakes protrude from the earth like pins from a cushion. The police are unfurling a yellow tape, sealing off the area.

"You've taken a good chunk off the top."

"Not enough," says Middleton. "The good stuff is way down. We're still finding last year's picnics."

"And bodies."

"Intrusive burial number one."

"Can't have a mound and not have intrusives," says Norris. "By the way, how is Mr. Mohr?"

"He's so cute," Middleton says.

"He's not doing too well. I doubt he'll be back out."

"That's sad," Middleton says. "I love the way he got all dressed up for us. It was sweet."

"A regular Schliemann," says Norris.

Palmer walks over with a cowled expression and sits down at the end of the bench. "Give me a cigarette," she says. Norris offers her his pack, and she fishes in it with a slender finger, addresses herself to her colleagues. "They're shutting us out."

"They're what?"

Palmer lights up, inhales deeply, then speaks, letting the smoke stream from her nostrils. "Until a forensics team has gone over the site."

"They'll ruin it," Middleton says.

Palmer nods, runs a hand through her chopped hair.

Middleton stands up. "What did you tell them?"

"What could I say? We found them a body. Now they want to take over."

"The whole site?"

"That's right."

"The whole fucking site? Why not just the burial?"

"The whole fucking site." Palmer masks her agitation with exaggerated coolness.

"We might as well clear out now," Middleton says. She is pacing, hands in her back pockets. "Shit. This'll put us back a week."

"They're talking two." Palmer says evenly.

"Two! What for?"

"For the bureaucracy. Our permit is suspended. We have to reapply."

"Son of a bitch! They can't do that to us."

"Tell the sheriff," Palmer says, smoking calmly. "Do you know what a grackle is?"

Norris is caught short. "A grackle?"

"Some kind of bird, isn't it?" says Middleton.

"That's right. A black bird. And this is some kind of grackle nesting ground, and the local grackle club is upset that we are out here messing it up."

"What's that got to do with anything? Christ! Look at that factory across the street! Are they upset about that too? I fucking doubt it."

"The sheriff thinks it is possible that it might come up during the review of the permit. They complained about not having been consulted the first time around."

"That's ridiculous. They're going to make us wait two weeks?"

"I'm not waiting two weeks," Middleton says. "I'll come back, but no way I'm wasting two weeks here."

"I need a drink," says Norris.

Detective Ross, the sheriff, and two people from the State Highway Patrol are conferring by the ambulance. "Don't go anywhere, Mister," the sheriff tells me. "I got some questions for you."

"For me?"

"That's right. Stick around."

I peer inside the back door of the ambulance. A wire mesh litter and on it an industrial olive-green bag. Zipped shut. A clump of grass and muddy handprints on the bag, mild reek of newly upturned earth and rubber. Ross approaches. "Been meaning to drop by Mr.—ah—Quintus, is it?"

"Lucian."

We shake hands. The detective scratches the back of his head. "Now, I don't recall . . ."

"I changed my name to Lucian of Samosata."

Ross reaches for his handkerchief. "Now, why'd you go and do that? I kind of liked Quintus Horatio Flackjacket." He is wearing his signature blue summer seersucker minus the jacket, tie loosened around his neck, collar unbuttoned. He peers into the back of the ambulance. "They think he's been buried there about a year. We'll see what the coroner says." He steps away from the ambulance, motions for me to follow. "Sheriff tells me you still been spending a fair amount of time out here."

"I walk out now and then."

"Remember seeing anything looked like a funeral?" He grins.

I shake my head.

"Down there, back around?" He points. "Underneath a bush?"

"No."

"Whoever put him there wasn't in too big of a hurry. They got down almost two feet."

"They said the body was decomposed. How do you know it was a man?"

"They're right about that. Never seen such a maggot-eaten mess my whole life."

"How do you know it was a man, then?"

"Don't too many women wear size eleven Nikes. They pulled him up in his damn running shoes. We'll know a lot more when the coroner finishes checking it out. How long he's been dead. How he died. Who he *was*."

The sheriff walks over carrying his clipboard and wearing an expression right out of television. "I want you to tell me how many times you've been out here in the last year."

"Exactly?"

"That's right."

"I can't say exactly."

"Try. Give me a number."

"Twenty. Maybe."

"You sure?"

"Give or take a few."

"Ballpark. Twenty."

I nod.

"Now tell me who else you've ever seen out here."

"You. You arrested me here, remember?"

"Besides me."

"Those two drunks last week and them." I point over to the archaeologists.

The sheriff writes. "That the only time you ever saw either one of them out here?"

"The archaeologists?"

"No. Schroeder and the woman."

I nod.

Ross looks on, amused. The sheriff glances at him, the outline of a dislike professionally underconcealed. "He's all yours, boss," the sheriff says. "We'll let you know when we have further questions." Pro-forma eye contact. "Have any travel plans?"

I shake my head.

"Good," he says. "Let us know if you plan to leave the area anytime in the next few weeks."

I shrug, stop short of agreeing. He turns to leave. "You coming back to the station, boss?"

"I'll be back later. Got a few things to check up on first."

The sheriff doesn't bother to turn around but marches away toward his car.

"Prick."

"He's your sheriff." Ross dabs at the back of his neck with his handkerchief. The archaeologists are still at the picnic bench. Palmer is gesticulating, cigarette between two fingers. Norris is slumped, fedora pulled over his eyes and stubby legs stretched out. Middleton is pacing and twirling her braid. "Them two you found out here last week—the woman, she was the same one that was raped."

"I know."

"And Schroeder. She's his girlfriend."

I shrug. Should I tell him about the gun? Put them on to Schroeder so they can put him away? Get rid of him, at least for the time being?

"People say she's one sweet bitch." Ross grins, mopping his neck. "Least that's what they say out at Jack's."

"Who says that?"

"Everybody I talked to out there. Deals a little coke on the side too. One dude told me they're thinking about installing her next to the cigarette machine."

I glare at him, resolved not to tell him anything now.

The ambulance pulls away; the sheriff, the deputy, and the highway patrol follow behind in convoy. Ross's expression changes. He motions for me to walk with him toward his car. "You remember telling me you heard some shots that day?"

I nod.

"And you saw some cars too."

"Did I say that? I don't remember."

"How many shots did you hear?"

"I don't remember. Two or three."

Ross pulls open the door of his car and settles behind the wheel. "Try and remember. Two? Three?"

"I can't remember exactly."

He pulls the door shut with a grunt, twists the key in the ignition. "I have it written down somewhere. I suppose that's about it for now. See you around, ah, Luke, is it?"

"Lucian."

"Right." He lifts a fleshy hand from the wheel and then pulls away, tires spurting dirt and gravel. I watch the car bounce onto the roadway and speed off. Is it possible that he knows more than I do? Has he made a connection between this body and Sylvia and Schroeder? A whir of factors and considerations kicks up. Does he know I know? Does he know I know he knows?

Palmer and Norris are still smoking cigarettes at the bench. Middleton is loading equipment into the back of the van. I leave without saying goodbye.

The clock at the bank reads three-thirty. Sylvia is nowhere to be seen. At three-forty I decide to go in to get the money before the bank closes for the weekend. Maybe she was delayed, went off to sleep and forgot. But maybe she is afraid to come into town. Maybe she knows. Maybe the police have her. Maybe she doesn't want the money.

Derringer is startled when I tell him how much to withdraw from my account. "You want a bank draft?"

"Cash."

"That's an awful lot of scratch to be carrying around. A bank draft would be safer."

"Cash. In hundreds."

He shrugs and fills out the withdrawal slip and goes to the cashier. I settle back in the air-conditioned coolness and look out the window, hoping to spot Sylvia and at the same time not wanting to. Derringer returns with two banded stacks of newly minted bills and places them on the desk. "Five thousand times two," he says. "You want to count it?"

"No." I put the money into my pack and zip it closed.

Derringer shakes his head in disapproval. "That's the worst place you could put it," he says.

"Don't worry about it." I get up.

"Mind if I ask what you're planning to buy with it?"

I shoulder the pack and pause for a moment.

Derringer is awaiting my answer. "Could it be? Finally? At long last?" An eager grin spreads across his face, and his eyebrows do a canny one-two bounce. "A car? You buying a car?"

"No. I'm buying a fuck."

Derringer's face registers shock, but in an instant he recovers himself, guffaws loudly with locker-room aplomb. It's the funniest thing he's ever heard from me.

Outside there is still no sign of Sylvia. I cross the street and sit on the bench in front of Town Hall to wait. Of course I'm buying something. I didn't have to, but I did. *Ordo amoris. Ordo amoris.* So clear and lucid in theory. The order of love and hate, a simple premise that contains the proper element of sweet and rational necessity.

The hand of the clock moves steadily toward the hour. I watch the traffic on Main Street. At five o'clock I stand up and cast my last glances up and down Main Street. Derringer emerges from the bank, locks the front door behind him, sees me, waves tentatively. I stand, shoulder the pack, and start for home.

At Liberty Street the hound catches sight of me and gives chase. He catches up, barking and leaping, then settles into pace alongside, tongue flying out the side of his mouth. Good boy. Good boy! Come on, now! Good boy. At West Street I feel an urge to turn around, to look back, but resist. I stop, pat the dog, but instead of sending the dog away, as I always do, I invite him along with a slap of the thigh—come on, boy—and with vigorous tail-wagging the dog trots along with me.

I arrive at my front door to find it locked and the house exactly as I left it. The dog sniffs at the edge of the crow's (or is it a grackle?) basket. "No. Away from there." The dog sneezes, waggles its tail, and follows me into the house.

I lift a bottle of wine from the case in the kitchen closet, dropping the pack on top. Open it, fill a glass to the brim, and sip, wandering out the kitchen door and into the early evening, dog shambling behind me. The newly green trees rustle. A breeze has picked up and on it the pungent smell of fertilized fields. The weather seems to be changing, the humidity easing. I wander to the edge of the lawn, sipping, wondering how it has come to pass that the *autarkeia* I have held to so stubbornly can have been so easily obliterated? The intentional sublimation of want and desire, the contempt for the instincts—the fucking and feeding and fighting and fleeing—has been replaced without the least effort—virtually overnight. I take down a large gulp of wine, abating consciousness, a pleasant easing inside. Sublimation suddenly seems less sublime, and *autarkeia*—the worthy goal of Cynics—seems too abstract to live by. Had I not striven to try and attain a portion of it I would be tempted, with another big sip of wine, to deny it altogether. Don't cynics hold all abstractions in contempt? My *bios theoretikos* is crumbling, falling gently to my feet, replaced by an elated longing to have Sylvia next to me again tonight, and maybe tomorrow. And the day after?

Exchanging my glass for the bottle, I march into the woods, swigging, the hound tagging faithfully behind. Presently I find myself near the tracks staring at the shallow grave containing my old clothes and boots. An animal has dug through and uncovered them. One boot lies gnawed and torn in the dirt. The dog sniffs it, paws it, roots around, then loses interest. I drink from the bottle, wiping my chin with the back of my hand, contemplating this grave of mine. A snatch of Horace comes to mind and I recite a few lines, feeling simultaneously silly and serious.

Quo me, Bacche, rapis tui.
Whither, Bacchus, am I swept on,
thus possessed by your wine.
What are the groves and caves
this new self of mine must behold?

I swig again. And again. Then I strip myself naked, toss my clothes onto the upturned grave, and walk back to the house, the dog barking, leaping about me.

"That you?" Sylvia's voice.

"Er. Yes." I put the bottle on the table, no leaping of heart, no urgent rush to embrace her. Cower in the kitchen, not knowing what to do.

She appears in the doorway. "Jesus Christ! What happened to your clothes?"

My face colors; I try to cover myself with my hands. "I took them off."

"I guess so." She leans in the door frame. "The question is, where did you leave them?"

"In the woods."

She nods in mock approval. Then laughs. "Didn't realize you were into, like, nudity. Turn around. Let me get a good look at you."

I slip past, heart pounding, and run upstairs to put on some clothes. When I return she is sitting at the kitchen table, wine bottle to her lips, her expression serious. She puts the bottle down. "Sorry I didn't make it to the bank."

I take two glasses from the cabinet, fill each to the brim, emptying the bottle.

"Did you get the money?"

I drink, avoiding her eyes. The dog paws at the door. I let it in, pat it on the back, good boy, raw disappointment making it difficult to respond, or even to look at her.

"They found a body at the Indian mound today." I watch for her response.

She sips from her glass, eyes cast down at the table. "They did?"

"It had been buried there for almost a year."

"Who says that?"

"The archaeologists who found it."

She drinks again. Says nothing.

"The cops were out there. Ross, the detective, he asked about you and Schroeder."

She avoids my gaze. Drinks more wine.

"Why would he be asking about you two?"

"I don't know. He probably thinks we did it."

"Did you?"

"Look. Do you have my money? I don't feel like being interrogated."

"Maybe I should ask Schroeder."

"Good luck." She drains her glass. "I don't know where he is."

I retrieve another bottle from the closet, shoving the pack into the corner.

"Look," she seems to fumble for words, twirls her empty glass by the stem. "What is it you want from me?"

I pour more wine. "I don't know."

"Then why all the questions? I thought you wanted to help me out?"

"I did."

"You did? You mean you changed your mind?"

"I still do. I think."

"You think? Shit, man. What do you think I came here for?"

A twinge. I ease it with a long, loud slurp, roll the liquid on my tongue. "Don't panic. It's all right. I want to help you."

An incredulous stare, then her nostrils flare, begin to pump, eyes well with tears, and she puts her head down on the table and begins to sob. I lean against the stove, watching her shoulders quake and her hair falling over arms and elbows, strangely, perversely satisfied. It is a cruel sort of pleasure, and I am neither proud nor relieved to be feeling it, but it has taken the edge off my disappointment, and because it is the truth I have no choice but to admit it. Why pretend otherwise?

"Did you kill the man who raped you?"

No response.

I press the point. "And did you bury the body out at the mound?"

No response. She won't look up, continues to sob, face buried in her elbow. Am I torturing her? The thought that maybe I am sends a thrill through me. Revenge and the unwitting discovery of another crime. The knowledge puts me in control of a weapon that I am free to wield as I choose. "You did kill him. And you buried him on the mound. Amnesia was a way to hide everything, to keep the police from interfering."

Her head jerks up. "No! I didn't. I wish I had, but I didn't!"

"Who did, then?"

"Tom did." As she says it regret writes itself across her features, and to hide it she lifts the glass, buries her face in it, drinking greedily. "I wanted to. I would have. I'm glad he's dead. But I didn't kill him."

"Why are you running away, then? You had a year to get away. Why the sudden rush?"

"I wanted to go with Tom."

"But he left you."

"He came back to get me. We were supposed to go together."

"But he left without you. Why'd he do that?"

She shakes her head, wipes her nose with her sleeve. "I don't know."

"Did he leave you to take the rap?"

"I said I don't know."

"He couldn't be long gone. The body was discovered this morning."

She leans over, takes a letter from the back pocket of her jeans. "Here," she says, handing it to me. "Read it."

I sit across from her, spread the letter on the table. She reaches for the bottle and fills her glass. "I don't care. I don't give a fuck about anything. Tell the cops. Tell the fucking cops. I don't care anymore." She drinks.

I read the letter.

Reward is due for secrets kept;
I would forbid a man who divulged the rites
Of Ceres' sacred mysteries to
Stand under rafters where I stood, or to
Put out to sea with me.

"I never knew he wrote poems," she says, wine dribbling down her chin. "Words and fucking music."

"He didn't write it." I slide the note across the table to her, sickened. "He didn't write it. He stole it. From me. From Horace."

"From you?"

I try to think of how to explain but can't, feel violated by Schroeder as never before, as if he has ripped pieces from me and sent them up in flames. "You should be glad to be rid of him."

"Why?"

"Because he's an asshole."

She looks at me with bleary-eyed disgust. "Yeah, right."

"As soon as the body is identified they'll come looking for you."

"So what? They can think whatever they want. I didn't do it. Besides, they'll have to find me."

I go to the closet, grab the pack and another bottle. "Here's the money." I toss her the pack.

She unzips the bag, reaches in, takes out the cash. She fans the two banded stacks with her thumb. "Holy fucking Christ! There's ten grand here!"

I pull the cork, drunk now, feeling the cheap elation of a bribe accepted, a beggarly victory.

"Ten grand." She seems unfocused and confused, thumbs the stacks again, then shoves them back in the pack. I feel a roaring, fill-the-glasses drunkenness coming on. But Sylvia does not roar along with me. She begins to cry.

"It's okay." I try to soothe her. "Don't cry." Her tears are not gratitude but humiliation, and I realize I am not saving her but dredging her in the mud. I put my glass down and walk on unsteady legs out to the porch to check on the crow. It is dusk, and the streetlights flicker on. I pull away the cover on the basket, venting a rank smell of rotten meat. The crow is dead, splinted wing pressed stiffly against the wall of the basket. I look around for the dog, but the dog is nowhere in sight; stand for an unsteady moment over the dead bird. I should have called Jane earlier.

Inside Sylvia is still sitting at the table. Reeling with wine, I watch her from the doorway, fighting an urge to embrace her. Then, a drunken inspiration. I throw open the closet and reach into the case for the last two bottles of wine, stuff them into the pack, and run upstairs for the gun.

"Come on!" I grab Sylvia by the arm, pull her out of the house. She doesn't resist but stumbles along.

"Where are we going?"

"Walk fast. We don't have much time."

It is dark now, and at the top of West Street I let go of her hand and begin to set a pace.

"Where are we going?"

"The airport."

She accepts this without comment. We walk at a brisk, sobering rate without speaking. Single file along the airport road. Cars flash past. The road is busy in early evening. We crunch along on the narrow shoulder, over discarded cigarette packs and cans and tumbling cellophane bags. Walking the road alone is easy. I feel invisible. In tandem it feels dangerous. The cars whoosh past; some slow down, curious, others swerve as if annoyed. In less than an hour we are standing in the high sulfur glare of airport parking-lot lights. I unshoulder the pack, remove the gun, and stuff it into my pants.

"Is that Tom's gun?"

"It's mine now."

"What are you doing with it?"

"Keeping it for collateral."

"Get rid of it. It'll get you in trouble."

I hand her the pack, and we cross the lot and enter the bright terminal building. The gun in my pants makes walking awkward. I still feel semidrunk.

The departure schedule lists one flight to Chicago.

"Guess I'm going to Chicago," Sylvia says.

In line at the ticket counter she asks, "You coming with me?"

"I can't."

"Why not?"

"I can't. Besides, you haven't told me where you're going."

"Mexico, man."

"Where in Mexico?"

"Anywhere where there's a beach."

At the ticket counter I begin to sense panic. Her eyes dart, her small spindle of a body sprung tightly, a waif, all limbs and shaggy clothes and tossed hair. The clerk at the counter beckons. "Can I help you?" His head tillers from her to me, waiting for a response. Sylvia fumbles with the pack, stalling for time. "A ticket," she says.

"To San Diego," I cut in.

"One way or round trip?"

"One way."

"Are both of you flying?"

"No," Sylvia says. "Just me." She rests the pack on the ledge under the counter. The clerk, plump and groomed sleek, begins typing. Sylvia leans toward me, whispers into my ear, "Why San Diego?"

"You don't have a passport," I whisper back.

"Yes I do," she says and reaches into her back pocket for the mangled little booklet and waves it at me. "Excuse me, sir."

The clerk looks up. "Yes?"

"I'd like to change that ticket."

"How would you like to change it?"

"I want to go to Acapulco."

"Acapulco?"

"That's right."

"One way? Or round trip?"

"One way," she smiles.

"No, she doesn't. She wants to go to San Diego."

The clerk frowns. "San Diego? Acapulco? What'll it be?"

"I want to go to Acapulco."

I pull her away, whisper in her ear while the clerk screws his porcine features into a customer-first look of fake amusement. "Go to San Diego. Don't give him your name. From there go anywhere you like."

She nods, approves the strategy, returns to the counter.

"San Diego," she says.

The clerk returns to his computer screen. I wander away to let her complete the transaction, stroll toward the waiting area with its little bucket seats and coin-operated television sets and murmur of Muzak and backlit advertisements for industries nobody should ever hear of. I think of my winter visit to the control tower, the flat expanse of Oblivion's single runway under feet of snow. I imagine lifting off from it, lifting into the air and flying away with Sylvia next to me, gazing out the window as the lights of Oblivion shrink away into darkness.

"Is Sea World in San Diego?" Sylvia is behind me, slipping her ticket into the pack. She is exited. "It is, isn't it?"

"I don't know."

"Sure you do. Where they have those whales and dolphins and other trained fish that do tricks." She slings the pack on her shoulder. "Come on. I'll buy you a drink." She takes my hand and pulls me toward the airport bar. "Let me buy you a couple of drinks."

We sit on tall stools at an elevated little table. She orders Jack Daniels and Coke. I ask for wine. Like the engines of a jet she is winding herself up, setting herself on some trajectory where anxiety conceals itself in exuberance and a barrage of excited talk. "Want to see my ticket?" She takes it out, hands it over. "Read it," she says.

"Sylvia Plath?"

"My favorite poet." She laughs. "The idiot at the counter didn't bat an eye."

I return the ticket, sip sour wine, look through the glass partition into the airport. "Take a bus into Mexico. Don't fly."

"Why?"

"It'll be too easy for them to trace you. Just go to the bus station and get on a bus."

"To Acapulco?"

"Go anywhere you like, Sylvia Plath."

Her exuberance fades. She jabs her finger into her drink, retracts it, and puts it in her mouth. "What will you say if the cops ask about me?"

"Nothing."

"What about Tom?"

I shrug. "What about him?"

"You want to know the truth?" She dips her finger again. "Will you promise not to tell?"

I nod.

"I was there when it happened. That day in the field. I ran." Her eyes begin to cloud. She jabs her finger into her drink. "I heard the shots, and I just ran and ran." She finishes her drink. The flight to Chicago is announced. "Sea World, here I come," she says.

"Why didn't you claim self-defense?"

She stands, shoulders the pack. "Because it wasn't."

"But you were raped."

She unshoulders the pack and takes out the wine bottles. "Here," she says, handing them over. I take them, and she kisses me on the forehead. "It wasn't supposed to get that far," she says. "Tom was late. It all happened too fast. I ran away."

Before I can ask her anything else she turns on her heel and strides toward the gate.

The flight to Chicago roars down the runway and lifts off, red lights beating counterpoint against the stars. I watch from behind the fence, from my bower of tall summer weeds, an open bottle of wine beside me and Schroeder's gun in my lap. I grip the gun by the handle, point it at the airplane banking in the distance, and squeeze the trigger. My wrist bucks, the gun leaps in my hand. I squeeze the trigger again. Another bolt of sound, then immediate roaring silence and ringing ears. I examine the revolving chamber, sniff the muzzle, hot, oily cordite. Drop the gun into my lap and swig another mouthful of wine. Sylvia Plath. Sylvia Plath and me. Me and Sylvia Plath. By legal snafu still Quintus Horatius Flaccus and going by Lucian of Samosata but feeling for the moment more like George Gordon—who was Lord Byron, who was the rowdy sixth Baron Byron of Rochdale—singing between fat mouthfuls, *I would to heaven that I were so much clay / As I am blood, bone, marrow, passion, feeling. / Because at least the past were passed away*—swig— */ and for the future (but I write this reeling, / Having got drunk exceedingly today. / So that I seem to stand upon the ceiling) /*—swig again—*I say*—and again—*The future is a serious matter / And so—for God's sake—Hock and soda water!*

Yippee! I swig again. Swallow, cough, and sputter. Hock and soda water. Hockheim on the River Main! Spatlese and spatchcocks and sprudel wasser sp-sp-sputtering away. All goddamned day . . . Yippee! Wave good-bye to Sylvia Plath winging her way toward the beaches of Mexico. And I—Don Juan, perhaps? Diogenes in the dark? Or Plato? Thomas of Erceldoune? Alfred Lord Tennyson? François Villon? Who knows? Who cares?—here to finish these bottles. Sylvia Plath, good-bye. And good riddance! I couldn't have withstood another fucking and, I know, could not have withstood you—your substanceless blue substancelessness—much longer either. Whoever you are—or were—or will one day be. I think.

I reassemble her story backward from final confession to cornfield and crows (no, grackles) and van Gogh and Hemingway and suicides. Try to picture Sylvia luring her cocaine creditor into the field with promises of repayment and him thinking only of a hot fuck. When did he tie and gag her? Was the roughhousing part of the bargain? Was Sylvia begging off by then? Wondering, then panicking, where the fuck Schroeder is? The prearranged white knight? Where is he? What is he waiting for? And then Schroeder finally does appear, stepping out of the corn like a vengeful demiurge. But too late. Guinevere is already violated and, delirious with fear, she flees.

So where was Schroeder? Was he wandering? Lost in the corn? Or was he waiting for them, concealed? Doubled over with his gun in his fist, watching Sylvia, his live porno queen, being bound and gagged and savagely fucked. And only *then* stepping out from his hiding place with gun ready and cock hard and ejaculating bullets into the Nike-shod beast. Could that have been what happened? *Pop pop pop.* Blackbirds and corn and van Gogh and Hemingway and not suicide but murder.

So where was Schroeder? Did he watch her being raped? Did he peek out from his hiding place and—for the thrill of it—wait until things got rough before intervening? And if so, is Sylvia aware of it? Or did he tell her he was scared? Maybe that's what he told her. He had doubts. Didn't want to commit murder. That's what happened. The trap was set and he began to doubt, couldn't go through with it. So he watched. Then, when it started going really badly for her, he put his doubt aside and rushed in. And Sylvia ran away. And Schroeder buried the body and went off to college.

I swig again. The blinking red lights of the flight to Chicago have long since vanished. I think I would like to kill him. And use his gun to do it. I heft the stupid weapon. No. I couldn't do it. I put the muzzle to my temple. Close my eyes. Feel the cold metal ring ready to blow an entrance into my brains. I count backward.

Five.

Four.

Three.

Two.

No. I can't. I can't do it. It makes no sense, and sense is all I have ever sought from things.

One.

I drink. I drink to make sense. I read to make sense. I walk and talk and telephone to make sense. Sense of everything. Sense of nothing.

I drink. C'mon, Lucian of Samosata. You ridiculed Peregrinus Proteus, the phony Cynic, for his public self-immolation at the Olympic Games. For love of notoriety, you said he did it. Well, here we are. Laugh at me. Finger on the trigger. Have a good laugh!

Or what about you, Horace? You, who departed this life like a diner replete from a banquet, rubbing your stomach and picking your teeth? Do it!

Do it!

C'mon! Whoever you are! Pull the trigger!

. . .

. . .

I can't.

He can't.

We can't.

It can't. The brain. It refuses to extinguish itself. Doesn't trust itself. Saved—for all its higher faculties and lowly instincts—to survive its own harsh acuity.

I drink. More dullness seeps in at the edges. It is comforting. Look up at the sky. Good-bye, Sylvia Plath. Good-bye and good riddance. Good-bye and thanks for fixing my *ordo amoris,* setting it straight in line with all the other objectively existing orders of things that may or may not be perceived or understood and that may or may not be doubted but that (drinks sloshing in our hands) we may repair to for comfort and, if we're lucky, a little peace of mind.

I finish the bottle and throw it against the fence. It breaks with a loud crash. Try to stand up, drunk now, exceedingly drunk, and feel in the grass for the last bottle. Let's go visit Mohr. Read him *Dr. Jekyll and Mr. Hyde.* Now, there's a story.

The house is dark when I arrive. It is long past midnight, judging by the moon. The walk has sobered me. I knock on the front door and wait, then rap on the office window, but nobody answers. I sit on one of the wicker chairs on the porch, legs heavy with wine and walking. The sound of canned television laughter filters through an open window above. It is humid. Warm and humid. The open expanse of lawn surrounding the house creates a feeling of exposure, like being out on a broad starlit prairie and having no place to hide. Welcome, the sign on the road says.

I get up and knock again, this time more aggressively. Then, after a few more minutes of waiting, return to the chair. A breeze picks up and blows across the porch, on it the smell of approaching rain. I settle into the chair and unfurl my legs, taunt myself for flirting with the gun and for bringing it to tempt Mohr. Will he understand the gesture or be offended by the melodrama of it? He must have decided against suicide long ago—preferring instead to come alone to this creaky old house and stiffen slowly in a rented room.

But maybe not . . .

I walk around to the back of the house, looking for Mohr's window. The monotony of the landscape makes it difficult to reconstruct the view from it. The house is large, and there are several windows to choose from, all facing southwest—so the tenants can warm themselves, I imagine, and count sunsets. I put the bottle down and rap gently on the third window from the corner. Rap again, then push up. The window opens easily.

The curtains billow. It is Mohr's room. The smell gives it away. I drop the bottle in the window. It lands on the floor with a loud thud.

"It's me," I call, listen for a reply, then hoist myself up through the frame, gun jabbing into my pelvis as I belly through, walking on hands, and drop onto the floor at the foot of the bed.

The room is still. I get up slowly. "Are you here?" The room is dark but for a weak cone of moonlight stabbing through the parted curtains. Eyes slow to adjust to the dark, I lean toward the tumbled sheets and pillows. "Are you there?"

No answer.

I fumble with the bedside lamp, twist it on with a noisy clack. His head is sunk among the pillows, mouth agape, eyes open. The tubes are gone from his nose, lie coiled on the floor beside the bed where he must have dropped them. The shocked look of him—as though suddenly extinguished—drives me away. I back off, feeling that I have intruded upon something I have no right to intrude upon, pace to the farthest corner of the room to take in the entire deathbed scene. I am unsure how to react. I have never seen a body so still, so absolutely still. After a few moments I return to the side of the bed to close his eyes. But I recoil from touching him, feeling that this too is some sort of violation. Then I realize that it is right that I, his friend, should be the one to close his eyes. An instinct for rite wells up and, solemnly, I reach out and close his eyes, even letting my fingers linger on the strangely yielding flesh of the lids and the orbs of his eyes underneath them, which also yield to the light pressure of my fingers and retreat deep into their sockets. To close the mouth I push upward on his jaw. The stubble on his chin produces an incongruous scratching sound underneath my fingers. But the lips part and his mouth opens slowly when I remove my hand. I try holding it shut, bent knuckle of my index finger under the chin, thinking that after a minute or two the jaw will lock into this position. But gravity pulls it downward. I pull the pillows out from underneath and his head falls back, chin tilted up at the ceiling. The mouth stays closed.

I retreat to the other end of the room again, wondering if I should go find the nurse. There is no hurry, I decide, and drag the high-backed leather chair over to the side of the bed, open the bottle of wine by pressing the cork down the neck. I glance around for *Treasure Island* but can't see it anywhere. Then intuition tells me where it is, and I pull back the covers. Mohr is holding it Biblelike against his breast. I lift the sheet back over, wondering if he has been holding it since I finished reading it to him or if he reached for it as he was dying—for comfort, or just for something to hold on to.

The bedside lamp casts a band of light across his gray face. I sit back, lift my feet onto the bed and the bottle to my lips, upending it to let the cork float away from the neck. The wine dribbles into my mouth and courses down my chin. I would like to dribble some wine into Mohr's mouth too but fear I might not get it closed again.

A recitation seems in order, and I flit through all the bits of written language stored in my memory for something appropriate, something wise and priestly. But it is not easy. And as I rummage through the detritus and debris of all my reading I begin to feel emptier and more desolate than I can ever remember feeling. I lift the bottle to drink, and it begins to dawn on me that this emptiness is the result and outcome of this mania for storage. And I can think of nothing to say because there is nothing there except the acquired scraps and imparted strands of a tired, epigonic self.

The muscles of my abdomen begin to tighten and roll, and an anguish I have never felt before breaks over me. I begin to cry. And then, as though a tiny, disengaged part of me is standing off to the side observing (he's crying now, look at him crying), I give in to the rolling tide, and the room collapses around me so that even the dead Mohr disappears and all that remains is me, alone, me and my own wine-beslobbered reflection into which everything dissolves like a fine powder in a swirling pool of water. Sobs fill the emptiness, fill it with a warm, wet music. People begin to approach from distant places, people I once knew and whom I recognize. My other selves. My eponymous selves. They smile, and I smile back, and they continue smiling, and I am touched by this and overcome by sadness and cry all the harder. I cry to forget them and cry that I have forgotten. I never knew them, and this little poignant piece of the truth makes me sadder, and I cry harder and all the more deliciously for ever having denied it. I love myself and am sad because I don't know who I am and not knowing who I am is all I will ever know. This cruel little solipsism makes me sadder still, and I cry all the harder for it. These other selves are my only conversation with whatever it is I can call myself, my unknowable self that exists only in conversation—with Chidiock Tichborne (who saw the world and yet who was not seen), with William Blake (who present, past, and future sees), with Quintus Horatius Flaccus (clear in the head—save when nursing a head cold), and now (Oh, the stupidity! Oh, the vainglory!) Lucian of Samosata. They are smiling as if to say everything is all right, that I should get it out of my system, purge myself of my self. And this uncomprehending, curious sympathy makes me cry. And crying makes me cry.

Then it is over. I am done. The room reassembles itself around me. Former selves clatter back into remoteness. They are gone. The sadness is gone. And I am alone, again face wet with snot and tears and across from me the vitrified body of Mohr the librarian.

I open the curtains, turn off the light, and return to the chair. A dim moonlight penetrates the room, and I wipe my face with an edge of the bedsheet, sip from the bottle, and drift into a drowsy contemplation—not of Mohr but of Sylvia and her fate. It is hard to fix her in my thoughts. Soon all that will remain of her is a cruel image of the unfortunate woman fleeing from misogyny to misogyny and looking neither back nor forward but simply stumbling onward through the brutal gauntlet of this world. I struggle to amend the image, to fix her into memory some other way, and now I see her in airports and bus stations, in bars and at the movies. I see her waiting in line and taking her turn, driving to work, and lying on the beach. I see her renouncing booze and taking up religion and then renouncing religion and embracing suburban quietude. I see her cooking and eating and running from place to place—alone or with children, it doesn't matter, because she will always be alone and she will come to know it and accept it, although people will crowd around her and want to convince her otherwise. It won't matter. I see her getting sick and recovering and getting sick again. I see her moving from place to place. I see her walking with the same unsteady wobble. I hear her praises being sung, and I see her being vilified by one and the same person. I see her wandering under the stars at night. I see her looking at herself in the mirror. Sticking out her tongue. Feeding the birds. Collecting wood for a fire. Riding an escalator. Digging in a garden. I see her growing old. I see her dying.

When I open my eyes again it is dawn. The curtains billow at the open window, and the morning air blowing through it has freshened the atmosphere. Mohr's features stand out clearly in this dull grey light. He seems more peaceful in this light than under the incandescent glare of the lamp. I stand and stretch on unsteady legs, my head still clouded with wine, my mouth dry. I glance at the bottle and resist the urge to finish it off, reaching instead for the plastic water pitcher on the bedside table and draining it in one long draft.

"Excuse me." The voice startles me. The nurse is standing in the doorway. "What are you doing here?" She appears startled as well and moves quickly into the room with an expression of disapproval. On seeing Mohr she checks herself. "Oh my," she says.

I put the pitcher back on the table. "He died last night."

"What time?"

"I don't know. He was gone when I arrived."

"When did you get here? How did you get in?" Her voice registers alarm. My shabby appearance is having an effect on her.

"I don't know what time it was, exactly."

She is flustered. "I didn't hear anything. Who let you in?"

I point to the open window. "It was that or sit outside all night. I hope it's not a problem."

She glances at Mohr, then hastens over to close the window. "As a matter of fact, it is a problem," she says, pulling the window shut. "You are trespassing. You had no right breaking in here."

"He was my friend."

"That's not the point." She moves over to the bed, picks up the coiled plastic tube lying on the floor, and hangs it on a hook by the bed; shoots me a look that is meant to entertain and dismiss her first cruel suspicion. "The point is that this is private property and you are trespassing." She picks up the bottle from the floor. "I suppose this is yours."

I nod, offer to take it from her, but she retracts it.

"Look. I don't know who you are, but if you don't get out of this house immediately I'm calling the police."

"I was here yesterday. Remember?"

"That's beside the point."

"Don't give me that beside-the-point bullshit. I'm a friend of his. A friend. Understand?"

She pushes past me and yanks open the door. "You're trespassing on private property. Now please leave." She holds out the bottle. "And take your liquor and your gun with you."

I look down to see the butt of the gun sticking out from under my shirt, tuck it back in feeling oddly exposed and unable to defend myself.

"Get out," she commands, and I obey, pausing at the door for one last look at Mohr. The nurse, assured now of her control, escorts me to the front door. "You can call to find out what arrangements have been made," she says.

"Arrangements for what?"

"For services."

"Who arranges for services?"

"We have written instructions." Then she closes the door.

The morning air is refreshing. There is nothing left but to clear my head and walk off my hangover. I leave the bottle on the porch steps and start for home.

Bright, cloudless dawn. The sun rising at my back, my shadow stretches long and spindly on the road ahead. A light dew covers the open fields, reflecting sparks and glints of morning light. I would like to take it all in, but my head feels tight, constricted, my vision pinched at the edges. It is not just the lingering effect of alcohol but some organic impurity of spirit and a general lack of conscious clarity that prevents me from attending to the quiet beauty of the morning. It is as though I were viewing the world through a rolled tube and breathing through that same tube and never achieving fullness of vision or aspiration and always aware of the limits and boundaries of this tight, conscripted subjectivity.

I pace along, watch the lengthened stride of my shadow on the pavement. A flock of birds erupts from a tree in the distance. I stop to watch as a huge sprinkler cuts on in the field to my right, an enormous wheel-mounted arachnid contraption that straddles the rows of corn and moves up and down them spraying in all directions. A generator pumps water through miles of bony pipe—*ftht ftht ftht*—a pickup truck speeds by, stirring a pungent smell into the air, the smell of manure and petrochemically fertilized earth and out of this the distilled odor of the world going diligently about its business, not meandering but working, working—even the corn working in the field and the big watering contraption roving up and down the rows like some cruel galley master shouting and brandishing a whip. Keep up the pace. Faster faster faster.

At the bend in the road I stop for a rest, mouth dry, sour wine in my stomach. A car drives past. The driver waves. I sit down on the bank of a narrow ditch that runs alongside the road. The sun is climbing. It is growing warmer. Dew is steaming off the fields and the wet shoulder of the road.

Another car blows past, then slows, reverses.

Ed Maver rolls down the window. "You all right there, buddy?"

I greet him with a tired wave. "Yes. Just resting."

"What are you doing way out here this time of morning?"

"Just out walking."

"You walked all the way out here?"

I nod.

"Goddamn, you must've been out walking all night."

I shrug.

"Hop in. I'll take you home."

"Thanks, no. I'll walk."

"C'mon there, give the old feet a break."

"No thanks." I stand up, brush the seat of my pants.

Maver eyes me. "You sure you're all right?"

"Do you have any water with you?"

He lifts a plastic-lidded mug from between his thighs. "Just coffee. Here, have some."

I accept the mug, drink a mouthful, and offer it back.

"Go on, finish it."

"You sure?"

"Sure I'm sure. Had two cups already this morning."

The coffee is warm and sweet. I drink it down in large, stomach-warming swallows. Maver looks on curiously, the bill of his cap tilted up.

I return the mug to him. "Thanks."

"C'mon now. Climb in and drive to town with me. We can stop for more coffee on the way."

"I would prefer to walk."

"Don't give me that would-prefer bullshit. You look like you tied one on but good last night. A dose of Maver's sure-fire hangover medicine'll set you right. Cold V8 and scrambled eggs. C'mon and get in! It'll take you all morning to get back to town."

"I'm not in a hurry."

Maver shrugs, returns the mug to a plastic holder suspended from the dashboard. "Suit yourself, buddy," he says and yanks down on the gearshift. "One of these days you're going to get sick of walking, and when you do I want to be right there to help you pick out a brand-new car."

"Thanks for the coffee, Ed." I wave, realizing that I've never called him by his name before.

"Sure thing, Horace," he says.

"Lucian," I correct him.

"Isn't your name Horace?"

"Not anymore. I changed it."

"I'll be damned." He shakes his head in friendly bewilderment. "Well, it's a free country," he says and pulls away, waving an arm out the window.

I continue on more steadily with Maver's coffee warm in my stomach and his last words in my head—free country. A free country. How so, free? And wherefore this flight of words? This fleeing from self to self? Name to name? Wherefore this alien body that subsumes itself in a multitude of names and never comes closer to knowing itself than when it casts a name aside and flees from it? Is that what free means? I can't say, and no one has told me. If you ask me I will admit that I am Chidiock

Tichborne and William Blake and Horace and Lucian of Samosata since they are all I have, my head, my arms, my legs—my only limbs. And I use them freely to navigate the open road that runs between Oblivion and oblivion.

As I near the curve ahead Tom Schroeder rides past me on his motorcycle. He skids and almost falls off before wresting control and coming to a stop by the side of the road. I walk past, ignoring him, but he pulls alongside, pedaling the ground with one foot. Our morning shadows stretch long on the road ahead. "Where's Sylvia?" he demands.

"She's gone."

"Where?"

"I don't know."

"Where'd she go?"

"I don't know. Mexico. Argentina. Anywhere."

Schroeder works the levers on the handlebars. I continue to walk. "Give me my gun back," he says.

I pull it out and offer it to him, holding it between pinched fingers in disdain.

He stops the bike and takes the gun. Stuffs it into his belt. "Did she tell you everything?"

I ignore the question and resume walking.

"What did she tell you?" He pulls alongside again, pedaling the ground with a dirty boot.

"Leave me alone."

"Why should I leave you alone?"

"Because you're an asshole."

"You going to turn me in?" He sends a wad of spit arching high in front of us, leans an elbow on the enormous gas tank, pedaling.

"Yes."

"What for?"

"Because you're an asshole."

"You tell on me and I'll kill you."

I ignore him, keep walking.

Schroeder lifts his foot from the road, kicks the machine into gear, and roars ahead. Then he swerves to the right and turns so that he is blocking the road, straddling his bulky machine like some grand iron horse.

As I draw near he yanks the gun from his belt and levels it.

I continue toward him.

"Tell me where Sylvia is."

"No."

He keeps the gun leveled. "Tell me where she is!"

I walk straight at him. And pass by. He revs up the machine and blows by me, then swerves and blocks the road. Again he levels the gun. "Where is she?"

I walk straight at him.

"*Bang!*" he shouts. "*Bang bang bang!*" He tucks the gun into his pocket, laughing, then revs up the bike and blows past. I slow my pace, expecting him to turn and repeat the charade. But he doesn't. He just keeps going. Headed on his noisy machine in the direction of the interstate.

Boethius, my parakeet, is singing loudly when I come home. He is always tuneful this time of day. Today his tone seems sweeter than usual. When I look into the cage I see that his seed dish is empty. Who says birds are dumb? Jane, the vet, gave me the parakeet as a present. Originally I wanted a crow. Then, for about a day, I considered getting a dog—until I realized that I couldn't bring a dog with me to the library. Crows don't make very good pets, Jane told me over the phone. A few days later she brought the parakeet. It's yellow and speckled with white and has a touch of purple. Can I let it out of the cage? I asked. Not unless you want it to escape, she told me. Thus the name: Anicius Manlius Severinus Boethius—not that I expect the bird to discover the consolations of philosophy. Remaining alive will be fine.

I fill the seed dish and water bottle. The cage hangs in a window, and Boethius has a nice view of the woods behind the house, brilliant now with autumn yellows and reds and browns.

It's Saturday. I have taken Mrs. Entwhistle's old job at the library. She hired me for it after a little arm-twisting in the form of a small fund I established, the Mohr Trust. Any guilt I may have had for buying myself the job has disappeared. Mrs. Entwhistle and I work very well together. She moved into Mohr's office one week after his funeral. Redecorated it. Hung curtains and potted plants. I preferred Mohr's chaotic jungle of boxes and paper, but Mrs. Entwhistle has put her own imprimatur on the place. She has turned out to be quite a good head librarian. I have no complaints.

I occupy the circulation desk five days a week, Tuesday through Friday, ten until six. Saturday from ten until two. It's busy work, but I have come to like it. What I especially like is knowing what people are reading. It never occurred to me that I might come to know the town so intimately—the quiet, unseen, reading life of it, that is. I have even infiltrated it in my own small way. A shelf of my own favorite reading stands near the circulation desk, where I can watch people browse. It took some time to catch on. People were wary. But now the books are being borrowed (and returned!) at a fairly decent rate. Even Claudian's *Rape of Proserpine* was finally borrowed, though it came back within a week and I have now returned that work by the last great pagan poet to obscurity in the classics section.

I go into the kitchen, put some rice on to cook, uncork a 1989 Gevrey-Chambertin that Anderson got in last week. Two cases, one for him and one for me. The wine is as big and grand and robust as Anderson promised it would be. I sip it slowly; the strong bouquet opens my sinuses. The days, it seems, evaporate up my sinuses. I drink. I eat. I pretend I was never here. But the voices in my head dissuade me.

Lucian?

Yes.

Horace?

Also yes.

William Blake?

Him too.

I reach for the telephone, dial a number. Then Boethius erupts in a chitter, and I put the telephone down and wander over to look at the bird. He cocks his head; a tiny bead registers my presence. I put my finger in the cage and he pecks at it for a moment, then loses interest.

Huc omnes pariter venite capti
Quos fallax ligat improbis catenis
Terranas habitans libido mentes,

Haec erit vobis requies laborum,
Hic portus placida manens quiete,
Hoc patens unum miseris asylum.

Come hither all you that are bound,
Whose base and earthly minds are drown'd
By lust, which doth them tye in cruell chaynes.
Here is a seat for men opprest,
Here is a port of pleasant rest;
Here may a wretch have refuge from his paynes.

I forget about the telephone and return to the kitchen to finish preparing my dinner. Boethius, my exemplar, has nearly persuaded me to do away with telephoning altogether. But I still feel an occasional cramping. He has also persuaded me of something else, namely, that the elements that go into the making of a full life—food and drink and a modicum of sanity and the slow accretion over time of the tiny facts that define us—are easy enough to come by, but never to the full satisfaction of that shadowy self that lurks underneath all experience and that seeks its definition apart from and sometimes in contradiction to the world of facts. Some call it spirit or soul, but I think of it more concretely as an eponymous self: that entity within from whom we borrow our name and take our identity.

I host these philosophical visitations less and less frequently these days. Boethius is my stand-in. I like to think of his little cage as my anteroom, where Lady Philosophy is received and detained. I run everything by the little bird first. It's not as crazy as it sounds.

Mrs. Entwhistle thinks she knows what I need. She doesn't mind telling me either. Over the course of the last few months she has become bolder and bolder in her assertions. It started out with lessons on the organization of my work and proceeded, gently but with a certain preordained vigor, to encompass areas of my private life as well. Lately she has told me that I need to find a woman and marry. She can't believe I can live alone as I do and be fulfilled or happy. I don't invite her observations, but I don't forbid them either. The other day I suspected her of trying to set me up.

A woman came into the library with two young children, a boy and a girl, both of them somewhere between five and ten years old. I've never been a good judge of children's ages. The woman sat the kids down in the children's reading room and then went straight to my reserve shelf and began a thorough perusal of it. I watched her from the corner of my eye as I checked in the previous day's returns and stacked them on the cart. The circulation desk—the heart of the library—is an apt metaphor. Everything passes by and through it. I now understand the peculiar obsession of librarians that nothing escape their notice.

The woman selected a book from the shelf and hurried back to the children's reading room. A short time later she appeared at my desk with the young girl.

"Tell the man what we read," she coaxed, then flashed me a broad smile. "This is Estelle. My aunt said you'd appreciate her gift."

I was only slightly surprised and beamed indulgently at the little girl. People, I've learned, are comfortable with and will confide almost anything to a librarian—all their eccentricities and obsessions. It's one of the more fascinating aspects of the job. I leaned over the desk. The little girl gripped her mother's hand, hung her head shyly.

"Come on, Estelle, it's okay. Remember what we talked about?"

Estelle nodded.

"She's a little shy," the mother said.

I can see why, I wanted to say.

Suddenly the little girl looked up at me—looked me straight in the eye. And began to recite. *Nil admirari prope res est una, Numici*—the entire first stanza of Horace's epistle! Word for word in her little girl's voice! No stumbling. No backtracking. Her pronunciation was awkward, but she didn't seem self-conscious in the least. Then she finished the Latin and, without so much as a pause, recited the English. I immediately recognized the translation. It was my old copy of Horace. I had donated it to the library to put up on the shelf with all my other recommendations.

Not to be awed to a stupor, Numicius, is almost the only
Notion conducive to winning and holding mankind to a happy
State of existence. This sun, and the stars, and the seasons in cyclic

Changes: there are people who, in the face of these things, are not stricken
Speechless with terror. What value, then, ought to be placed on the wealth of
Earth, on the sea that enriches the farthermost Arabs and Hindus,
or on the ludicrous games of applause and support of the voters?
How do you feel we should look on such things and how ought we to treat them?
Anyone dreading their opposites fares very nearly the same as
One who is greedy to get them; his fear is distressful in either
Case, and abrupt confrontation with either is vastly dismaying.
Happy or sorrowing, dreading or coveting, what does it matter,
If, upon seeing things better or worse than he hoped, he just hangs his
Head and does nothing but stand there dumbfounded in mind and body?
Even a wise man is really insane, and the just man is unjust,
Seeking for goodness and wisdom in quantities more than sufficient.

When she finished she became shy again and looked away.

"My daughter has a photographic memory," the mother began, as if explanation were necessary. "My aunt told me you had one too."

"Your aunt?"

"Mrs. Entwhistle. I'm sorry, I forgot to introduce myself." The woman's face colored slightly and she put her arm across her daughter's shoulders and drew her near.

I don't know what the expression on my face communicated, but by the woman's look it must not have been the benign, charmed look she had been expecting. Was it astonishment? Bewilderment? Disgust? I don't know. "Thank you," was all I could bring myself to say.

The little girl peered up at me.

"It's all right, Estelle," the mother said. "You can go play now." The little girl detached herself and ran back to the children's section.

"I'm sorry if I embarrassed you," the woman said. "I only meant . . ."

"No. Not at all."

"I just thought . . ."

"Don't apologize. It's fine. Really. I'm just a little surprised. Astonished."

"I hope you don't think I go around showing her off."

"No. I didn't think that."

"We're here visiting my aunt. The kids and I."

"I see." There was nothing I could think of to say. The woman stood there, somewhat awkwardly, for another minute. She seemed to be waiting for me to say something; just stood there, her fists jammed into the pockets of a bright red nylon windbreaker. She had an air of sporting good humor about her that apparently, I had just undermined. She seemed both delighted and bewildered by her daughter's precocity—didn't strike me as the sort who would exploit or show it off.

"Did she pick it out?" I asked.

The woman shook her head. "Not exactly. We picked it out at random. The poem. It wasn't my idea, really. My aunt said you liked Horace."

"Does she understand the words yet?" As I spoke Mrs. Entwhistle walked past the reading-room door, waved at us with a knowing smile, and started upstairs.

"Oh, you'd be surprised how much she understands," the woman replied.

They stayed in the children's section for another half hour or so. Then came to say good-bye.

"Say good-bye," the mother instructed them, placing the volume of Horace on the reshelve pile.

"Good-bye," they chimed together.

"Good-bye, Estelle." I picked up the volume of Horace and offered it to her. "This is for you."

"Say thank you," Mother chirped and took the book from me on her daughter's behalf.

"Thank you," Estelle said.

"Are you sure?" the mother asked me, hefting the book in her hand.

I nodded.

I was sure.

A sharp wind picks up outside, a cold front moving in. Before she left the library this afternoon, Mrs. Entwhistle told me that a snowstorm might be on the way. She was worried about it, worried that snow would fall and winter would come upon us even before the leaves had fallen. It's something I have come to like about her. That she worries. There's a war brewing in Africa, and she worries about that. A two-year-old in California has been missing for a week. Weapons-grade uranium has been stolen from a facility in Russia. She has worried to me aloud on each of these topics, buttoning up her overcoat, wrapping her scarf around her head. Whenever she does, I try to imagine someone in China doing exactly the same thing, putting on an overcoat, preparing to go home, worrying about things beyond the horizon.

I eat, finish the wine, and sit at the kitchen table for a time. Before going upstairs to bed, I cover Boethius's cage.

Someone is flying a kite up on the mound. It is a bright, windy Sunday morning. No snow. Not even a threat. The kite is flying high on the breeze, so high that it is hard to tell what color it is. Just a dark speck in the sky. The university van is parked at the base of the mound. I follow the path to the top and find Dr. Norris, the big-bellied archaeologist. He waves to me, a cigarette dangling from the corner of his beard.

"Couldn't resist," he says.

"It's up there pretty high."

"Five hundred feet," he says, indicating the empty spool of string at his feet.

"You're back to dig?"

"Start tomorrow. Came up to make some measurements. Got distracted." He plucks the cigarette from his mouth, drops it on the ground.

"Still expect to find something?"

"Besides a dead body, you mean?" He grins, fishes a cigarette pack from inside his down vest, shakes one out, and offers it to me. I accept, put it in my mouth.

"Here. Hold on." He hands me a short stick around which the kite line is wrapped. I take it, surprised by the force. The kite seems firmly anchored to the sky. I watch it, mesmerized, while Norris hunches over to light his cigarette. I return the line to him and he gives me his lit cigarette. I puff my own cigarette to light, return his. Norris plants it in the corner of his mouth and concentrates on flying the kite.

I sit down in the grass, remembering a dream I had during the night in which I turned into a border collie after flying under the great arch in St. Louis.

"What are you looking for?" I ask after a while. "More pipes?"

"Maybe. It's impossible to predict."

"You must have some idea." The wind seems to be getting stronger. "What do you expect to find?"

Norris turns his head so that the ash is blown from the cigarette in his mouth. The wind begins to blow in strong gusts. Norris squints up at the tiny speck sailing against the sky. Then, suddenly, he lets go. Line and stick are jerked from his hand. He watches the tiny kite float away, then turns to me. "Clues," he says, indicating the ground at his feet. "All the way down."